DELIA'S SHADOW

Delia's Shadow

Jaime Lee Moyer

TOR®
A Tom Doherty Associates Book
New York

For my grandmother Lorene,
who loved family and life in equal measure

This is a work of fiction. All of the characters, organizations, and events portrayed in this novel are either products of the author's imagination or are used fictitiously.

DELIA'S SHADOW

Map of the Pan-Pacific International Exposition courtesy of SanFranciscoMemories.com

A Tor Book
Published by Tom Doherty Associates, LLC
175 Fifth Avenue
New York, NY 10010

www.tor-forge.com

Tor® is a registered trademark of Tom Doherty Associates, LLC.

The Library of Congress Cataloging-in-Publication Data is available upon request.

ISBN 978-0-7653-3182-3 (hardcover)
ISBN 978-1-4299-4948-4 (e-book)

First Edition: September 2013

Printed in the United States of America

0 9 8 7 6 5 4 3 2 1

ACKNOWLEDGMENTS

The acknowledgments page in any novel is a chance for the author to say thank you. I've been fortunate to have the friendship and support of many talented members of the science fiction and fantasy writing community. I can't express my gratitude to all of them in this space, but that doesn't mean I've forgotten.

But I can thank the usual suspects: my friends through thick and thin, Elizabeth Bear, Jodi Meadows, Rae Carson, Amanda Downum, Kat Allen, Celia Marsh, and Katherine Miller, who were always there when I needed them; the Million Monkeys, Charles Coleman Finlay, Tobias Buckell, Paul Melko, and Tom Barlow, who taught me structure and made me like it; my faithful and true critters on the Online Writer's Workshop for Science Fiction and Fantasy, P. J. Thompson, J. R. Hockman, Teresa Frohock, and Josh Vogt, who helped me see what worked; writers and poets extraordinaire Marcy Rockwell and Samantha Henderson, who were always willing to help; all the denizens of The Zoo both past and present; Steve Mancino, who took me seriously and taught me so much; and my daughter, Stephanie Irwin, who fell in love with Delia and knew this was the one.

Finally, I need to thank my tireless, hard-working agent, Tamar Rydzinski, who never gave up, and my partner in crime and life, Marshall Payne, who kept telling me this day would come.

OUTLINE MAP OF SAN FRANCISCO
PACIFIC
OCEAN
GOLDEN GATE
FORT SCOTT
BOULEVARD
PRESIDIO
U.S. MILITARY RESERVATION
EXPOSITION GROUNDS
FORT MASON
SAN FRANCISCO BAY
GOAT ISLAND
TO SAUSALITO AND MT. TAMALPAIS
TO OAKLAND
TO OAKLAND
COLUMBUS AVE
CHINA TOWN
CALIFORNIA ST.
FILLMORE AVE
VAN NESS AVE
MARKET ST.
MISSION ST.
TOWNSEND ST.
CIVIC CENTER
CLIFF HOUSE
LINCOLN PARK
FORT MILEY
RICHMOND
FULTON STREET
GOLDEN GATE PARK
LINCOLN WAY
SUNSET DISTRICT
SLOAT BLVD.
MISSION
POTRERO
SOUTH SAN FRANCISCO
MISSION ROCK
SEA WALL
INDIA BASIN
SOUTH BASIN
BALBOA PARK
INGLESIDE TERRACES
N
S
E
W
KEY TO LETTERS.
A. Ferry Station.
B. So. Pacific Station.
C. Telegraph Hill.
D. Nob Hill.
E. Lone Mountain.
F. Twin Peaks.
G. Buena Vista Park.
H. Mission Dolores.
I. Mission Park.
K. Alamo Squre.
L. Lafayette Square.
M. Jefferson Square.
N. Union Square.
M. Alta Plaza.
The Baldwin Piano Co.
310 Sutter Street, near Grant.

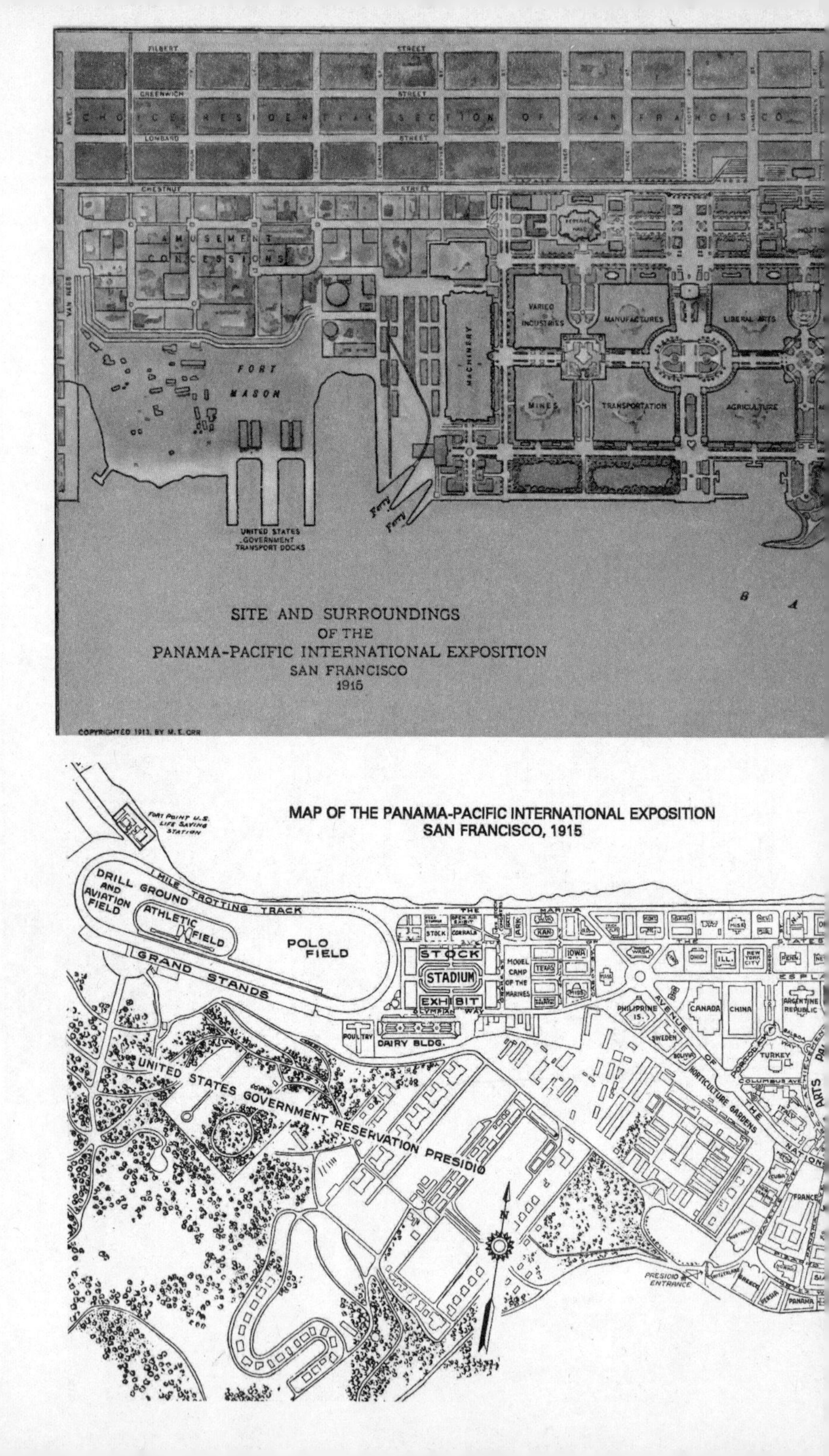
SITE AND SURROUNDINGS
OF THE
PANAMA-PACIFIC INTERNATIONAL EXPOSITION
SAN FRANCISCO
1915
COPYRIGHTED 1913, BY M. E. ORR
FILBERT
GREENWICH
LOMBARD
CHESTNUT
STREET
CHOICE RESIDENTIAL SECTION OF SAN FRANCISCO
VAN NESS
AMUSEMENT CONCESSIONS
FORT MASON
UNITED STATES GOVERNMENT TRANSPORT DOCKS
Ferry
MACHINERY
VARIED INDUSTRIES
MANUFACTURES
LIBERAL ARTS
MINES
TRANSPORTATION
AGRICULTURE
MAP OF THE PANAMA-PACIFIC INTERNATIONAL EXPOSITION
SAN FRANCISCO, 1915
FORT POINT U.S. LIFE SAVING STATION
DRILL GROUND AND AVIATION FIELD
MILE TROTTING TRACK
ATHLETIC FIELD
POLO FIELD
GRAND STANDS
STOCK STADIUM EXHIBIT
STOCK
CORRALS
MODEL CAMP OF THE MARINES
IOWA
TEXAS
OLYMPIAN WAY
POULTRY
DAIRY BLDG.
PHILIPPINE IS.
SWEDEN
BOLIVIA
CANADA
CHINA
ARGENTINE REPUBLIC
TURKEY
OHIO
ILL.
NEW YORK CITY
PENN.
AVENUE OF HORTICULTURE GARDENS
UNITED STATES GOVERNMENT RESERVATION PRESIDIO
PRESIDIO ENTRANCE
FRANCE
PANAMA
N

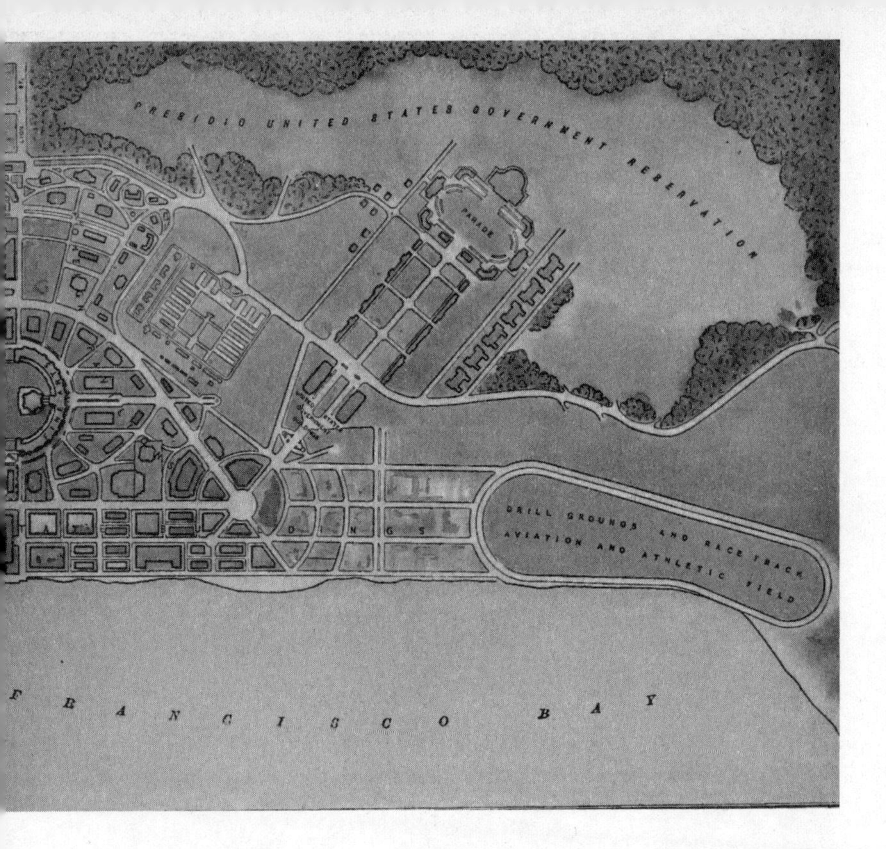
PRESIDIO UNITED STATES GOVERNMENT RESERVATION
PARADE
DRILL GROUNDS AND RACE TRACK
AVIATION AND ATHLETIC FIELD
FRANCISCO BAY

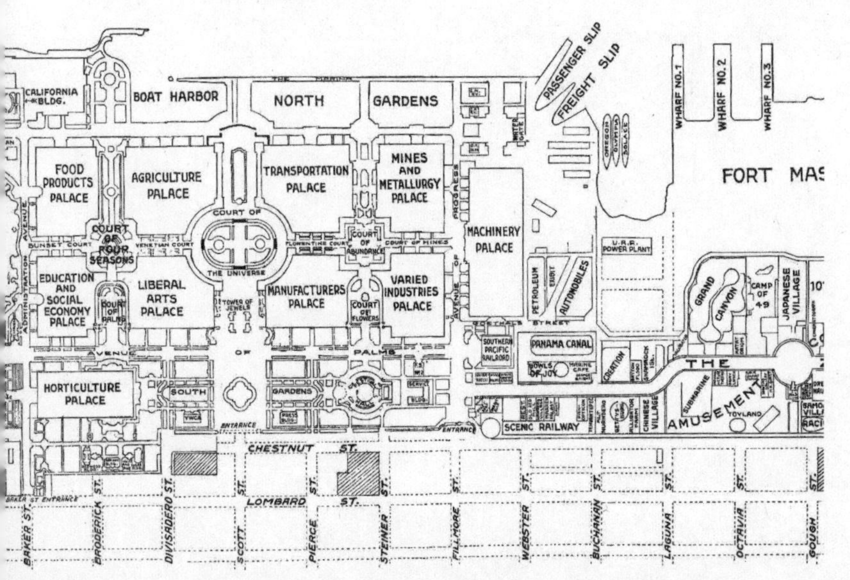
BAY OF SAN FRANCISCO
THE MARINA
CALIFORNIA BLDG.
BOAT HARBOR
NORTH
GARDENS
PASSENGER SLIP
FREIGHT SLIP
WATER GATE
OREGON
OLYMPIA
SOLACE
WHARF NO.1
WHARF NO.2
WHARF NO.3
FORT MAS
FOOD PRODUCTS PALACE
AGRICULTURE PALACE
TRANSPORTATION PALACE
MINES AND METALLURGY PALACE
MACHINERY PALACE
COURT OF FOUR SEASONS
SUNSET COURT
VENETIAN COURT
COURT OF THE UNIVERSE
FLORENTINE COURT
COURT OF ABUNDANCE
COURT OF MINES
AVENUE OF PROGRESS
U.R.R. POWER PLANT
EDUCATION AND SOCIAL ECONOMY PALACE
LIBERAL ARTS PALACE
COURT OF PALMS
TOWER OF JEWELS
MANUFACTURERS PALACE
COURT OF FLOWERS
VARIED INDUSTRIES PALACE
ADMINISTRATION AVENUE
PETROLEUM
AUTOMOBILES
GRAND CANYON
CAMP OF 49
JAPANESE VILLAGE
GOETHALS STREET
SOUTHERN PACIFIC RAILROAD
PANAMA CANAL
BOWLS OF JOY
CREATION
AVENUE OF PALMS
HORTICULTURE PALACE
SOUTH GARDENS
Y.W.C.A.
PRESS BLDG.
FESTIVAL HALL
SERVICE BLDG.
ENTRANCE
SCENIC RAILWAY
CHINESE VILLAGE
THE AMUSEMENT
SUBMARINE
TOYLAND
CHESTNUT ST.
LOMBARD ST.
BAKER ST. ENTRANCE
BAKER ST.
BRODERICK ST.
DIVISADERO ST.
SCOTT ST.
PIERCE ST.
STEINER ST.
FILLMORE ST.
WEBSTER ST.
BUCHANAN ST.
LAGUNA ST.
OCTAVIA ST.
GOUGH ST.

CHAPTER 1

Delia

The locomotive engine belched billowing clouds of steam, a black-iron dragon chained to the tracks. Warm air ruffled my hair and vanished before I became sure I'd felt it. Foggy, late-spring nights in San Francisco were cold, something I'd conveniently forgotten.

Sam, the elderly porter who'd looked after me all the way from New York, took my satchel and offered his hand as I came down the rickety train-car steps. "Will you be all right on your own, Miss Delia? I can wait until your friend comes if you'd feel better."

"I'll be fine." I shook out my skirts and took my bag. "This is home. I won't get lost."

He doffed his cap and smiled. "You take extra care anyway. Lots of strangers in town for the fair."

I tipped Sam a dollar and moved away from the tracks, facing my fear head on and confronting the reason I'd left home three years ago. San Francisco was full of ghosts. Long-dead children trailed after sad and worn-looking women, and young mothers carrying newborn babes followed proper-looking gentlemen with new wives on an arm. Each restless soul clung to someone they'd loved in life, unwilling to let go. Others walked purposely through train cars and walls, following paths they'd walked before or stopping to cross streets that no longer existed.

Ever since I was a small child I'd caught glimpses of people my parents couldn't see, or faces peering at me from corners in an otherwise empty room. More than once I'd run to my mother frightened and certain that some stranger had crept into our house. Each time she'd stopped whatever she was doing and taken my hand, walking me from room to room so I could see no one was there. She thought the ghosts I saw an overabundance of childhood fancy, something I'd outgrow in time.

My mother was seldom wrong, but growing up didn't cure me of seeing spirits. After the earthquake and subsequent fire nine years ago, I began to see them everywhere. Some ghosts were translucent with no more substance than the fog, barely in the world of the living. I'd no way of knowing for certain, but I thought them the oldest or with the fewest ties to loved ones. Others were so close to solid looking I might have thought them made of warm flesh if not for the old style of their clothes and ability to walk through objects.

Going to New York was an attempt to escape spirits and find respite, however brief. That respite lasted almost two and a half years. Long enough to think I might have a normal life.

I dropped my monogrammed satchel on a bench and gathered courage to search the faces on the platform for Sadie. My shadow stood before me, appearing so alive I expected to see her breathe. Thinking of her as a shadow made me feel less insane. I'd never wanted to believe in ghosts, not really. After six months of being haunted by one, I clung to every scrap of sanity I could.

She watched patiently and waited to follow as soon as I moved away. Long dark hair was plaited and coiled neatly on the top of her head, exposing delicate ears and a pale neck. Slender fingers clutched a thin shawl closed over her old-fashioned white cotton blouse. A gold cross glittered at her throat, tiny and easily missed. Dark-blue skirts brushed the top of her scuffed shoes. Green eyes met mine, aware that I saw her.

I didn't know her name or why she followed me; she'd died before I was born. She'd found and laid claim to me just the same.

Since the morning I awoke to find her standing at the side of my bed, I began to see spirits everywhere again. My hopes for a normal life had vanished. I couldn't help but feel a touch of panic at the thought of being haunted. But everyone had a shadow, perfectly normal people who never gave the bit of darkness following them a thought. Normalcy was something I desperately craved. Returning home might give me a chance to find it again.

The train station was new since I'd left three years before. Tall stone columns held up a ceiling decorated with plaster medallions carved into intricate leaves and flowers, the designs overlaid with gold leaf to catch the light. Oval windows along the front wall were framed in dark wood, beveled glass held in place by strips of soldered lead foil.

Nightfall meant clouds had moved in off the bay, smothering the city in a curtain of gray mist. Fog rolled through the arched double doors open at the end of the platform, wisps flowing across soiled tile floors and leaving a slick film of moisture behind. Dampness glistened on wooden benches framed with iron, filmed flickering electric lamps, and the four-wheeled carts porters filled with luggage too large to carry.

A deep breath brought the salt-tang of the bay and of fish offloaded on the docks, overlaid with the oily scent of cinders darkening the track bed. The fire had changed the look of the city, ripped away familiar places and replaced them with new buildings, but the air still smelled of home.

"Delia! Over here!" Sadie waved and plowed through the crowd, living and dead. Tall and slim, Sadie's wide-brimmed hat was tipped to show off a heart-shaped face and ocean-blue eyes. She was always in fashion, wearing the latest styles to sweep the city. I'd no doubt the fur-trimmed wool coat, the black kid gloves, and beads looped around her neck were all the rage. She'd cut her hair as well and curls the color of sun-ripe wheat foamed out of the hat. I felt like the poor country cousin in my traveling garb.

I kept a smile on my face, knowing she wouldn't understand my flinch as she walked through the middle of a gold-rush miner and a Chinese railroad worker. My shadow stepped aside or Sadie might have ended up standing inside the ghost.

"It's so good to see you." I shut my eyes and hugged Sadie, unnerved at seeing my ghost hovering behind her. "Three years is a long time."

She held me at arm's length, glee barely contained. "I'm not the one who took a teaching job on the other side of the country. You've no one to blame for being deprived of my company but yourself. I might even forgive you for going away if you show proper appreciation for my surprise."

"Surprise?" She was the same old Sadie, bubbly and bright, brimming with secrets and infectious good humor. I really was home and laughing easy. Being haunted suddenly didn't seem as horrible. "Are you going to tell me or make me wait to find out?"

Sadie tugged off her glove and shoved a hand under my nose, grinning and obviously pleased with herself. A sapphire and garnet ring sparkled on her finger. "Look! Isn't it glorious?"

"Oh, yes, completely glorious." I held her hand where I could view her finger without my eyes crossing. The ring was beautiful, stones catching the light and glimmering like captured stars. "From Jack I assume. I hope you'd have written if you'd tossed him aside and taken up with a new suitor."

She laughed, knowing me too well to think my words anything but teasing. "Of course it's Jack. Now let's get home. You must be exhausted and Mother's waiting up to see you. I've got a cab parked at the curb. Do you have another bag?"

"Somehow my trunk got put on the wrong train when I transferred in Denver. The rail company assures me they'll send the luggage on and deliver it to the house." I hefted the small satchel and threaded my other arm through Sadie's. "I'll survive until it arrives. How is Mama Esther?"

Sadie's frown was an unfamiliar visitor on her face. "Weaker. The doctors tell me that hanging on through the winter was a positive sign. I'm sure she pays them to lie to me and thinks I don't know." She squeezed my hand and smiled. "I'm glad you came home for the summer. Seeing you will brighten the house for all of us. And I'm counting on you to talk some sense into me about wedding plans."

I laughed again and we started for the door, my shadow a step behind. More ghosts crowded the lobby now that the train was empty, far more than I'd seen in one place before. None wore the face of those I'd loved and lost in the quake, and I was very grateful. I steeled myself to walk normally and not try to steer Sadie around spirits. She couldn't see and wouldn't feel them, but I didn't have that luxury.

Each ghost that passed through me deepened the clammy chill that shivered over my skin. Voices filled my head and faded again. I heard cries of pain and pleas for help from those trapped under rubble after the quake, felt the heat of the fire steal a last breath. Age and sickness stole life as well, seldom peacefully. Touching death again and again brought me closer to tears. I gritted my teeth and held on. People would truly think me insane if I began to cry for no reason.

Fog swallowed the ghosts as soon as we stepped outside, all but my shadow. I caught my breath, grateful they'd vanished and not caring why. Sadie chatted about mutual friends all the way to the cab, filling me in on all the gossip and scandals I'd missed. We'd been friends since the age of ten and our time together was always the same, her talking a blue streak and me listening.

The cab driver took my bag, tucking the satchel into the footwell of the driver's seat before helping Sadie and me into the cab. My shadow drifted into view as well, sitting next to Sadie and watching me with the expectant stare I'd come to know. I'd become more certain she wanted something from me as the months went by. What the ghost expected I'd no idea, but coming home was the first step toward discovery.

Sadie waited until the driver whistled the horses into motion, and the four-horse hack lurched away from the curb before she pounced. "Fess up, Delia. You didn't come home just to see the exposition. Tell me what's wrong. Did the boy you were seeing break it off? For the life of me I can't remember his name, but you know the one I mean."

"Jonathan?"

"Yes! That's the one." She leaned forward and touched my hand. "You didn't mention him in the last letters you sent. I thought that must be the reason, that he'd ended the engagement. That sort of thing is always so dreadful."

"Nothing so dramatic as a broken engagement, Sadie. We never got to that point. And if you must know, Jonathan didn't break off courting me. I told him I didn't see a future for the two of us." I leaned back against the cold leather seat, surprised that Sadie thought a broken heart would send me running for home. "Do I need a special reason for coming to visit?"

She crossed her arms, bunching the fur collar on her coat and peered at me from under the brim of her hat. Nothing put Sadie off once she'd caught the scent of even a hint of gossip. "This is me, Dee. That story might work on Mother, but I know better."

My shadow had turned away, staring out the cab window as the horses labored up hills, past neighborhoods newly built since the fire and through pockets of streets spared by the flames. Watching the ghost's wistful expression, I could well believe that she'd come home as well. Perhaps she had.

I smoothed ash-gray skirts over my knees, stalling another moment. "All right. I did want to see the fair, that part is true. And I've missed you terribly, but that's not the entire reason."

Sadie leaned forward, eyes sparkling. "I knew it. Keep talking and don't make me pry it out of you."

Of all the people in my life, Sadie was the one I felt sure would believe me. My parents hosted a society benefit at our house one night when we were both twelve. Sadie came to keep me company and we spent the night up in my room, trading secrets. Clouds covered the moon and wind whipped rain and tree branches against my window, making the atmosphere decidedly spooky. She hadn't believed my claim of seeing ghosts at first, so I'd tried to frighten Sadie by describing the haunts wandering through the churchyard across the street, wildly embellishing to make them sound more gruesome. Instead of being scared, she'd sworn to keep my secret and begged me to teach her how to see spirits as well. I knew then I could trust her with anything.

That didn't make telling her any easier or take away the worry of what she'd think. I folded my hands in my lap and swallowed back tears. "What would you say if I told you I thought—I knew—that a ghost was following me? That I was being . . . haunted."

"Haunted? Really?" Sadie bounced in her seat, face lit with delight. "Tell me you mean it and that you're not teasing."

"I mean it, Sadie. I've never been more serious." I'd hoped she'd believe me, but I hadn't anticipated enthusiasm. "She follows me everywhere and I've no idea why."

"Where is this ghost now?"

I nodded at the spirit, still transfixed with the scene outside the window. "Sitting next to you. She seems taken with the scenery at the moment. Most of the time she stares at me."

Sadie grabbed both my hands. "A real ghost! How exciting. What's her name?"

"I don't know her name or anything about her, just that she wants me to do something. I've had the feeling since she came to me that something terrible happened to her." My shadow turned from the window, her face a study in patience. I saw something new in her green eyes as well—sorrow. Not at all sure why, I began to cry, wiping tears on a sleeve and embarrassed that I couldn't stop. "Then a few weeks ago I started dreaming about being in San Francisco. She was always there, just as she was in New York. But instead of following she was . . . leading me toward something. I woke up one morning and knew I had to come home. So here I am. Crazy, isn't it?"

"Oh, Dee." Sadie sobered and passed me a lace-trimmed hankie from her bag. "No, it's not crazy and neither are you. You did the right thing. I know a person who can help, someone with a real connection to the spirit world. We'll find some answers and the ghost won't need to haunt you."

"I knew I could count on you. Thank you." I dried my face and balled the damp handkerchief in my hand, still sniffling, but calmer now that she knew. Underneath Sadie's foolish exterior was a good heart. "Call her Shadow. It's more dignified and respectful, at least until we discover her true name. I can't bring myself to think of her as just another ghost."

Shadow went back to her silent vigil and I watched out the window as well, reacquainting myself with home. Fog softened brick and glass storefronts, the sharp corners not yet worn by storms or wind rounded by mist-shadows. Empty lots were a swirl of pearly gray. The familiar was there, but so much was new and jarring, so much gone. I could name each missing storefront on the blocks I'd walked summer evenings with my first beau. The ice-cream parlor was gone and a butcher shop in its place, the candy store where he'd bought me taffy replaced with a tailor's shop. Each loss was a fresh stab of pain.

New houses filled this side of the hill, built in the style of the homes lost to the fire. Tall turret rooms and bay windows overlooked the street, and columned porches graced the front. Even fog couldn't soften the sheen of too-bright paint on wooden siding and the scalloped trim dangling from the edge of roofs, or framing windows. In time the paint would fade, the harshness so evident to one who'd grown up in the city gradually become less noticeable. Now each new dwelling was a fresh wound, bleeding and garish.

Three years away hadn't prepared me or cushioned the blow. If the city was Shadow's home, I couldn't imagine what San Francisco looked like to her, or how much the changes hurt.

The cab stopped in front of the small house atop Russian Hill. I gathered my skirts and slid out after Sadie, digging coins from my handbag to pay the driver before my friend could stop me or protest.

I turned for my first look at home, the house I'd missed for three years. On the outside everything appeared exactly the same. Morning glory vines ambled up one side of the porch and across the top, blossoms shut tight against the night and ready to open at sunrise. Nasturtiums spilled out of window boxes in ribbons of yellow and orange flowers and saucer-shaped leaves. My father and mother's will made Esther my guardian, and provided me with a substantial trust as well as income from my father's real-estate holdings. I could afford to buy a house of my own in San Francisco or anywhere I chose, but this place and the people inside held my heart. This was home.

But even if things appeared unchanged, I knew that wasn't true. I couldn't resume my old life and go on as if I'd never gone away.

Shadow was already waiting on the walk, stoic and expectant.

Gabe

Gabe pulled back on the reins just enough to slow the horses to a walk. The buggy crept past the house, allowing him to keep Jack's fiancée and her friend in sight until the front door closed behind them. He poked his partner with an elbow. "Sit up, Jack, and stop worrying. Sadie's safe inside and the cab is gone. They won't go out again tonight."

Jack uncurled from his crouch and sat on the seat properly. He slicked back unruly red-brown hair and settled his hat down tight. "Thanks for your help. I wanted to take a few hours' leave this evening and go with her to meet Delia's train, but Sadie wouldn't hear of it. She's perfectly capable of getting to the train station and back, but with all that's happened—I just didn't feel easy about her being out alone."

"If that was Victoria I'd do exactly the same thing right now." Saying her name never got easier. Nine years had passed since Victoria and their unborn child had died in the fire that swept the city after the quake. Gabe mourned each and every day. He might have saved them if he'd been home and not out on patrol when the quake struck. Not knowing added guilt to his grief.

Gabe guided the horses around the corner at the end of the block, away from the well-to-do houses on Russian Hill and toward Nob Hill's mansions. He watched the shadows for movement and anything that didn't belong. On a workday evening, most of the residents were tucked in for the night. Anyone skulking near houses or walking the streets most likely didn't belong. "Have you told Sadie anything?"

"Not yet. I don't want to frighten her, not until I've no choice. I keep hoping one of us will catch the killer and telling Sadie I've been keeping secrets won't be necessary." Jack yanked his hat off again, raking fingers through his hair and adding to his disheveled look. The dampness in the air only made his hair and mustache curl tighter. "Patrolling this neighborhood is a waste of time. It gave me an excuse to follow Sadie home tonight, but that's the only good I can see."

Gabe gestured at the well-kept mansions, manicured front gardens, and ornamental iron fences. "Police patrols until the 'unpleasantness' is resolved will keep San Francisco's leading citizens off the mayor's back."

"I doubt the esteemed citizens of Nob Hill know anything about what's happened." Jack fell silent for half a block, the scowl on his face deepening with each darkened house they passed. "Is the paper going to print the latest letter? The editor and the chief were still yelling in Cap's office when I left."

Three letters sat in Gabe's files, each addressed in a careful hand to the editor of *The Examiner,* and detailing how the killer's victims suffered. If the person writing the letters were telling the truth, there were more victims than the police knew. A lot more.

Gabe's hands curled into fists, the reins digging furrows into his skin. He was positive the handwriting on the pale blue envelopes and cheap stationery was identical to the old letters in his father's files. The muscles in the back of his neck twitched each time he thought of the symbols drawn in place of a signature. "The newest message threatened people visiting the fair if the letters aren't on the front page by tomorrow. Printing them could cause panic. Not printing them means people could die. The chief is in a bad spot either way. And I don't know how the mayor thinks he can keep this quiet."

"I don't know how we're expected to catch this killer, either." Jack smothered a yawn with the back of his hand. "Not if every detective on the force is watching the wrong neighborhoods. This butcher's been one step ahead for weeks."

The buggy crested the hill. Gabe hesitated at the top before turning away from gated mansions and rich people sleeping soundly. No one would miss them if they spent the last two hours of their shift driving other neighborhoods. Parts of the city never slept. Those were the streets they needed to be on.

"We won't be patrolling up here much longer, Jack. Time is running out." He smiled, grim and without humor. "People from all over the world are in San Francisco for the Pan Pacific. Printing his letters won't stop him from expanding his hunting ground. He wants the attention a killing in a public place will bring him."

Jack put his foot up on the buggy front and rested an arm on his knee. "And what's to stop him from moving on again when the entire police force converges on the fair?"

"Nothing. But I don't think he will." Gabe shrugged. "Call it a hunch, but I think he'll stick around as long as he's getting the publicity he wants or we catch him."

"Then I guess we better catch him. Any idea how we go about that?"

"Not yet." Gabe's stomach churned, his father's stories whirling in his head. Captain Matthew Ryan worked five years on the letter writer's murders and the killings stopped as suddenly as they'd started. That he'd never brought the killer to justice still haunted his father. "We'll find a way. I'm not letting him get away."

He bit his tongue before the words "not again" slipped out. Gabe hadn't told Jack about the letters in his father's files, not yet. He'd needed to satisfy his doubts about the similarities and that his memory was sound. Until then, it was only a hunch. His father had taught him hunches had no real place in police work.

Someday Gabe might even believe that.

CHAPTER 2

Delia

I set my bag down in the front hall and the house settled around me, wrapping me in familiar things. Smells drifted from the kitchen: the scent of fresh-baked bread and cookies, roast beef and honeyed yams from dinner. The wallpaper had faded more but otherwise hadn't changed. Tiny roses still marched in straight rows to the high ceiling, the pattern disappearing into gloom the lamps never chased away.

No ghosts filled the hall or the parts of the sitting room I could see from the door, none but Shadow. Home might be more of a haven than I'd hoped.

Sadie hung her hat and coat on the hall tree near the door. A shake of her head and the curls settled perfectly into place. "Are you hungry? I know Annie planned on keeping food warm for you."

"Starving." My hair didn't curl and shaking my head the way Sadie had would gain me a face full of straight, mouse brown strands, not angelic charm. I tugged off my hat and brushed fine wisps that had escaped hairpins off my face. "But I don't want to keep Esther up too late. Food can wait until I've said hello."

She took my hand and led me up the curving staircase. "Don't be surprised if Mother's sleeping when we reach her room. She sleeps more than she's awake most days. And, Dee, I should warn you. She's awfully thin and her memory's not what it was. Don't be offended if she doesn't know you right off."

"Your last letter warned she was growing worse." I trailed fingers on the darkwood banister, oil from my skin leaving streaks on the polished surface. Sadness mixed with the joy of coming home. Change happened when you weren't watching. "I'm prepared."

"You think you are, but you're not." Sadie squeezed my fingers. "I've seen her every day of the three years you've been gone and I'm not prepared for what I find each morning. Do your best. I can't say it gets easier, but you learn ways to cope."

A glance over my shoulder showed Shadow right where I expected her to be, gliding a few steps behind. Her attention was fixed on the top of the stairs and she leaned slightly forward, her expression anxious, as if she wanted to rush ahead. The ghost had changed since we arrived in the city, more alert to her surroundings and showing me more than an unchanging, placid stare.

Counting steps kept me from thinking too hard about what that might mean. Facing Esther's decline came before puzzling over my problematic ghost.

My mother had been Esther Larkin's best friend, just as Sadie was mine. Esther had invited me on a grand adventure during the spring of 1906, a present for my sixteenth birthday. Traveling with her and Sadie down the coast was my first trip away from my parents, and I felt quite grown-up. We spent the last week in a red-roofed hotel in Coronado, its sweeping porches and round-topped turrets combining to make me feel as if I slept in a storybook castle. Eating breakfast on the terrace, waves whispering over sand yards away, added to my feeling of being the princess in a fairy tale.

We got news of the quake the day before we were to start for home. Esther held me together while I waited for word from my parents, word that never came. Once we were allowed to return home, I moved in with Sadie and Esther. She stepped into my mother's shoes and I was as much her daughter as Sadie.

Sadie went into the bedroom ahead of me. Esther was awake, scribbling in one of her journals as she had every night for as long as I'd known her. Her curly hair had thinned as much as her body and the color had leached away, leaving puffs white as milkweed down. She looked up and smiled, shaky and frail, but bright as her daughter.

"Delia! Come in, come in." She set the journal aside and patted the bed. "Sit with me and visit. I'm glad you came home early this evening. It's been too long since you came in to say good night."

Sadie and I traded looks. Esther knew me, but didn't remember I'd been gone. Maybe morning would be better, after she'd rested and wasn't so tired. I leaned to kiss her soft cheek, determined to make the best of it. She smelled of talcum and rose water. "You're right; I should come in more often. I'll try to do better, Mama Esther."

She patted my face with a shaking hand, confusion clouding her eyes. Confusion did little to dim her smile. "I wouldn't deny you time with your friends. You need to see more of that polite young man who likes you so much, not waste your evenings with an old woman. But when you get in early enough, peek in before bed. I sleep easier when I know both you and Sadie are home safe."

Tears burned my eyes and I cradled her hand between mine. "How was your day? Did Annie bring up any of the cookies she baked?"

"My days seldom change. I won't bore you with the story of my promenade down the hallway and back." Esther peered about my shoulder. "Delia, where are your manners? Leaving your friend standing in the hall is extremely rude. Please invite her in and introduce me properly."

Shadow stood on the threshold, hands folded at her waist, watching Esther intently and ignoring me. She didn't step any farther into the room even after being invited and I was glad. The ghost loomed like a shadow of death in the doorway, poised to claim Esther. That I'd led her here, even unknowingly, suddenly felt like a betrayal.

Sadie sucked in a quivering breath, on the edge of tears. She'd guessed who Esther saw. "Mama, we didn't bring anyone home. You're having another one of your spells. I think it's best if I tuck you in so you can get some sleep now."

"You didn't?" She peeked around me again, certainty wilting. The light went out of Esther's faltering smile and I knew Shadow was gone. "I could have sworn . . . I know I saw a girl standing in the doorway."

"You're just tired." Sadie turned off the big floor lamp in the corner, leaving only a small light on near the door. Her cheerful smile might fool Esther, but not me. "A good night's sleep will make a world of difference."

Sadie and I eased her mother down on the pillows and tucked the coverlet around her. I kissed Esther on the cheek again. "Sleep well. I'll come eat breakfast with you in the morning. Would you like that?"

She nodded, brow crinkled in puzzlement. "If you like. Who are you again?"

"I'm Delia. Remember?" I smoothed her hair, keeping my voice calm and struggling to smile. Calm was far from how I felt. "I've come home again."

Esther shut her eyes, tears pooling in the corners. "Oh, Delia . . . I'm so glad you're back. They told me you died in the quake."

She thought I was my mother. Each breath stuck in my throat so that I couldn't speak. I fled into the hallway, exhausted and unable to bear more. Sadie murmured to Esther, soothing her as you would a small child, and shame joined grief. I'd broken in five minutes. Sadie had borne the burden alone for nearly three years.

Hugging arms over my chest did little to warm me. The air in the hallway had turned so cold I expected to see my breath cloud. Shadow stood at the end of the hall, keeping her distance from the bedroom door, but positioned to keep me in sight. Green eyes stared at me, the ghost's gaze intense and aware, trying to convey a silent message. "Say something," I whispered. "I don't know what you want. Tell me."

She glided a step closer, hand extended. The memory of brushing death again and again was too fresh and raw for me to brave taking Shadow's hand. I stepped back, shaking my head. "No, I can't do that. Find another way to tell me. Find a way to speak so I can understand."

The ghost dropped her hand and didn't pursue me. She looked toward the bedroom again, drawn by Sadie's soft voice and Esther's mumbled answers, and her fingers wrapped around the cross at her throat. Shadow's eyes met mine for a moment in silent pleading. Then she was gone.

Gone for now, but I knew not forever. I slumped against the wall, shivering in the lingering chill.

Sadie stepped into view and closed the bedroom door softly. She leaned against the wall with me, offering companionship. "Mother's already asleep. Dee, I have to ask . . . the girl Mama saw in the doorway . . ."

"Shadow was watching us talk. I'm surprised, but I think Esther saw the ghost." I took a breath, unwilling to think too much about possible answers, all of which came back to how little time Esther had left. I wasn't ready to face that. Not yet. "I can't explain how or why. As far as I know Shadow hasn't shown herself to anyone but me. But I'm far from an expert on ghosts."

She chewed her lip for a moment and nodded. Sadie understood the implications perfectly. "Come on, Dee. Annie will feed you and then you can get some sleep. This was a rougher homecoming for you than I'd imagined."

"I'm fine." I took a breath and brushed hair out of my eyes. "Hungry, but fine."

Sadie raised an eyebrow, looking down on me from her height advantage of two and one quarter inches. "No, you're not. But I'm not going to quarrel with you about putting on a brave face tonight. I'll save that for breakfast. You'll be able to argue back and hold your own once you've rested. It's more fun that way."

"I'm sorry, Sadie. I'd have come home sooner if I'd known." I led the way down the stairs, hunger a burning coal in the pit of my stomach. Food and sleep would help set things right, just as long as I could swallow past the lump in my throat. "It's not fair you've coped alone. Now that I'm home, I'm staying."

"I wasn't alone, Annie was here. And I had Jack to help. He's good with Mama." Sadie smiled shyly and ducked her head. I'd only heard of Jack through letters, but the softness of her expression while saying his name made me like him sight unseen. "I haven't been left on my own."

"I'll be staying in any case." Shadow's seeking me out put an end to the foolish notion that I'd left ghosts behind by leaving San Francisco. Spirits would find me no matter where I was and I needed to face up to that. Whatever the reason she led me home, I was grateful. I didn't want to miss Esther's last days. In any case, the students at Saint Celia's School for Girls wouldn't even notice I'd gone. "I'll send a telegram to the school and have the rest of my things sent."

We reached the bottom of the stairs and my stomach rumbled loudly enough to make Sadie laugh. She slipped an arm around my shoulders. "I'm glad you're not going back to New York. I've missed you. And I wouldn't want to attempt planning this wedding without you. Jack and I have talked about marriage for a long time, but we only made it official last Friday. We both agreed to skip the engagement party and go straight to the wedding. There's a great deal to be done in the next six weeks."

I paused at the kitchen door. Annie always knew everything that went on in the house, but I still lowered my voice. "Six weeks is a scandalously short engagement. People will talk."

Sadie's chin came up, haughty and proud. People much older than either of us wilted when she turned that look on them. "Let them talk. When Daddy's heart began to fail the doctors swore he had years left, but we lost him in less than a month. I can't risk waiting. I want my mother at my wedding. Six weeks might be all the time I have to spare. Mama won't remember a thing about what went on, but I'll know she was there."

She wore the brave face now, but I'd not bet against Sadie Larkin taking on San Francisco society and winning. And I'd be right beside her, ready to battle with anyone who breathed an untrue word.

I pushed open the kitchen door and held it for her. "We'll get started in the morning. First we'll eat breakfast with Mama Esther and have that quarrel over my bravery if you're still keen on it. Afterward we should visit a seamstress to see about a wedding dress. Making a dress and fittings will take the longest, so we should see to that immediately."

Sadie's eyes swam with tears. "I won't forget this, Dee. I promise."

I gave her a gentle shove into the kitchen and put on a smile for Annie. My heart was too full, all the words I could have said in answer gone. Leaving home had been a mistake. I'd not lost my problems, if anything I'd gained more in the form of Shadow and the mystery surrounding her. All I'd lost was time with the people I loved.

Six weeks. Such a short time to plan the start of Sadie's new life and prepare for Esther's to end.

The dream began like all the others I'd had, but the ghost didn't follow behind, waiting for me to find an answer. This time I was inside her skin.

Shadow rushed down streets gray with fog, cold seeping through the thin soles of her shoes and numbing her toes. The night was moonless and darker for it. People hurried past, vague shapes that loomed into view and disappeared again, heads down and bundled against the chill. Fog deadened the sound of footsteps, the creak of wagons and harness.

Hissing gas lamps stood on corners, a small oasis of yellow light puddled on damp brick sidewalks. She crossed a street and Shadow looked behind, the feel of someone watching tickling the back of her neck. The shape of a man winked in and out of view back the way she'd come, skirting the edge of gaslight and vanishing into the fog again. He kept his head down like all the other people on the street. She saw him turn a corner, no doubt in a hurry to reach home and a fire.

Shadow pulled her shawl tighter, the deeper cold near the wharfs making her wish for her heavy wrap. Fishing boats rocked gently on the incoming tide. Mooring ropes groaned as they pulled tight and water sloshed against the hull. She turned into a gravel-lined alley, a shortcut she never took after dark, but she'd worked late and longed for her own fire.

The coins she'd earned in tips jingled in her skirt pocket. Saturday nights were busy at the tavern. Sean had given her a quarter for staying an extra shift and offered the use of the cot behind the kitchen. She'd slept there other nights and Patrick knew not to wait up on Saturday, but the baby was teething and fussy. They'd both be up walking the floors and waiting on her.

More than cold made her walk faster. Shadow tried not to think of the stories men told over mugs of beer and glasses of whiskey. Darkness pressed in as the alley narrowed. She wrapped a chapped hand around the cross at her throat, muttering prayers under her breath.

A cat yowled, running from between two houses and across her path. Shards of stone and grit flew away from the cat's paws and stung her cheek. Shadow touched her face and drew away bloody fingers. She found the scrap of handkerchief in her pocket and worked it out, careful not to spill her hard-earned coins on the ground.

Shadow moistened the handkerchief with her tongue, scrubbing at her fingers and walking faster. The streetlamp at the end of the narrow alley, a beacon marking the street and the last block home, blinked out.

Tall and broad-shouldered, a man stepped out of the mist, standing toe-to-toe with Shadow before she saw him. She stared, heart pounding in terror and breath coming in gasping sobs.

A cloth hood covered his head. She couldn't see his eyes, his mouth.

She couldn't see if he smiled.

I scrabbled off the bed, running from a threat that began to fade as soon as my eyes opened. My feet tangled in sheets and the hem of my nightgown, tripping me. Slamming into the table next to the bed tipped the lamp, but I caught the heavy brass base before the whole thing crashed to the ground.

Light chased away more panic, enough that I stopped wanting

to flee the room. The house was still silent with sleep. I hadn't screamed, Sadie or Annie would have come running. Shaking, gulping air, and crying, I huddled in the overstuffed chair, grateful not to have an audience for my humiliation and the privacy to sort through what had just happened.

The dreams had started in New York, mere glimpses of Shadow hurrying down a darkened street or following me wherever I went. Urgency had always been there, coupled with fear and panic and the need to get away. Details of those dreams were as fuzzy and murky as the fog. They'd changed little by little as the months wore on and I'd begun to follow Shadow instead of the ghost trailing after me. The sense of urgency, that there was something vital I needed to do, increased until the day I knew I had to come home. Still, I'd never understood why Shadow was afraid or why the ghost felt the need to show me these things.

Distance played a part in the dreams being fragmented and unclear. I was in San Francisco now, my home as well as Shadow's, and the details of this dream were as sharp and clear as a freshly minted coin. That made what I'd seen twice as frightening.

Shadow stood at the foot of my bed, hands folded at her waist. Watching and waiting for me to speak.

"Dear God in heaven. I'm so sorry, Shadow. So sorry." I understood the sorrow in her eyes now and some of the reasons she followed me. She'd never gotten home. Shadow needed someone, needed me, to know why.

Why was important, I understood that. What she expected from me now that I knew baffled me.

CHAPTER 3

Gabe

Gabe unbuttoned his suit coat and let the front hang open. The slope wasn't steep, but the climb in the morning sun was enough to make him sweat. Grass and tiny white daisies, granite headstones and flowers left by loved ones glistened with moisture deposited by last night's fog. Each step kicked up water droplets that soaked into the cuffs of his trousers and the tops of his socks. His feet were getting wet inside his shoes.

This early in the day the Presidio was empty of visitors wanting to pay their respects to fallen soldiers. A crisp breeze blew off the bay, the air cold enough at the top of the hill that Gabe decided against abandoning the jacket for shirtsleeves. His squad worked efficiently if somberly, voices subdued and their normal gallows humor missing. Bright sunlight reflected off the patrolmen's brass buttons and the numbered badges pinned to their uniforms, an illusion of warmth that didn't live up to its promise. Even if the wind hadn't chilled him to the bone, the bodies lying side by side atop one of the graves would do the job.

Jack stood in the shade of a redwood not more than fifty feet away, questioning the man who found the bodies and scribbling notes in the battered moleskine he kept in his pocket. The gravedigger was older, his dark hair gone mostly gray and skin suncreased. He twisted his cap in shaking hands and kept his back to the murder victims. Death was harder to confront outside a sealed casket.

An officer from the Presidio, a captain, hovered behind Jack's shoulder. The Army brass scowled, his opinion of civilians investigating a crime on his base and infringing on his territory clear. Jack ignored the captain's silent fuming and did his job, patiently prodding the gravedigger for information and writing down the answers.

Shock would drown the memories of what he'd seen soon. All the old man would remember then was the blood.

Gabe left his partner to prying loose information. He walked a slow circle around the dead couple, always careful to stay clear of the patrolman taking photographs with a folding Kodak. Concentrating on the details was a detective's job, searching for patterns and similarities between open cases. His father taught Gabe that was how the toughest crimes were solved, gathering and piecing together odd fragments of information until you had the picture clear in your mind. A murder investigation was a macabre jigsaw puzzle, splashed with blood and the remnants of someone's life.

Focusing on details let him ignore the sewer stench of punctured bowels that filled each breath, coating his tongue. Collecting information let him pretend not to see the way blood drew insects, how flies swarmed around stab wounds or crawled over the dead man's open eyes. Thinking about anything but how the bodies were posed was a rookie mistake.

He hadn't been a rookie in ten years. Gabe swallowed away the burning in the back of his throat and vowed to keep his breakfast down.

The man and woman lay on their sides facing each other, hands bound behind their backs. Neither one wore shoes or stockings. A hangman's noose looped each of their necks, the length of rope that tightened the knot running down their backs and tied around their ankles. Skin was scraped raw and bloody around the ropes at both wrists and ankles. Gabe swallowed again, suddenly reminded of animals gnawing off their own legs to escape a trap.

Strips of red fabric were rolled and stuffed into their mouths to muffle screams. They'd screamed around the gags, he was certain of that, and probably tried to plead with their killer. The woman's gag was pulled tight and cut into the corners of her mouth, tearing skin enough to bleed. Each scream did more damage, drew more blood.

They'd suffered before dying. The wounds Gabe saw were nonlethal, shallow stab wounds inflicted for pain and not to kill. Not right away. Movement would tighten the rope around the victims' necks, slowly choking them, and staying still through the punishment they'd taken was next to impossible.

A coroner's report would confirm what Gabe already knew: the dusky color of their skin meant the couple had suffocated before they could bleed to death. The killer never meant for them to die quickly or easily.

The symbol carved into their foreheads, a circle divided into quarters, matched marks on the first two victims found: a man in Chinatown and a woman near the Ferry Building. Weeks separated those murders from these, but the killer left his victims where he knew they'd be found. He wanted to send a message and make sure the police took him seriously.

Gabe took this man very seriously indeed.

"Lieutenant Ryan?" Jack motioned him over. The gravedigger was heading down the hill toward the gates, but the Army officer still glowered behind Jack's shoulder. "The captain would like a word, sir."

Gabe took one last look at the tableau staged for them. "Patrolman Henderson!"

The tall and skinny young rookie broke away from a line of men searching between headstones and trotted across the grass. "Yes, Lieutenant?"

"I think we're almost done here. As soon as Baker finishes taking his photographs, cover them up. The coroner and his men will be along soon. Gather a few of the officers to give them a hand getting the stretchers down the hill."

"Yes, sir." Marshall Henderson stared at the bodies, sweat beading on his forehead. "It's him, isn't it? The one sending the letters."

"Yes." Gabe clapped the boy on the shoulder, feeling like a grizzled veteran and much older than thirty. Henderson had only been on the force six months, but he'd dragged the new patrolman into the investigation from the start. For a rookie he had good instincts and so far, he hadn't panicked. "Get the blankets over them and set someone to watch for the coroner."

Gabe stuffed his hands deep into his pockets and took his time strolling to where the captain and Jack waited. The captain meant to force a confrontation of some kind and throw his weight around. Summoning Gabe like a private caught sneaking out after curfew guaranteed the captain would get exactly what he wanted.

That soured Gabe's mood further. The mayor and the base commandant were old friends. Getting in a row with a high-ranking officer would come back on him, right or wrong. He'd have to dig deep and find a scrap of diplomacy and patience.

The look Jack gave him was a mixture of warning and exasperation. "Captain Irwin, this is Lieutenant Ryan. Lieutenant Ryan is the detective in charge of the investigation."

Irwin appeared to be about forty, tall and well-muscled, compact and not going soft around the middle. Squint lines surrounding pale blue eyes and skin tanned to the color of tobacco spoke of days spent outdoors, not sitting at a desk. A training officer perhaps, accustomed to barking orders and instant obedience. Jittery bounces on his toes and a disapproving scowl made his annoyance plain.

Gabe didn't much like men like the captain, not since the quake and the desperate days after. So far Irwin hadn't given him a reason to reform his opinion. He forced a smile and stuck his hand out. "Pleased to meet you, Captain Irwin. Is there something I can do for you?"

"I need your men gone within the hour, Lieutenant." The captain's handshake was as brusque as his manner of speaking. "The colonel is hosting a group of European military officers and their wives. His schedule calls for speeches at fourteen-hundred hours, a wreath-laying ceremony, and escorting everyone to the fair once the ceremony is complete. I have a squad waiting to set up the podium and chairs. Your men are smack in the middle of where they need to work."

Jack tapped the edge of his notebook with a chewed pencil, a sure sign he was tense or on the verge of losing his patience. "I explained to the captain that this was a murder investigation and couldn't be rushed. He insisted on speaking to someone in authority."

"Sergeant Fitzgerald's word is as good as mine, this can't be rushed." Gabe slipped his hands back in his trouser pockets, working at looking relaxed. He had a hunch; he wanted to be wrong. "You're not exactly short of scenic views, Captain. The Presidio is a big place. Surely you can find another suitable location for the colonel to give his speech."

"Lieutenant, it's not a matter of scenic views or we wouldn't be having this conversation." Captain Irwin gestured with the riding crop in his hand, waving it in the direction of the victims. He never really looked at the dead couple or saw how their heads lined up precisely with the grave markers. "The colonel is scheduled to lay a wreath on the graves of the first base commandant and his wife. I can't move the ceremony without moving the graves."

Having his hunch confirmed left a bitter taste in Gabe's mouth. The killer wanted to send a message all right, but he might be the only one listening. "The mayor and Commandant Blair have already come to an agreement about jurisdiction. They both feel the police are best equipped to find this killer. I won't be responsible for a haphazard investigation that allows him to escape. My men know what to look for, Captain. They will leave once they're sure nothing's been missed. Not before."

Irwin glowered, pulled himself up straight, and smacked his riding crop against his leg repeatedly, a pose designed to put the fear of God and Captain into young troopers. That he thought intimidation would work on Gabe was almost amusing. Almost.

"You'll regret not being more cooperative, Ryan. I'll be making a full report to the colonel and Commandant Blair."

"You do that, Captain." He smiled, baring his teeth. The small amount of patience he'd mustered was gone. "Finding two people butchered before noon will be the only thing I regret about this day. Rest assured I'll be filing a full report as well."

The coroner's men trudged up the hill; canvas stretchers on sturdy wooden poles folded in half and balanced in one hand. They opened out the dull ivory rectangles on the grass, one near the man's bulky body, the other next to the woman. He stepped away from Irwin's outraged sputtering, watching silently and doing the dead couple honor that the captain didn't seem inclined to show.

Henderson directed two patrolmen to help lift the blanket-shrouded bodies. Rigor mortis had set in before the couple was found, making the task easier. They struggled to lift the stocky dead man's weight and settle his rigid corpse on the stretcher. The woman was easier to move, slightly built and not very tall.

Gabe saw a scrap of blue flutter in the grass. The wind sent the envelope tumbling across the hilltop, sticking in blades of grass for an instant and whirling in the air again. Marshall Henderson reacted first, already in hot pursuit before he could yell.

Henderson caught the envelope within a few seconds. He pinched the blue square tight between two fingers, turning it to examine both sides. Color bleached from his face. “I’ve got it, sir. You need to see this.”

He left Jack to deal with Irwin and met his promising rookie halfway. The cheap blue stationery was splotched with the woman’s blood, but not enough to obscure the handwriting or that the letter was addressed to Lieutenant Gabriel Ryan.

Gabe wrapped the envelope in his handkerchief, tucked the note in a jacket pocket and buttoned the flap. He had cotton gloves and fingerprint powder in his desk. Nothing had shown up on any of the other letters, but he kept hoping overconfidence would make the killer sloppy.

His men knew their jobs and could finish up without him. He strode past Irwin without a word or a glance, his mouth dry and his heart pounding. The killer was raising the stakes, making this personal. He couldn’t summon the willingness to be diplomatic with the captain.

Jack caught up before Gabe got more than a hundred yards down the hill. His partner tucked the ever-present moleskine into an inside pocket, whistling a cheerful tune.

A catchy melody penetrated Gabe’s funk after a moment and recognition made him smile. The song was a hit in the saloons and bawdy houses near the docks, the lyrics lewd and not fit for decent company. Undoubtedly in poor taste considering the situation.

That made the song perfect in Gabe’s eyes. They’d stayed partners for ten years because Jack knew when to give him a moment to breathe and when to make him laugh.

Some of the tension bled out of his shoulders and he unclenched his fists. "Better not let Sadie here you whistling that song. She'll start questioning where you learned it."

Jack grinned. "Who do you think taught me? Sadie taught me all the words, too."

"I should have known." He chuckled and shook his head. "You two were made for each other."

The air was clean away from the murder site, filled with the familiar seaweed and sand scent of the bay, the smell of pinesap and wet grass crushed underfoot. Noise from the Pan Pacific carried into the Presidio, voices and music an insect drone in the distance. Fog built an iron-gray wall outside the Golden Gate, biding its time until sunset. The killer would bide his time, too, using darkness and murk as cover to hunt.

The men from the coroner's office and two of his patrolmen passed them, each man holding the stretcher handles tight or gripping the canvas sides to get the bodies safely down the hill.

Gabe paused to let the stretcher bearers get ahead and watched them go. "May God have mercy on their souls. With luck, we'll turn up something that identifies them so their families can be notified. They deserve a decent burial."

"And someone to mourn them." Jack kicked at the grass, his cheerfulness gone. "We won't get any clues in the letter he left. Not if it's like the others."

The driver who'd brought him from the station house waited at the bottom of the hill. Sunlight glinted off the windscreen of the black motorcar and the wire-spoke wheels. Gabe still preferred buggies, but the chief was determined to replace all the horse-drawn vehicles the department owned with automobiles. He and Jack ambled downhill, neither of them in any hurry to overtake the procession of stretchers.

"This letter isn't exactly like the others, Jack." Gabe's hand strayed to his pocket, touching the bulk of handkerchief and envelope inside, mindful of the letters addressed to Captain Matthew Ryan in his father's files. "He addressed this one to me."

"A mash note then, like the letters you told me about." Jack tugged off his plaid cap, beating the hat against his leg with each step. "It's been almost thirty years since your pop got those letters, Gabe. This can't be the same."

"It isn't the same." Unlike his father, he didn't have a wife and baby to threaten for one. The fire took Victoria and his unborn child from him. He didn't have anything left worth losing. Gabe opened the car door and waved Jack inside. "Thirty years is too long. But it tells me this man is still a step ahead and knows more about us than we know about him. Frankly, that gives me the willies."

The car jerked away from the curb, gears whining as the driver followed the twisting road that led off the base and back into the city. Gabe leaned his head back and tipped his hat over his eyes. Thinking, trying to put the puzzle together.

"Gabe, I still haven't said anything to Sadie." Leather seats and springs creaked under Jack's weight. "If this man knows as much as you think . . . Should I be worried about Sadie and her family?"

He lifted the brim of the hat and looked his partner in the eye. "I'll assign some men to watch the house and keep an eye on things. I can't force an escort on her, but if Sadie consents I can assign officers to take her shopping or anyplace she needs to go. Talk to her. See if you can get her to agree."

"How much should I tell her?"

Gabe thought of Victoria and pulled the hat back over his eyes. "Tell her all of it and put the fear of this man into her. Do whatever it takes to get Sadie to agree to police protection."

Knowing his men were watching over Sadie would let him

sleep better. He didn't want to see the empty, wounded look in Jack's eyes if anything happened to her.

He saw that look in the mirror every morning. That was enough.

Delia

The front room of the dressmaker's shop was stifling. Fanning myself with one of the brochures on the showroom table moved little air and did less to relieve the heat. I'd suffocate before Sadie emerged from the dressing suite.

I'd left my chair once to open the front door, hoping to let in some air, but the plump clerk behind the counter shut me in again immediately.

"We can't leave the door open, Miss." She eased the door closed, a faint touch of disapproval in her smile. Her square hands were smaller than mine, nails trimmed short to keep from snagging the fabrics, and pale against the dark wood frame. "Mademoiselle says the moisture is bad for the silks. And you never know who might come wandering in that don't belong. Would you like a cup of tea?"

"Yes, that would be nice. Thank you." I'd settled in my chair again, resigned to waiting on Sadie's pleasure.

Telling the girl that I didn't belong here would only confuse her. This was the fourth shop we'd visited in two days and the fourth to prove I still lacked Sadie's sense of style and fashion. I was adrift in a sea of swatches, pearl buttons and bobbin lace, following where she led.

Shadow stood near me, hands pressed to her stomach and eyes all too aware. The shawl she'd worn since coming to me was tied around her waist, as if the ghost found the room too warm as well. A silly notion, but she continued to change from the silent spirit

I'd known for six months. Closeness to home and the life ripped away from her had to be the reason why.

She watched buggies and motorcars pass on the street with great interest, studied the faces of people walking past the windows and the few women who came into the shop. Looking for someone, perhaps searching for a face she knew.

Ghosts mingled with the people on the sidewalk, going about their business as they had in life. Whalers from San Francisco's earliest days, Russian fur traders and troopers dressed in Civil War garb, they all took turns walking through the two women chatting outside the window. Some areas of the city were thick with restless dead and in others I never saw a spirit. None but my personal ghost. She never left me for long.

I watched Shadow, mulling over my nightmare and trying to understand what she wanted from me. What I'd learned in the dream brought me no closer to solving the puzzle she represented. Knowing how she'd died didn't tell me how she'd lived or who she was in life. The need to discover all I could about her was growing stronger, becoming a compulsion. I didn't know if that desire came from the ghost or from inside me.

Accepting that the ghost was real and haunting me was hard enough; that she might be influencing my thoughts made me uncomfortable. All that kept me from contemplating the possibility of insanity was that Esther had seen her too.

The door to the dressing suite swung open and Sadie finally appeared. Tears filled my eyes and I forgave all the waiting. She'd never looked more beautiful.

Sadie stepped up onto a round platform centered in front of a wall lined with mirrors. Mademoiselle Fouche shook out the full silk skirts of the wedding dress, settling the lace overlay into place. Long organdy sleeves reached her wrists. Lace appliqués, roses and lilies, and tiny pearls covered the silk bodice. The fabrics were a soft cream, not stark white, and set off Sadie's coloring perfectly.

"What do you think, Dee?" She grinned and twirled round once, a curly-haired kewpie doll with roses blooming in her cheeks.

"I think Jack will faint dead away when he sees you in that dress." I went to stand near Sadie and gazed at her reflection in the mirror. Trailing behind from shop to shop was worth seeing her so radiant. "Be sure to warn the best man. He'll need to be ready."

Mademoiselle set a matching silk cap and lace veil on Sadie's head. She stepped back, smiling broadly and obviously pleased. "There. You will be a most beautiful bride, Miss Larkin. A few small alterations and it will be as if the dress was made just for you. I can have it ready for you within the month. Excuse me while I write up the order and prepare the bill."

The dressmaker disappeared into the back room, leaving Sadie to preen. She fussed with the neckline, head tipped to the side and eyeing the fit of the bodice with a practiced eye. "This is excellent work. The girl who ordered the dress canceled at the last minute. Mademoiselle Fouche is letting me have it for half of the original price." She twirled again so that the skirt floated around her, gleeful and happy. "It's perfect, Dee! There couldn't be a more perfect dress."

Shadow left her place near the windows. The ghost glided in slow circles around the platform, eyes fixed on Sadie. She extended a hand to brush the full skirt, fingers passing through lace and silk without stirring the fabric.

Sadie never noticed. The ghost looked to me, her eyes begging for me to understand.

"What's wrong?" Sadie squeezed my hand. Her gleeful look was gone. "Is Shadow here?"

"Shadow is always here." I managed a smile and steered the conversation to safer ground. "I've been home for three days now.

When do I get to meet this fiancé of yours? I'm beginning to think you made him up."

She laughed. Mentioning Jack was all it took to make her happy again. "You'll meet him tonight. Jack and his partner Gabe are coming to escort us to the fair. We'll have supper out and then see the sights. The four of us will have a marvelous time."

"Scheming are you?" I folded my arms over my chest and peered up at her sternly, determined to look cross. "It won't work you know. It never has."

"Delia Ann Martin, I'm hurt. Scheming is the furthest thing from my mind." She fiddled with the veil and pouted prettily. Pouting always worked on her beaus and admirers, and no doubt Jack was helpless in the face of her trembling lip. I was made of sterner stuff. "Gabe Ryan is Jack's best man. You'd have to meet him sometime before the wedding. I thought the four of us could have a bit of fun tonight while you got to know each other. What's the harm in that?"

"No harm at all. Not if a bit of fun's all you've planned." Sadie would never admit to matchmaking or that her scheming was doomed to failure. "And meeting Mr. Ryan means I can warn him about Jack fainting. He can begin planning his strategy for catching the groom."

Sadie stepped off the platform and beamed at me, scenting victory. "Let me get changed and settle up with Mademoiselle. We can visit with Mama and tell her all about the dress before the boys call for us. This will be fun, Dee, I promise. You and Gabe will get along swimmingly."

"Yes, great fun. I'm sure of it." That I muttered to the closed door of the dressing suite didn't matter. Sadie would heed my tone about as well as the door. "I'm sure Mr. Ryan has no idea what he's gotten himself into."

I shivered, suddenly chilled in the overheated room. Other

ghosts, women dressed in evening finery, shopgirl frocks, or dance-hall costumes that barely satisfied decency, shimmered into view atop the fitting platform. More ghosts appeared in the mirrors lining the wall, all standing and staring at me. Each spirit wore the stoic expression of my ghost, each mirrored Shadow's waiting pose and the sorrow in her eyes. They all had secrets or obligations from life left undone, wrongs they needed set right before they could rest.

The weight of their need pinned me in place and I couldn't speak, or turn away. All these lost souls wanted my help, as Shadow did, and left me with just as little idea of what they expected me to do.

The bell on the shop door jingled, announcing another customer, and the chipper voice of the dressmaker's assistant greeted two older women. One by one the ghosts faded, releasing me and letting me breathe. I sat on one of the small chairs to wait for Sadie, fighting the need to curl over my knees and cry.

Shadow stood in her place by the window again, the shawl draped around her shoulders and one hand clutching the cross at her throat. She waited, patience personified.

CHAPTER 4

Gabe

Gabe leaned back in his creaky swivel chair, rocking and staring at the piece of blue stationery centered on his desk blotter. Imagining the letter taunting him to decipher what the killer's message really meant wasn't hard.

The precise handwriting in black ink matched the three letters sent to the newspaper. This letter was longer, two double-sided pages, but Gabe never questioned that it was written by the same man. The symbols on the bottom of the last page convinced him if nothing else.

Not knowing what the symbols meant bothered him. They might be nonsense, the meaningless creation of a deranged mind. That was the conclusion his father came to when he'd worked the letter murders case years ago, but Gabe wasn't so sure. More than a hunch prodded him toward thinking he'd seen similar pictures before. Trying to remember when and where he'd encountered the symbols kept him awake at night.

The killer had repeated his demands to reprint all his letters on the front page of *The Examiner* and escalated his threat to hunt people on the Pan Pacific grounds. That was a sure way to start panic if word got out. The murderer had to know the mayor and the chief would never agree to publish any part of the letters. Gabe had a sick bet with himself that the killer was counting on that.

No trace of fingerprints appeared on either page or the inside of the envelope, but he hadn't really expected to get that lucky. He'd found what he thought he'd find: raving that made little sense, threats and bragging, right down to the methodical detail of how the couple left in the Presidio cemetery were murdered.

All that set this letter apart was his name on the envelope, and that the killer laid the responsibility for the couple's death, and any future victims, at Gabe's feet.

That he wasn't really to blame didn't stop him from brooding.

Jack rapped on the half-open door to get Gabe's attention. He held up a brown paper grocer's sack. "Baxter and Henderson found something after we left. A lady's handbag and a pair of shoes."

"Come in and shut the door." Gabe slipped the letter and envelope under the desk blotter. "Did they touch anything?"

"No, Henderson knows better. He looked inside the bag to see what was there and didn't go any further. Baxter follows his lead." Jack set the sack on the corner of the desk. "If we're not careful the kid will have our jobs soon."

"Marshall Henderson's too smart to want our jobs."

Gabe pulled two pairs of cotton gloves out of his desk and tossed a pair to Jack. The paper sack had been used before, worn and soft at the top from being rolled and creased. Oily stains that smelled faintly of sausage soaked one corner and partway up the side. The bag looked like trash, a discarded sack used to carry lunch once too often.

A black grease pencil had been used to draw the same symbol carved into the victim's foreheads on one side. The killer's calling card.

He pulled up the roller-shade on the window behind his desk. The sun would set soon, but the sunlight that remained brightened the desktop more than his lamp. "Where did they find this?"

Jack had laid sheets of clean typing paper over the dark green blotter, a trick they'd figured out years ago. Anything that dropped off the bag or the contents would show on the white surface. "Henderson dragged Baxter with him all the way to the edge of the Pan Pacific grounds. He made Baxter search around every headstone, bush, and park bench with him. They spotted the bag on top of a headstone near the boundary fence. Soon as Henderson saw the drawing, he knew the killer left it sitting in plain sight for them to find."

Another message: *catch me if you can.*

Gabe gingerly lifted a small pair of brown leather shoes out of the sack. The straps on one shoe were broken, torn loose from the side and not unbuckled. A heel was missing from the other shoe, tossed into the bottom of the bag and rattling around. The shoes were clean, no mud or grass sticking to the soles or lodged in the straps. He set them on the paper and pulled out the handbag.

The square handbag was made of soft brown leather to match the shoes, framed at the top in etched brass. A round ball clasp in the center held the top closed, while a small hinge on each side let the metal frame pivot to open the bag. Two dime-sized rings mounted on the top corners of the metal frame anchored a short chain handle.

Gabe felt like a voyeur peering inside the dead woman's purse. He tipped the bag up and emptied it onto the paper-covered desk. The scent of gardenias filled the office: her perfume. He inventoried the contents, ticking off what was left of a woman's life. "A change purse, a comb, gloves with pearl buttons, a small bottle of cologne, and a lipstick. Nothing to tell us who she was." He ran his hands along the inside and turned the handbag inside out. "There's a pocket here."

The flap was held closed with a small jet button. Gabe laid a mother-of-pearl calling card case and a tarnished silver compact on the desk with the rest of the woman's things. He opened the compact to find face powder more than half-gone and a cracked mirror.

Inside the card case was a stack of embossed visiting cards, each with a small yellow rose printed on the bottom right corner. Flowery script spelled out Miss Elaine Meadows.

He held a card up for Jack to see. "Elaine Meadows. We'll send some of the boys around to other station houses and see if anyone's reported her missing. If we find her family maybe we'll get a lead on the man with her."

"You're assuming the handbag and shoes belong to the woman we found this morning. I can't believe identifying her is that easy. The murderer is just as likely to leave the belongings of a victim we haven't found yet." Jack emptied the coin purse onto the desk. "Streetcar tokens, about two dollars in coin, and a house key. The number eighty-four is engraved on the key."

"That's a start. If no one filed a missing person's report I'll send men out to start checking buildings numbered eighty-four." Gabe scooped everything back into the handbag. Paper sack, handbag, and shoes went into the deep bottom drawer of his desk and were locked away. He remembered the letter and envelope under the blotter, and secured them with the rest. "How many can there be?"

"No more than one on every block. Shouldn't take the squad more than a month to check them all. By then we'll be hip-deep in bodies and no closer to catching him." Jack stripped off the cotton gloves and dropped them in the drawer Gabe held open. "We should get moving if we want to get to Sadie's on time."

Gabe checked the office one last time, making sure all the file drawers and his desk were locked, and pulled the shade down over the window. He slipped on his coat and waved Jack toward the hall. "I can't believe I agreed to this. Escorting Sadie's friend to supper and the fair is above and beyond best man duties."

Jack lounged against a wall, twirling his cap on two fingers while Gabe locked the office door. "You'd have to meet Delia sometime before the wedding. Might as well be tonight, Gabe. And it won't kill you to leave that garret of yours for one evening. You spend too much time alone."

"It's not a garret. Mrs. Allen runs a perfectly respectable rooming house."

"That she does. And you live in the smallest room on the top floor. I think that qualifies as a garret." Jack gave him a sideways look. "It's been nine years, Gabe. Time to rejoin the world."

"So you've said before." Buttoning his coat gave his hands something to do other than shake with memories of smoke and fire. Gabe took a breath. "One night at the fair won't kill me. Just don't expect this to become a habit. Whatever Sadie's plotting won't work."

Jack's eyes widened in mock horror and he put a hand to his chest, fingers splayed wide. "My girl? Plotting? Heaven forefend."

Gabe couldn't help laughing. "If you don't walk faster we will be late."

They moved past a line of office doors, a frosted window set in the middle of each shellacked pine frame painted with a detective's name. The hall was dimly lit this time of day. All the offices were closed up and the shades pulled over the windows, shutting out any light that might leak in from outside. Day shift was headed home and the men working nights were already out on the streets.

The station lobby was quiet, too. A few people sat patiently on the battered oak benches waiting to speak to an officer, while others unable to sit still paced near the front desk. Gabe viewed change of shift as the eye of a hurricane, an hour of calm before the storm winds hit again. The drunks and rowdies brought in for fighting, and pickpockets preying on tourists would fill the holding cells before dawn. All of them would come through the lobby first, fill the benches, and kick up a fuss. Quiet never lasted.

Luck was with them. A cab pulled up to drop someone off in front of the station house as they stepped outside. Jack gave the driver Sadie's address and they were off.

Gabe stared out the cab window. Dusk settled over the city, the thin layers of salmon-colored clouds that streaked the sky gradually darkening to indigo. Windows on shopfronts began to glow and street lamps came on one by one, their light shimmering up the steep hills like earth-bound stars. The bright glass globes lured swarms of moths as twilight deepened, an attraction that ended in death.

He looked away. Too much death stalked his city in darkness.

"So." Gabe cleared his throat. "What do I need to know about Sadie's friend before I meet her?"

"I've never met Delia. She took a teaching job in New York the year before I met Sadie. I know Sadie dotes on her and thinks of her as a sister, not a friend." Jack pulled on the end of his mustache, deep in thought. "She's very protective of Delia, too. I know Sadie was really concerned about how Delia would react to the way Esther has deteriorated in the last year. She wrote letters to soften the blow, but she knew Delia would take her mother's condition hard."

He picked at the crease in his trouser leg and frowned. "Is she that close to Mrs. Larkin?"

"Delia was on a trip with Sadie and Esther to San Diego when the quake hit. She lost both her parents. Esther took her in and adopted Delia as a second daughter. They are that close."

"That is rough." Losing those you loved once was bad enough. Twice seemed unfair. "Did Sadie say how she was handling it?"

"We haven't had time to talk, just quick notes. This will be the first time I've seen Sadie since Delia came home." Jack gathered his coat and plaid cap. "We're here."

The cab parked in front of the house and Jack hopped out to ask the driver to wait. Gabe stood on the walk staring at the front door and rooted in his pocket for a handkerchief. It took a moment to remember he'd left the handkerchief in his office. He stuck his hands deep in his trouser pockets to wipe his sweaty palms dry, annoyed and chiding himself. Meeting and having supper with Sadie's maid of honor shouldn't make him that nervous. He scowled and wiped his hands again. Maybe Jack was right, maybe he did spend too much time alone.

Jack clapped him on the shoulder and he flinched. "Relax, Gabe. No matter what Sadie might be scheming, there's nothing riding on this evening. Just try to remember that Delia's not a suspect. Don't interrogate her."

Gabe stared and the knot in the pit of his stomach pulled tighter. "Do I do that? Interrogate people, I mean."

"Sometimes. I think it comes from spending too much time in a garret. You forget how to talk to people outside of work. Sadie adores you anyway." Jack shoved him toward the front door. "Let's go. Just say hello and leave the rest to Sadie. She'll talk enough for all of us."

Delia

The cab ride to the fairgrounds was both amusing and strained. Sadie chatted away as always, steering the conversation and determined not to let silence linger for more than a few seconds. Jack let her talk, casting amused glances my way when she focused her smile on Mr. Ryan. He knew exactly what she was up to but he wasn't going to spoil her fun. I liked him a great deal. He really was perfect for Sadie.

I didn't know what to think of Gabriel Ryan. Sadie had neglected to mention Lieutenant Ryan was tall and good looking, with a strong jaw and eyes that changed from brown to hazel depending on the light. A small bump suggested his nose had been broken sometime in the past. That and a crooked smile rendered his face handsome rather than pretty.

He didn't smile much, added little to the conversation and did his best to politely deflect Sadie's onslaught of charm. That only encouraged her to put forth more effort to draw him out. He was losing the battle and didn't seem to notice.

Shadow hovered next to Sadie, poised on the edge of the seat and watching all of us. That the ghost heard and understood everything was clear. Her eyes were always aware, but now her whole face was animated and expectant. Twice she reached toward Jack, pulling back before touching his face or his hand. Each time the ghost brushed Sadie's cheek in passing. Sadie remained oblivious.

"Delia!" Sadie laughed and grabbed my hand. "You're not listening to me at all."

"Sorry." The poor light in the cab hid the rush of heat to my face. Or so I hoped. Everyone was staring at me, including Shadow. She faded, tattering around the edges and growing thinner until she vanished. I swallowed and met Sadie's eyes. "I was thinking of something else and didn't hear you. Could you please say that again?"

Sadie knew the ghost held my attention; it was always the ghost. Her smile dimmed, but didn't disappear. "Remember the spiritualist I mentioned when you first came home? I'd tried to get in touch with her, but she didn't answer my notes. Jack's just told me that she's working at the fair. Isn't that marvelous? We can go talk to Madame Bobet about your problem with Shadow right after supper."

"Shadow?" Mr. Ryan hadn't spoken to me before, but now I had all his attention. "That's an unusual name, Miss Martin, not one I've heard before."

Jack cleared his throat and Mr. Ryan glanced over at him. He turned back to me, suddenly sheepish. "I don't mean to pry. It just struck me as odd."

"I don't really know her name. Shadow is just what I call her." I looked to Sadie for rescue, but I saw right off I'd get no help from that quarter. The smile on her face as she looked on was positively blissful. Now that Mr. Ryan had made the first conversational move, she'd sit back and be quiet. I clung to my own brittle smile and stumbled onward. "Sadie believes her spiritualist friend can help me discover Shadow's real name and who she was."

"I see." He brushed at his trouser leg and glanced at Jack again. Sadie was whispering in Jack's ear and if Mr. Ryan sought his own help, he didn't find any. "How do you know . . . Shadow?"

She chose that moment to reappear, hovering in the space between seats in the cab. Shadow's green eyes bored into mine, relentless in demanding my attention. She wanted me to tell him, I was certain of that. I was just as sure he'd scoff. "Do you believe in ghosts, Mr. Ryan?"

He half turned on the seat so he could look at me straight on. "I'm not sure in all honesty. There was a time I'd have said no, but you see strange things working the streets late at night. I can't explain all of them and a good detective learns to keep an open mind."

Sadie and Jack had stopped whispering. The two of them held hands, watching me and Mr. Ryan. I couldn't interpret the expression on Jack's face, but there was no question with Sadie. She was perched on the edge of the seat, no longer smiling, but vibrating with controlled eagerness. "Tell him, Dee. No one here will laugh."

"You won't laugh, Sadie. Best not to make promises for others."

With Shadow staring at me I couldn't deny her existence. I took a breath and set about finalizing my humiliation. "Shadow is a ghost, Mr. Ryan. I can't explain her either and I'd dearly love to. I've seen strange things most of my life, but I never really wanted to believe in ghosts haunting people. Unfortunately, Shadow leaves me little choice but to believe in her."

"I won't laugh at you, either." He smiled, rueful and appearing a little embarrassed. "If we're going to exchange ghost stories perhaps you should call me Gabe."

"I'd like that." I didn't know anything about Gabe Ryan, other than he was Jack's best friend. But if Sadie was determined to throw us together, first names would be easier. "Call me Delia."

Gabe sat back and listened to my tale of how Shadow came to be with me six months before and why I'd journeyed home. He nodded when I hesitated, but otherwise let me tell the story my own way. Jack listened intently, but didn't ask any questions. They took me seriously, that much was obvious, but what they thought of the story still made me nervous. A good detective took all witnesses seriously; at least to their face.

Before I'd gotten to my nightmare, the cab was at the front of a queue of horse-cabs and motorcars waiting to drop people at the fair entrance. No one spoke until we'd all climbed out. I was just as glad not to be the center of attention, at least for the moment.

Jack squeezed Sadie's hand. "Wait here with Gabe and Delia. I'll pay the cabbie and see if I can get him to come back for us later."

Sadie wore another fashionable broad-brimmed hat of blue silk to match her outfit. Peacock feathers bobbed on top and her perfect curls just peeked out round her face. She tipped her head to one side and blew Jack a kiss, flirting playfully. "I promise not to run off with strangers. Hurry, darling. I'm famished."

I expected him to melt at her feet. Instead, Jack exchanged looks with Gabe, his smile suddenly strained, and hurried toward the driver.

We moved back from the curb to wait, Shadow hovering behind my shoulder as always. I tried my best to ignore the feel of eyes on the back of my neck and enjoy the sights. The crowd was larger than I'd imagined for a weekday evening. Men, women, and youngsters streamed through the entrance, all smiling in anticipation of an evening of wonders. I'd read in the papers that people from all over the world had come to San Francisco for the Panama-Pacific Exposition. That was an easy thing to believe.

Conversations around us were held in a variety of languages, French blending with German and Japanese, or even what I guessed might be Italian. Faces and costumes were just as varied, kimonos and saris as prevalent as skirts and evening wraps.

Spotlights played over the tallest building just inside the entrance. Multicolored glass gems hung on all the walls and tiered columns, and continued to the top of the central tower. Mounted on a mirrored backing made to sway freely in the breeze, each jewel sent sparks of light in all directions. Aptly named the Tower of Jewels, the effect was dazzling. Other buildings, each in a unique style, could be glimpsed through the entrance.

The excitement in the air was contagious. Like the wide-eyed children all around us, I didn't know where to look first. I'd never been abroad to tour the Continent or ventured to the Near East. But if I closed my eyes and listened to the voices of the crowd, the music carried on the wind from The Zone and other attractions, I could well imagine I was in an exotic country rather than San Francisco.

I threaded my arm through Sadie's. "This is marvelous; I've never seen anything like it. You were right to drag me out for an evening. What shall we do first?"

Jack rejoined us and Sadie took his arm, abandoning me with an apologetic smile. "Supper first, I really am starving. Then we can find Madame Bobet. Didn't you say her tent was in The Zone, Jack?"

"That's what Officer Finlay told me. She's supposed to be in a red tent with gold banners." He patted Sadie's hand. "We'll find her after supper. I have a café all picked out in the Court of Flowers. The Zone is a bit of a walk from there, but that will give us a chance to see more on the way."

Once we got through the press near the entrance, the crowds thinned. People headed off in all directions, some rushing straight for The Zone on the far end of the fair, while other groups strolled leisurely or made their way toward one of the main exhibits.

Jack and Sadie led the way, Gabe and I a few yards behind. She always brimmed with good cheer and stood ready to take on any adventure, but in Jack's presence Sadie positively glowed.

"They get on well." Gabe strolled with hands stuck deep in his pockets, looking relaxed for the first time. "I'd given up hope Jack would find someone he could be himself with. I'm glad to be wrong."

I studied my friend and her beau, head-to-head and pointing out the sights to each other. In the presence of strangers and those she didn't know well, Sadie wore charm like armor, but she'd no need for protections or defenses with Jack. The two of them were comfortable in each other's company. I smothered a spark of jealousy, ashamed I'd allowed the feeling to sneak in. "Sadie's never lacked for suitors, but they all expected her to change for them. I knew right off Jack was different. She gets this besotted smile on her face at the mention of his name. I've never seen her so content."

"Jack's over the moon for her, too." He looked away, chewing his lip. "I hope nothing happens to change that for either of them. They deserve to be happy."

A shimmer of movement caught my eye, resolving itself into the ghost of a young woman. Her ghost was tied firmly to this world and appeared near as solid and lifelike as Shadow. She was no more than nineteen or twenty with long, dark hair loose around her shoulders. Her round face wasn't overly pretty, but open and good natured, with large hazel eyes. Barefoot and dressed in a nightgown, she was visibly pregnant. She followed Gabe. The way she watched him and the longing in her face almost brought me to tears.

Telling Gabe would be cruel. He had no idea she followed.

Only someone he'd loved deeply and lost suddenly would haunt him that closely. Shadow appeared at the girl's shoulder, her face a picture of sadness. I stared into Shadow's eyes and the certainty I'd guessed right settled on me. Gabe's wife and child had died in the quake, along with my parents.

His reticence to socialize in the face of Jack and Sadie's happiness came into focus. Gabe wished our friends well, but their joy was a painful reminder of all he'd lost. He still grieved. I understood that all too well.

Shadow touched the young woman's face. The ghost looked away from Gabe, startled and confused until Shadow took her hand. Light flared and they were gone.

My ghost continued to remind me how little I knew about spirits or how they moved through the world. Shadow was like the puzzle box my father kept in his study, all the secrets locked inside until you found the key piece. Talking to Madame Bobet might give me the key I needed and begin to answer some of my questions. Guessing only frustrated me.

Gabe peered at faces in the crowd, looking hard at the people we passed and unaware of ghosts, or that I blinked back tears. He noticed me watching and blushed, embarrassed at being caught out. "Sorry. Jack's always telling me I need to learn how to be a civilian."

"Don't apologize. I'm curious about what you're looking for." The crowd was a sea of men, women, and their children to me, a few with the faint wisp of a ghost hovering near. I gestured at a couple on a bench. They sat shoulder to shoulder, but neither looked at the other. "That man and young woman sitting under the streetlamp. What does a policeman see that I don't?"

Gabe stared for a moment and went so far as to take my arm to walk closer, stopping right in front of them. He pointed at the building behind them. "Nod and pretend I'm telling you all about the architecture."

I did as he said, amused and wondering at the bit of playacting. We didn't stand there long before Sadie noticed we'd stopped and called to me. "Delia, whatever are you doing? Hurry or all the tables will be spoken for."

Gabe took my arm again, smiling and tipping his hat to the woman on the bench before we hurried to catch up with Jack and Sadie. I managed not to laugh until we were out of earshot. "Well, what did you see? Don't keep me in suspense."

We closed the gap with Jack and Sadie before he told me. "They're married. I saw matching wedding bands, but no engagement ring. I'd guess they've quarreled and that's why they aren't looking at each other. Judging from his boots and her hat, I'd say they might be from someplace out of the country." Gabe grinned. "Tourists in other words, and lucky you pointed them out to me. A pickpocket was sizing them up. I stood there that long to make sure Harry knew I was on to him. Once he got a good look and realized who was watching, he ran off."

"Harry is the pickpocket?" I looked over my shoulder. Shadow was back and followed me, but the bench and the couple were out of sight. "I didn't see anyone."

"You're not trained to notice those things." He took my arm again briefly, putting himself between me and the crowd around a knot of musicians. "With a little practice you'd learn. Besides, I know Harry from my foot patrol days. I thought he'd retired, but I guess this crowd is too rich for him to pass up."

Gabe was right; the temptation for a retired pickpocket would be enormous. Crowds became larger the deeper we went into the fair grounds, and it became obvious that many of the men and women around us were people of means. I could well believe that half of San Francisco society had decided to visit the exposition on the same evening. The organizers had chosen the location not only to draw in visitors from all over the world, but to entice the citizens of San Francisco to come see the sights.

Chestnut Street marked the southern edge of the fairgrounds, a wide avenue that allowed a steady stream of cabs and motorcars. San Francisco Bay bordered the northern side and on clear days gave visitors a spectacular view of sailboats skipping before the wind, or majestic steamers bound for Oakland to unload cargo from all over the world. The Presidio nestled tight against the fences to the west. Monterey cypress and redwood trees graced the slopes of the military cemetery overlooking the fairgrounds, both a beautiful and sobering sight. I'd read in the papers that they'd considered holding the Pan Pacific in Golden Gate Park, but settled on filling in the mud flats on the northern end of the city instead. Three years had gone into constructing the grounds and the buildings, a major undertaking that did San Francisco proud.

After dark, the fair appeared truly magical. Everywhere I looked was full of movement and color. Thousands of hidden, colored spotlights made the buildings glow in soft blues, reds, and greens. A barge the newspapers named the Scintillator floated on the Bay, holding an array of spotlights in seven different colors that the operators shone into the sky after sunset. Another floating platform held a locomotive that generated steam to reflect the lights from when the skies were clear. On nights fog crept in from the sea, it served the same purpose, glowing and swirling with colors.

Some reporters called the exposition the Domed City and it was easy to see why. Domes on the Palace of Fine Arts, the Liberal Arts Palace, and other buildings I didn't yet know names for gleamed under colored spotlights. Elaborate archways led from the main buildings into the courts between, all of which were full of fountains and flowers, and the most beautiful statues.

We'd reached the café and Jack held the door open for Sadie and me. The attendant led us to a table by the window in the back corner. Candles flickered on blue saucers in the center of each white tablecloth, yellow flames swaying as we passed. Chandeliers hung from the ceiling, small round electric bulbs inside crystal tulips providing soft light. The excitement I'd felt outside carried over to the diners. Couples traded bites of food they'd never tried before, smiling at the new tastes, and children grinned over dishes of ice cream.

Statues and fountains in the adjoining courtyard were lit by spotlights, cascading water catching the light and transformed into a spray of diamonds. The gardens were in full bloom, roses a soft blur of yellow and pink at the edge of the shadows. Blue and white pansies filled the window boxes near to hand, sweet alyssum billowing between the plants and hiding the soil under a carpet of tiny, white flowers. Normally I'd have thought the view peaceful and lovely.

But the courtyard was full of ghosts. Not ghosts as I normally saw them, looking as they had in life and reenacting some remembered day. These ghosts shambled, dazed and confused, covered in blood and ash. Dozens of them crowded the space near the window, wounded and dying, and looking me in the eye.

One by one the ghosts changed as I watched, turned to dust

swirling on the wind or became grains of sand that streamed away, vanishing into the hourglass of years since the quake.

"Delia?" Gabe held a chair for me, a perplexed expression on his face. Sadie was already seated and pulling off her gloves, but Jack stood behind his chair, waiting for me to sit. They all watched me. "Will this seat do or would you rather sit across from Sadie?"

The ghosts were gone, the courtyard empty. Even if my companions weren't questioning my sanity, I was.

"No, this is fine. Thank you." I took a breath and sat across from Jack. Gabe pushed the chair in and I smiled, too embarrassed and shaken to try to put a good face on things. "You must think me quite strange. I'm not usually this distracted. Normally there's no need to repeat things for me."

Sadie leaned across the narrow table, hands folded at her breast and earnest as any ingénue playing Juliet on her balcony. "No one thinks you strange. Truly we don't."

Jack rested an arm along the back of Sadie's chair. He regarded me just as seriously. "For what it's worth, I believe your story about Shadow and the other ghosts. I've told Sadie stories about things I've seen late at night, especially near the docks and around Chinatown. I don't know how to explain them, except as ghosts." He traded looks with Gabe before turning back to me. "I think you'd be hard-pressed to find a beat cop in the city who doesn't believe in spirits."

Shadow stood at the end of the table, hands pressed to her stomach, watching and aware of the conversation. She gave Jack special attention. For an instant I wondered if she'd grown tired of me and perhaps she'd haunt him instead. My ghost turned her head to stare at me again, as focused on making me understand as ever. Thinking she might leave was a foolish notion, one born of fear.

Being haunted by a ghost who carried secrets she was desperate to share wasn't an easy thing. What I'd learned already about her murder, the other spirits I saw and how close death was at all times frightened me. Gazing into Shadow's eyes, I knew I'd only be drawn in deeper. I'd not served my purpose yet.

The waiter arrived to take our order and the conversation came to a halt. Sadie asked him to explain how some of the more exotic dishes were made, giving the rest of us time to pore over the menu. We settled on sharing a dinner of curried lamb, braised chicken, a platter of dolmas and yogurt, and rice with roasted red peppers. Gabe and Sadie wanted to try honeyed figs for dessert, Jack and I ordered spice cakes with sweet cream.

Once we'd given our order, the waiter set tall goblets of water on the table and hurried off. Gabe toyed with his cutlery for a few seconds and cleared his throat. "I promised to trade ghost stories with you, Delia. You've told me some of yours. It's only fair I tell one of mine." He glanced at Jack and Sadie before going on. "As long as no one objects."

Sadie was unable to contain her excitement. She smiled broadly and leaned forward until Jack took her hand. "Oh, please tell, Gabe, we all want to hear. Don't we, Dee?"

I sat back, hands out of sight under the table and twisting my napkin around my fingers. The fine-spun cotton was soft against my skin, smooth and cool. Enthusiasm for ghosts was hard to muster on my part. I smiled at Gabe in any case. Not a very bright smile, not brimming over with charm, but the best I could manage. "I don't object. We did say we'd trade."

He regarded me solemnly, perhaps sensing this wasn't a game to me in the way it was for Sadie. Gabe nodded. "We did. One story and then we can find something other than ghosts to talk about."

Shadow drifted round the table to stand between Gabe and the window. I couldn't avoid looking at her there, not without being rude as Gabe spoke. She'd positioned herself in that spot for a reason, as she did everything for a purpose. I twisted the napkin tighter and numbness deadened the tips of my fingers.

Gabe took a sip of water and shifted in his chair to face me. "Back when Jack and I were still rookies we did a full year of night duty. The sergeant in charge of the station house usually gave rookies the worst assignments."

Sadie frowned and rested her head on Jack's shoulder. "That doesn't seem fair."

"It was a test," Jack said. "Sergeant Marsh wanted to know if you'd follow orders and fit in. If you complained or he decided you were a troublemaker, you kept walking the toughest beats. The sergeant didn't like Gabe and tried to persuade me to take a new partner. I said no. Marsh punished us for more than six months."

"Really." Sadie smirked at Gabe and I knew he'd never live it down. "I'd never have guessed you for a maverick, Lieutenant Ryan."

Gabe put on a dignified expression and straightened his tie. "I assure you, Miss Larkin, it's not true. Now if your fiancé is finished tarnishing my good name, I'll go on with the story."

Jack grinned and gestured for Gabe to continue.

"For six months, we walked the same beat near the docks. The area was pretty rough, full of taverns and burlesque houses that catered to merchant seamen, dockworkers and soldiers who wandered over from the Army base." Gabe toyed with his spoon again, absently spinning it in circles on the tablecloth. "Before the quake and fire, a maze of alleys ran behind buildings from one block to another. Nothing good ever happened in those alleys once the sun set."

Shadow drifted closer to Gabe, hovering at his shoulder. She'd lost the shawl and the neat plaits on top of her head were bedraggled, strands trailing down her neck and into her face. Muddy smudges soiled her blouse and a bruise darkened one side of her jaw. Her hand clamped around the cross at her throat, tugging until the chain pulled tight. She stared into my eyes and opened her mouth as if to speak. Shadow began to unravel, threads of mist drifting away until there was nothing left.

Gabe's breath hitched in his throat and he shivered. I trembled, too, wondering if she'd touched him in passing and if he'd felt her die.

He squared his shoulders and went back to his story. "You never knew what you'd find in those alleys. All of them were bad, but there was one in particular that made my skin crawl. I hated going in that alley."

Sadie pulled closer to Jack, the bright eagerness gone from her face. "Why was that?"

"It was haunted, sweetheart." Jack toyed with the peacock feather on her hat. His matter-of-fact tone didn't match the frown he gave Gabe. "We always heard and saw odd things on nights the fog was heavy. Sometimes I'd hear a scream or glimpse a woman running from the middle of the alley toward the docks. She'd always disappear before she got to the street and I was never sure I'd really seen her. Once or twice I thought I saw the shadow of someone behind her. For the longest time I thought the fog was to blame. Sound can carry a long way and it's easy to mistake what you see. Then Gabe admitted he saw odd things, too."

"I need some air." I shoved back my chair and stood, dropping the crumpled napkin on the floor and rocking the table. Water sloshed out of my glass, dampness spreading in a dark circle. "Please excuse me. I . . . I need air."

Waiters dodged out of my path, heavy trays laden with food tipping precariously. Sadie called my name and people turned from their dinners to stare, but I didn't stop.

I couldn't. I'd be sick if I stayed inside. Pushing through the door to outside was a relief.

My coat and handbag were still at the table. An icy wind off the bay sliced through my dress of summer cottons and tried to carry off my hat. Gooseflesh rose in concert with deep muscle tremors. I huddled over my knees on a bench near the door, hugging myself tight and gulping mouthfuls of chill air. Cold forced back the nausea, sparing me still more disgrace. I shut my eyes, rehearsing what I'd say when I went back inside.

Footsteps slowed and halted in front of me. I opened my eyes enough to see black calf-length boots, gray trousers neatly tucked into the tops, and the bottom of a wool coat. The man continued to stand there and I imagined him staring. Ignoring him was rude, I knew that, but I was in no mood to engage in conversation with strangers. I kept my head bowed and hoped he'd leave.

Hinges on the café door squealed and the black boots hurried away. I lifted my head, expecting to see Sadie come to take me back. Instead Gabe Ryan stood there, my coat clutched in one hand and a goblet of water in the other. I sighed and sat up straight. The odds of a pit opening up to swallow me were slim, but I wished on the brightest star overhead, just in case.

Gabe handed me the water and draped the coat around my shoulders. "Are you all right?"

"Aside from dying of embarrassment, I'm fine." Sipping cold water settled my stomach, chasing away the last shaky, queasy feeling. "You've caught me on a very bad night. I don't usually make dramatic exits from restaurants, either."

He sat next to me, blocking the worst of the wind. "I can't help but feel this is my fault. I upset you with that story. I'm very sorry, Delia, that wasn't my intent."

"There's no reason to be sorry. You're not to blame. Neither is your story, not entirely." I sipped more water, dredging up courage from my toes and worked at meeting his eyes. "Tell me if this is right. The alley in your story was gravel lined, with brick buildings on both sides. Rooms to let on the top floors, but no windows looked into the alley. The only light came from a streetlight at one end. On foggy nights it was especially dark."

He frowned. "That's exactly right. How did you know?"

I sipped more water, all I'd seen of how Shadow disappeared so clear. "Shadow showed me that alley in a dream. A nightmare. She never took the shortcut after dark, only that one night. I'm sure she was the woman you and Jack saw running. He found her in the alley and took her away. She never made it home to her family."

Shadow stood in front of us again, dressed as I usually saw her, and I couldn't say how long she'd been there. Only the dead could display the patience in her face, or the stoic way she stood with hands primly folded and waited.

"Delia . . ." Gabe raked fingers through his chestnut hair, glancing at people passing by and lowering his voice. "Explain this so I understand. Who took her?"

"The man in the mask. He murdered her, Gabe." Brushing the edges of a murder, even one that happened so long ago, made me nauseous again. All the fear and panic from my nightmare rushed back, made worse by knowing what I'd seen was real. Bright lights and happy people vanished. The sorrow in Shadow's eyes engulfed me until sorrow was all I saw. "Dear God in heaven, he killed her and her family never knew. They never knew."

CHAPTER 5

Gabe

Gabe sat quietly, watching the crowd and taking note of anyone who showed too much interest in them. Delia still wasn't feeling well. Rushing back inside and assaulting her queasy stomach with the smell of food didn't seem wise, and in any case, he wanted a peaceful moment to think. Once they rejoined Sadie and Jack any hope of quiet was gone.

A man had hurried away from the café front as Gabe first came out. The man was tall, swaddled in a greatcoat with the collar flipped up against the wind, a red plaid muffler, black leather gloves, and a bowler hat pulled down low on his forehead. In the time it took to reach Delia's side, Gabe was left with a view of the man's retreating back and nothing else. That made him pay even more attention. Every instinct screamed for him to chase after the stranger, but he couldn't leave Delia alone.

Catching a man staring at Delia, a man that he couldn't recognize, woke all of Gabe's worst fears. He could probably pull ten men out of the crowd and other than the flipped-up collar, half of them would be dressed almost identically. Hiding in plain sight was the perfect way for the killer to move through the crowd at the Pan Pacific.

The stranger wasn't the only thing unsettling him and making him edgy. As soon as Delia mentioned the man in the mask, he'd known he couldn't dismiss her story. That piece of information was buried deep in his father's case files, part of a witness report from thirty years ago. Gabe still wasn't sure he believed in ghosts, not completely, or that he wanted to believe, but he was at a loss about how she'd known about the mask. That report was written before Delia was born and the details never made public.

More to the point, however reluctantly, Delia believed Shadow gave her the information. He didn't have a better explanation. Until he found one, he wouldn't try to change her mind.

A couple came out of the café, holding tight to each other and laughing. Gabe stood and offered Delia his hand. "Sadie was going to have them hold dinner. We can sit here as long as you need, but if you're feeling well enough maybe we should go back inside."

"We should." She wobbled for an instant, but let him steady her before pulling her hand away. Delia's smile was as uncertain as her footing. "You may have forgiven me, but Sadie won't be as generous if she misses dinner. She's quite fierce unless fed at regular intervals."

Gabe pulled the door open and smiled, hoping to ease her nerves and lighten her mood. She had plenty of reason to be unsure and nervous. So did he. "I don't think you need to worry too much. Jack asked the waiter to bring bread and crackers to hold her over. She'll be somewhat pacified."

"Jack's a good man. I'll be sure to thank him." Delia paused in the doorway. She turned back to look over the fairgrounds, watching something in the distance.

He looked too and saw nothing. "What are you watching? Is it Shadow?"

"No, Shadow's gone for now, but the city is full of ghosts. I see them as well." Colored lights reflected in her soft brown eyes, caught glints of gold in her hair and shimmered on the rhinestone brooch pinned to her coat. Her cheeks, already pink from cold and wind, flushed darker. "I can't help but watch them. It's not curiosity on my part. It's more that I don't have a choice. That sometimes frightens me."

"That's a reasonable thing to fear. Being able to see the dead walking around would scare me." He followed her in, hovering protectively and never letting her get more than a foot or two ahead. She was shaky, her steps unsteady. Gabe was afraid she'd faint and argued with himself over whether holding Delia's arm would offend her. He settled for staying close. The few café patrons who dared to stare at her got his best policeman's glare.

Sadie bounced out of her seat and rushed to meet them as they neared the table. She wrapped Delia in a hug. "Are you all right, Dee?"

"I'm cold, but the madness seems to have passed." Her sardonic tone reassured him. Delia let Sadie put an arm around her shoulders, though Gabe had a hunch that was Delia's way of letting Sadie feel useful.

Gabe held her chair, making sure she was seated and secure before he took his place. He saw the look Jack gave him as he fussed. After insisting he should be the one to go out and find her, Gabe was sure he'd hear plenty later.

Delia settled in and gave all of them an apologetic smile. "I'm sorry to have left so suddenly and made you all wait for dinner. I hope you can forgive me."

"There's nothing to forgive. And don't fret over making us wait, the busboy kept us well supplied with bread. Sadie didn't starve while you were gone." Jack signaled the waiter. The older man raised a hand and hurried back toward the kitchen. "I'm just glad you're all right."

"That you feel better really is most important, Dee." Sadie took the last slice of bread from a crumb-filled basket and tore it in two. She dropped the smaller piece on Jack's plate. "If you're not up to walking after dinner we'll go home. We can see the fair another night."

"All I need is some food and to warm up a bit. I'm fine now, promise. And I'm eager to meet with Madame Bobet tonight if possible. Hearing what she has to say feels more important than ever." Delia glanced at him. Gabe nodded, hoping he looked encouraging, and she turned back to convincing Sadie. "Do you remember the nightmare I told you about?"

"Of course I remember." Sadie frowned at the piece of bread she held and dropped what was left on her plate. "It sounded horrid. I still wish you'd woken me."

"It was horrid, but maybe there was a purpose, too." Delia's hands were tucked in her lap, but Gabe saw her twisting the edge of the tablecloth around her fingers. "I think there's a very good chance the woman Jack and Gabe saw in that alley was Shadow."

Jack looked up sharply from buttering his scrap of bread. "What makes you believe that?"

"Don't interrogate her, Sergeant. Take it on faith that she has good reasons." Gabe looked his partner straight in the eye, confident that Jack would understand from his tone and expression that this wasn't a joke. Now wasn't the time to question her. "No more talk about ghosts until later. Let's have a pleasant dinner first."

Jack gave him a considering look and tugged his mustache. "A good idea. They're bringing the food now."

The waiter and two helpers approached the table, each of them carrying a heavily laden tray with dishes piled high or steaming platters of lamb and chicken. Gabe wasn't sure the narrow table would hold all the food, but with some rearranging they managed. They passed plates round in a circle, each person heaping on food from the dishes closest before passing the plate on. The scent of curry spices tickled his nose and with the first bite strange tastes burst on his tongue, sweet and bitter at the same time. At first he wasn't sure he cared for the texture of the dolmas paired with yogurt, but they grew on him. The rest of the meal was heaven on a plate.

Sadie steered the conversation back to wedding plans and plotting an extravagant honeymoon. Before too long Delia's color was back to normal and she joined in the conversation, poking good-natured fun at both Jack and Sadie. Gabe threw in his share of quips, but mostly he watched to make sure Delia ate and was suitably distracted. He still felt responsible for upsetting her and doubly guilty for knowing he'd have to do so again soon.

Details were his job and Gabe couldn't ignore the truth; he needed all the details Delia remembered. He'd seen too much in his ten years on the force not to be open to the idea of things he couldn't explain, but Delia's story had pushed him closer to outright belief than he was comfortable with. The idea that Shadow might be a victim of the killer his father hunted for five years spooked him.

That the ghost had chosen to reveal her secrets to Delia added to the unease roiling in his chest. He couldn't shrug that off as a hunch. The timing, with a new killer roaming the city, disturbed him most of all. Even as the four of them ate and joked Gabe couldn't stop thinking about the possible connection.

Busboys swooped down only seconds after they'd finished eating and carried off empty serving dishes, soiled plates, and the paltry fragments of lamb and chicken left. Their waiter returned a moment later with coffee and their desserts.

Gabe let the first bite of honeyed figs sit on his tongue, sorting out the sweetness of honey from the dusting of spices: cinnamon and clove, with just a touch of ginger. If he could remember by the time he saw her at breakfast, he'd tell his landlady. Mrs. Allen loved to cook for him and the other boarders and a new dessert from the fair would excite her.

"How are you feeling, Dee?" Sadie rested her elbows on the table and cradled her water glass in both hands. She peered at Delia over the top of the glass. "You've no need to be brave about it either. No one will be upset if you need to go home. We can make arrangements to see Madame Bobet in a few days."

"You've no need to fuss, I feel fine." Delia pushed her empty plate away and folded her napkin neatly. She brushed a wisp of light brown hair off her face and smiled sweetly at Sadie. "Not ordering more spice cake will require bravery, so if you're truly concerned, perhaps we should go."

Gabe took the bill from the waiter and paid for dinner over everyone's protest. They gathered their coats and left. He reached the door first, blocking the exit for a few seconds to scan the area for anyone who looked out of place. Searching for a man he wouldn't recognize.

"Something wrong, Gabe?" Jack's tone was casual, but he moved a half step in front of Sadie.

"No, nothing wrong." Delia regarded him solemnly over Jack's shoulder, her expression wary. He wouldn't fool her any more than he'd fool Jack, but he'd keep up the cheerful facade for Sadie. Gabe pushed the door open and held it for his friends. "Old habit from my patrolman's days. Sometimes I can't help but watch people."

Sadie arched an eyebrow at Gabe on the way out, but didn't say anything. She threaded her arm through Jack's and they led the way again. If Jack kept her that much closer when the street grew especially crowded or held her arm a tiny bit tighter, she'd never notice.

Gabe noticed. He wished he hadn't.

Delia

The closer we came to The Zone, the more crowded the walkway became. Supper hour was over and everyone wanted to make the most of the evening. Fathers chased down errant children and dragged them back to their mothers. Couples, old and young, strolled arm in arm marveling at the lights and the sculptures commissioned for the Pan Pacific. Packs of young boys rushed for the rides, free of parental supervision for a short time and wild as puppies. Girls about the same age were more constrained and followed close behind their parents, faces sticky with cotton candy.

Fog hung over the mouth of the bay, but hadn't worked its way to shore. The wind was brisk and carried the smell of popcorn, coffee from the Hills Bros. exhibit, and food of all sorts. Lights outlined the front of buildings, the tower holding the Aeroscope and arched on long wires over the streets. Spotlights illuminated sculptures and fountains. All but the most distant corners of The Zone were awash in bright colors, music, and movement.

We stopped to watch the Aeroscope as it came into view over the top of the buildings. Broad at the base, the tower narrowed gradually until the top was a slender spire. The square iron cage rose slowly, an electric star ascending to the sky. Once at the top, the cage hovered in place so the people inside could see the whole of the exhibition laid out at their feet. I'd read in the paper that the cage held five hundred people and was always full, day or night.

"Oh, Dee. I want to go to the top." Sadie was entranced, watching the cage descend again and bouncing on her toes. She still clutched Jack's arm and he bounced with her, but not by choice. "We'll talk to Madame Bobet and then ride the Aeroscope. What do you say?"

"I think it's perfect for you. You'll have oodles of fun." I eyed the fragile-looking enclosure slowly sliding down the tower. Imagining the Aeroscope hurtling at high speed to its destruction was all too easy. "I wouldn't dream of trying to stop you, but my feelings about high places haven't changed. I'll find a nice bench firmly anchored to the ground and wait for you."

Gabe cleared his throat, his usual prelude to entering the conversation. "You won't need to wait alone, Delia. I'm not keen on heights myself. Jack's the daredevil. Perhaps you and I can tour one of the exhibits nearby and meet them when they've finished."

Sadie beamed at me, a sure sign she thought all her scheming was coming to fruition. Gabe had handed her matchmaker heart all it ever dreamed of and he was only being polite, nothing more. That would never occur to her.

"That's very kind, Gabe." I ignored Sadie's victory smile. She'd be cross with me for dashing her hopes soon enough. "But if you'd rather take in the view from the tower, go with Jack and Sadie. I'll be fine on my own."

"Gabe really is terrified of heights. Remind me to tell you about the time we had to chase a pair of shoplifters up a fire escape and over a rooftop." Jack's forced laugh hit a false note, making me suspect he'd joined Sadie's conspiracy. The longer I let this go on, the more pressure my loving friend would apply.

A distraction was in order. I pointed to the deep crimson tent not far ahead, lightning-bolt banners on the roof snapping in the wind. "Is that Madame Bobet's tent?"

Sadie didn't disappoint me. "Oh, I think that must be. I hope she's not too busy."

We set off again. There were mercifully few ghosts in The Zone and those I saw were mere wisps of memory, faded to the point of passing out of this world completely. Shadow hadn't reappeared, but her presence tickled the back of my neck and an ache filled my chest. I didn't need to see the ghost to know she was with me.

Gabe watched the crowd as we walked, chewing his lip and frowning. His story of old habits grew harder to believe, but I trusted he had a reason to pretend all was well. I wouldn't question him just yet.

The signboard in front of Madame Bobet's tent announced "*Madame Isadora Bobet, World Acclaimed Seer and Spirit Guide. Fortunes Foretold, Advisor to the Brokenhearted, Messages Delivered to Loved Ones in the Spirit Realm.*" Pictures of pyramids, coffins painted with the likeness of Egyptian kings, and spirits rising from crystal balls decorated the sign as well. It was all very exotic and strange.

A tall young man with hazel eyes and skin the color of burnished bronze guarded the entryway. Dark curls framed his face and brushed the back of his neck. He was dressed in baggy black cotton pants tied at the ankle, leather sandals, and a red brocade vest that hung open across his well-muscled chest. A gold hoop pierced one ear and a red silk sash wrapped his waist.

"Daniel! It's been ages since I've seen you." Sadie rummaged in her handbag and produced a calling card. She smiled and offered it to him. "Would you be a dear and see if Madame Bobet can fit us in?"

He took her hand as well as the card, bowing and kissing her fingers. Daniel's smile was quite breathtaking, but Sadie took it in stride. Charm was wasted on her, she had too much of her own to wield. "Anything for you, Sadie. Isadora is finishing up her last appointment for the evening. She'll be happy to see you and your friends. I'll show you to the waiting lounge."

The inside of the tent was divided with heavy velvet curtains of royal blue and burgundy, trimmed in black braid and edged along the top with gold fringe. Filmy silk scarves dimmed electric lights mounted inside brass lanterns, keeping the atmosphere mysterious. Small tables set along the velvet walls held crystal dishes of dried rose petals or brass incense burners. The smell of sandalwood coated the back of my throat.

Daniel kissed Sadie's hand again and left us in a lounge furnished with a fainting couch on one side of the room, a small settee near the entrance and large cushions stacked in heaps. Two of the small teak tables and incense burners sat at either end of the room. Sadie and Jack perched on the edge of the fainting couch and I shared the settee with Gabe. We sat in silence for no more than a minute or two before Madame Bobet made her entrance.

Flamboyant was the only word for Madame Isadora Bobet. Tall and waif thin, she had high cheekbones that set off her deep blue eyes and her finely chiseled nose. Her black gown swept the floor, layers of airy silk falling from a high waist and rippling over straight shantung skirts. A beaded shantung train spread in a half circle behind her. The bodice was embroidered with silver moons and set with crystal stars that glimmered in the low light. A satin turban, beaded with small pearls and more crystals, covered bobbed blond hair that just brushed her chin. Long streamers of crimson silk trailed from the turban, flowing down her back to the floor.

She was younger than I'd supposed, no more than a year or two older than Gabe. Perhaps because Sadie had referred to her as Madame Bobet from the first I'd pictured someone closer to Esther's age, heavyset with silver rings and a stern expression. Instead she appeared elegant, dramatic, and self-assured. Yet under the outer facade, I thought her somewhat fragile.

Madame Bobet posed in the entry for a moment, staring off into the distance, one hand holding back the plush-velvet curtain and the other an ivory cigarette holder. She slowly turned her head toward us and grinned. "What do you think, Sadie? Does the outfit work?"

"Stunning as always, Dora." Sadie went to Isadora and gave her a hug. "I've been trying to find you for days. When you didn't answer my notes I got worried."

Isadora held Sadie at arm's length; her lip stuck out in a pout the equal of Sadie's best. "Forgive me? Your notes are on the hall table at home. I've just been swamped and never had time to open them. But you're here now and we can talk it all out in person." Her gaze swept all of us, lingering an instant too long on me and then Gabe. "Introduce me to your friends. I'm already charmed by your handsome fiancé."

"How are you, Dora?" Jack kissed her on the cheek. "I had one of my men track you down when Sadie told me she couldn't locate you. I was getting worried, too."

"My, my. All this concern for my welfare will turn my head." Isadora abandoned Sadie to stand in front of Gabe. She looked him up and down and held out a hand. "You may call me Dora. What should I call you?"

Gabe shook her hand and flinched. He let go as soon as was polite. Madame Bobet wasn't what he'd expected either and his stunned expression was rather comical. "Lieutenant Gabriel Ryan. I'm Jack's partner."

"So you're the detective he speaks so highly of." Her eyes widened as she studied him. The wince before her smile brightened was so slight I thought I'd imagined it, but the step away from him was real enough. "It's a pleasure to meet you, Gabriel."

She turned to me next, cigarette held out to one side. Dora stared at me but didn't speak, and her mouth pulled into a tight line. I stuck my hand out and stepped forward, determined to make the best of odd behavior and not be rude. "Delia Martin. I'm sure Sadie's told you plenty about me as well. All lies, I assure you."

Dora smiled at that. "She has said a word or two, yes. Forgive me for not taking your hand, Delia. It's been years since I've encountered a ghost as strong and willful as the one following you. I'd rather not risk becoming entangled."

"You can see her?" I looked over my shoulder and Shadow was back, silently watching all of us in turn. Her hair was tidy, the shawl neat and straight on her shoulders. The cross lay outside her blouse, easier to see than usual.

"I see her, but not exactly as you do. I know she was young when she died, with dark hair and green eyes. She wore blue skirts, a gray shawl, and white blouse, a tavern maid's or a shopgirl's clothes. There's a lot of energy surrounding her and it's difficult for me to look at for long." Dora took a deep drag on her cigarette, staring at the place Shadow hovered. She exhaled smoke in a cloud that rose to the top of the tent in straggling wisps. "Now I know why Sadie brought you to me and that I should have read her notes. I'd be prepared if I had, but we'll work things out. How long has she haunted you?"

"More than six months. Shadow is the reason I came home." Shadow stepped around Gabe to stand between me and Dora. I'd come to associate patience and the ability to wait endlessly with Shadow, but the placid face I'd grown used to had changed, become impatient.

Restlessness and a need to do something *now* swept over me. The change in Shadow affected me as well, her need growing to become mine. That she held that much control over my emotions frightened me.

"Tell me why you call her Shadow. Explain to me how she found you." Dora moved between me and my ghost, and I found myself looking into the spiritualist's bright blue eyes. The pressure in my chest eased. "Talk to me, Delia. Don't let her inside without a fight."

Gabe couldn't see Shadow, but he avoided walking through her as if he could. He stood next to me, hands shoved deep into his trouser pockets and frowned. "Is Delia in danger from this ghost?"

"No, I don't think so, not directly. I don't sense any malice toward Delia. This ghost emanates sorrow and fear, and a strong need to set things right. She's very afraid of someone or of something happening that's happened before." Dora never took her gaze from my face. She was an anchor, keeping me from being swept away on the current of Shadow's will. Sadie hadn't exaggerated Dora's abilities. "Tell me what you know, Delia. I'll help if I can."

"Shadow is what I call her, I don't know her name." I told Isadora about the last six months of my life, how I woke one morning to find Shadow standing next to my bed and how she'd changed since coming back to San Francisco. My voice broke telling Dora what the ghost had shown me about her murder and how closely the dream matched Gabe's story. Relating Esther's ability to see Shadow was hardest of all, as if that confirmed my fear Esther edged closer to death.

Things I didn't tell—the ghosts outside the café window, knowing Gabe's wife haunted him—felt like guilty secrets. I'd keep those for now.

Frowns in differing degrees of severity graced my friends' faces when I'd finished. Sadie looked the most complacent, but she'd heard the entire story before. And she shared my fears about Mama Esther already. We both knew time was short.

"I'm glad you won't let Shadow touch you. That was very wise." Dora stabbed her cigarette into an incense burner, holder and all. She wrapped her arms over her chest, pacing the small lounge and watching the ghost. "She gives me the heebie-jeebies, Delia. She's too strong for a casual haunt and I don't think she picked you at random. You're right, she wants something from you. I'm uncomfortable not knowing what she wants or what she expects you to do."

"Shadow won't hurt me." I felt the truth in the words, but where that came from I couldn't say. "She won't hurt me."

"But this thing she wants you to do might." Gabe raked fingers through his slicked-back hair and traded looks with Jack. "I'd wager it has something to do with the way she died and the man who killed her. Otherwise, why bring you back to San Francisco to show you? She's tangling you in what happened to her. I don't like that."

Shadow's stare jerked away from me, her attention captured by something outside. Voices and music from The Zone, muffled and hushed by the thick tent walls, became a cacophony of deafening sound. The air in the small lounge grew icy, heavy and thick with the ghost's anger. Breathing became difficult, each gulp of air a struggle. The room began to blur and I sank onto the settee, sick to my stomach from how my head spun. Sick as well from the fear overwhelming me, terror I couldn't claim as just my own.

Wind keened through the tent, ripping silk scarves off the lights and setting the electrified lanterns swinging violently. The tables rocked side to side and Sadie's hat blew off, crashing into the far wall. She clung to Jack, wide-eyed and pale. Dora's skirts whipped around her legs and the streamers on her turban snapped and fluttered, a mirror of the flags atop the tent. Gabe stayed beside me, one hand on my shoulder as if keeping me from blowing away.

Shadow turned back to me, a hand stretched toward me. Her eyes plead with me, stark with a need and desperation I'd not seen before. She drifted closer and the noise from outside quieted.

"Help them. Please . . ."

Sadie's gasp and the way Dora's eyes narrowed let me know they'd heard, too. I dug my fingers into the settee cushion, fighting to keep myself separate and not drown in Shadow's eyes. "I still don't know what you want. Tell me what to do. Tell me who to help."

The ghost's appearance changed. Blood trickled from a split lower lip and dripped onto her filthy white blouse. One eye was nearly swollen shut. She was barefoot, wrists and ankles scraped raw and bloody, her shawl and cross gone. She reached toward me again, her hand oddly curled.

Her fingers were broken. I choked back nausea and tears. "Tell me!"

"Please . . ." Shadow looked over her shoulder, face frantic with fear. The wind rose again, howling through the lounge and flinging stacks of heavy cushions in every direction. Both tables fell over, scattering smoldering sticks of incense across the carpet. Shadow vanished, taking the wind with her.

I found myself staring into Jack's eyes. His mouth was set in grim lines and he cradled Sadie against his chest, petting her hair. She was pale and frightened, but unhurt. I imagined I looked much worse.

Gabe patted my shoulder. "Sit still and rest. We'll have a fire if I don't get that incense off the carpet."

Jack sat Sadie down next to me and went to help Gabe. She rested her head on my shoulder, tiny shivers and the unnatural lack of chatter all the signs she gave of how frightened she really was. Sadie was tougher than most gave her credit for, myself included.

Dora shoved tattered silk streamers out of her face and stepped into the center of the room. She surveyed the damage, hands on hips and turning in a slow circle. I ignored the muttered profanity, deeply grateful she'd aimed well and I didn't have to duck when she kicked a cushion across the room. Dora pulled her foot back to kick another when something caught her eye.

"Damn, I need a drink. Where did this come from?" Isadora bent to pluck something off the carpet. She held out her hand, a small gold cross on a broken chain dangling from her fingers.

Then Madame Isadora Bobet fainted dead away. I didn't blame her in the slightest.

CHAPTER 6

Gabe

Gabe drummed his fingers on the arm of the overstuffed leather chair, his need to move growing stronger the longer he sat still. Good manners glued him to his seat or he'd be pacing Sadie's sitting room. He'd no valid reasons to be this restless, but he couldn't shrug it off, or get past the feeling he'd left something important undone. For the life of him, he couldn't think what that might be.

Sorting the chaos in the spiritualist's tent after Isadora fainted had taken time. Once a doctor was summoned and Sadie was sure Dora was in good hands, they'd all decided that going home was for the best. Neither Delia nor Sadie had said as much or complained, but it was obvious both of them were shaken and exhausted. They had good reason.

Gabe had a patrolman summon a car to take them home. It was a silent drive for the most part, attempts at conversation brief. Sadie remained subdued and rested on Jack's shoulder, and Delia had huddled in the corner, staring out the window.

Truth was that he and Jack weren't in much better shape. Gabe had no idea what had really happened in that tent or why. That was a big part of his unease, not knowing. The need to understand why Shadow reacted as she did itched as badly as a case of poison oak.

And if he allowed himself to think about it for too long, the sudden appearance of the cross would terrify him, for buried in one of the evidence boxes stored on his father's farm was a similar necklace. The cross and chain had been slipped into one of the letters sent to Gabe's father, a letter meant to taunt Matt Ryan with details of how the woman suffered before she died and that the police would never find the body.

Gabe had taken the broken chain and gold cross from the tent floor, wrapped them in a silk scarf and buttoned the tiny bundle into his coat pocket. Then he'd worked hard at reining in his imagination and convincing himself that it couldn't be the same necklace. There had to be a logical explanation.

Dammed if he could think of what that was.

His father had never discovered which of the killer's victims the cross belonged to. Now Gabe was afraid he knew. What touching the necklace did to Dora made that fear stronger.

Sending Dora home with Daniel and two patrolmen to watch outside her house until morning was all he could do for her tonight, but a trace of guilt lingered nonetheless. Unwittingly, she'd been drawn into the circle of those who might draw the killer's attention. Tomorrow he'd convince Isadora to accept full-time protection and work out duty assignments with the desk sergeant.

Jack was in the parlor with Sadie now, explaining about all the extra duty the last few weeks and the secrets he'd kept. Convincing Sadie that the threat was real and her life needed to change until the killer was caught might be difficult. All she had was Jack's worry and no real proof she was in danger. As independent and stubborn as Sadie was, that might not be enough. He wouldn't wager any money on who would win that argument.

Once Delia came downstairs, Gabe would have his turn talking to her. He had a hunch she'd agree to protection without a fuss. She'd only told him a little before leaving the fairgrounds, but Shadow's appearance, the blood and the injuries, and the cross on the carpet had shaken her deeply. Delia had proof that the threat was real.

At this rate half his squad would be watching people he thought might be in danger. He'd pull men from other squads if necessary. All Gabe cared about was that everyone, Jack and himself included, got through this investigation unhurt.

He rubbed his forehead, trying to wipe away the headache throbbing over his right eye. A few hours ago he wouldn't have believed the wind whipping through Dora's tent and the overturned tables were caused by anything as outlandish as a ghost. He'd have thought it all a trick of some kind, a hoax staged for the benefit of a gullible audience. But he'd been right in the middle of what happened, witnessed the manifestation from beginning to end, and all the lingering skepticism he'd harbored about Shadow was stripped away. That made him slightly ill.

The housekeeper, Annie, bustled back into the sitting room, balancing a wooden tray loaded down with cups, a big coffee pot, a sugar bowl and cream pitcher, and a china platter filled with more of the cookies she'd given him earlier. She fit the tray back on the top of a rosewood butler's table close to his chair, putting everything in easy reach.

Gabe guessed Annie must be older than fifty, but by how much he couldn't say. Her deep-brown skin was smooth and young looking, the only wrinkles he saw fine lines around her mouth and large, dark eyes. Thin and wiry, with a long, sharp nose, she was taller than either Sadie or Delia by a good four inches. Her iron-gray hair was streaked with white and pulled up in a tight bun on the top of her head, making her look taller still. A starched white apron covered an older style chicory-blue cotton dress.

She'd asked before going back to the kitchen how he took his coffee. Annie stirred in two sugars and handed him a cup to go with the half-empty plate of cookies balanced on his knee.

Gabe smiled. "Thank you. The cookies are very good. What did you say they were called?"

"Spice jumbles." Annie's warm smile crinkled the corners of her black eyes. "My mama taught me how to make those cookies when I was nine years old. If you like them I can write the recipe out for your wife. There's nothing special to making them. Takes almost no time to mix up the dough and she can throw in what sweet spices she has on hand to taste."

"If it's not too much trouble, I'll take the recipe for my landlady. She enjoys cooking for her boarders." He cleared his throat and struggled with not letting his smile become a grimace. "I lost my wife in the quake, Mrs. Fletcher."

"I'm grieved to hear that. Sometimes God tests folk awful young." Annie sat in the chair across from him, her shoulders slumped as if she carried the burden of his loss. "You're not much older than Sadie. Your wife couldn't have been much more than a child at the time."

"Victoria was nineteen." Looking back from thirty, nineteen sounded very far away. Gabe couldn't face counting the years ahead he'd spend without her.

He just couldn't. "Losing her was hard."

"Lots of us lost folk then, Gabriel. My husband was already gone, God rest his soul, but my oldest, my William, he died running from the fire. One of the Army men saw this Negro boy running down the street carrying something and thought he was a looter." Annie fussed with her crisp white apron, no longer looking at him. "I guess they'd never seen a lunch bucket before. Shot Willie and left him lying in the street for the fire to take. All he was trying to do was get home to me. I'd never have known but a neighbor saw and told me."

She sounded numb, not angry. Gabe decided he'd be angry for her. He'd had lots of practice in the last nine years. "I'm sorry, Mrs. Fletcher. That never should have happened."

"You can call me Annie if you like. No reason for Sadie and Dee's friends to be formal." Annie stood and settled her ankle-length skirts. She refilled his plate from the big platter of cookies and smiled. "God tells us to forgive and I've done my best. I've got to get back to the kitchen and start the bread for morning, but I'll bring the recipe in before you go." She patted his shoulder on the way past. "Give it to your landlady with my blessing. Jack and Sadie are still talking, but I checked on Delia and she'll be down shortly. You won't be sitting by your lonesome long."

Gabe had finished off a second plate of cookies and most of his coffee before he heard Delia's heels clicking on terra-cotta tile floors in the large entryway. He was already on his feet as she came into the room.

She waved him back into his seat and sat in Annie's chair. "Sit down, Gabe. I didn't mean to keep you waiting for so long, but Esther was awake and I needed to get her settled." Delia gestured at the cookie platter and his empty, crumb-covered plate. "I see Annie treated you to her best cookies. She must like you."

"I'll have to make sure to stay on her good side." He leaned forward, forearms resting on his knees and hands clasped. Putting this off would only make it harder. "I know it's been a long night already, but we need to talk, Delia."

"Officially, you mean." Delia sat up straight, hands folded in her lap. "Given the shouting coming from the parlor, I'm going to guess Jack is having a similar conversation with Sadie."

He'd heard muffled voices a few times and one loud crash, but no more than that. Not enough to tell him if Jack was holding his own. "Who's winning?"

She smiled, just a little. "I didn't linger long enough to eavesdrop. But just based on volume, I think Jack might be ahead. I'm not willing to count Sadie out just yet." Delia looked him in the eye, all traces of humor gone. "Go ahead and tell me, Gabe. I'm not as excitable as Sadie. You have my promise not to yell."

"I won't hold you to that promise." Gabe cast about for a place to start, all his careful rehearsal forgotten. Telling her about the murders and asking his questions was so much easier when it all happened in his head. "Jack and I have been working on a series of murders for the last three months. We don't have much in the way of leads and catching the killer will take time. I—Jack and I—feel that having men from our squad watch this house until we find this man is a wise precaution. I'm also going to urge you to accept a police escort anytime you leave the house."

She tipped her head to one side, her expression carefully neutral. "You really think this is necessary because of the case you're working on?"

Gabe nodded. "I do. Jack agrees. He's telling Sadie the same thing right now."

Delia took a deep breath before she spoke. "The two of you have been detectives for years. You must work on murder cases all the time. I'm willing to believe that you honestly think we need protection, but I need to know why. What frightens the two of you so much?"

He'd told Jack to tell Sadie everything. Gabe couldn't do any less, especially not with the memory of a stranger watching Delia at the café so fresh. "There is a chance—there is a strong possibility that people close to the detectives working the case are in danger. We're afraid that you and Sadie might draw this killer's attention."

Her chin came up, a challenge in her eyes. "That's all well and good, and I'm sure you have your reasons. But you still haven't told me why, Detective Ryan. I'd like to know what kind of danger Sadie and I are in."

"This is an ongoing investigation, so I can't give you all the details, but I'll tell you what I can. It's not pleasant. A lot of it will be hard to hear." Gabe closed his eyes briefly and rubbed his forehead again. The headache was worse. "I know you're tired, but I need to ask some questions when I'm finished."

She stared over his shoulder for an instant, her eyes losing focus, watching the ghost. Delia shivered and turned back to him, a flush blossoming in her cheeks. "Go ahead, Gabe. I'm listening."

Gabe gave Delia all the information he could about the murders, stressing how the killer moved through the city and took his victims seemingly at will. And even though he questioned the wisdom of doing so, he told her about the letters, explaining that the latest one was addressed to him, making the killer's taunts personal. He didn't gloss over how horrible the victims' deaths were.

And he didn't attempt to conceal the murderer's claims that there were more victims still undiscovered by the police, or hide that he believed those claims. She flinched at some of what he said and swallowed hard, but didn't turn away.

Not until Gabe finished. He waited for her to speak first, giving her time to come to terms with the idea that the killer could come after her or Sadie. His questions could wait another few minutes.

Delia brushed at her eyes and squared her shoulders. "If Sadie insists on being difficult, I'll do what I can to convince her. She's an innocent in many ways. Recognizing the ugliness of the world is difficult for her. Now ask your questions. I'll do my best to answer."

He poured more coffee, offering Delia a cup that she declined. Stirring in sugar turned into a delaying tactic, so he took one sip and abandoned the cup on a side table between their chairs. "I have some questions about Shadow and the nightmare you had. A big part of my job is piecing the fragments of a case together until they form a picture that makes sense. Any of the details you remember from your dream or what you saw of Shadow tonight could be important. I wouldn't put you through this if it could be avoided, but you're the only one who can tell me what I need to know."

Delia watched a spot just behind his left shoulder, her eyes tracking the ghost as Shadow moved around to stand next to him. A chill tendril of air brushed his cheek. Gabe shivered and clamped down on his imagination.

She pulled her gaze away from Shadow; the weary set of her mouth made clear the effort required to separate herself. "Be honest with me. Do you think what happened to Shadow is related to the case you're working on?"

"I don't know." He shrugged and tried to smile, remembering the fine line between witness and friend. Right now he wasn't sure which side of the line to stand on. "I think if a connection exists, it's from sometime in the past. But I won't know until I hear what you have to say."

"That's fair." She tucked a strand of hair behind her ear with a shaking hand, a sign of nerves let slip. The trembling lip when she smiled was a bigger tell; her bravery was a thin facade. "Do your worst."

Gabe perched on the edge of his seat and looked into Delia's brown eyes, baffled about where the sudden impulse to hold her hand came from. They'd only known each other for one evening, but he already knew she wouldn't welcome that kind of attention or thank him for coddling her. He sternly reminded himself of professional distance, and that the needs of the investigation came before sparing her feelings, or that he was attracted to her.

Honesty demanded Gabe admit to himself that he wanted to make an attempt to know Delia better. A pang of disloyalty, to Victoria and her memory, hit him simultaneously. Rejoining the world of the living carried a lot of guilt.

He rubbed his sweaty palms on his knees and held professionalism between them like a shield. "I'm going to ask you about the nightmare you had. Any thing you can remember could be important. You said the man who took Shadow was wearing a mask. What was it made of?"

She shrank back deeper into the chair, hands bunching her skirts tightly. Delia chewed her lip, remembering. "Cloth of some kind, rough and light-colored." Her eyes opened wider. "Thick canvas, like a scrap of sail from one of the fishing boats. Shadow grabbed the mask while trying to get away."

"That's good. Those are the kinds of details that help." Canvas could mean a fisherman or a merchant seaman, even a sailmaker, but Gabe mistrusted the obvious. He pushed a little harder. "Now tell me what the mask looked like. Could Shadow see any part of his face around it? The color of his eyes?"

The answer was immediate. "No, Shadow couldn't see his face. The mask fit over his head like a . . . a flour sack. Small slits over his eyes let him see out, but she couldn't see past the openings. A design painted on the front was all she really saw. That stood out even in the dark."

His mouth went dry. "A design?"

"Yes." Delia drew the design in air with a finger. "A circle divided into quarters, drawn on white canvas with black paint. There was something else, too. The paint was smudged and she couldn't make it all out, but small pictures were drawn at the bottom of the circle."

Gabe patted his pockets down, silently swearing at himself for not being as meticulous as his partner about carrying a notebook.

He finally came up with a pencil and a flyer for a local grocer, Mrs. Allen's shopping list of the previous day scribbled in a corner. "Can you draw what Shadow saw? It doesn't have to be perfect, but even a rough sketch will help me understand."

Delia quirked an eyebrow over the grocery list, but turned the flyer face down on the side table and sketched on the back. She paused, added a few more lines, and held the flyer out. "I drew all the time while at school, but I'm badly out of practice. That's near as I can come to what I remember. I hope it's clear enough."

"It's perfect." The killer's calling card stared up at him from the creased paper. Two small figures, enough like the signature used by the murderer to twist his stomach, sat at the bottom. Gabe pointed at the largest one. "Do you know what that is?"

She shook her head. "Not for sure. I went to an exhibit at the Natural History Museum in New York last year. This reminds me of the Egyptian picture writing I saw. Hieroglyphics, I think they're called."

His coffee cup rattled on its saucer, sloshing lukewarm coffee across the tabletop and bouncing his spoon onto the floor. For an instant, the word *earthquake* was on his lips, but the pictures on the wall remained still and the two small chandeliers on either end of the sitting room didn't sway. If not for the flash of fear in Delia's eyes and the puddle of coffee he hastily mopped with his napkin, Gabe might have thought the incident was all in his head.

The doorbell at the front of the house chimed as he dealt with the spill. Annie answered before he had time to worry or wonder. Gabe couldn't make out all the words, but her clipped tone made it clear what she thought of late callers. He heard a man's voice ask for him and the door closed again.

Gabe was on his feet, the flyer and pencil tucked into an inside pocket, and buttoning his coat as Annie led Marshall Henderson into the sitting room.

Henderson's hat was clutched in one hand, long fingers curled tight around the rounded brim. The young rookie nodded to Delia. "I'm sorry to disturb you and your family so late, Miss. The desk sergeant told me that Lieutenant Ryan and Sergeant Fitzgerald might still be here."

"I think we can forgive you, officer." Delia exchanged looks with Gabe before turning back to Henderson with a smile. "I'm sure this is important or you wouldn't interrupt their evening off."

Marshall blushed, obviously flustered by her attention even if he had spoken first. "I'm just following the lieutenant's orders, Miss."

Another murder. He'd left instructions that he was to be notified, day or night, and that was the only reason Henderson would hunt them down this late. A bitter taste rose in the back of his throat and his heart began to race. Less than twenty-four hours had passed since they found the last victims.

"Annie, can I impose upon you to tell Jack we have to leave?" Gabe asked. "I'll come by and get the cookie recipe for my landlady tomorrow if that won't be a problem."

"You come calling anytime you like, Gabriel." She eyed Henderson standing awkwardly to one side, pale and sweating in his blue wool coat. "Wrap up the rest of the cookies on that plate in a napkin and take them with you. Jack didn't get his share. This young man would probably like a few, too."

Gabe scooped the cookies into a white linen napkin and handed them to Henderson. "Put these in your coat pocket for now and be sure to share with Sergeant Fitzgerald. Now tell me where we're going." The young rookie glanced at Delia and hesitated. Gabe nodded, signaling his approval. "Go ahead, Marshall. You can speak in front of Miss Martin, but stick to generalities. Specifics can wait."

"Golden Gate Park, just off 36th Avenue. Baxter's out front with a car." Sweat glistened on the patrolman's face, rolled down his neck and into his collar. "Ruby Diamond was working the corner of 36th and Fulton. She took a customer into the park to conduct business. They didn't go even a hundred yards from the street, but she picked that clump of trees because they'd be out of sight. The gentleman with Miss Ruby walked into a body in the dark. She says he ran off screaming. He wasn't anywhere to be found by the time we arrived."

Ruby Diamond was well known to all the beat cops and patrolmen who spent any time at all on the waterfront. Normally Ruby worked closer to the docks, but the fair was luring everyone from their usual haunts with the promise of easy money. "Is Ruby all right?"

"She's shaken up, but won't go home." Henderson pulled a handkerchief from his back pocket and wiped his face. "Miss Ruby insists on speaking to you first. Maxwell is looking after her and keeping her out of the way."

Jack and Sadie came into the sitting room, hand in hand, Annie right behind them with coats draped over an arm and holding Gabe's hat.

"Thank you, Annie." Gabe slipped on his overcoat before retrieving his hat from Annie. "I'm really sorry the evening didn't work out the way you'd planned, Sadie. If you and Delia are game, we can try seeing a bit more of the fair one day soon."

The smile that spread across Sadie's face almost chased the worry of Jack's being called away from her eyes. "No one's to blame for what happened this evening, but I'll hold you to that offer. You and Jack work out the details. An excursion with a little less drama would be nice."

Gabe caught his partner's eyes. "Go on out to the car with Henderson and he can get started on filling you in. I need to have a word with Delia."

"Don't take too long." Jack buttoned his coat and forced his cap over his wild mop of red hair. "I won't be held responsible if I'm forced to listen to Baxter's theories for long. We'll see ourselves out, Annie."

Jack kissed Sadie good-bye and followed Henderson to the door. Gabe hung back, waiting to speak to Delia and make arrangements to finish what they'd started, hopefully without an audience. Sadie eyed him for a moment, openly curious, but Annie intervened, filling Sadie's hands with dirty plates and shooing her toward the kitchen. Delia stood, a hand resting on the high, curved back of a chair and her expression equally as curious as Sadie's.

He fiddled with the brim of his battered fedora, reaching for professionalism again. "The drawing you made is a great help. I have a friend, Colin Adams, who is a professor of antiquities at Stanford. He might be able to tell us if the drawing on the mask really is a hieroglyphic and what it means. I plan to go see him tomorrow afternoon. If you're not busy, I'd like you to come along. There are some letters with similar drawings I'd like both of you to see."

"Letters?" Understanding shone in Delia's eyes. "You mean letters from the murderer."

Gabe nodded. "We haven't released that information to the press yet. You don't have to make the trip tomorrow, but I thought you might find what Colin has to say interesting. I'm hoping he can give us both some answers."

"I'll come. It does sound interesting and I'd like to see this through." Delia sank into a chair again, tired smudges under her eyes. She peered up at him, face perfectly serious and solemn. "Tell me what time you'll call round and I'll be ready. And is this a strictly professional request for my company? I'd like to know how to dress."

Gabe didn't know what to say. He hunted for a hint in the way she watched him that she was teasing. Some dimly remembered and rusty social skill took over, and he answered without thinking. "The request for your assistance is professional, but wanting to spend time in the company of a new friend is wholly selfish on my part. Is twelve-thirty too early?"

"Twelve-thirty is fine. I'll see you then." She stared at a spot behind him for an instant before giving him a shaky smile, throwing him more off balance. "Be careful tonight."

"I will. Good night."

Gabe hurried across the empty entry hall, footsteps a muffled echo against the high ceiling. He shut the front door softly and paused on the step to flip up his collar. Fog-laden air hung in a damp veil between him and the car at the curb, dark shapes forming and vanishing again in the constantly moving mist. Faces peered at him, hauntingly familiar, and melted back into the swirling wall.

Ghosts of a different sort, made from fallen clouds and memory. He'd face them later.

CHAPTER 7

Gabe

Gabe rubbed his hands together briskly to get some of the blood moving and regretted leaving his gloves at home. Damp and cold penetrated his overcoat, soaked through his suit jacket, and seeped through skin to the bone. The calendar might say June, but summer fog carried winter in its heart. He'd worked many a December night and not been near as miserable.

He'd handpicked his squad, looking for men who followed orders but thought for themselves as well. That always paid off in ways both big and small, and tonight was no exception. He and Jack arrived to find the murder scene closed off and the investigation well underway. That gave Gabe hope he might get to bed before dawn.

One of the men had driven two patrol cars over the grass to the edge of the grove and trained the headlights on the body and the surrounding area. It was probably still too dark for Baker's pictures to expose properly, but Baker snapped away with his Kodak and Officer Turner set off the magnesium powder in the flash pan when given the word. The two men were a good team. If anyone could get photographs of the murder scene on a foggy night, they could.

Gabe's stomach flipped. What he saw in the shifting fog and

uncertain illumination of headlights was bad, worse than he'd ever seen. At least one of the men had been sick. Dirt and old leaves scuffed over the splash of vomit didn't hide the sour smell. It blended with the scent of blood and piss into an unnaturally foul odor, held close by the fog and not allowed to dissipate.

Cops who survived long term on murder squads found a way to shut out the gore and the smells, and turn off their human side that recoiled and wanted to run. Gabe had learned to become an observer, distancing himself to note facts, patterns, and record details. Observing let him do his job and if he dealt with nightmares later, that was on his own time.

He'd have nightmares about this victim.

A sturdy, middle-aged man hung upside down from the tallest tree in the small grove. His shoes were gone, his white shirt and trousers cut up and tattered, but the victim still wore his wool coat. The bottom of the coat brushed the ground behind the man's head, a dark drapery that hid his pale face from anyone approaching from the street. A hat rested against the tree trunk, trampled on until its shape was unrecognizable.

The rope knotted tight round the man's ankles had been tossed over a sturdy branch to haul him up, looped three times to keep the victim from slipping to the ground and tied off around the trunk. His arms were unbound and dangled next to his head, congealed blood sticky on the backs of his hands and hanging in long strings from the end of his fingers. Dark urine stains soaked the front of his trousers and open eyes stared, the knowledge he was going to die frozen on the murdered man's face.

He'd been strung up, gutted, and field dressed as if the grove were a forest and the victim a hunter's prize kill. His entrails lay on the ground, tossed aside in a slimy coil. The killer hadn't bothered with a gag this time. Cutting out the man's tongue worked just as well.

The magnesium flash stripped away the shadows, each burst of white light burning a new image on the back of Gabe's eyes. Unlike the other victims, a quartered circle had been carved on the man's chest, not his forehead.

Jack busily took notes and drew small sketches in his Moleskine, documenting what he could in case Baker's nighttime photographic efforts failed. Taking notes and asking questions was the way his partner survived and kept his sanity.

Gabe gestured toward the tattered remains of the victim's white shirt. "That shirt is soaked in blood. He was alive when the killer carved that symbol."

"I think the poor bastard was alive for most of it." Jack cleared his throat and took a step back. "What I want to know is how our boy managed to overpower a man that big and string him up like that. Makes me wonder if he had a partner."

"Don't buy trouble." Gabe worked his way around the tree, dodging his men and working toward the edge of the light thrown by the headlights. His eyes scanned the ground, looking for footprints or anything the squad might have missed. "I want day shift out here at first light. The man who moved those cars into place did the right thing, some light is better than none at all. But it's still almost impossible to see out here."

"What time do you want me at your boarding house with a car?" Jack bent to pick something up, but tossed it away. "An acorn. Probably not important."

"You get to handle this one on your own. I need to pay Colin a visit to chase down a piece of evidence. I'm taking Delia with me." Gabe stopped where the light began to fail and turned back to watch his men working. Pausing also gave Jack time to think about Delia going along. He never doubted that his friend and partner would have a comment to make. "I'll sleep better knowing you'll be here to supervise in the morning."

Jack didn't say anything at first, but his pencil beat a staccato rhythm on the edge of his notebook. "I can run the investigation in the morning, that isn't a problem. But is taking Delia to see Colin wise, Gabe? I'm not sure involving her in this case is good for either one of you."

"Let me show you something. Then you can decide if involving Delia is wise or not." Gabe dug in his pockets and found the grocer's flyer with Delia's sketch on the back. He moved closer to the light and angled the paper so that the headlights shone full on her drawing. "She drew this from memory tonight while you were with Sadie. It was part of a nightmare she had about Shadow."

By the time Gabe finished telling Jack about Delia's nightmare, the mask, and her guess about hieroglyphics, his partner was shaking his head.

"Forget I said anything. You'd think I'd know better by now than to second-guess you." Jack pushed his cap back with the end of his pencil. "The coroner's wagon is here. Let's go talk to Ruby and distract her while they cut the body down."

Gabe found Henderson and asked where Maxwell was looking after Ruby. Marshall pointed them toward a bench on the far-side of the grove.

They found Maxwell and Ruby only a few yards from the sidewalk and inside the dim circle of light cast by a streetlight. The young officer watched the street and the darkened park warily, obviously aware of being visible while not being able to see anyone approach. Gabe gave Maxwell credit for letting Ruby have the comfort of the streetlamp and not making her wait in the dark.

Ruby sat with her legs crossed, skirts hiked up almost to her knees, and one foot jiggling rapidly, as if keeping time to music. Smoke from her cigarette curled up to join with the fog. A pile of snuffed out and discarded cigarette butts littered the ground at her feet, none smoked more than halfway down.

"Lieutenant Ryan." Maxwell's relief was obvious. "I've offered to see her home several times, but Miss Diamond insisted on waiting to speak to you."

No one called Ruby Miss Diamond, not even Ruby, but pointing that out would only hurt Maxwell's feelings. "You did just fine, Maxwell. Report to Officer Henderson and have him find something for you to do. Sergeant Fitzgerald and I will make sure Ruby gets home."

Gabe traded looks with Jack. His partner sat next to Ruby, arm draped casually along the back of the bench. Gabe stood in front of her, feet planted far apart and hands stuck deep in his overcoat pockets. Ruby glanced up at him, a quick, guilty look, and went back to concentrating on her cigarette. He'd let her finish this one before expecting her to speak; he had patience enough for one.

Jack put his hand over hers when Ruby tossed the cigarette away to stop her from lighting another. "You told Officer Henderson you wanted to talk, Ruby. If you've changed your mind, just say so. No harm in that, we won't be angry. I'll have one of the boys see you home and the lieutenant and I can get back to business."

Ruby pulled in on herself, suddenly looking older and scared. "You've got nice boys working for you, Gabe. They took good care of me."

"That's their job, Ruby. I'm still glad to know." Gabe crouched down, putting his eyes level with hers. She was crying and trying to hide it. "You can tell me anything you know. Jack, too. I promise that whatever you say stays right here with the three of us. But we can't help you unless you tell us what you're scared of. Tell us what happened."

Ruby took a deep, shuddering breath and brushed at her eyes. "The man hanging from the tree, I know him from back when I first started working the streets. His name's Terrance Owens, married with a couple of nice kids and another on the way. Terry used to run a few girls out of a rooming house near the docks, but he got away from that life years ago. Saved his money until he had enough to do something better."

Gabe thought he understood now why she insisted on talking to him. Ruby wouldn't want any of the young officers to see her crying. He took her hand. "I'm sorry you saw any of this. And I'm especially sorry your friend died."

Sympathy made her cry harder. Jack pulled a clean handkerchief from his pocket for Ruby. He let her dab at her eyes for a few seconds before asking the next question. "What did Terrance do for a living?"

She wiped her eyes again, sitting up straighter and speaking to Gabe. "He drove a single horse cab for his wife's father until he could save up for his own. The last five, six years, Terry drove a four-horse hack, a fancy one with leather seats. Nights when the fog's thick and business slow Terry would give me a ride home. He never wanted anything in exchange. Just took me to my door and went home to his wife and kids."

He glanced at Jack and saw the same thought in his eyes. Neither one of them knew what to say to Mrs. Owens about how her husband died. "Knowing who he was is a big help, Ruby. We'll be able to notify his family so they know what happened to him. Did Terry have a priest or a minister? It might help Mrs. Owens to have someone familiar there when she hears the news."

"Father Joe, over at Saint Catherine's." Ruby clutched Gabe's hand. "Terry's name isn't all I need to tell you. I saw a man drive off with Terry's hack."

"Are you sure, Ruby?" Gabe sat next to her, looking over the top of her head to meet Jack's gaze on her other side. "Finding his body had to be a shock. I'm not sure anyone could tell one cab from another in the fog, especially after an experience like you had."

Ruby yanked her hand back and scowled at him. "That's an awful nice way of telling me I was out of my head and seeing things. Except I know what I saw. I didn't imagine seeing someone drive off with Terry's rig."

"Gabe's sorry." Jack shook his head and put a finger to his lips when Gabe started to speak. "He didn't mean it that way. The lieutenant just doesn't know how to talk to a lady. Tell us what you saw."

She sniffled and gave Jack a grateful look. "I chased the man I brought to the park out to the street. I was mad as blazes he left me here alone. He was dressed like a gentleman, but the coward refused to go looking for a policeman. I got to the bench here in time to see a strange man sitting in the driving seat of Terry's cab. My customer scrambled inside and slammed the door closed. They drove straight off."

"Thank you, Ruby. You've been very helpful." Gabe's headache came back twofold, joined by a cold knot in his stomach. Running after her customer to give him a piece of her mind and a whack or two sounded exactly like Ruby. His doubts about her state of mind spun away into the fog. "Answer one last question for me, then I'll have a patrolman take you home. How did you know for certain the cab you saw belonged to Terry?"

"He had a yellow rose painted on the door and another on the back. For his wife. Rose is her name." Ruby stared at the empty street, tears rolling down her face. "I didn't make a mistake. That was Terry's rig."

Jack helped her to her feet. "Come on, Ruby. Let's get you in a patrol car. Your ride home tonight is on the mayor's tab."

Gabe trailed behind them, the lump in his stomach growing colder. A dead cab driver and Ruby's word about what she saw on a dark foggy night were all he had to hang theories on. He could hear his father's voice lecturing him, repeating over and over that he should deal with facts, evidence. The only way to solve a case was to pile that proof up so high, no one questioned your conclusion.

His faith died with Victoria. Gabe hadn't seen much point in praying since, but he prayed now, asking God to listen this once and for Ruby to be wrong about seeing someone else drive off with Terry's rig. He desperately wanted the cab driver to be just a cab driver.

What he wanted didn't silence the refrain in his head: *I see you, but you won't see me. Catch me if you can.*

Delia

Shadow's head hit the wagon bed with a sharp thump. The split in her lip opened wider, pain spiking down her jaw and blood dripping off her chin to cool under her cheek. She remembered that he'd hit her hard, knocking her to the ground and making her woozy.

Dust and the smell of fish and crab rushed at her from the splintered boards of the wagon, unsettling her stomach. Weighted nets, damp rope, and dirty buckets shared the back of the wagon with her, adding to the stench. She moaned, unable to stop the sound from rising into her throat or escaping. The stranger punched her again with a gloved fist. Pain spiked the side of her face, her cheekbone shattering with a grating sound and all Shadow remembered afterward was darkness.

She came to as the wagon stopped, struggling to get a breath under the heavy tarpaulin covering her. The wagon bed dipped under his weight. Shadow laid still and limp, drifting in and out of consciousness; too dizzy to lift her head or think of escape. Certain, too, that if she moved he'd keep hitting her until there was no chance of her moving again.

He tugged the tarpaulin away and grabbed her ankles, dragging her to the open wagon gate before tossing her over his shoulder. Pain woke with the movement, sharp but bearable. The mask was gone, but hanging head down so she couldn't see his face, only the back of his coat. A laborer's plain coat, smelling of pork sausage and sweat.

His boots clumped up muddy pine steps to a narrow porch. The building was a house, dark inside, the embers of a fire banked on the hearth and lamps unlit. Shadow caught glimpses of sturdy furniture in the main room, books piled on a table next to an armchair and photographs of a woman and young boy in oval frames.

The stranger moved quickly down a short hall and into a small bedroom. He kicked aside a rag rug next to the bed, grabbed the iron bedpost with his free hand, and slid the bed away from the wall. Shadow heard him grunt, the muscles in his back straining to hold her and lift. A trapdoor swung open at his feet. The hinges moved smoothly, well-oiled so as not to make noise. He took a lantern from atop a chest of drawers and stepped down into the opening.

Two deep steps and a third to the bottom, and he dumped her off his shoulder. She cried out, the excruciating pain in her face and jaw ripping down her neck and into her shoulder. Blood oozed from her swollen lip.

He struck a match and lantern light dazzled her eyes. The stranger grabbed her ankle and dragged Shadow through an open door and into a dirt-walled room under the house. Boards braced the walls. Timbers and joists, the foundation of the house and floors, made up the ceiling.

Shadow struggled not to pass out again, to kick at his knees, to claw his hands when he shifted his grip to her wrists. He yanked on her arms, dragging her to the far end of the dug-out space and the thick wooden post driven into the ground. Metal rings were bolted to two sides and pieces of hemp rope knotted around each ring. He jerked her arms over her head and began to tie her.

"No . . . please, no. I have a baby at home, he needs me." She knew she shouldn't beg when he smiled, a chipped front tooth gleaming in lantern light. "Don't do this! Let me go home."

Pleading was useless, he wouldn't release her. Shadow's heart thudded against her ribs, panic over being shut underground driving away dizziness and overcoming the sick pain in her head. She screamed, splitting her lip wider, and used all her strength to twist side to side to pull free. One arm slipped from his grip and she raked nails down the side of his face, leaving bloody scratches.

Pale blue eyes regarded her coldly, the absence of emotion terrifying her. He wrenched her arm up again, tying the rough hemp ropes so that they dug into her skin with the slightest movement. A dirty red bandana from his pocket was stuffed into her mouth and knotted tight behind her head.

The stranger tossed Shadow's shoes and stockings into the corner near the door. He stood in the doorway for a moment, lantern in hand, and stared at her.

Calm eyes were the last she saw before he shut the door, taking the light with him.

I screamed, thrashing against bindings and shoving away the hands holding me down, panic a metallic taste coating my tongue. My only thought was escape, to find a way to win free. I didn't want to die in the dark.

"Delia! Wake up now, sweetheart. Annie's here. Wake up and talk to me."

Trembling and gasping for breath, I opened my eyes. Light

from the small lamp on my dressing table chased away images of crumbling dirt walls. I was in my bedroom, a prisoner of tangled sheets and coverlets, but safe, not locked underground.

Bursting into tears might not be the bravest response to waking from a nightmare, but I wasn't the heroine of a dime novel. Sobbing seemed the only sane reaction. I don't think I could have stopped myself from crying no matter how hard I tried.

Annie sat on my bed and gathered me into her arms, rocking me just as she had when I was sixteen. I'd had many a nightmare that first year I came to live with Esther and Sadie.

She saw my eyes were open and the sharp tone used to wake me left Annie's voice. "You're all right, darling. Nothing in a dream's going to hurt you."

Sadie stood just inside the doorway, wide-eyed and twisting the belt on her dressing gown around her fingers. She looked near as frightened as I was.

"I . . . I'm sorry. I didn't mean to wake you." My hands shook badly, but with Annie's help I struggled free of the sheets and dangled my feet off the side of the bed. The room was cold, raising gooseflesh on my skin. "Please, go back to bed, both of you. I'll be fine."

Annie pulled a cotton throw off the end of the bed and draped it over my shoulders. "I can sit with you until you're ready to sleep. And don't go fussing about being too grown-up for me to take care of you. Tell me about your dream and we'll chase it out of your head, just like we used to do. Sadie, would you be a dear and fetch Delia a glass of water?"

Sadie was pale with exhaustion, bruised circles under her eyes calling into question how much sleep she'd gotten even before my scream brought her running. "Would you like anything else, Dee? I can bring up a snack, too, or even make tea."

"Water is fine." I tried to think up a wisecrack, a funny remark to chase some of the concern from her face. My wit had deserted me with my composure. "Once that's done, please go back to bed. No reason for all of us to lose sleep."

Esther tottered out of the darkened hall behind Sadie, a barefoot, white-haired apparition, wearing an over-large nightgown. She leaned heavily on a cane for support, her free hand trailing along the wall. Being whisper thin and weighing no more than a sigh didn't rob Esther Larkin of determination. She wobbled to the center of my room and began to shout.

"Leave my house!" Esther flailed the air with her cane, coming close to toppling over. "I won't have you haunting my girls and bringing them trouble. Get out!"

Pressure in my chest told me Shadow was near, but I couldn't see her. It scared me that Esther might. Death came closer each day, stole a bit more from her.

Sadie caught her mother round the shoulders and eased the cane out of Esther's hand. She gave me a bleak look before she led her mother away. "Come back to bed, Mama. I'll make you some hot milk to help you sleep."

Annie and I sat quietly for a moment once Sadie left the room. A few brief seconds of silence gave me hope that if I stalled long enough, Annie wouldn't ask about the dream. I knew better, but I clung to the foolish belief she might have softened over the last three years.

That was folly.

"Talk to me, Delia. Getting hurtful things out into the light's always better." She took my hand, rubbing warmth back into my fingers. "I know Sadie was having trouble sleeping after speaking with Jack for so long. Did your talk with Gabriel bring bad dreams?"

"No." I cleared my throat, trying to swallow air suddenly sticky as honey. "Gabe isn't to blame."

"The ghost then, the one you and Sadie whisper about. She needs to stop bothering you." Annie's mouth set in a thin line. "My Gran showed me the trick of running off ghosts causing trouble."

Shadow shimmered into view, clean and neat with the shawl draped over her shoulders, and every hair in place. The blood and bruises so evident in my nightmare had vanished again. She hovered in the same spot where Esther had stood, hands folded primly at her waist. Her throat was bare, the cross I'd grown accustomed to missing.

A soft wind began to blow through the room, stirring the curtains and my hair. No anger filled the air, only the fear I'd let Annie send her away.

I stared into my ghost's pleading eyes, unable to turn away from her desperation and certain she understood our every word. Certain, as well, that the grief and sorrow I felt were my own. I couldn't help thinking about her child, how she'd pleaded with the killer that her baby needed her. Shadow deserved justice and to rest in peace. I'd do my best to give her both. "No, she needs to stay a little longer. We're not finished yet."

I slept until after nine, waking to brilliant sunshine and the sound of sparrows and finches squabbling under the eaves. Their quarrels died away as they got down to the business of feeding nestlings and males singing their territory. The cedar tree outside my window was home to many of their nests. Drooping green needles and tightly shut cones scraped against wooden siding and the window frame with each touch of the breeze. Birds perched on the branches and flitted off again: purple finch, juncos not yet gone for the summer, crowned sparrows and mourning doves. Reciting the names was a familiar summer morning ritual, one I'd started at sixteen.

Listing birds also kept me from thinking of ghosts and nightmares, of sorrows past and present. I was all in favor of that.

Annie carried Esther's breakfast tray past my door before I'd managed to force myself out of bed. Cutlery rattled against china plates and bowls in time to her footfalls, and the smell of bacon, muffins, and coffee drifted into my room. She hummed an old spiritual, the sound comforting and familiar. Esther's raspy voice and Sadie's laugh followed soon after. I threw off the covers, put on my dressing gown, and went to join them.

Sadie came to my room after breakfast, a bit of company and moral support while I got ready for my excursion to Stanford. The thought of what we might learn from Professor Adams both excited me and made me nervous.

Nerves were determined to carry the day. My teasing of the night before became all too real a problem as I stared into my armoire. Clothing I'd left behind three years before, now dreadfully out of fashion, stared back at me. I promptly went into a panic over what to wear. "Oh, no . . . I completely forgot my trunk still hasn't arrived."

"What's wrong, Dee?" Sadie appeared at my shoulder, viewing my small assortment of skirts, blouses, and my lone garden party dress with puzzlement.

I gestured at what some might call my wardrobe. "This is what's wrong. Normally I don't give two figs about what I wear, you know that. But I made the mistake of teasing Gabe last night about how I should dress to visit Professor Adams and he took me seriously."

"You were teasing Gabe Ryan." Sadie crossed her arms and quirked an eyebrow. "I'm certain your conversation with him was at least as grim as mine was with Jack. Of course Gabe took you seriously. He takes everything seriously, not that you'd know. Whatever did you say?"

Now I felt doubly foolish, but if I dove under the bed to avoid answering, Sadie would just pull me out again. "I asked if wanting me along was strictly a professional request for my company. And then I said that I'd like to know how to dress . . . depending on his answer."

Sadie stared at me for an instant before she burst out laughing. "Delia Martin, I can't believe you were flirting with him! What did Gabe say?"

"I think I shocked him at first, because he just stared. He finally managed to say that asking for help with the investigation was professional, but that wanting to spend time with a new friend was completely selfish on his part." I sank onto the vanity chair in front of the dressing table, reconsidering my plan to hide under the bed. "It all got so complicated. I didn't think I was flirting. I certainly didn't think Gabe would take it that way. Maybe I shouldn't go after all."

She grinned impishly, obviously enjoying my discomfort. Equally delighted, I was sure, with seeing her schemes come to fruition with no effort on her part. I'd put my own head in the noose.

Sadie got a hand under my arm and dragged me to my feet. "Too late to back out now, Dee. Gabe will be here in an hour. We'll find something of mine for you to wear. By the time I finish, you'll knock Gabe Ryan out of his shoes."

I dug my heels in and refused to budge. "I've only known him for a day. I'm not sure I want to knock him out of his shoes."

The grin faded. An earnestness I rarely saw in Sadie crowded out the glee. "Jack is Gabe's oldest friend, just as you're mine. I want the two of you to be friends as well. What's the harm in that?"

What Sadie didn't say is that after the wedding she'd have little free time for me and Jack would have just as little for Gabe. That was the way of newly married couples, all their attention was focused on each other.

Her intentions were good; she didn't want Gabe or me to be lonely. I relented somewhat. "No harm in being friends I suppose, I do like Gabe. But that's as far as I'm willing to go. I want a promise you won't be plotting romance and matchmaking behind my back."

She took my hand, still solemn and earnest. "I'd never think of matchmaking behind your back. You've my word on that."

"Just try to remember this is more fun for you than for me or Gabe." The clock in the parlor chimed the half-hour. Another brief moment of panic gripped me until I remembered the clock ran fast. "We'd best get on with finding me something suitable to wear. I think I've settled on trying for friendly looking, but serious enough for visiting a university. Do you think we can manage that?"

Sadie beamed, glee restored. "I think we can do a little better than friendly. You'll look stunning."

I'd never looked stunning in anything, but I didn't argue. Sadie tugged me into the hall and toward my doom, telling me all about current fashion and what colors might look best on me at midday.

Shadow stood outside Esther's door, hands pressed against her stomach, the picture of eternal patience. She turned to look at me for an instant, her eyes full of sorrow, and went back to watching Esther sleep. Tears filled my eyes, the brightness of Sadie's chatter dimming. I knew what the ghost was waiting for, what it meant.

I wished I could believe that Esther had a guardian to show her the way and wouldn't be alone. Much as I wanted that to be true, I wasn't ready to make that leap of faith. There was too much I didn't understand about ghosts, too much uncertainty about what Shadow wanted from me.

Even if I felt the need to find an answer to the riddle Shadow represented, I didn't trust her. I wasn't sure I ever would.

CHAPTER 8

Delia

I was tempted to wait for Gabe on the front porch. That seemed the only way to avoid Sadie looking on from the sidelines and gauging Gabe's reaction to her handiwork. She'd dressed me in a deep burgundy summer suit, a hat with a wide cream-silk brim and black silk gathered on the crown. The skirt fell to just above my ankle, wide, boxy pleats making it fuller than I was used to wearing. Jet buttons closed the jacket and the wide lace collar of a cream-colored batiste blouse filled the square neckline.

The effect wasn't what I'd call stunning, but I had to admit I looked less like a frumpy girls' school teacher when she'd finished. Sadie was very pleased with her handiwork, too pleased for my peace of mind. Allowing her to fuss over dressing me once meant I could look forward to more of the same. That was probably the least pressing of my worries, but the safest to think about.

Fretting about the nightmare, remembering Shadow's pain and fear, and knowing I had to tell Gabe added to my overall case of nerves. Avoiding tears might be impossible and crying would embarrass me, but I'd lived through embarrassing moments before. What the ghost showed me was important, I knew that, and somehow tied to the case he was trying to solve. Gabe needed to know all the details, no matter how painful I found the telling.

"You look wonderful, Dee. Tomorrow I'll take you shopping. That way you won't have to worry about having something suitable to wear until the rail company brings your trunk. We'll work on updating your wardrobe and find a special outfit for you to wear when the boys take us to the fair again." She fussed with my collar and adjusted the hat. "Something in a deep green and a cut to turn heads, I think."

"Turning heads is your area of expertise. You love playing the peacock." As soon as she took her hands away, I laid the collar back the way I'd had it. "I'm more comfortable in plainer plumage."

The doorbell chimed. Annie let Gabe in, her warm hello one she reserved for people she liked. Footfalls came toward the sitting room, hollow sounding against the high ceilings. That my heart beat a bit faster was enormously silly and not knowing where to stand even more so. I ended up next to Sadie, stiffly facing the door.

Confronted with the two of us posed side by side, Gabe looked confused. Sadie greeted him straightaway with a bright smile and a kiss on the cheek. "How are you, Gabe? I hope you and Jack weren't out too late. Did you sleep well last night?"

"Well enough, thank you. We weren't out too late considering. Jack dropped me off just after midnight." Gabe turned to me and smiled. He appeared genuinely pleased to see me, but still firmly anchored in his shoes. "Are you ready, Delia?"

"I'm ready." I gathered my gloves and my handbag. Ignoring Sadie beaming at the two of us like a fond maiden aunt was difficult, but I managed. "Do you think we'll be back by suppertime? I should let Annie know whether to expect me or not."

"I'm hoping we can get to Stanford not long before Colin's lecture ends at three. When we start back depends on how quickly he finds the information we need." Gabe glanced at Sadie before clearing his throat. "I know a nice restaurant not far from the campus. It's not fancy, but the food's good. We could have supper there after we finish with Colin and then drive back. Does that sound all right? I don't want to inconvenience Annie more than I have already."

I expected Sadie to jump in, but she kept her promise and stayed quiet and blameless. How awkward I felt making social arrangements with Gabe wasn't his fault or Sadie's. The foolish mistake I'd made the night before made me uncomfortable and afraid to speak without thinking carefully beforehand. "That does sound like the best solution. Yes, that would be nice. Let me tell Annie and then we'll go."

Sadie spoke up then. "Go ahead and leave, Dee. I'll tell Annie not to expect you. Jack's coming over after work to visit Mama. That will give Annie plenty of people to feed and fuss over."

"Thank you." I took a breath, nervous again now that we were setting out. "That will save us some time."

She patted my shoulder on her way out. "I'll see you tonight. I expect you to tell me all about your day."

Bright sun made me squint as we stepped outside and I tipped the hat brim to shade my eyes. The young officer who'd come to find Gabe the night before, Henderson, held the car door for me. I settled myself while Gabe got in on the other side, searching the backseat for the glimmer that meant Shadow was going to show herself. The back of my neck itched with her nearness, but the telltale shimmer of air that preceded her presence never appeared.

We were pulling away when I noticed a second patrol car parked in front of the Bourke's house across the street. One of the officers touched the brim of his hat as we drove off and nodded to Gabe. It was an odd sort of comfort to know someone was watching the house. Disquieting as well, and a reminder that life had grown dangerous.

The car roof was up and a glass screen separated us from the driver's seat up front. Henderson wouldn't be able to overhear what was said and I wouldn't have to shout over the rush of wind. Both of those things made me feel better. Finding a way to open the conversation and to recount the dream was the problem. The longer silence stretched between us, the more difficult breaking it became.

Gabe took off his hat and set it on the seat between us. He stared out the window on his side, chewing his lip and appearing deep in thought. I took in the scenery on my side, not ready to disturb him yet. We moved off Russian Hill, down Powell past Chinatown, and into downtown. Horse-drawn buggies, wagons, and cabs vied with motorcars for space once we turned onto Market Street, slowing progress to a crawl.

Crowds filled the city sidewalks at midday: women lugging home brown-paper parcels from a morning trip to the grocer or butcher, bankers in suits and bow ties, sailors strolling in twos and threes, tourists in town for the fair taking in the sights. Shopkeepers' wives helped unload goods from wagons in front of their husband's stores, guarding small mountains of bags and boxes on the sidewalk until the men carried it all inside.

Ghosts milled in groups on the same walkways and in the street, pointing and staring at unseen spectacles. Other ghosts moved with purpose, going from one remembered place to another. Unless I looked closely or the ghost had faded, picking out the dead from the living was sometimes difficult.

Gabe studied the crowds intently. Last night's talk convinced me that he searched an ocean of strangers' faces for a killer, and perhaps, wondered who among the people we saw might be the next victim.

I wondered as well. "Gabe . . ."

Surprise was followed by the sheepish expression I'd seen before. He'd forgotten I was there. Gabe blushed and put his back to the window. "I get so wrapped up thinking about this case . . . but that's no excuse for rudeness. Forgive me, Delia. What did you want to say?"

"No harm done. Your case or something near is what I need to talk about." My fingers curled around the edge of the leather seat, holding tight to something solid. "I had another dream. A horrible dream."

His relaxed, friendly manner fell away. A policeman's distance and caution came over Gabe, pulled him up straighter. "A dream about what happened to Shadow?"

I nodded and he ran a hand through his chestnut hair, leaving it tousled and trying to curl. How much he resembled Jack that way startled me. I hadn't noticed that they looked enough alike to be brothers until now.

"Are you able to tell me about the dream?" Gabe asked. "I'll understand if it's too soon."

"I intend to try. This will be difficult to tell, Gabe, but I'm afraid I'll lose my nerve if I wait. You need to know what I saw." I nursed the flicker of courage inside, trying to coax it into a flame. "Shadow didn't die in that alley. The man in the mask took her somewhere, to a house. She was still alive then. What he did . . . what I saw was terrible."

Gabe's eyes widened, but he'd risen to the rank of lieutenant for a reason; he was good at his job. His voice remained calm, professional. "Did Shadow know where the house was? The district it might be in?"

"Let me think." Shutting my eyes to organize my thoughts was a mistake. I jerked them open again immediately, desperate for sunlight. Shadow's memories of darkness and numbing cold shut out the warmth and brightness of the day, filled my mouth with the taste of salty dirt and the need to keen with terror. Breathing was difficult. The weight of earth and the house above, and the fear I'd die alone in the dark, left me gasping for air.

Isadora's admonishment not to let Shadow inside so easily, to keep myself separate and in control, came back to me. I needed to anchor myself or I'd be lost in the ghost's life and not be able to speak at all. That I couldn't see her didn't seem to matter.

This was Shadow's panic I drowned in, not mine. I fought to remember light and that the horrors crowding my head all happened long ago. "The stranger wore gloves and . . . he kept hitting her until she stopped moving or making noise. She was unconscious and covered by a tarpaulin in the back of a wagon. Shadow didn't come around until they reached the house."

Gabe let me stumble through describing all I remembered: the smell of the wagon and the stranger's coat, what Shadow saw of the house and the pictures on the wall, the trapdoor in the bedroom floor. Telling him about the room under the house, how the stranger watched Shadow from the door and left her in the dark was hardest.

My voice quavered relating Shadow's plea to go home to her baby, but I won the struggle not to cry. Gabe took my hand when I'd finished, both a kind gesture and a reminder that I wasn't the one shut underground.

We sat quietly for a time and I watched out the window, fighting for composure. Once Henderson negotiated the narrow streets of downtown, leaving the city proper didn't take long. A wide, two-lane road went south from San Francisco, winding down the peninsula past fields green with newly sprouted lettuce, corn nearly knee-high, and pumpkin vines beginning to sprawl across earth dark with moisture. Farmhouses and barns sat in the center of a patchwork of soil and growing plants, rising dust marking where farmhands worked. Lean-tos at the side of the road sported hand-painted signs, each promising fresh produce for sale later in the season.

Sunshine, warm air, and new growth made Shadow's memories of darkness and cold bleak in a new way. I mourned her, grieved that she'd never seen her child grow and that he'd never known his mother. Parents and children lost each other, I knew that first-hand, but this was an especially cruel way.

"Remembering that took courage. Thank you." Gabe squeezed my fingers and released my hand. "I'm fairly certain that I know when Shadow died. My father was a homicide detective, too. Almost thirty years ago he worked on a series of murders almost identical to the ones Jack and I are investigating. The killings stopped as suddenly as they started. Based on what you just told me, I'm almost convinced the same man has started killing again."

"After thirty years?" I stared, grappling with the idea. Giving Gabe information was part of what Shadow wanted from me, I was certain of that. Why was becoming clearer. "Where has he been? For that matter if it is the same man, why did he stop killing when your father was hunting for him?"

"I can't answer either of those questions yet. I'll be honest. The idea of the same murderer coming back gives me a serious case of the shakes. And believing the ghost of one of his victims is giving me clues makes me fear for my sanity. I really do believe and that makes it worse." Gabe sighed, sounding tired and a bit defeated. He pulled a packet of light blue envelopes out of his inside pocket. "I brought these to show Colin. Dad has letters in his files just like them. I'd be a fool to ignore the similarities between my father's cases and what's going on now. I'm not willing to risk Sadie's safety or yours by refusing to see what's right in front of me."

"If it makes you feel any better, Lieutenant Ryan, I've been questioning my sanity for years. You grow accustomed to it." I slumped back in the seat, forgetting good posture and all the deportment lessons my mother worked so hard to teach me. "As long as we're sharing delusions, perhaps you can tell me more about the letters your father received. What makes you think all the letters come from the same person?"

He started to say no, I saw it in his eyes. Sharing evidence and confidential information with me was against the rules, and the little I knew of Gabe Ryan pointed toward him always playing by the rules. Something changed his mind. Perhaps Sadie's charm was rubbing off on me.

Gabe tucked the letters back into his pocket. "I'm trusting you with this, Delia. You can't tell anyone, not even Sadie."

"No one would believe me. I have a problem with insanity." The twinkle in his eye suggested he didn't take everything as seriously as Sadie thought, but I gave a serious answer in any case. "I won't tell, not Annie, and especially not Sadie. You've my word on that."

He glanced at Henderson and back to me. "There are obvious things that started me thinking about this. Both sets of letters are written on the same blue stationery. I haven't compared side by side, but the handwriting is exactly the same as I remember. So are the symbols he uses instead of a signature. But the pattern is what really started to convince me."

Listening to Gabe explain helped push back Shadow's memories and fear. More than that, I got a glimpse of how his mind worked when presented with a puzzle, and likely, how he did his job without going mad. "What kind of pattern?"

"Both for my father's cases and mine, the first few letters were sent to the newspaper. The killer claimed a string of victims the police never found and demanded front-page coverage. Dad believed him and so did I, but we never made the letters public." Gabe frowned and raked fingers through his hair again, waking more curls. "Then a new set of letters arrived, addressed to my father instead of the papers. The last letter my squad found was addressed to me personally. In Dad's case, the murderer went one step further. He began sending proof to my father that he was telling the truth."

Shadow appeared, faint and ragged, almost not there. Neat plaits were undone, uneven chunks of hair hanging in her face and hiding some of the bruises. She cradled her broken hand to her chest and sorrowful green eyes stared into mine, making sure I'd seen. The ghost vanished.

I choked back the burning in my throat and the desire to be sick. "Dear God in heaven. What kind of proof?"

"Locks of hair, buttons, a wedding band, and a gold cross. Trophies he took from his last victim. I thought that cross was still in the files my father has at his farm. Seeing it on the floor of Dora's tent was a shock."

Gabe ran a finger along the crease in the crown of his hat, studying the old fedora as if he'd never seen it before. I thought he'd finished, but he cleared his throat and started again. "It got worse. The last letter, the one with the cross, was slipped under the front door of our house and threatened my mother. Dad and his partner took turns sitting up all night in our front room for three days. As soon as Dad could make arrangements, he sent my mother and me away. The killings stopped, but Dad didn't bring us home for six months."

"That's why you ordered protection for Sadie." He nodded, still seeming to pay more attention to the hat than me. I wasn't fooled. "And for Dora."

"I have men watching over my landlady, too. I'd station a man in every doorway of the city if I thought that would slow this killer down." Gabe stopped his nervous fiddling and smiled, wry and without a trace of humor. "Keeping this man from repeating the rest of the pattern might be impossible, but I'm going to try. He's won every move so far. That can't last. Every killer makes a mistake sooner or later."

I was fascinated and terrified simultaneously. He was resigned to contesting with fate, even if he was likely to lose. The handkerchief twisted tight around my fingers, digging grooves in my skin. "You make tracking a murderer sound like a chess game."

The university was just ahead, green lawns and gravel pathways glinting in the sun. Gabe slicked his hair back and stuck the fedora down tight. "Playing chess is easier, Delia. With chess I can see the board."

Gabe directed Henderson along a series of side lanes to the eastern portion of the campus. The roads were narrow, more pathways designed for bicycles or small carts than automobiles. Students stepped off the crushed gravel path into the grass to stare as the patrol car rolled past. A visit from the police couldn't be a common sight on the quiet campus and I didn't blame them for being curious.

Not many of the students were women, but those I saw were bolder than I'd been at that age. Young women pointed at Henderson and held hurried, giggling conversations behind upraised hands. Some of them must have spoken loud enough so that he heard or shouted things after the car passed. He looked straight ahead, but blushed furiously.

The antiquities building sat alone at the end of a long tree-lined lane. A half-circle drive in front, paved with white flagstones and edged with marigolds, let Henderson park near the base of the marble front steps. The building appeared newly built since the quake, three stories tall and faced with redbrick. Arched windows on the front of the building and brass handles on the double doors reflected sunlight into my eyes. A constant stream of students left the building and rushed off across the lawns, their classes ended for the day.

Gabe opened my door and offered his hand. "Colin's office is on the second floor. We'll give the crowd a few moments to make their escape and then we'll go up."

"I've never been to Stanford before." I tipped the brim of Sadie's hat down, shading my eyes so that I could look around. A large pond peeked from behind the building, shimmering in the sun. Tall trees grew next to benches along walkways and cast pools of shade on neatly trimmed lawns. "The campus is much bigger and more open than I imagined."

"Leland and Jane Stanford's only child died of typhoid. The story goes that the two of them decided to found the university as a memorial to their son." Gabe stuck his hands in his pockets and rocked back on his heels, squinting up at the building. "The Stanfords traveled all over the world, visiting great universities and colleges, and came back to build this place. They made it their life's work to educate other people's children."

"I hadn't heard that story before. How very sad." I turned in a slow circle, taking in the open space, lush plantings, and magnificent architecture. "And yet it's such an admirable thing to do with grief. I don't know if I'd have the strength."

"I suspect you have more strength than you realize." He watched me with a melancholy half-smile and a look in his eyes that I couldn't interpret. "We all find personal ways to deal with loss. And if we're lucky, we find work to do that means something." Gabe offered his arm and the sadness went out of his smile. "The stampede for the door seems to be over. I think it's safe to go up to Colin's office now."

The corridors were empty and our footsteps echoed in the cavernous entryway. Paintings hung on the white plaster walls in the corridor, mainly landscapes depicting scenes from all over California.

Portraits of people I didn't recognize decorated the stairway walls off to the left. Glass cases full of ribbons, trophies, and photographs stood on either side of the doors.

Hand-painted banners announcing a dance on Saturday night spanned the width of the hallway. The smells in the building reminded me of school: the sweet scent of ink and paper, shellac on desktops, and the sour smell of damp string mops the janitors used to clean floors.

We started up the wide staircase that went to the second floor. The wooden risers carried a thick coat of wax, clouded and scuffed long past the point of being slippery. I imagined hundreds of students tromped up and down all day, grinding bits of gravel and mud from the soles of their shoes into the stairs. That the oak wasn't worn down to splinters was something of a miracle.

The second floor hallway was filled with classrooms on one side and large, quiet offices for professors on the other. Open classroom doors gave me glimpses of chalkboards and rows of empty desks. Most of the offices were closed up for the day, roller shades drawn over the door's window that had the professor's name painted in gold. The corridor was quiet and even our footsteps were muffled. Twice I thought I saw a ghost walking through a wall or turning the corner ahead of us, but the spirit moved too quickly for me to be sure.

Professor Adams's office looked to be empty as well. Gabe rattled the brass doorknob several times and knocked on the door frame. "Colin? Colin, are you in there?"

"Perhaps he's been detained." I twisted the handle of my handbag around my hand, thinking of all the time spent making the trip. Time Gabe could have put to use tracking the killer. I didn't know Professor Adams, but I hoped he wasn't the kind of person to forget appointments.

"We'll give him a few more minutes." Gabe rattled the knob

again and leaned against the wall in defeat. "He's probably talking with some of his students."

Our wait was brief. A tall, thin man, in a shabby brown suit, came huffing around the corner at the far end of the hall, his long legs taking strides twice the length of mine. Thinning black hair was combed straight back from his forehead and a pair of spectacles perched dangerously close to the end of his nose. He raised a hand and waved. "Gabe! I'm so sorry I'm late. The department chairman needed a word with me and I couldn't break away."

Colin Adams fumbled in his pockets for keys, dropped papers out of the stack balanced on one arm, and had to retrace his steps to retrieve them. By the time Professor Adams came to a halt in front of us, Gabe was smiling.

"You're always late." Gabe shook Colin's hand before introducing me. "This is Miss Delia Martin. Miss Martin is Sadie's best friend and the maid of honor for the wedding. Delia, this is Professor Colin Adams."

Colin smiled and offered his hand. Despite the balding patches in his hair, his face was youthful and his green eyes bright. "I'm pleased to meet you, Miss Martin. How do you happen to be here? Gabe doesn't usually arrive with charming young women in tow."

"Please, call me Delia." I shook Professor Adams's hand and glanced at Gabe, a bit uncertain about Colin's tone. Gabe's hands were stuffed in his trouser pockets and he looked rather unsure himself. "Gabe asked me to come along. He thought I might find it interesting."

Professor Adams fumbled his key into the lock and gave Gabe an appraising look. "Does Miss Martin have a special interest in Egyptology?"

"Delia was the one who suggested the drawings might be hieroglyphics. I thought she deserved to know if her hunch was right or not." Gabe pushed the door open and waved me inside. "After you."

I'd imagined Professor Adams's office as a dark and dreary cave full of Egyptian artifacts, odd specimens floating in jars and smelling faintly of formaldehyde. His office turned out to be quite pleasant. Big windows took up most of one wall, letting in plenty of sunlight and showing a view of wide lawns, trees, and the tranquil pond at the back of the building. Two of the casements were opened halfway, letting in fresh air. The scent of honeysuckle and jasmine came in with the warm breeze, vanquishing the musty smell of old books and leather bindings.

Wooden bookcases were built into the longest wall, the fronts framed in ornately carved molding. Deep shelves stretched from floor to ceiling, but Professor Adams's books were stacked two and three deep. Glass cases sat under the window and along the wall behind the door. Ornately painted pottery, wine jars, and etched clay tablets filled the inside shelves. Some of the images reminded me of the painted sign outside Isadora's tent.

Small animal mummies—a hawk, a dog, and what looked to be a small crocodile—sat on top of the largest cabinet. A small painted coffin, much like one made for an infant that I'd seen at the museum in New York, rested on top of the other case. The thought of a tiny mummy resting inside made me uneasy.

The centerpiece of the room was an old mahogany desk. An inkstand of carved oak sat at the top of a dark brown blotter, inkwells capped and pens laid neatly in a wide groove chiseled in the front edge. A small calico cat slept in a desktop tray on one corner, curled tight in a sunbeam with a paw over her eyes and determined to ignore visitors. She purred as I scratched behind one of her ears, taking it as her due, but didn't open her eyes.

"The cat's name is Nefertiti. She's convinced this office belongs to her and I can't dissuade her of the idea. Nor can I get her to stop sleeping on my correspondence." Professor Adams dropped his stack of papers on the desk. The cat opened one eye to glare balefully at him and promptly went back to sleep. "Take my advice, Delia. Never name a cat after a powerful queen, even one long dead. They do their best to live up to the name."

Colin rooted around under his stack of papers. A bottom drawer was searched next. He came up frowning, patted down his oversized jacket pockets, and wandered over to the bookshelves. "There was a book I wanted to show you, but I think I left it in the lecture hall. I'm going to beg your indulgence for another few moments, Gabe. I'll be back shortly."

He left and I turned to Gabe. "Is he always this . . . this scattered?"

"Always." Gabe grinned and took his turn petting the cat. She lifted her head long enough to lick his fingers, a sure sign of favor, and went right back to sleep. "Colin is one of the best at the research he does, but when it comes to practicalities like remembering a book, he's hopeless."

More artifacts cluttered one section of bookshelves and several small tables in the room. I wandered the office studying each piece, as fascinated with Colin's collection as I'd been with the museum exhibit. Many of the pottery pieces in Colin's office were in better condition, the colors brighter and the designs sharper.

Amongst the figurines and clay shards on one shelf, I found a tarnished silver frame holding the photograph of a young bride. She was slim, still more girl than woman in appearance, and I guessed her to be no more than seventeen. Dressed in a white silk gown and a lace veil that trailed to the ground, she clutched a huge bouquet of roses and lilies. My mother always said happiness made all brides beautiful. Gazing at the photo and the bride's radiant smile, I'd no reason to doubt the truth in that.

"Is this a picture of Colin's wife?" I took the frame off the shelf and held it up for Gabe to see, unable to keep myself from smiling back at the fading photograph. "She's very pretty."

Gabe froze in the act of petting Nefertiti. Deep grief twisted his face with pain and vanished, a glimpse of something private he locked away again. He smiled, but his voice cracked on her name. "Victoria was my wife and Colin's sister. That portrait was taken on our wedding day. I—we—lost her in the fire."

"Oh." I'd missed the resemblance to the sad ghost trailing after Gabe. Time and pregnancy had changed her face, transformed the girl into a woman. I held out the photograph, not knowing what to do or say. "I'm so sorry, Gabe. I didn't mean . . . I'm sorry."

"It's all right, you couldn't know. I've never mentioned her to you. Jack's always telling me I should talk about her more." He came and took the frame. Gabe cleaned dust off the glass with a sleeve, staring at the photograph for a few seconds once he'd finished. He brushed a finger over Victoria's face and set the frame back on the shelf. "I'm starting to forget what she looked like."

Sadie was half-right in her campaign to push us together. Gabe needed friends and I liked him more the longer I knew him. Guilt over causing him pain, however unwitting, weighed on me. "Jack has a point. You should talk about her and share your memories. Perhaps you could tell me about Victoria over dinner. I'm a very good listener."

He tipped his head and studied me, that unreadable look in his eyes again. "I'm not sure I have the right to impose on you that way."

"You're not imposing. I asked you to talk about Victoria. We've become friends and I'd really like to know." The awkwardness I'd felt earlier returned, but I pressed on. "And I truly am a good listener. I'd have to be in order to survive living with Sadie."

Gabe looked away, a hint of a smile beginning to form. "On my best day I'm not a match for Sadie. I can't promise that talking about Victoria will be easy or that I'll manage more than a few words. But two friends should be able to come up with something interesting to talk about over dinner. Discussing something other than ghosts and this case would be nice."

"Never fear, Sadie keeps me well supplied with gossip for occasions like this." I couldn't bring myself to tell Gabe that speaking of Victoria didn't truly turn the topic away from ghosts, not for me. The prospect of normal conversation was daunting, but I'd find a way to rise to the occasion. What I couldn't do was stand in that spot another second. I went back to petting the sleeping cat. "I can even dredge up a juicy scandal if you like. Name any public figure and I'm sure Sadie's told me something about them."

"That could be useful." He sat in a visitor's chair near the desk. A glint of mischief showed in his eyes. "What do you know about the mayor?"

The office door opened and Colin hurried inside, the gilt-edged book in his hand held high. "I've got it. Now we can get to work solving your mystery."

We gathered around Colin's desk. Gabe pulled the packet of letters from his inside pocket. He shuffled through them and spread pale blue sheets of stationery across the desk blotter. The drawings at the bottom of each page were crisp, clearly drawn in dark ink.

The sharpness of the images made it easier to recognize the blurred figures from the mask. Paint had run and smeared on the canvas, but the lines and flourishes framing each one were the same. I was certain they'd been drawn by the same hand. My heart beat faster and I leaned against the desk to keep from trembling. "Gabe, I've seen some of these before."

He looked up sharply. "Are you sure?"

"I'm certain." I pointed, careful not to touch the paper. Shadow's memories were still close to the surface. Contact with something touched by her killer might strip away my hard-won control. "This one, this, and this."

"May I?" Colin asked. At Gabe's nod, he picked up one of the pages and studied the drawings with a magnifying glass. He set the paper aside and leafed through his book, settling on a page with a triumphant smile. "You should congratulate Delia on her perception and excellent memory. These are hieroglyphics. A reasonable reproduction at that. Have you made a study of the Egyptians, Delia?"

Colin knew nothing of ghosts and dreams. I wasn't about to tell him, but I didn't want to lie either. "No, not formally. I attended an exhibition at the Natural History Museum in New York last year. The hieroglyphics fascinated me."

Gabe spoke up, stopping Colin from questioning me further. "Knowing what the pictures are is only the first step. Can you tell me what they mean?"

"These figures are representations of Egyptian gods." Colin laid the open book on the desktop. He pointed to the drawings in the book and each corresponding figure on the letters in turn. "This is Anubis. He was most often drawn as a man with the head of a jackal. And this is Horus, shown with the head of a hawk. Both of them were sons of this man, Osiris, king of the underworld. This last one, the ibis, is Thoth. All of them were involved in Egyptian legends about the judgment of the dead."

"No wonder Dad thought the symbols were deranged gibberish. That's not general knowledge, which makes me wonder how our killer knew." Gabe turned to me with a tentative half-smile. "I'm in your debt, Delia. I'd never have thought to show these to Colin without your suggestion. Knowing what this means doesn't tell me who this man is, but it's a step forward."

Colin picked up the letters one by one, examining each one with a deepening frown. He finished and tapped a sheet of stationery with a finger. "Are the killer's letters all signed this way? With the symbols in this order?"

Gabe gestured at the letters and envelopes spread across the desk. "Every one. What does that tell you?"

"This is only a guess, Gabe. I can't know for certain what this man is thinking." He sighed and pushed his spectacles back into place. "But . . . your killer could be more deranged than your father thought. He might believe he's enacting judgment in the court of the underworld."

The pressure in my chest increased, a warning of the ghost's nearness, distress, and fear. That alone was enough to convince me that Colin had guessed right. I hugged my pocketbook to my chest and silently entreated Shadow to stay away a little longer.

"Explain that to me." Gabe rubbed the back of his neck and peered at the letters with narrowed eyes, as if he might coax secrets from ink and paper that way. "I don't see what you see."

Colin touched a symbol. "It's the pattern. Anubis is always first. His job was to escort the dead to Osiris's court for judgment. The deceased's heart was weighted to see how heavy his sins were in life and the results recorded by Thoth. Then Horus takes the newly judged to Osiris for the final verdict. If a person's sins weren't too heavy, he passed through to the afterlife. The heart of any who failed the test was fed to a beast, Ammut, and denied eternal life. If Ammut ate your heart, you became a wandering spirit."

"Ghosts." I met Gabe's eyes across the desk, thinking of Shadow and being locked in darkness. "Those who fail his test become ghosts."

Others had died in that cold, dirt-walled room. I prayed at least one had found the strength to haunt the man who killed them and that he knew. He deserved a taste of their fear.

Nefertiti leapt up from sleep, back arched and hissing. The cat streaked across the desk, disappearing out the open door into the hallway. Envelopes and blue stationery fluttered in all directions.

"Blasted cat." Colin crawled under the desk to retrieve an

envelope, grumbling under his breath. "I don't know what gets into her."

Shadow shimmered into view near the corner of the desk, her shawl draped neatly over her shoulders and across her chest. Her hands hung loose at her sides. She stared at the stack of letters in the center of the desk. The ghost understood what the letters were, what they meant.

Shadow understood better than any of us.

CHAPTER 9

Gabe

The inside of the restaurant was smaller than Gabe remembered, but the lunch counter up front was new and took up space once occupied by tables. On a weeknight like this the counter was empty and only two other couples, both older, sat at a table. He left Henderson seated on a high-backed stool at the counter, reading a menu and with instructions to order anything he liked. Marshall could have his own supper and still keep an eye on the car from there.

Their waitress was young, high school–aged at most. She wore a white bib apron over a gray cotton dress and a lacy frilled cap, starched to stand stiffly. A hand-lettered name tag labeled her Kari Lynne.

Gabe stopped himself from lecturing her about displaying her name openly. He couldn't afford to start thinking that every shop-girl, every woman serving food or drinks in taverns and cafés was being stalked by the killer. Everyone was prey, from dockworkers and men working the rail yards, to cab drivers like Terrance Owens. He couldn't lose sight of that.

Warning everyone he spoke with would accomplish nothing,

aside from spreading fear. Catching the murderer and ending the threat would let all of them live normal lives. Gabe included himself in that assessment.

Kari Lynne led them to a small table near a window. The wide expanse of plateglass offered a view of the East Bay hills far off in the distance. Early evening sunlight tinted the hilltops, grass already browned by the beginning of summer heat glowed rose and apricot. Purple shadows gathered in sheltered hollows, cuts eroded by winter rains, and shallow canyons, a prelude to nightfall.

Gabe held Delia's chair, letting her get settled before he took his own seat. The waitress offered menus and a smile. Kari Lynne's white, straight teeth added even more charm to freckled cheeks and dimples. She might have been the model for an advertisement touting the health benefits of country living. "Let me know when the two of you are ready to order. Can I bring water or coffee while you decide?"

Delia tucked her gloves into her handbag. "Do you have tea and lemon? I'd like some if you do."

"Tea and lemon." Kari Lynne scribbled on her order pad. "You, sir?"

"Coffee, please." Gabe gestured toward Henderson. "The officer at the counter. Would you make sure his order goes on my check?"

She made another note on the order pad before hurrying off. "I'll remember."

Discussing menus and ordering took up time, stirring sugar into coffee and sending Kari Lynne back for the lemon she forgot took up a little more. Gabe toyed with his spoon, out of excuses and reasons to stall. Conversation of some kind couldn't be that hard.

He cleared his throat. "How's the tea?"

"It's very good." Delia took another sip and set the gold-rimmed teacup on its mismatched saucer. She looked around the room, smiling at the older woman who nodded in greeting. "This is a very charming place. My father used to enjoy discovering out-of-the-way restaurants and neighborhood cafés. My mother found most of them disreputable, but I loved exploring with him. I think Papa would have liked this one."

"What did your father do for a living?" Gabe wrapped his hands around the coffee mug, annoyed that they wanted to shake and needing something to hold. She'd given him something to talk about, but Jack's warning stuck with him. "If my asking makes you uncomfortable we can talk about something else. I don't mean to pry."

"I'm not that complex or devious, Gabe. If I didn't want to talk about Papa I wouldn't mention him." Delia leaned back in her chair, tracing squares on the red-checkered tablecloth with a fingertip. She glanced up at him and smiled, her face soft with memories. "My father was a banker. He was very good at his job, but Papa always told me the best thing about managing the bank was being home by four every afternoon. That gave him more time to paint."

Gabe loosened his death grip on the mug and rested his hands on the table, reminding himself to breathe. He'd been eighteen the last time he'd been this nervous talking to a woman. That woman had been Victoria and he hadn't made a single attempt to get to know any women since her death, not even as casual friends. Outside of work, he'd kept to himself.

And Gabe wanted to know Delia, to have a friend if nothing else. He needed to make this work. He needed to breathe. "I can't imagine my Dad or my banker with a brush in their hand. What did your father like to paint?"

"Most of his work was landscapes and seascapes. We'd spend the day at some scenic locale and Papa would fill his sketchbook to set the scenes in his mind. Later he'd transfer the ones he liked best to canvas. He was very talented." She gazed out the window, sunlight waking glimmers of gold in her brown hair. "Papa loved to do portraits, but I was young and sitting still was boring. Mama only sat for him once, not long after they were first married. He painted dozens of pictures of colleagues and friends, but the painting he did of Mama was always my favorite. Other than my parents, it's the one thing I wish the fire had left me."

Tears filled her eyes, but didn't spill over. Gabe didn't know how to comfort her or if he could, but he kept talking, hoping he'd stumble over the right words. "You must miss them a great deal. I wish I'd had a chance to meet him and your mother. Your father sounds like he was an interesting man and I have a hunch your mother was just as strong as her daughter."

"I'll take that as a compliment, Lieutenant Ryan. Mama ran two hospital charities and bred roses in the back garden, but she never thought of herself as accomplished. Papa and I knew better." Delia studied him, sober and solemn, nothing in her expression hinting at what she might be thinking. She surprised him then and took his hand, her small, soft fingers wrapping tight around his. "I've done all the talking so far. You promised to tell me about Victoria and I'm going to hold you to that. How did the two of you meet? I'd really like to know."

Gabe silently counted up the long string of days that mounded into years of mourning Victoria and their child. All the happiness and laughter they'd had together had been lost in his misery. He needed to remember something joyful about Victoria before those memories vanished, fading like the memories of her face.

Delia opened all the doors for him, the least he could do was walk through.

Even when it hurt.

"Colin introduced us," Gabe said. "He and I both love baseball and we became acquainted watching the Seals play out at Recreation Park. After watching a few games and having supper after, Colin and I started making plans to meet. One Saturday I arrived to find Colin had dragged his younger sister to the game. Victoria came back the next week and every week after for the entire season. She knew the rules as well or better than I did, and before long she was arguing with me over plays. A year later we were married. We had two years together."

Grief took hold again. He couldn't say "before I lost her," not without choking on the words. Not yet.

Delia squeezed his fingers, pulling him back. "Colin sounds as much of a matchmaker as Sadie."

"Oh, he was." Gabe shook his head, remembering Colin's declarations of innocence and was amused all over again. "I didn't mind so much, but Victoria was convinced Colin thought she couldn't find a beau on her own. That was far from the truth. I was lucky she liked me enough to overlook her older brother's plotting. Colin redeemed himself with Victoria eventually."

"I'm glad to hear." She smiled, gentle mischief in her eyes. "Otherwise I'd feel obligated to turn Sadie loose on him. I'm sure she knows someone Colin's age."

He laughed. "That might do him some good."

Holding Delia's hand while talking about Victoria was both strange and comforting, a confusing sensation Gabe didn't examine too closely. Delia was the only person who hadn't known Victoria in life he'd been able to talk to and that must mean something. He was afraid if he thought too hard about any of it, all his fears would surface and he'd back away.

He didn't want to back away. Gabe grew more certain of that every hour he spent in her company. That Delia hadn't pulled her hand away gave him hope she didn't, either. He'd stumble forward, one step at a time.

Friendship couldn't be that hard.

Delia

The waitress brought our dinners and the smell of chicken and dumplings, roast beef and hot rolls made my mouth water. Once she was certain we had all we needed, Kari Lynne went back to hover near Henderson. She refilled salt and pepper shakers lined up on the counter, giving herself a reason to be near enough to chat and not be too obvious about flirting. Henderson didn't blush talking to Kari Lynne. I imagined that even with the distance, he might visit her again.

No ghosts paraded past the windows or lingered inside the diner to distract me, a blessing. Shadow had vanished before we left Colin's office and hadn't reappeared, though not being visible didn't mean she wasn't with me. She was always there, a presence I couldn't deny.

Victoria's ghost hadn't appeared either and I was profoundly grateful. I'd encouraged Gabe to talk about her, but at the same time I'd been afraid that his pain and grief would act as a summons. How I'd react knowing Victoria was there, listening and watching, was an open question and one I'd rather not have answered.

There was always the chance that the night Shadow led her away, Victoria had gone for good. Why some ghosts roamed the world of the living, restless and unsettled, was a puzzle I'd still not solved. I hoped Victoria was at peace. Gabe had loved her very much.

I cast about for a safer topic of conversation, one that didn't involve ghosts or chasing murderers, or people we'd lost. Watching Henderson with the young waitress gave me one. "Do you know how Jack and Sadie met? Sadie is so crazed with planning a wedding and making guest lists I haven't heard the story. Anyone can see the two of them belong together, but I can't imagine Jack as part of her usual social circles."

"Jack doesn't mingle with San Francisco society by choice, but his family insists he has an obligation. Unfortunately for him, his stepmother has always dragged him back into the social whirl each time Jack tried to escape." Gabe took the last roll from the basket, the corners of his mouth twitching toward a smile. "His stepmother was overjoyed when he took up with a girl from a suitable family. But until I got to know Sadie, I couldn't see Jack getting serious about her or any other socialite."

"Really?" I stared, more surprised than I wanted to admit. Embarrassed, as well, both for making assumptions about Jack's family and not stopping to think. "Who is Jack's stepmother?"

"Katherine Norton Fitzgerald, one of the most sought-after hostesses on Nob Hill. That's how Sadie and Jack met. They were both at one of Katherine's garden parties." Gabe grinned and set aside his bread. "Jack introduced himself by spilling a full water tumbler of punch down the front of Sadie's dress and trying to clean her up with a napkin. His usual method for surviving Katherine's social functions was to add whiskey to his punch and he wasn't entirely sober. So not only was her dress ruined, but Sadie smelled like a brewery. She retaliated by dumping a half-full punch bowl over Jack's head."

"Oh, poor Sadie. And poor Jack." I slumped back in the chair, helpless with laughter. One of the older couples near us frowned and looked on with disapproval, but I ignored them. "He's lucky Sadie didn't break the bowl over his head. That would be just like her."

"Jack arrived on her doorstep the next day with a bouquet of roses to apologize. He wouldn't leave until she took them." He tore the bread roll into little pieces, but left them on the plate, lost in his own thoughts. "He'd already fallen for Sadie. I recognized the signs."

"Roses were a wise choice." I sipped my tea, not wanting the lighthearted mood to slip away. "Sadie's the social butterfly and makes the rounds of all the parties, but I've never met Katherine Fitzgerald. I've read items about the family on the society page and I'm sure Sadie's passed on gossip, but I don't recall hearing of a stepson."

"I'm not surprised." Gabe finished his coffee and gestured to the waitress. She spoke to Henderson before starting toward us. "Jack didn't find out Katherine was his stepmother until his father passed away when he was fifteen. He was too young when his mother died to remember her. For some reason his father thought keeping his mother's death a secret was in Jack's best interests."

"Oh, how horrible for him. What a shock that must have been." The taste of tea and lemon soured on my tongue. I set the teacup on the saucer, vaguely unsettled. "I can't imagine a good reason. How did Jack's mother die?"

"Cholera. Jack's never really forgiven his father for letting him grow up thinking Katherine was his mother. Even as a child, he's never gotten on with her." Gabe lowered his voice, frowning. "My mother lost a sister in the same epidemic. Jack and I are only a few months apart in age, so I was an infant at the time. Mom was always grateful the weather turned cooler and the epidemic never spread to our part of the city."

Kari Lynne arrived to refill Gabe's coffee and clear away empty plates. "Would you folks like dessert?"

I leaned back in the chair, hands folded in my lap and feeling much more relaxed in his company than when we'd arrived. "I don't know if I could manage a whole dessert alone. Would you be willing to share something, Gabe?"

We ordered cherry pie à la mode and two forks, and set about becoming better friends. I told Gabe about the three years I spent in New York teaching. He told stories about growing up near Mission Delores and summer vacations camping in the Santa Cruz Mountains. We talked long after the waitress cleared away the dishes. All the worries and cares that were such a part of my life retreated into the background, lost in stories of happier times.

Stars filled the sky by the time we finally left the table, a glimmering sea of silver strewn across the darkness. I waited near the big window next to the door while Gabe paid the bill. Shadow stood next to the parked car and watched me with knowing eyes, patient as always.

My troubles hadn't wandered far after all.

Gabe

Gabe opened his door as soon as Henderson parked in front of Sadie's gate. The patrol car still sat across the street from the Larkin house, headlights off. Night shift had started and the men keeping watch had changed, but he knew them both so that was all right. Habit and caution still caused him to pause for a look around the yard, peering into murky corners before opening Delia's door.

Jack sat on Sadie's front step, huddled deep into his overcoat. Anything that caused his partner to be here this late and waiting for him outside couldn't be good.

Gabe offered Delia his hand. She didn't let go once she was out of the car. That was a strange feeling, but one that made him smile. "Jack's waiting for me. I'll say good night at the door and not come inside after all. Please give Annie and Sadie my apologies if they're still awake."

"I'm going to guess that Jack sitting on the step doesn't bode well." She opened the gate herself and led the way up the walk, still holding his hand. "Something to do with your case is my guess. Even if Sadie gave him the boot, Annie would offer him shelter in the kitchen."

Jack met them at the base of the front steps. He eyed Gabe before greeting Delia, obviously amused and doing a poor job of hiding it. "I'm sorry to pull Gabe away, Delia, but duty calls. Annie's gone to bed, but the front door's unlocked for you."

She leaned and kissed Jack's cheek. "Thank you for guarding the door until we got back. I'm sure Sadie's pacing a hole in the carpet waiting for me to get inside. The curtains on her window have twitched four times since the car pulled up."

"That's my girl." Jack stuffed his hands in his coat pockets and started down the walk. "I'll wait in the car, Gabe. Take your time saying good night."

They'd talked for hours, both in the diner and on the drive home, all the silences between them comfortable ones. Now that it was time to say good night all the ease Gabe had felt in her company deserted him. He couldn't deny that some of his nervousness came from being on display and knowing his men were watching. The rest was worry over what Jack needed to tell him.

But his concerns about the case had nothing to do with Delia. Constantly letting his job come between them would end their friendship before it started; Gabe wouldn't let that happen. "I'm glad you came with me to see Colin today. The evening turned out to be a lot of fun." He almost left it at that, but something nudged him to take the next, slow step. "I'd like to do that again, if you're willing. I promise our next excursion will have nothing to do with tracking down evidence."

Delia clasped his hand tighter. This time he knew without a doubt she wasn't teasing. "I'd like that a great deal, Gabe. I had a wonderful evening. But I won't hold you to that promise just yet. I suspect it's one you might not be able to keep."

She released his hand and opened the front door. Light framed her face, the gentle lines of her profile and the soft shimmer of her hair reminding him again how lovely she was. Her beauty was quieter than Sadie's, but no less real.

The bemused look on her face jerked Gabe back to the moment and the realization that he was staring. He ducked his head, grateful that he hadn't made a total fool of himself yet. "I'll say good night now. Jack's waiting."

"He is. I hope the two of you aren't out too late." Delia touched his hand, a quick brush of her fingers that filled his chest with loneliness. "Be careful, Gabe."

The door closed and Gabe stood on the porch for a moment, thinking. He didn't have to sort through his feelings or make decisions now. Breathing was still all he need do, all that was required.

He took the steps two at a time and hurried to the car. Jack had left the curbside door open for him and Gabe slid inside, strangely apprehensive about where they might be going. Henderson pulled away as soon as the door closed.

Jack tugged on the end of his mustache and watched out the window. He glanced at Gabe, the flicker of streetlights and shadow across his face concealing his expression. Tricks of light couldn't hide how much Jack enjoyed teasing him. "I'm glad you and Delia had a good time. Sadie will be very pleased. She might even stop matchmaking and inventing reasons to throw the two of you together."

"No, she won't. You know that as well as I do." Gabe tugged his hat off and balanced it on his knee, trying to ward off a headache. Each faint pulse in his temple pulled the old fedora tight as an iron band. "We had a great time once we left Colin's office, but try to keep Sadie from pushing too hard. I like Delia a lot, I really do, and we're friends now. But I need to leave things at friends for a while, without any pressure from you or Sadie, or anyone else. Can you make her understand that?"

"I'll make sure Sadie goes easy. She'd never want to hurt you, Gabe." Jack's amusement disappeared. "What about Delia? Does she know about Victoria?"

"She knows. She found a picture of Victoria in Colin's office. He still keeps Victoria's wedding portrait on his bookshelf." The pain of saying her name was still there, but blunted just a little. Maybe given enough time and practice, he wouldn't need to brace himself against the ache first. "Delia asked me to tell her about Victoria over dinner. I told her how we met."

"It's a step, Gabe." Jack watched him closely. His friend knew him too well. "The next step will be easier."

He took a deep breath to clear his head. "Yes, it's a step, but forgive me if I don't believe this will get easier anytime soon. Now tell me where we're going and what was so important neither of us gets to go home."

Now it was Jack's turn to take a breath. "The handbag Henderson and Baxter found did belong to the victim left in the Presidio. Elaine Meadows was reported missing by her sister Jodi this morning at the Gough Street station. She hadn't heard from Elaine in a week. Miss Meadows lived in a small cottage behind the house at 85 Pine Street."

"Let me guess. The cottage address is 86 Pine." Gabe wiped a hand over his face, hit hard with the memory of perfume wafting from her handbag and filling his office. The killer wouldn't lead them to Elaine's house without a reason. "Did her sister have a key?"

"No, the one found in Elaine's handbag and a spare kept by the owner of the cottage are the only keys as far as her sister knows.

I was at the murder scene in the park until after four. The desk sergeant at Gough Street sent two men over to the cottage on Pine. They didn't have a key and no one answered their knock, so they broke down the door." Jack hunched deep into his coat. "Someone died inside that cottage, Gabe. Not Elaine, but someone else. The killer wanted us to find her house and see what he'd done."

"He's playing with us. I've never thought this man was completely sane. After the information Colin gave us today, I think he's crazier than I imagined." Gabe explained Colin's theory about the Egyptian court of the dead and then gave Jack a brief account of Delia's latest nightmare. They were entering Pacific Heights and only a few blocks from Pine by the time he'd finished. "One other thing you should know. I've changed my mind about this not being the same killer. I'm convinced we're looking for the same man my father tried to find thirty years ago."

Jack frowned. "Your hunches usually pan out, I have to give you credit for that. But the same man coming back and killing again seems like long odds."

"It is long odds, but two different men, following the same pattern and killing the same way feels wrong. This is more than a hunch. I know I'm right." He shrugged, but Jack's skepticism was always welcome. His partner kept Gabe honest and forced him to think things through. "Right or wrong, it won't change how we conduct the investigation enough to matter. But the more we understand about him, the better our chance of catching him becomes."

As soon as they turned onto Pine, Gabe saw the house. Police cars blocked the road and horses from the mounted patrol grazed on a neighbor's neat lawn. Lights blazed in all the windows of the large front house, floor lamps and wall sconces casting streaks of flickering yellow into the yard. Officers moved in and out of that light, silhouettes going about their jobs. He thought he recognized a few members of his squad, but the distance was too great to be sure.

Henderson pulled the car to the curb three houses down, as close as he could maneuver. Gabe stuffed the fedora back on his head and got out. Dread of what he might find set his heart to racing, making him sweat despite the cold night air.

Curious neighbors craned their necks from upper-story windows and front yards, straining to see if the new arrival was someone of note. Death and its aftermath was a spectacle, something to gawk at if the tragedy didn't touch you directly. Gabe would never get used to that.

"Lieutenant?" Henderson stood near the front wheel, one hand on the corner of the windscreen. "Should I see if I can help or stay with the car?"

Uniformed officers swarmed over the yard and in and out of the house, but Gabe waved the rookie toward them anyway. After spending the entire day waiting by the car, Marshall Henderson deserved his chance to feel useful. "Go. Find me something I can use to catch this bastard."

The rookie took off at a trot. Jack joined Gabe on the sidewalk. "A gravel drive goes down the side of the house to the cottage in back. From the size and the position, my guess is the carriage house was converted to living quarters. That was pretty common the first couple of years after the quake."

Gabe nodded. "I remember. My parents lived in a neighborhood like this before they moved to Santa Rosa. Those who still had a safe place to live shared with family who didn't. Who lives in the front house?"

"Elaine's landlord, Gerald Robinson. We haven't been able to locate him." Jack coughed and cleared his throat. "There's a question among the neighbors about the exact nature of their relationship. The older woman next door, Mrs. Knickerbocker, liked Elaine and thought she was a nice girl. She's more than happy to explain how Gerald took advantage of a younger woman if you're interested."

"I'll pass for now." Gabe glanced at his partner. "I'll bet you lunch for a week that our male victim was Gerald Robinson. There's probably a photograph in either the house or the cottage."

Jack pulled his moleskine and a pencil from an inside pocket. "Bet with the rubes who don't know you, Lieutenant Ryan. I already checked the photographs. Mrs. Knickerbocker doesn't need to worry about Gerald corrupting another young woman. I've already got men searching for next of kin."

They moved toward the house and the organized chaos of a preliminary investigation. Gabe slipped his hands into the pockets of his overcoat, set his shoulders, and settled into a relaxed, purposeful stride. His father had taught him from his rookie days that if you looked like the person in charge, that's who you were. That mask of command was habit now, one he seldom need think about.

None of the neighbors tried to speak to him; instead they stepped back apprehensively to let him and Jack pass. The officers he knew nodded and kept working. Most of the men were strangers, sent out from the local station house. That meant their commander was likely here, too.

"Front house or the cottage, Jack? And was Parker here when you left?"

"He was here. Go down the drive and to the cottage first. Stick close to the hedge. Maybe we can get back there without being seen." Jack muttered so only Gabe could hear. "If we're lucky, Captain Parker's gone home to rehearse giving his report to the mayor."

An older man dressed in a dapper, double-breasted suit and a gray-serge coat detached himself from a knot of men near the front of the house and started toward them. Parker's coat hung from broad shoulders and stopped just shy of dragging the ground, making him look squared off and shorter than he was. He leaned forward when he walked and bounced off his toes, an odd gait more than one rookie made fun of when they thought no one could hear.

"Too late." Gabe flipped his collar up and pulled his hat low over his eyes. "Walk faster and pretend you don't see him."

Parker raised a hand and called out. "Lieutenant Ryan! Over here."

He'd no choice but to stop and wait, but Gabe was damned if he'd come when summoned. Captain Parker was in command of the Gough Street station, not Gabe and not his men.

As the older, more experienced detective, Parker had tried to convince the chief to let him conduct the investigation into the murders. He'd been humiliated when the chief turned him down. Now he went out of his way to make Gabe look bad.

He waited until Parker came to a halt before acknowledging him. Gabe nodded, but didn't offer his hand. "Good evening, Captain. What can I do for you?"

"Explaining where you've been until now is a start, Ryan. It's after eleven." Parker made no attempt to keep the conversation private and more than one patrolman turned to scowl at the captain's back. Not all of them were Gabe's men.

"Pursuing other areas of the investigation." Gabe stood easy and kept his hands deep in his pockets, concealing they'd curled into fists. He was tired and still had a murder scene to face, but snapping at Parker would only make things worse. "Is that a problem? Sergeant Fitzgerald and my men have everything well in hand."

Parker's hand swept out to the side, the gesture encompassing all the work going on around them. "I've got men working a double shift waiting for you. You're the officer in charge of this investigation. Regulations say I can't dismiss them without your permission."

"I beg your pardon, Captain." Jack took a half step forward. The tap of his pencil on the side of the moleskine grew faster, a sharp contrast to the flat, professional tone in his voice. "As Lieutenant Ryan's second in command, I do have the authority. I gave your men permission to go off shift before I left to apprise the lieutenant of the situation. They could have gone hours ago."

Gabe stepped in before the storm brewing on Parker's face broke over his partner. "Send your men home, Captain. I appreciate their assistance, but Sergeant Fitzgerald is right. There's no need to keep them from their families. We can handle everything from here."

"The mayor expects results, Ryan. So far you're not handling this any better than your father did in his day." Parker glared, trying to provoke a reaction. When he didn't get one, he barked an order over his shoulder. "Andersen! Gather the squad and send them home."

Gabe spun on his heel and started down the drive again. If he stood there one second longer Parker might get what he wanted. Jack was right with him, red-faced and breathing hard. Neither of them could afford to let Parker goad them into losing their tempers.

Roses climbed a trellis against the side of the house, filling the air with a peppery summer scent. Gravel crunched under their shoes, the sound vaguely reminiscent of eggshells cracking or walking on seashells mounded up on a beach after a storm. He listened hard to that sound, using it to drown out Parker's voice shouting orders.

Jack nodded to the men on their way to the street and home. "What was that about?"

"The remark about my father?" Gabe shook his head. "Parker

takes every opportunity to remind me that Dad never found the killer."

The cottage door was propped open with a high-backed kitchen chair. Light spilled across the threshold, shining on an older man leaning over the low iron fence between houses. Marshall Henderson stood on the cottage side, scribbling down what the old man told him. Movement off to the left turned out to be Maxwell, on his knees under a window in the cottage wall and mixing plaster of Paris to make a mold of a footprint.

His men knew their jobs; so did he. Gabe's anger at Parker flared, but he let it die. This case was hard enough without nursing a grudge.

He paused in the doorway before stepping inside, noting details and setting the scene in his mind. Narrow stairs to the left of the front door went to a second story. The small living room had been ransacked, furniture overturned and destroyed. Braided rugs were bunched and flung against the fireplace, cushions on the green and gold settee slashed and stuffing scattered. The few paintings hanging on Elaine's walls had suffered the same fate.

Strips of canvas hung from broken frames, limp as wilted flowers. Draperies were torn from the windows on either side of the fireplace. Gabe's face was reflected back at him, ghostly pale against the darkness outside. He turned away. "What's behind this cottage?"

Jack flipped through his moleskine. "A veranda, some flower beds, and a rather tall stone wall. All very private. Beyond the wall is an alley and an overgrown lot. If you wade through the weeds to the farside, you come out in the play yard for the local parish school."

"Is there a back door? A gate in the wall?"

"No gate. The back door is in the kitchen." Jack gestured at a plastered arch to the right. A pale yellow beaded curtain hung by one corner, open cupboard doors showing beyond. "Be careful if you go in. There's broken glass and china all over the floor."

"I'll take your word on it. Even if I went outside I couldn't see anything." Gabe stepped around an up-ended table to stand in the middle of the room. He turned in a slow circle, surveying the pattern of damage. "He was angry when he did this, furious at someone or something. This was all for him, not anything he planned for us to see."

"No. That's upstairs." Jack cleared his throat. "He left his message in the bedroom."

The odor of wet paper and mildew hit Gabe as soon as he stepped onto the landing at the top of the stairs. Dampness glistened on the hall floor in front of the bathroom, the wood already saturated and dark. A runner down the center of the hall squelched with each step.

He nudged the bathroom door open with his toe. Books and newspapers filled the washbasin, soaked and swollen by a steadily running tap. More newspapers and magazines floated in a bathtub full of ink-stained water. The steady drip of water echoed against tile floors and walls.

What he took to be streaks of gray newsprint smeared on white plaster walls resolved themselves into symbols the longer Gabe stared. Rough sketches of Anubis and hawk-headed Horus were drawn over and over.

"We didn't follow his instructions. The newspapers didn't print his letters, so he destroyed them." Gabe plucked the corner of a newspaper from the sink and held it up. The print had run together, smeared and unreadable. He let it drop and wiped his hand on his coat. "How bad is the bedroom?"

Jack pushed back against the wall to let Gabe pass in the narrow hallway. "Not as bad as it could be. The park was worse."

A breeze fluttered blood-splattered lace curtains on the open windows. Coverlets and sheets were stripped from the bed and tossed into a corner. The mattress ticking was soaked in blood, days old and dried to the color of rusted iron. A faint odor filled the room, but if Gabe breathed shallowly, he almost didn't notice. Corpses smelled the same, sweet with rot and decay. They hadn't found a body. That didn't mean one hadn't lain here.

More pictures decorated the walls, drawn in blood: Anubis and Osiris on a crude throne, Horus and a dog-headed beast that must be Ammut. Scales large and small filled the spaces between the Egyptian Gods. These were rendered with more skill, more detail.

On the night table sat an apothecary's scale, tipped out of balance by a feather on one side and a square wooden box on the other. Blood had seeped from inside, swelling the dovetailed joints that held the corners together and turning the yellow pine black. The source of the smell was suddenly clear. Gabe didn't need to open the box to know it held a human heart. The question was whose heart, which victim hadn't they found.

The killer's message was clear as well. Propped against the base of the scale was a pale blue envelope, addressed in crisp black ink to Lieutenant Gabriel Ryan.

He wrapped the letter in his handkerchief, the singsong refrain he associated with the killer running through his head. That was the true message.

Run, Gabe, run. Catch me if you can.

CHAPTER 10

Delia

Since the day they'd started, Annie had invited the young officers Gabe sent to watch the house inside for breakfast each morning. Duty rosters rotated among the squad and the faces outside changed every few days, but with Gabe's blessing, Annie cooked for all of them. She was in her glory, a mother bird with a nest full of chicks always willing to be fed. Jack confided that guarding our house had become the most coveted duty in only a week.

Sadie and I took turns taking breakfast up to her mother or helping in the kitchen. I'd gone down early and piled Esther's breakfast tray with fresh strawberries, eggs, hot biscuits, coffee, and cream. She wouldn't eat half, but I'd help. I felt sure that Baxter and Henderson would make short work of the rest if I offered what was left in the serving dish.

Esther's thin, breathy voice carried down the hall. I paused outside her door, knowing that Sadie was in the kitchen, and listened. She was talking to ghosts again.

I'd caught glimpses of the ghosts in her room over the last week, a dark-haired man, a girl of three or four, but they vanished as soon as I entered. The feeling they belonged in the house and with Esther was too strong to ignore. Perhaps that was why random spirits never wandered through; the house had its compliment of restless dead. Still, my feeling of home being a safe haven was shaken. Eavesdropping had convinced me that Esther carried on conversations with her ghosts. The give and take of asking questions, and waiting for replies, was unmistakable. Seeing spirits was disturbing enough. I was glad I couldn't hear their answers.

That Shadow no longer stood watch outside her door was a relief. Esther's new companions seemed just that, company to fill empty hours and not harbingers of death. All I need do was see the stress in Gabe's face and the anxious way Jack hovered over Sadie, or count the policemen eating in our kitchen to be reminded how death stalks all of us. I didn't need more reminders.

I rattled the coffee cups, all the warning I could give, and put on a cheerful smile. Esther watched the door as I came in, confused and lost looking. Pretending all was well grew easier as the days passed and I found ways to cope with her failing memory, just as Sadie said I might. Sadness waited for when I'd left her room.

"Good morning, Mama Esther." I set the tray on the butler's table near the bed and leaned to kiss her cheek. "I've brought breakfast. Are you hungry?"

"You again." She narrowed her eyes, peering at me suspiciously. "Where did Teddy go? Did you send him away?"

"I didn't send him away, I promise." I spread a small tea tablecloth over Esther's lap and tucked a napkin into the neck of her nightgown. She couldn't hear the roaring in my ears, but I heard little else. "Who is Teddy? Can you tell me about him?"

"Teddy Coleman . . . Beryl and Teddy went to church in the buggy, but I wasn't feeling well and stayed home." Esther slumped back on her pillow, the fight in her seeping away as I watched. She picked at the hem of the napkin, eyes unfocused. "I lost them.

There was an accident . . . a delivery wagon or a horse. I can't remember now."

I'd known Sadie's father, a tall, burly man with thinning ginger hair named Andrew. He'd doted on his only child. Andrew Larkin died of a failing heart and a case of pleurisy when Sadie was not quite fourteen. If Esther had been married before and lost husband and child both, I felt sure my mother or someone would have spoken of it. It was possible my mother never knew, or that Esther had reasons to keep a prior marriage secret, but I couldn't imagine her with a sordid past or involved in scandal.

Spooning eggs into a dish gave me a moment to wrestle with my doubt. The ghost was real; I'd seen him several times. I couldn't say for certain what part Teddy played in Esther's past, only that he had strong ties to her. She wanted Teddy with her and in the end, that's all that mattered.

I smoothed the hair off her face and kissed her cheek. "Eat some breakfast now. You'll feel better and you can have a nap afterward if you like. Teddy will come back to visit soon."

On some mornings, Esther was eager to feed herself, the portion of her that remembered family determined to lift part of the burden from them when she could. Today she let me feed her, listless and staring toward the corner of the room. I chatted on, telling her what Annie had planned for dinner, small bits of gossip from Sadie, and describing the walk I'd taken with Gabe last evening. Nothing cheered her or drew a response.

My appetite faded as she withdrew further. I felt responsible and that my asking about Teddy contributed to Esther's melancholy. Her need for the ghost worried me.

Esther's ghosts knew I saw them, were as aware of me as Shadow. Perhaps if I gave permission they'd return. Summoning ghosts was a frightening thing to think of doing, but if it comforted her, I was willing to try.

I put the dishes aside and took her hand. "Mama Esther, tell Teddy it's all right if he'd like to sit with you at breakfast. I don't mind. And I promise not to send him away."

Her gaze came back to me slowly. Understanding took longer still. "Teddy's afraid she'll make him leave too soon. He can't go yet."

Esther's small hand weighed nothing as it rested in mine, her aged bones hollow as a bird's wing. I squeezed her fingers gently and smiled. "I gave him my promise. Even if I wanted him to leave, I wouldn't know how to send Teddy away. He can come back when he likes."

She came straight up off the pillow and clutched my arm tightly enough to hurt. "No, no, no . . . that other girl, the one who follows you. It's not fair for her to make him leave. She watches over her boy and . . . and I need Teddy here. He can't go yet."

Esther thought Shadow meant to send Teddy away. I couldn't say she was wrong. Now I wondered if my ghost spoke to her too and how Esther knew Shadow was watching over someone. Being afraid of upsetting her more made my voice quiver, but I had to ask. "I don't think she'd send Teddy away, not if you need him. Has she told you her name? Or who it is she's protecting?"

Shadow shimmered into view at the foot of the bed, the first time I'd seen her in more than a day. She was clean and neat, the shawl over her shoulders and hands hanging at her sides. The ghost never showed the punishment she'd taken at the killer's hands where Esther might see. I was the only one who saw her bloodied and bruised.

The ghost glided down the farside of the bed, her eyes fixed on Esther and a hand reaching for a cross that wasn't there. Shadow stood out of Esther's reach, her face a mask of sorrow and grief. She didn't want harm to befall anyone in our house, I was as certain of that as I was that my parents had loved me.

Esther looked into Shadow's eyes and her fingers slipped off my arm, her body going limp. "She stares and won't talk to me. But Teddy knows. Teddy's afraid. He shouldn't be afraid in my house."

I eased her back on the pillows and smoothed wispy white hair off her face. Each day she faded more, grew thinner and more confused. For the first time I lied to her, seeking to give her a moment's peace and comfort. That I desperately wanted the words to be true didn't make it so. "Everything will be all right, I promise. Rest now. Annie will be up soon to sit with you."

She muttered under her breath for a moment, garbled sounds and words that made no sense, and shut her eyes. I held her hand until her breathing grew quiet and I knew she slept.

Shadow drifted closer to Esther and watched her sleep, hands pressed to her stomach in the stoic pose I knew well. The ghost remained mute, all her secrets locked behind green eyes. She couldn't tell Esther those secrets. Shadow needed to share them with me, but I'd been too frightened to accept the full burden.

Other people's lives might depend on what I could learn. I needed to find the strength to face Shadow's memories without losing myself to them. Asking Dora for help was a good first step.

I gathered up dishes, tea cloths, and napkins as quietly as I could, a now familiar ache settling in my chest. Grief was an old friend.

Fear of what tomorrow might bring was new. I didn't relish becoming acquaintances.

Gabe

Gabe checked the time and switched off his desk lamp. The clock chimed five o'clock as he gathered up the files and papers scattered over the green blotter, stacking them neatly before adding the files to the pile in his bottom drawer. Locking the desk was his final official act for the day. He'd read the coroner's reports and viewed Baker's photographs a hundred times, the killer's letters at least that many times.

Reading them another hundred times wouldn't show him anything new. Gabe could recite every scrap of information, every clue and threat in the killer's letters from memory. He needed to stop obsessing about this case before he became incapable of anything else. There were more pleasant ways to fill his time.

He'd found an excuse to visit the Larkin house almost every evening for the last two weeks. Taking reports from the men on duty, checking with Annie to make sure the patrolmen weren't imposing on her offer to feed them, and giving her the duty roster for the next week were all valid reasons for him to be there.

And all completely unnecessary. Reports and duty rosters were handled in the station house, and Jack kept a sharp eye on the men outside the house. Gabe knew none of his squad would push Annie's hospitality too far. He'd handpicked the men on guard, only choosing officers he thought trustworthy in any situation.

Lying to himself lasted all of one day. Gabe made up excuses because he wanted to see Delia. He couldn't deny his eagerness to spend time in her company and get to know her better.

She appeared just as happy to see him. They'd gotten into the habit of taking long walks each evening, discussing anything and everything but the murder case. Arriving to see her under the pretense of duty left him feeling slightly guilty. Once he'd started, Gabe couldn't find a graceful way to break the pattern.

The only reason Gabe saw for going on like this was cowardice. That changed tonight. If he wanted to see Delia or take her to supper, he should just say so. He pulled down the roller shade and grabbed his coat and hat off the rack.

Jack lounged against the wall outside Gabe's office, coat over his arm and cap in hand. "I was going to give you five more minutes before I came in after you. We have a cab waiting at the curb."

Gabe's mood sank. He stuffed the fedora on his head, determined not to take the sudden spell of grumpiness out on Jack. "Where are we going?"

"Delia and Sadie are having supper with Isadora. We've been invited to join them." Jack gave him a sly smile. "I took the liberty of accepting for both of us. I didn't think you'd mind."

The tension knotting his shoulders and the back of his neck eased. He was always on edge now, waiting for the call to the next murder scene. Two weeks had come and gone since the night he'd walked through Elaine Meadow's cottage and gone back to his office to read the letter addressed to him. Gabe had no illusions that the killer had stopped hunting victims. They just hadn't found the bodies.

Gabe shrugged on his coat as they walked, his good mood restored. Supper and conversation with Delia was just what he needed. "That was good of you, Sergeant. I foresee a bright future for you as a social secretary. Is Henderson driving the girls to meet us?"

"That's what Sadie's note said. One of the officers assigned to Isadora will drive her to the restaurant." Men arriving for night shift passed them in the hall and nodded. Others going home for the day hurried toward the station's main room. Jack lowered his voice. "Baxter's staying at the house with Annie and Esther. Everyone's taken care of."

He nodded, but didn't answer.

Shift change was in full swing, the main room crowded and noisy. The desk sergeant waved as they left, but he was too busy assigning patrols and taking end-of-shift reports to do much else. That was fine with Gabe.

A brisk wind whipped down narrow streets as they stepped outside, carrying the scent of the ocean into the heart of the city. Fog would follow the wind in from the sea. The bite in the air was damp as well as cold, and Gabe flipped up his collar for the short walk to the waiting cab.

Jack pointed down the block. "The cab's in front of the tailor shop. I promised an extra tip if he'd wait."

The cabbie drove a small, two-horse hack and no roses decorated the doors, but the memory of Terrance Owens strung up in the park punched Gabe in the gut. He stopped in the middle of the sidewalk, staring at the man in the driving seat. "Jack, starting tomorrow we both carry pistols. On or off duty, I want you armed. See what you can do about getting sidearms issued to the men in the squad who don't have them. Make sure the men guarding Sadie and Dora are carrying weapons by morning."

"I'll take care of it." Doubt clouded Jack's face, but orders weren't questioned. Voicing his doubts would come later. "What about Mrs. Allen?"

"Her sister is ill. She went to Sacramento to help out with the children. I don't expect her back for close to a month." Gabe started toward the cab again, the jitters in his stomach settling once he got a good look at the cabbie. The driver was no more than twenty-two, skinny, and with barely enough muscle to control his horses. He wasn't the murderer. "I put her on the train myself early this morning. We'll worry about her once she's home again."

Jack gave the cabbie the name of the restaurant and they climbed inside the shoddily kept hack. They were forced to slam the door several times before the latch caught. The cab lurched away from the curb, merging into the flow of traffic heading deeper into downtown. Gabe sat back and a spring poked him in the back through the thin upholstery. He slid forward to the edge of the seat, thankful they weren't going far, and waited for Jack's questions.

He didn't wait long.

"Why the pistols, Gabe?" Jack frowned and tapped his fingers against the side of the cab. "Why now?"

His partner respected Gabe's decisions and rarely asked for explanations, believing there were good reasons behind them all. Even with Jack, he didn't want to push that belief too far. "We found Terrence Owens's body more than two weeks ago. A few days later we found Elaine Meadows's cottage but there's been nothing since. He's still out there, Jack. I don't trust how quiet it's been. You read that last letter."

"Calm before the storm." Jack watched out the window for a moment, scowling fiercely. "You could be right. He made a lot of threats in that letter. Without finding bodies, there's no way to know if he's carried any of them out."

"He did. The heart in that box came from someone." The conviction that the killer was biding his time and planning his next move had been growing in Gabe for days. Just because they couldn't see the results didn't mean nothing was happening. "This man threatened you and me by name. That means everyone close to us is in danger as well. I'll feel better if all the officers on this case go armed until we catch him."

"If we catch him. He might decide to disappear again."

"I don't think he'll stop killing this time. My father always believed something happened to drive the killer away and I think Dad's right. We'll find him." The only thing that kept the nightmares at bay and let Gabe sleep at night was the belief they'd catch this killer. He didn't know if he could live with himself if the murderer slipped away. "Right now he thinks he's smarter than we are. You and I are going to prove him wrong."

Delia

Officer Henderson opened the door for us and Sadie swept into the restaurant, a curly-haired conqueror no man could hold against. I thanked Henderson and followed at a slower pace. Watching heads turn was half the fun.

I wasn't disappointed. People at tables near the front did watch Sadie strut past, but this restaurant was designed for nefarious meetings. That limited her audience. More than half of the tables were set against a wall of the building and enclosed by latticed walls on two sides, creating secluded dining areas closed off from view of the other patrons.

Brocade curtains in rich greens and golds covered the entrance of each alcove. The unoccupied dining rooms were dark, curtains looped over brass hooks on one side. Unlit candles sat in crystal holders in the center of the dark-wood tables and in seashell wall sconces.

The curtain was still drawn back in the room Isadora had chosen. She sat with her back to the wall and directly in front of the door, taking deep drags on her cigarette and blowing clouds of smoke toward the ceiling. Rhinestones glittered on the bright blue cloche covering her blond bob. The matching blue dress she wore was simple and not near as flamboyant as the outfit I'd seen her in last, but fortune-telling called for a certain dramatic flair. Supper at the Stone Rose was a more sedate occasion.

Her eyes narrowed as we drew closer, no doubt watching Shadow trail behind me. The sense she was good at what she did and not a sham was stronger than the first time we'd met. Dora saw ghosts differently, but her world still teemed with spirits. We had that curse in common and I trusted her as a result. If anyone could help me pry secrets from my ghost, Isadora Bobet could.

"Dora! You look stunning in that outfit." Sadie spread her arms wide, folding Isadora into a hug and kissing her cheek. The way Dora held the cigarette out of the way showed long practice with Sadie's greetings. "You picked the perfect place for all of us to have supper. The boys should be here soon. Jack promised they'd arrive on time even if he had to drag Gabe out of his office. Is Daniel joining us?"

"No, he stayed home to lavish attention on the bird. Tom-Tom's been languishing in his cage while we work the fair and Daniel feels guilty. He's afraid the silly creature will start plucking his breast feathers again out of spite." Dora turned to me with an apologetic smile. "We have a parrot. The wretched bird is nothing but trouble, but Daniel adores him."

Sadie took the chair next to Dora. The two of them traded gossip about friends they held in common, none of whom I knew. I listened to distract myself, amused at the shocked tone in Dora's voice as Sadie related some minor social scandal. The waiter circled the table, filling water goblets and laying menus out at each place. He kept his head down, but his eyes seldom left Sadie.

Dora exchanged looks with me, rolling her eyes as if to say "another one," and picked up talking to Sadie without missing a word. I choked back a laugh. She really was Sadie's friend.

The waiter left and I went back to silently rehearsing what I'd say. This supper meeting was my idea. Now I found myself growing nervous. Sadie didn't know about Esther's ghosts and recounting the last nightmare to Dora was necessary, but wouldn't be pleasant. I wanted the hard parts over, including asking Isadora for help. That might prove to be the most difficult task of all.

My back was to the door, but the way Sadie's face lit up let me know Jack had arrived. I took a sip of water and fiddled with the napkin spread over my lap, all so I wouldn't turn too quickly to see if Gabe had accepted the invitation for supper.

How relieved I was to see him following Jack was complete foolishness. We'd spent every evening together for the last two weeks, but supper tonight was entirely different circumstances. I'd a right to be nervous.

Sadie stood to greet Jack, the embrace she gave him far different than how she'd hugged Isadora. Jack brushed fingers lightly over Sadie's cheek before sitting next to her. They clung to each other more now then when I'd first come home, touched and held hands more often.

We'd talked after Gabe put guards on the house and I knew how frightened Sadie was something might happen to Jack. This wasn't a normal case. The danger was always in the back of her mind, as it was in mine. Late at night, when the house was quiet and outside sounds were dulled by fog or distance, I thought of little else. The fear something might happen to Gabe stopped me from getting closer, I knew that. Knowing made me angry.

Gabe took off his coat for the waiter to hang up and smiled. "Good evening, Delia, Sadie. Jack says I have both of you to thank for inviting me."

Sadie beamed and leaned forward. "Inviting everyone to supper tonight was Delia's idea. She has something very mysterious she wants to discuss with all of us. I couldn't pry the secret out of her."

Dora extended a hand to Gabe and gave him a lascivious smile. "Lieutenant Ryan, how lovely to see you again. I'm so glad you could join us."

She meant for him to kiss her hand, but Gabe barely touched her fingers. Even so, I saw a blue spark snap between them. Dora winced and Gabe drew his hand back sharply. "Good evening, Dora. I thought we'd established last time that shaking hands wasn't a good idea."

Isadora pouted, sticking out her bottom lip almost as prettily as Sadie. "I'd hoped that was a fluke, Gabe. I guess I'll have to concede the field."

Gabe ignored her and took his seat. He turned to me, smiling and openly curious. "Should we hear what you have to say or order first? This meeting was your idea and it only seems fair to let you decide."

I knew Gabe well enough now to guess he meant to put me at ease. It didn't work. Blushing wouldn't kill me, but being the center of attention felt odd and slightly uncomfortable. "Ordering first might be best. And perhaps we should ask the kitchen to delay sending the food out. This isn't a conversation I want to have while eating."

Dora ground her cigarette into the pot of sand behind her. Her teasing manner dissipated with the last of the smoke curling around her head. "How much of this concerns the ghost? You call her Shadow if I recall."

Shadow appeared behind Sadie and Jack, standing so that I was forced to look into her eyes. "Almost all of what I have to say concerns Shadow."

"Do you want me to send her away, even temporarily? I can do that before you start if you find it easier." Isadora reached across Gabe and pulled my chin around, forcing me to look at her and not the ghost. "Look at me when you answer, Delia. You still let her too far inside."

"No, I don't want her sent away. Shadow's part of this." Dora dropped her hand and sat back in her chair, arms crossed over her chest. I met Shadow's stare again, certain I saw relief in her eyes. "I need your help to let her inside without losing myself in her memories. She knows who the killer is. I have to find a way that she can tell me."

Sadie clutched Jack's hand, worry for me stealing the light from her eyes and the color from her face. My guilt grew, knowing

I had sadder things for her to hear. "Are you sure that's wise, Dee? Dora seems to feel it's dangerous."

"It is dangerous. Once you let a ghost in getting them to leave again can be dicey." Isadora pawed through her handbag, coming up with a tortoiseshell cigarette case and a box of matches. She lit a cigarette and inhaled deeply. "Ghosts aren't known for being truthful, Delia, especially ghosts that manifest as strongly as Shadow. I agree she wants something, but I'm not sure that what she wants is to find a murderer. There's more to it, I can feel it."

"Shadow's trying to protect someone. I've sensed that for a long while." I broke away from Shadow and looked Dora in the eye. "Until Jack and Gabe find this killer, that person is in danger. So are we."

Gabe reached for my hand and threaded his fingers with mine, earning a raised eyebrow from Dora. Then he took my side. "Give Delia a chance to tell you everything before you make up your mind. She's already learned important information about this case from Shadow. I didn't want any of this made public, but this isn't an ordinary investigation. If she thinks telling you will help us catch this killer, I'm inclined to trust her judgment. All I ask is that this doesn't go any further than the five of us."

Jack kissed Sadie's hand and let go to tug a notebook and chewed pencil out of his pocket. He flipped through to a blank page, wrote the date at the top and then my name. Witness notes. "Gabe's right. Listen to her, Dora."

"Well, well . . . two champions. I feel properly put in my place." Dora laughed and sat back in her chair, cigarette hand out to the side and the other arm folded over her stomach. "Obviously I've missed things while shut up in that stuffy tent at the Pan Pacific. Summon the waiter, Jack. We'll order and get on with this."

Ordering only took a few moments. Dora asked the waiter to close the curtain over the entrance, giving us privacy. She leaned forward and squinted at me, seeing more than what was on the surface. "Go ahead, Delia. I'm listening."

Some of the story I'd told that first night at the fair, but I started at the beginning, afraid I'd leave something out. Building my case and convincing Isadora to help me was important. I told her about all the dreams, starting with the first few in New York where all Shadow did was lead me down dark streets. Detailing the first nightmare was difficult, relating the second one had me struggling to stay calm enough to speak. Even with Gabe holding my hand, I felt the weight of Shadow's underground prison pressing in, cold and dark.

Jack scribbled down everything, even what I was sure he already knew. Gabe explained about the hieroglyphics the killer used as a signature and how I'd helped him discover what they meant. Dora frowned, but didn't interrupt.

Then it was time to tell about Esther's ghosts, Teddy and Beryl, and what Teddy told her about Shadow. That was most difficult, worse than describing Shadow's injuries. I tried not to see Jack wince or how Sadie leaned against him with her eyes closed. She'd heard her mother talking to herself as had Annie, but not known what it meant. I hoped Sadie would forgive me for keeping that from her until now.

I'd felt certain Isadora would believe me, she knew much more about spirits than I did. But I'd had doubts about the others. Their expressions reassured me I needn't have worried.

Dora had worked through two cigarettes and had started a third by the time I'd finished. She slumped back in her chair, mouth pulled into a thin line. "I'll concede that you're probably right and Shadow has a connection to the killings. She was a victim and would want her killer brought to justice. But everything you've told me has been planted in your mind or in Esther's mind by a ghost. I'm not convinced Shadow isn't looking to live her life again through you. Even to extract revenge by using you if she can. That's very dangerous, Delia."

A stiff breeze swirled through the dining room, guttering candles and fluttering the brocade curtain across the entrance. Anger built in the room, a storm centered on Isadora. She sat up straight and snapped commands at Shadow, a note in her voice I'd never heard before. "No, not this time. Hear me now, spirit. Stop immediately or I will banish you. I'm not as kind-hearted as Delia nor as willing to believe."

The wind died instantly. Shadow hovered behind Jack's shoulder, green eyes staring into mine and imploring me for help. "Show her," I whispered. "Dora isn't the enemy. Show her and make her believe."

Isadora watched warily as the ghost drifted closer. Pins worked loose from Shadow's neat plaits, sending hair straggling into her face. All the punishment she'd taken at the murderer's hands, the bruises, the split and swollen lip came into view. Dora flinched as Shadow held up her broken hand, flinched again at the festering animal bites that appeared on the ghost's arms and neck. I'd seen what he'd done to her before, but I forced myself not to turn away. Anger at how she'd suffered gave me more resolve.

Shadow looked more solid, more real with each second. Sadie gasped and buried her face in Jack's shoulder. Gabe scowled and swore under his breath, gripping my hand tighter. They saw the ghost now, too.

Jack held Sadie and watched the rest of us, perplexed and confused at our reactions. He couldn't see Shadow, that was obvious, but I didn't understand why. Dora noticed as well. She studied Jack's face and frowned before turning her full attention to the ghost.

The small dining room grew cold, chilled to the point of being able to see my breath and shivers rippling through me. Gabe put an arm around my shoulders and pulled me close. Other spirits shimmered into view behind Shadow: young men from the docks and older women who might be storekeeper's wives, or housekeepers from well-to-do neighborhoods. All were dressed in old-style clothing, beaten or wounded in different ways. I knew them to be more lost souls, victims of the killer never found by the police or their families.

More than a dozen spirits filled the corner of the room when Shadow stepped forward. She changed again as we watched. Mud flaked off her blue skirt, bruises faded, and the filthy white blouse became clean again. Shadow put a hand over her heart and stared into Dora's eyes.

A spot of blood showed under her fingers, small at first, but spread until the front of the white blouse was stained crimson. Blood seeped between the ghost's fingers and fat drops wept onto the floor. Shadow pulled her hand away, staring at the blood smeared on her palm and dripping down her skirt as if surprised.

She stretched a bloody hand toward Isadora and whispered, "Help them . . . please help them."

A gust of wind fluttered the heavy curtain over the entrance and blew out the candles on the wall. The ghosts vanished.

We sat in silence for a moment, wisps of smoke curling toward the ceiling from blown out candles. Sadie was pale and trembling, but she wouldn't cry. Not here, not yet. Jack helped her to stand. "I'm taking her outside for air. I'll send the waiter in to relight the candles."

Isadora stared as they pushed through the curtain into the main room. "Well, well . . . I wonder." She looked pensive, but I'd no way to know what she was thinking and Dora wouldn't speak until she was ready. That was fine. Sorting my own thoughts and emotions was difficult enough.

"God Almighty." Gabe squeezed my shoulders. "You told me,

but I didn't know, Delia. I couldn't see before. I didn't know and I'm sorry."

Dora drummed long fingernails on the tabletop. "None of us knew, only Delia. The question now is what to do about this ghost."

My hopes plummeted. "You're not going to help."

"Don't be silly. I can't leave you at the mercy of a spirit that strong and determined." Isadora lit another cigarette, took one long drag, and let it dangle from her hand. "But I need to think. Once supper is over we can all adjourn to my house. Your ghost won't be able to manifest and bring her friends along inside my walls."

Gabe traded looks with me. He lifted his arm off my shoulders and took my hand again. "What do you have in mind?"

"Something I control, not the ghost. Spirits should be tame and docile, unlike men." Dora smiled flirtatiously and leaned closer. "Have you ever engaged a spiritualist and dabbled in séances, Lieutenant Ryan?"

He cleared his throat and shook his head. "No. I can't say that I have."

Dora leaned back, her smile satisfied and slightly smug. "Good. It will be more entertaining that way."

CHAPTER 11

Delia

Isadora lived in a neighborhood at the top of Potrero Hill. We turned into her gate and entered a far country, distant and isolated.

Dora's home was set back at the rear of a big, wooded lot. Pine and cedar trees swayed in the breeze, branches creaking and needles scenting the air. A long front drive, tall black-iron fence, and hedges hid her sprawling, two-story cottage from view. Her house was cut off from both passersby and the neighbors on either side, an island of solitude.

"Living here must be lovely." I glanced at Dora and went back to watching the lights of her house shimmer behind the trees. "Your neighbors are so far away I imagine it's like living on a country estate."

"A little like that, yes. Or at least as close as I can come and still be near the city." She nodded at Gabe, sitting in the front with Officer Polk. "If I lived in a boardinghouse like Gabe or even a neighborhood like yours, I'd need an asylum within a year. All that humanity and their emotions would drive me mad."

I must have looked shocked. Dora patted my hand, amused

and patient. "Most people don't understand there are different tiers of the spirit world, different energies that intersect with our world. Spirits of the dead, ghosts, are the only tier you sense and see right now. I have the misfortune to sense and see them all, and strong emotions seek me out. Extreme pain and fear are the hardest to weather. I need a retreat to recover and shield myself from the worst assaults."

"Does that hurt?" Dora lifted an eyebrow, peering at me quizzically. I suddenly realized what I'd done. "I don't know what just came over me, I sound like Sadie. Please forgive me, I'd no right to ask something that personal. I'm so sorry."

She laughed, utterly delighted. "Don't be sorry. I was a bit surprised, but not offended. You're the first person to ever ask me if what I do causes pain. The answer is yes, sometimes what I sense does hurt. Tell me, could you see what happened between Gabe and me tonight?"

I nodded. "A spark jumped between you. From the way you and Gabe flinched I got the impression it hurt."

"You see more than I thought. We'll have to watch that carefully." The car with Sadie and Jack stopped ahead of us. We waited farther down the semicircular drive at the front of the house for them to get out and Henderson to drive away. Dora pulled off the blue cloche and shook her hair out. "The energy from all the death surrounding Gabe's job seeks him out, clinging to his aura. Touching me grounds him. Unglamorous as it sounds, I'm the lightning rod for his lightning. Gabe is only the second person that's ever happened with. The first was a priest."

"Why Gabe?" I straightened the seams on my gloves, fiddling to keep from appearing anxious and more than a little afraid of the answer. "Why not Jack? He's working the same case."

"Sometimes spirits seek a strong protector. That was certainly the case with Father Dylan. With Gabe, my guess is they sense he could bring them justice and put their souls to rest." She frowned. "And Jack isn't being haunted. The ghost that sometimes follows Gabe will attract more spirit energy."

"Gabe was married before the quake, but he lost Victoria in the fire. Shadow led the ghost away the night I met him and I'd hoped she'd found rest. If you've seen her then she's not gone, she's still haunting him." I swallowed, but it didn't help. Truth left a bitter taste in my mouth. "He doesn't know. I haven't been able to bring myself to tell him."

The car stopped. Officer Polk came around to open Isadora's door. She held the handle, forcing the door closed again, and looked me in the eye. "You did the right thing, Delia. All you'd accomplish by telling Gabe is to hurt him. His wife's ghost will leave when he's ready to let go, not before. Now, let's go inside."

She let Polk open the door and help her out. I slid out behind her, relieved that Gabe had been too involved in giving Henderson instructions to notice our conversation. That relief was rooted in guilt over keeping secrets, even if Dora did think them best.

Jack and Sadie stood to the side, head to head and deep in their own intense conversation. Not wanting to intrude or appear to eavesdrop, I turned away. I needn't have worried. Until Dora called to them, they saw nothing but each other

Shadow shimmered into view on the porch, blocking the way into the house. Dora took my arm and marched me up the steps, pausing one step down from the ghost. "Go. I've no plans to surrender Delia to you, now or ever. You won't cross my threshold until I call you. Now leave."

Green eyes sought mine looking for a reprieve, but I echoed Dora. "Go until she calls you. It won't be long."

She came apart, shattering into a pearly powder that swirled away on the wind. The ghost hadn't gone far. Shadow's presence was still there, a second heart beating in my chest. She never left me.

Isadora winked at me before turning to address our friends. A change came over her, something more than the flamboyant persona she donned for visitors to the Pan Pacific. The gestures and the stance were equally dramatic, but I couldn't put aside the sense that this was more than playacting. Fear rippled up my spine, unexpected and out of place. "Friends." Dora extended a hand, naming each of us in turn. "Sadie, Jack, Gabe, and Delia, come inside. Welcome to my home."

We stood there for a few seconds, staring at her and one another. Dora threaded her arm through mine again, the air of being more than just a fortune-teller gone. "I need a drink. Who wants to join me?"

She held my arm tight and practically dragged me over the threshold. The sensation of something oily sticking to my skin made me jump. Gabe brushed at his cheek and looked puzzled, but Sadie and Jack didn't react at all.

Dora whispered in my ear. "Keeps out the boogeyman. Relax, nothing will hurt you."

A parrot squawked loudly from deeper inside the house, followed by the sound of Daniel yelping and the clang of an iron cage door slamming shut. The screech from the bird that followed was earsplitting, even from a distance. Daniel screamed right back, but in a tongue I didn't understand. After a few seconds of man and bird both yelling, the noise died down. Either Daniel had thrown a cover over the cage or they both got tired.

"I don't know which is worse, Daniel or the wretched bird." Dora sighed and hung up her coat. "At least we'll be in my workroom where it's quiet."

Daniel chose that moment to come padding down the hall and into the entryway. He was barefoot, dressed in a pair of loose cotton trousers tied below his waist, and wasn't wearing a shirt. His dark curly hair was mussed, as if he'd been sleeping and come back down to tend to the bird. Sadie and Dora didn't seem bothered by his state of undress, but no doubt they were used to seeing him this way. I stared at a painting on the wall, cheeks burning, reminding myself sternly that this was his home and we'd intruded on him.

He nodded to the rest of us and held his hand up to show Dora. "Blasted bird bit me again."

"Ungrateful creature." She kissed the bright red welt on his palm and trailed her fingers down his chest. My blush burned hotter, but I don't think either of them noticed. "Go on up to bed, darling. Let me take care of this séance for Delia and I'll join you."

Daniel kissed Sadie's cheek in passing and nodded to the rest of us again. He yawned broadly and started up the carpeted staircase, tugging the loose trousers up as he climbed. "Have a good evening, everyone. Call me if you need anything, Dora."

Gabe waited until Daniel disappeared and cleared his throat. "How long have the two of you been married?"

Dora sidled over to him, smiling coyly. "We're not married, Lieutenant. I'm afraid Daniel and I have rather bohemian views when it comes to marriage."

For an instant, I thought Jack was going to choke trying not to laugh at the look on Gabe's face. Sadie swatted him on the shoulder. "Behave, Jack. Dora, stop teasing Gabe. Start the séance so we can get the unpleasantness over with."

Dora let out a dramatic sigh, but sobered right away. "You're right, it's late and the sooner this is done the better. I don't want to be in the middle of a summons at midnight. Follow me."

Isadora led the way down the darkened corridor, back the way Daniel had come from. She opened a door, the oiled wood dark with age, and waved us all inside. "Delia, sit between me and Gabe if you would. That will lessen the static."

He gave both of us a puzzled look, but didn't say anything. I followed Sadie in, curious about what Isadora's workroom was like.

The room smelled faintly of sandalwood and cinnamon. A round table sat in the center of a fringed carpet. The table was draped in blue velvet that fell to the floor and a shorter, white silk square canted at an angle on top. White candles filled freestanding iron candelabras in all four corners of the room. I brushed a hand over one and any fears I had of it tipping vanished. The stands were near as tall as me, with a heavy base that weighed as much or more than Sadie.

Heavy white damask drapes covered the windows. The walls were bare with the exception of one large mirror, mounted in a heavy gilt frame carved with vines and flowers. It hung in an odd spot, not centered on the wall but closer to a corner. Two cherry cabinets sat underneath the mirror, doors closed.

Finding the chair I was meant to take was easy. A large crystal ball, mounted in a cast silver stand, marked Isadora's place. I sat in the chair to her left, Jack to her right, and Sadie took the chair between Gabe and me.

Dora left the room and returned with a wicker basket of bread and apples. The basket went in the middle of the table, behind the crystal ball. Isadora lit the candles and took her seat. The scent of cinnamon grew stronger.

"Sadie and Jack know this, but I need Delia and Gabe to pay attention." Candle flames swayed in the breath of air that seeped past the drapes, and fingers of alternating darkness and light caressed Dora's face. A normal thing, not in the least tied to ghosts, but one that still stirred quivers of uneasy in my stomach. "Once we start it's imperative that you stay in your seat and not drop the hand of the person on either side. You're perfectly safe as long as the circle remains unbroken."

Skepticism was the kindest word I could think of for Gabe's expression. "What happens if the circle is broken?"

"That depends entirely on the spirit who answers the summons. Some try and possess a person in the circle if the medium's control is broken." She shrugged. "It's not unheard of for a ghost to take up residence in the house where the séance was held. I'd rather not have my house haunted. Getting a haunt to leave again can be difficult."

Gabe looked to Sadie and Jack. Their expressions were equally as serious as Dora's, full of belief. "You're not joking this time. You really mean this could be dangerous."

"Yes, Gabe, I really mean it. Keep in mind that this ghost, Shadow, might not be the only spirit to answer the summons. Not all entities are benign. And I still have my doubts this ghost is harmless as she appears to be." Isadora leaned forward, arms resting on the table and hands wrapped around the crystal ball, any hint of her earlier playfulness gone. "We all know the spirit following Delia is strong enough to take over her dreams. It takes a great deal of energy to become visible to a group of people, but Shadow managed that today as well. But unless I'm mistaken, she's only spoken twice and both times all five of us were together. Am I right, Delia?"

"I hadn't thought of it, but yes." I kept my hands folded and tucked in my lap, an act of self-control that kept me from twisting the velvet tablecloth. "If Shadow was able to speak to me, I might have had answers long ago."

Dora rubbed the crystal globe with her thumbs, staring at her reflection. "I'd guessed as much. That tells me she's pulling power from the living to do so, but needs more than Delia alone. Something about the makeup of this group allows her to gain that power. This ghost is strong, but not as strong as I feared."

Jack's puzzled frown grew deeper. "I'll admit I heard a voice both times, in the tent and at the Stone Rose. But I haven't seen anything. Sadie told me about what happened in the restaurant on the way over. Why didn't I see the ghosts, too?"

"Maybe you're just not her type." Dora smiled, impish and teasing. That she'd made light of his question caused me to pay closer attention. "I can't say for certain right now, but with luck we can find out. Let's get started. Hold hands everyone and don't let go until I say."

I took Isadora's hand first, then Gabe's. The shock I'd half expected didn't happen, a relief that must have showed on my face. Dora squeezed my fingers and took Jack's hand, closing the circle.

"Spirit, we bring you gifts from life into death. Commune with us, help us learn your name, and move among us." Isadora's voice grew louder. "Show us if you hear my summons. Make your presence known."

Three times she repeated her summons and then fell silent. We listened for some sign Shadow had answered. I listened inside as well, searching for a change in the constant pulse that was the ghost's presence.

We didn't wait long. The table jerked sharply, rocking and jumping as if trying to fly toward the ceiling. I jumped as well and almost dropped Dora's hand, but she held tight and didn't let me go. Gabe held tighter as well.

"Do you remember your name and who you were in life, spirit?" Dora kept her eyes on the crystal ball, her gaze intense and focused. Vague shapes moved inside, glimmers in the gloom. "Knock once for yes, twice for no."

A hollow sounding rap came from under the table, as if Shadow knocked on an empty box and not the solid wooden top. Shadow's presence itched along my skin, stronger than I'd felt before, but I couldn't see her. Dora's control or the protections on the house kept the ghost contained and from showing herself until called. Isadora had said as much, but I'd still expected the ghost to appear.

Dora asked more questions, testing to be sure the ghost answering really was Shadow and not some other wandering haunt. I was satisfied long before Isadora, but I could sense the ghost's agitation, her impatience to get to the reason she'd sought me out at the start. Shadow's turmoil filled me, her struggle to resist Dora's constraints and fill me with her memories welling up in my chest, and edging me toward panic. I was the center of a tug-of-war between them, a prize to be claimed by the strongest.

Isadora won and Shadow's surrender let me regain some calm. I clung to Dora's hand and Gabe's, mindful of the warning not to break the circle or her concentration. A hundred years before people might have called her a witch, communing with the dead a forbidden talent, viewed as a mark of evil and best hidden. Spiritualists and séances were in fashion now, but Dora still hid much of what she was capable of doing.

I didn't blame her. Fashions changed and people still feared what they didn't understand.

"Show yourself, ghost. Tell us your name and deliver your message," Dora whispered now, each word a piece of ice sliding down my spine. "Fill the mirror so that all can see you and hear you speak."

The odd placement and why the mirror was the only ornament on the walls became clear. None of us had to do more than turn our heads to have a clear view.

The center of the mirror grew opaque, swirled with wisps of gray, flashes of yellow light and a deeper gloom in the background. I stared, struggling to make sense of what I saw. The images were blurred, edges blunted and objects indistinct. Then I knew what I saw. Fog and a night-darkened street.

The start of my nightmare.

"Oh, dear God." I risked a glance around the table. Jack stared as raptly as the rest of us. He saw this time, I was certain of it. The scene in the mirror was the same when I turned back, an instant from the past frozen in place. "I think I've seen this before."

"The dream you told us about." Dora squeezed my fingers. "The mirror gives her a portal to communicate with the living. Watch and see if Shadow shows us more or something different. You're the only one who will know."

Images grew clearer the longer I stared: lighted windows on the front of a building, a sign advertising beer a nickel a mug, hot baths or a room for a quarter. Sounds came from the mirror scene as well, muted voices and laughter, a foghorn and the deadened clop of horses' hoofs on cobblestones. We watched the outside of a tavern, seeing the scene as Shadow had. This was the true start of the nightmare, the minutes before she left work and started on her way home.

Light shone around the double doors at the front entrance, cheap pine hung crooked and not plumb in the frame. One swung open and Shadow stepped onto the street. She surveyed the thick fog and darkness, dismay settling on her features. Lines pulled at the corners of her mouth and her shoulders slumped, and I saw just how tired she was.

I felt her weariness as well. Another glance around the table showed Gabe, Jack, and Sadie giving the mirror all their attention, but they didn't feel the ache in Shadow's calves or the way her shoulder burned from carrying heavy trays through two shifts. But Isadora's eyes met mine and I knew she was there with Shadow as well, living those moments with the ghost. We shared that curse, a kinship I felt sure either of us would relinquish gladly.

Shadow tugged the thin shawl tight around her shoulders and started off. The tavern door opened again and a dark-haired, broad-shouldered man stepped out. His nose had been broken and healed crooked, and his bushy mustache made that more obvious. A stained barkeeper's apron was held around his ample waist with thin ties that wrapped around twice, the apron itself long enough to flap around his calves when he ran. "Allie! Wait a tick."

She stopped, but frowned and hugged arms over her chest. "It's cold, Sean, and I'm tired. Have your say and be quick. I've the need to get home to Pat and the baby."

"No call for snapping at me. Hold out your hand, I've something for you." Sean put a quarter on her palm and folded her hand around the coin. "I almost forgot the extra I promised you for staying the extra shift. It's been a busy night and you deserve the little bit more."

Allie sighed and slipped the quarter into a skirt pocket. "I'm sorry, Sean. It's my own fault you needed to come after me and no reason to be cross with you. I was in such a hurry to be off I'd forgotten. Five o'clock again tomorrow?"

"Five is fine." She started to go, but Sean put a hand on her shoulder and turned her back to face him. "Aileen, come back inside. If I can't talk you into sleeping in the backroom tonight, wait until I finish closing up. Let me walk you home. I don't like you out this late on your own. Not with all the stories about people disappearing floating around the bar."

She hesitated, but shook her head. "Pat's after me to quit and stay home like a proper gentleman's wife. He says this contract he signed with the railroad's going to make him rich. Maybe he's right or maybe it's another of his blue-sky schemes. I'll stick with what I know until I see the money. I've got the little one to think of feeding."

"Patrick Fitzgerald's got a fair head for business. Wish I could say he wasn't a bloody fool when it comes to his wife." Sean reached for Aileen's hand, but she stepped back. "The offer still stands, Allie. You and the baby can come to stay for long as you're willing if things turn bad again. Just say the word."

"You're a good man, Sean McGuire. But I said my vows and I'll live with them." She pulled the shawl tighter, eyeing the foggy street. "Pat half thinks Jackie belongs to you as it is. If not for that wild red hair on the boy, he'd be sure of it. I best get home now."

"Oh, dear God, that's my mother. Pop said she died of cholera. Dora, stop this. Stop it right now." Jack was half out of his seat, breathing hard and fast, and on the verge of running from the room. "He lied to me! I can't sit and watch this, I have to leave. Make it stop now!"

"Sergeant Fitzgerald!" Gabe's voice cracked with command, a tone I'd not heard before. He got Jack's attention and the snap in his voice went away. "Sit down, Jack. You're putting Sadie and Delia in danger. Close your eyes if you need to, but give Dora a chance to end this safely."

Jack's face was pale and he looked ill, but he nodded and sank into the chair. Sadie leaned toward him, whispering rapidly. The concern on her face grew deeper when Jack didn't answer. Gabe watched the two of them, worry and confusion in his eyes. We were all confused.

All but Isadora. She glanced at me and muttered under her breath. "Damn it. A blood-tie was the reason he couldn't see the ghosts. There are times I hate being right."

Dora began the chant to send the ghost from the mirror. "I release you with our thanks. I will not hold you here nor will your blood and kin. Go in peace, Aileen Fitzgerald. May you find rest soon."

She broke the circle then. Jack shoved his chair away from the table, shaking so hard I wasn't sure he could stand, and retreated to the corner. Sadie followed. He kept his back to the mirror and took her into his arms.

I continued to stare at the mirror, understanding why the ghost sought me out, making what I saw even harder to bear.

Shadow—Aileen—looked down on the room, hands folded at her waist, hair neat and the shawl draped over her shoulders. The ghost was aware of all that happened, all that was said, as she had been since we returned to San Francisco. Aileen had been dead thirty years, taken from her child when he was just a baby, but I'd no doubt she'd watched over Jack his entire life. Now she watched her son and Sadie embrace, and I saw tears glisten in the ghost's green eyes.

Help them, she'd said to me. Help them. What she'd meant was protect them. The danger had pulled even closer, become more terrifying by being real and that we still don't know who to look for. That frightened me most of all, the not knowing. But I wasn't alone and I needed to remember Gabe and Dora were here, too. That was a comfort, small as it might be.

Aileen was still here as well, patient and waiting to share the rest of her secrets. I just needed to learn how to hear them.

CHAPTER 12

Gabe

Gabe waited until the patrol car with Jack and Sadie pulled away before going back inside. He eased Dora's heavy front door closed quietly, determined to avoid waking Daniel. There were enough disturbing things about this night. Isadora's paramour parading half-naked in front of Delia a second time would only add to the list. He wanted to avoid that if at all possible.

The door to the workroom was closed, but the lingering smell of cinnamon filled the darkened corridor. He couldn't see details in the paintings hung at regular intervals along the wall, only that they were bucolic scenes, probably the European countryside. The carpet runner down the center of the hall was thick and lush, and he sank into the pile with each step. Like everything else in the house, the carpet was expensive and spoke of more money than a fortune-teller might be expected to earn.

An inheritance or the settlement from an early marriage was his best guess. Gabe wasn't going to pry into Dora's background without reason, but he couldn't help wondering.

Lights burned in the sitting room at the end of the hall, chasing shadows down the corridor. All the lamps and the chandelier in the small room were lit, more lights than necessary and probably more than normal, but he wouldn't say a word. Gabe wasn't awfully fond of the idea of sitting in the dark tonight. From the looks of things as he came back into the room, Dora wasn't, either.

Isadora Bobet was curled up in a huge overstuffed leather chair, shoes kicked off and feet tucked up under her full skirts. A cigarette dangled from one hand and the other cradled a glass of whiskey. She looked wretched, all the brightness and energy normally in her face sapped away by the séance. Any doubts Gabe had about her being a fraud had evaporated with the first hint of movement in the mirror. Her obvious misery added to his conviction Dora was for real. He was pragmatic enough to believe what was right in front of him, no matter how improbable.

The first thing Dora had done after they'd retired to the sitting room was open the rosewood bar cabinet and pour herself a drink. Cocktail glasses and liquor bottles filled the shelves, glittering amber and brown liquid reflecting the glow of lamps. She'd offered drinks to the rest of them as well, but they'd all declined.

All except Jack. He'd downed a full shot and held his glass out for more. Isadora put the bottle away after refilling the glass a second time. Jack was steady on his feet when he left with Sadie, but once he got home to his own liquor cabinet that wouldn't last.

Gabe could use a shot of whiskey, too, but the need to see Delia home stopped him from accepting. Keeping a clear head was wiser.

Delia sat huddled in a corner of the black leather settee, hugging a crimson throw pillow and chewing on her bottom lip. He'd seen that expression often over the last two weeks. She was thinking, trying to sort things out and make sense of the senseless. He hesitated in the doorway, unsure of where to sit and not wanting to impose if Delia wanted to be alone.

She saw him and the gloomy, preoccupied expression on her

face brightened with a smile. Gabe let out the breath he'd held without realizing, the smile all he needed to decide. He sat on the settee, not crowding her but close enough to take her hand.

How used he'd grown to holding her hand when they were together astonished him if he thought about it. She'd taken his hand on all but the first of their walks over the last two weeks, the gesture natural and unforced. He didn't think about it often, afraid that examining their relationship too closely would stop friendship from becoming something more. Nor did he let himself think beyond merely holding her hand. That seemed unfair to Delia, at least until he admitted to himself that what he felt was more than friendship. "How are you holding up?"

"Enormously tired, but fine otherwise." Delia set the pillow aside. She reached for his hand and he took hers gladly. "Jack's the one I'm worried about. There was no way to soften that blow for him, but I still feel guilty. I keep thinking I should have guessed who Shad—who Aileen was protecting before now."

"Don't be silly. None of us could have guessed she was Jack's mother. If he wasn't already dead I'd plant a curse on Pat Fitzgerald for being a liar and a cad. Not telling Jack the truth about Aileen is inexcusable." Dora angrily snubbed the cigarette out in the brass ash-stand next to her chair. She swung her feet down to the floor and held out her empty whiskey glass. "Gabe, be a dear and pour me another one. You can go right back to holding hands, I promise."

Delia fixed Isadora with a disapproving look and didn't blush, or let go of his hand. "I was under the impression you planned to help. If all you're going to do is drink and tease Gabe, we should leave. I'd hoped the three of us might make progress toward getting the rest of the answers we need."

Dora blinked owlishly for a few seconds, mouth gaping half-open. She mastered surprise, cleared her throat, and raised her glass in salute. "Your pardon, Delia. I forget that the quiet ones always have the sharpest teeth. I do want to help. Jack and Sadie are my dearest friends. But I need another drink and if I attempt to pour my own, I may embarrass myself. I'm getting old and that summons took more from me than I want to admit."

Gabe stood and took the glass from Dora. "Allow me. Water or straight up?"

"Two fingers, straight. It's a sin to dilute good whiskey with water." Her hand was steady when she took the glass back, but fatigue showed in her eyes and the way her mouth drooped. She wasn't faking. "Thank you, Lieutenant. Now we can get down to a serious discussion."

Dora sipped her whiskey and waited until he'd settled next to Delia again. "As I was saying, you couldn't have known what the ghost wanted to reveal. I can guess why Jack's father lied to him about his mother's disappearance, but it muddies the waters even more. The question now becomes how we get more information from Aileen Fitzgerald's ghost. It might be a week before I'm up to another séance and we'd have to pull in people from outside. Subjecting Jack and Sadie to that again would be callous."

"There might be another way." Delia hesitated and wrapped her fingers tighter around his. She was obviously nervous, but pushed ahead anyway. "You can teach me how to hear what Aileen has to say. Show me how to control letting her inside."

Isadora frowned. "I'm still not entirely comfortable with you opening yourself to her, Delia. Controlling the ghost and confining her to the portal was difficult, and I have years of experience. I'd like to find another way if possible. Putting you at risk is a last resort."

Delia's chin came up. "I'm already at risk. All of us are at risk. We have to find this man and stop him from killing more people. Letting Aileen give me her memories is the only way I know to get answers. If you're not comfortable with that, give me another way."

Gabe was only a bystander when it came to dealing with ghosts, a witness to a series of strange events he was forced to believe were real, but that he'd never understand. Delia and Isadora lived at the center of all the strange occurrences. He had to trust they did understand, help when asked, and keep them safe while they dealt with spirits. His skills and experience as a cop were useless for anything but watching over them.

"Let me think." Dora's nails tapped on the side of the whiskey glass, the rhythm eerily like a heartbeat. "Maybe we can bypass the ghost all together. A man who's killed this often will have attracted a great deal of energy to his aura. I can't say for sure, but at least a portion of that energy should rub off on anything he touches. We might be able to find him that way."

"But for some reason you're not certain you can find him. Is that right?" Gabe saw a look pass between the two women. "Both of you appear to know what you're talking about, but I don't. Explain it to me."

"Every person has an aura. Some draw and hold energy, others shed every scrap almost as fast as they encounter it. A murderer would draw negative emotions, anger, pain, and a desire for vengeance. That isn't the kind of energy that dissipates quickly. Traces should linger on anything he touches." Dora tucked the whiskey glass between her right leg and the side of the chair, and fished her cigarette case out. She lit a cigarette, but let it dangle from her hand. "But there is always the chance someone in his life grounds him and bleeds that energy and emotion away. I'm not sure we can discount that possibility entirely."

Delia let go of his hand abruptly and stood. She paced, arms hugged over her chest and frowning. "Someone in his life. You mean this killer could be married? Have children?"

"Yes, that's exactly what I mean. To the rest of the world he likely looks perfectly normal." Isadora took a long drag off the cigarette and blew out a cloud of thin blue smoke. She watched wispy circles swirl toward the ceiling. "He could be married, have a job and a family. His neighbors likely believe him to be a model citizen. Murderers don't often wear their desire for blood on the outside for all to see."

Gabe perched on the edge of the settee and leaned forward, hands resting on his knees. He wanted to question Isadora about how she knew so much about killers and where she'd gained the experience, but she wasn't on trial. If she wanted him to know, she'd tell him. "What do you need, Dora? I have access to all the evidence from this case. Just say the word and I'll make sure you have a chance to see any or all of it."

She retrieved the whiskey glass and drained it in one swallow. Dora licked her lips and smiled, turning all her slightly drunken charm on him. "Seeing the evidence won't be enough, Gabriel. I'll need to hold things he's touched and handle the victims' effects. It will take me two or three days to prepare for that. Aileen's cross took me by surprise, but I know what to shield against now. I won't be much use to you if I faint again."

Gabe was aware of Delia settling next to him, of the cushions shifting under her weight, the sound of her breathing, the fragrance of her hair. He pushed it all into the background, giving Isadora all his attention and focus. This is where being a policeman became useful. He knew how to take care of a prize witness. That's what Dora was now: not merely a friend, but a person with information that might help him solve the case. He'd feel obligated to try and talk a friend out of taking a risk, especially a risk she deemed too great for Delia.

He'd fail if he did try. Isadora might be slightly tipsy, but the determination to go through with this was real. He needed to draw on that vein of trust again and believe that Dora knew how to protect herself. "What can I do to make this easier for you? Tell me how to help."

"Arrange a place outside the station house if you can. Someplace neutral." She set the glass aside and buried the cigarette butt in the white sand filling the ash-stand. "Trite as it sounds, too many criminals around will make sorting guilt more difficult. And the older the evidence, the more chance I have of weathering the storm. Don't bring anything from the latest victim."

"Gabe." Delia touched his hand. "What about the files at your father's house? Those would be the oldest and hopefully the safest for Dora to touch."

"If they aren't too old for her to use, yes, those might be safest. And Dad's house is a neutral place, too." Gabe took Delia's hand and addressed Dora's inquisitive expression. "My father was a detective, a captain. Jack's mother wasn't the only person this man murdered thirty years ago. Dad was in charge of the investigation. He has boxes of evidence and files at his house in Santa Rosa. Can you use something that old?"

Dora rested her head against the back of the chair and shut her eyes. "Aileen's cross laid me flat, Gabe. I'm sure anything your father has in his files will more than serve the purpose. Will the day after tomorrow be too short of notice for your family?"

"Dad would be fine with five minutes notice. Two days will give Mom time to cook enough food to last a week. She's like Annie, happy when she has people to feed." He wanted Delia to come as well. Any thought of asking her made his hands sweat and his stomach clench. The trip to Santa Rosa was part of an official investigation, but Delia meeting his parents for the first time still felt laden with importance. "I'll arrange for a car and driver to take us out there."

Dora intervened, almost as if she knew Gabe was working up

the nerve to speak and saved him from feeling like an awkward schoolboy. The reason was perfectly logical, but Gabe couldn't shake the feeling Isadora intended to smooth the way for him. "Delia, I want you there as well. You're more attuned to Aileen's ghost and her reactions, and I'll have my hands full with victims' pain and the killer's energy. I can't keep track of her ghost as well." She opened one eye and peered blearily at them. "You don't have plans, do you? We can do it the next day if Sadie needs you for anything wedding related."

"No, no plans. We meet with the dressmaker tomorrow afternoon for Sadie's fitting, but the next day is free." Delia glanced at him and a hint of color crept into her cheeks. "I'll consult Sadie about the proper clothes to wear for dinner with your parents and combing through files on old murder cases. She's the expert on these things."

He relaxed. If Delia could make jokes and tease him, he had no reason to be nervous. His parents would dote on her and that presented an entirely different set of problems. Gabe needed to think through that ahead of time. His father wouldn't say much, but his mother would ask a lot of questions. "Remind Sadie my folks live out in the country. Egg ranches aren't known for being overly formal."

"No ball gowns then." Delia kept a straight face and appeared perfectly serious. Knowing her the way he did now was all that kept him from falling for it. "Perhaps I can borrow a pair of coveralls from the gardener."

Dora sighed and sat up, eyes bloodshot but wide open. "Don't be offended, but watching the two of you being adorable is exhausting. Go home, both of you. Pick Delia up before you call round for me, Gabe. No earlier than tenish, please. And don't bother acquiring coveralls for me. I've no plans to spend time in the chicken house and I assume your mother doesn't keep them as house pets."

Delia gave Isadora another look and stood. "I left my handbag in your workroom. Will fetching the bag myself cause problems?"

"No, you'll be fine." Dora made shooing motions with her fingers. "Go. You're safe in my house."

Gabe hesitated before following her. "Is there anything else you need before going through Dad's files, Dora?"

"Sage and white candles. I'll gather those myself." She smiled, teasing him again with Delia out of the room. "Candles and herbs aren't standard issue for murder investigations, but useful to have at hand none the same. I'll want to cleanse your parent's house when we're done. Waking remnants of the killer's aura and leaving them roaming loose wouldn't be wise."

That was something else Gabe didn't understand. If he was going to trust Dora, his confidence in her had to extend to everything she did. His father's reaction to Isadora cleansing the house of evil spirits worried him, but he'd find a way to smooth things over. "Delia and I will be here around ten morning after next. Get some rest."

He turned to leave and Dora spoke again.

"Gabe, one last request." She slid down in the overlarge chair and curled up with her head resting on the arm, limp as a small child after a tiring day. "Put a bottle of brandy and some glasses in a picnic hamper for the trip back to the city. After touching pain and death all day, I'll need something to drink on the way back."

He almost asked why, but thought better of it. Delia would know; he'd ask her. "Any special brand?"

"Ask the liquor merchant for his recommendation." She covered her eyes and sucked in a weary breath. "Please, go now. I'd rather you didn't see me cry."

Gabe did as she wanted. That Dora had asked him to leave didn't make him feel less a coward.

Delia

The dressmaker's shop was warmer than the last time I'd visited with Sadie. Dressing suites in the back were as overheated and airless as the sun-drenched waiting area in front. I'd learned after our first visit and dressed lightly. Even so, I wasn't prepared to swelter in temperatures that would do the Southern California deserts proud.

Mademoiselle's apple-cheeked assistant bustled around in her heavy waist-shirt and skirts, pinning hems and marking tucks at Sadie's bust and waist, and taking no notice of the heat. The smell of lavender and face powder wafted behind her in an oppressive, floral cloud. She chattered nonstop as well, asking Sadie endless questions about the wedding ceremony and honeymoon plans. Each time the assistant pulled a grudging answer from Sadie, she cooed and positively glowed with triumph.

The frown on Sadie's face went entirely unnoticed by the inquisitive shopgirl. Any other time I'd have laughed. Not today. That Sadie had held her temper in check this long made me proud.

Aileen's ghost stood near the door, watching the fitting with all her intense attention. I thought I understood why Aileen focused on Sadie. The desire and the need to watch over Jack's bride must be near as strong as her need to protect him. That the ghost turned from Sadie and gave me imploring looks confused and frightened me.

I'd told Dora we were all at risk, something I believed with all my heart. In the light of day, with Aileen haunting Sadie as much as me, I feared the risks weren't equal.

Mademoiselle's assistant tugged Sadie's arms up to shoulder height and slipped more pins into the lace and silk bodice. "Now stand just like this, Miss Larkin. If you lower your arms I'm afraid you'll get stuck. Mademoiselle needs to come have a look and make sure these adjustments are correct before I baste them in place." She hurried to the door, walking through Aileen's ghost without flinching. "Keep still now! Mademoiselle is with another client, but we'll be back to you as quick as we can."

The door opened and closed again so swiftly behind the assistant, not a breath of cooler air had a chance to sneak in. I'd begun to wonder if there was money to be made in suffocating brides and their maids of honor.

"Keep still she says." A low growl rumbled in Sadie's throat. "She leaves me strung up like a rose tied to a trellis and I'm supposed to wait cheerfully. I'm sorely tempted to let her have a turn at being the pincushion."

I didn't blame her in the slightest, but we'd be released faster if she didn't make a scene. "Try and be patient a bit longer, Sadie. They might almost be finished tormenting you."

"I certainly hope you're right. I'm wilting in the heat and I don't know how much more chatter I can stand." Sadie forgot and lowered her arms, but the pins gave her a sharp reminder. She grimaced and jerked them right back into position. "You'd think a girl working in a shop like this would show a bit more sensitivity to customer's moods."

"I imagine most brides are slightly more chipper and welcome a chance to gush about their wedding." A pitcher of water and two glasses sat on a small table in the corner, given to us grudgingly by the clerk in front when I insisted. I poured a glass for Sadie and put it in her right hand. "Be fair. You can't really blame her for your foul mood."

She sighed and sipped more water, her arm held at an odd angle to avoid the pins. "No, I can't blame her, but she's not helping, either. I can't get Jack out of my mind or stop worrying about him. I've never seen him so upset and angry, Dee. Jack wanted to go straight to Katherine's house last night and confront her about his father's lies. I finally convinced him to wait, but it was a near thing."

I sipped my own water and gazed into Aileen's placid green eyes. Her appearance of serenity was a lie. She held more secrets, not just about the man who took her life, but about Patrick Fitzgerald as well. I was certain of that, my belief rooted deep in a manner that came from the ghost. In very personal ways, those secrets had as much power to harm Jack as the killer stalking the city.

Aileen didn't want to hurt her son, I was sure of that as well. This was partly my fault and Dora's, but if anyone was truly to blame for Jack's upset, his late father carried the burden. "I never knew Jack's father and I know I shouldn't judge. But lying about how Aileen died and who Jack's real mother is—well, it's cruel. I can't fathom a sane reason to do something that heartless to his son. Does Jack have any idea why his father kept so much from him?"

Her shoulders slumped and Sadie looked well and truly miserable. "Not the slightest. Jack had his normal share of disagreements with his father, but all fathers and sons argue. The upset of finding out Katherine is his stepmother was minor compared to how angry Jack is now. I think that's what hurts him most. He doesn't understand."

Aileen drifted closer, a hand stretched toward Sadie. Misery, regret, and a need to comfort, the ghost felt them all and so did I. She brushed a hand over Sadie's hair, offering comfort as I'd seen Esther do a thousand times.

Sadie didn't feel her touch, didn't react or know Aileen was there. That made the gesture all the sadder.

The door to the fitting suite opened and Mademoiselle and her plump assistant entered. For an instant I caught a glimpse of

Marshall Henderson in the waiting area, filling one of the petite chairs to bursting and thumbing through a magazine. A chill breeze whispered around my head, making me shiver. Then the door closed and I was shut into the overheated room again.

"Good afternoon, Miss Larkin. Time to see how well Elise has followed my instructions." Mademoiselle smiled broadly, showing almost perfect teeth. "If all goes well I'll have the dress ready for your final fitting a week before the wedding. We can pin the hem once I'm certain the rest of the alterations are satisfactory. Your ceremony is in the evening and the gown will be ready that morning."

The assistant fussed with pins and made more adjustments, delaying the dressmaker's appraisal of her work. I took Sadie's water glass before she dumped the remains on the assistant's head. "Pardon me, Mademoiselle, but that's cutting things a bit fine. Perhaps you could just pin the hem now. Then Miss Larkin and I wouldn't have to worry about mishaps or unforeseen delays."

Mademoiselle recoiled. "Oh, I couldn't do that. The alterations to the bust and waist will change the drape and the fall of the skirts. Hemming the dress now would be a disaster. I won't take that risk."

"Of course not. Mustn't be rash." Waiting until the morning of the wedding to bring the dress home made me uneasy. Too many things could go wrong. We were at the dressmaker's mercy and there was nothing to be done.

I traded looks with Sadie, silently urging her to be strong, and replaced the water glasses on the table. Muttering snide comments under my breath wasn't polite, but my patience had melted away. "We don't want to ruin the drape or the fall of the skirts, and cause a scandal. Better to risk the bride going down the aisle in her second-best suit. Much safer."

Sadie struggled heroically not to laugh. If she'd heard me, the dressmaker had as well. I retreated to stand next to the door, out of the way and hopefully able to resist the temptation to make any further remarks.

Other temptations I had no intention of fighting. The door opened easily. Mademoiselle frowned, but I gave her my brightest smile and stuck my foot in the gap. I didn't think the dressmaker or her assistant would go so far as shutting the door on my foot, nor would they wrestle the handle from my grasp.

Air flowed into the fitting room, marginally cooler at best, but letting me breathe. The small opening let me look out into the empty waiting area. Henderson had moved to the front counter to talk to the clerk. I didn't think he was flirting with her; his expression was much too sober and hers too earnest. Henderson took whatever was being said very seriously.

"Dee, what do you think?" Sadie preened before the mirror, studying the bodice with a practiced eye. "Is the top too tight?"

I eased the door within a handspan of closing and took a step closer. She really was the most beautiful bride. "Stop worrying, Sadie. The fit is perfect."

A bell jangled over the front entrance. I heard Henderson say hello and the clerk start to scold a deliveryman for not using the tradesman's entrance. A gust of wind slammed the door before he answered her.

Aileen's ghost stood against the far wall, shawl crossed over her chest and hands folded at her waist. Three other ghosts stood with her, young women every bit as prim and proper as my ghost in their stance, and every bit as patient. The room was still stifling, but I shivered.

Each of the ghosts stared at Sadie, their gaze serene and patient. Haunting her now, as Aileen haunted me.

CHAPTER 13

Delia

We ran a few errands on the way home from the dressmaker's shop. Henderson was awfully good about driving Sadie anyplace she asked to go, always cheerful and smiling in the face of waiting in florist shops, or stopping at the butcher shop for Annie. He never complained and I counted us lucky to have him. I'd made sure Gabe knew how well he got on with all of us.

Our street was unusually crowded once we reached home. The iceman's wagon was parked in front of the McAllister's and dripped a steady stream from underneath, darkening the paving stones. Delivery wagons and a large furniture van filled other spaces along the curb. Henderson was forced to park the patrol car down the block.

He got out and stood by the driver's side, frowning and craning his neck to look around for what felt like an excessively long time. The neighborhood looked peaceful as always, but his expression warned of trouble.

Sadie gathered parcels into her arms and reached for the door handle. I stopped her. "Sadie, sit still. Wait for Marshall to open the door."

She stared at Henderson and slouched back against the seat. "I think this is when you tell me not to panic, Dee."

"Don't panic." Laughing would be unkind and under the circumstances, I didn't feel much merriment. "I'm sure everything is fine, he's just doing his job. We're a half block or more from the house, so Marshall is just being extra cautious. He's good at what he does and we can trust him."

I believed what I'd said. Gabe wouldn't assign him to our detail unless he knew Henderson was able to take care of us. I trusted Gabe even more.

We sat there another moment or two before Officer Henderson opened the door on the street side and leaned in. "I'd like both of you to get out this side if you would. We're going to walk down the center of the street, not on the sidewalk. If one of you could carry the roast in for Annie, I'll come back for the other parcels after you're safely inside the house."

Neither of us argued. We slid out, me with the dinner roast in my arms, and waited for him to give us instructions. Once he'd helped us out of the car, Henderson took his sidearm out of the holster. The barrel of the pistol pointed at the ground, but I'd no doubt that would change instantly if he felt threatened.

Aileen and her trio of sister ghosts shimmered into view a step behind Henderson. They stared beyond me, down the street and toward home. Anxiety pooled in my chest, making breathing difficult, and the thought of stepping away from the car made me tremble. For the first time, I wasn't sure if the fear came from the ghost or if seeing Marshall Henderson with a gun in his hand had stripped away all my courage.

"What's wrong?" I swallowed, trying to moisten a mouth gone dry. "We'd both feel better knowing."

"Officer Casey and the other car are gone." Henderson glanced at me and went right back to watching the street, seeming to look everywhere at once. I'd seen Gabe do the same at the fair. Habit Gabe had said, probably picked up early in his career, as Marshall had picked watchfulness up from him. "This doesn't feel right. Aaron wouldn't leave his post voluntarily."

I put the roast in the crook of my arm and reached for Sadie's hand. Annie and Mama Esther were in the house and the need to know they were all right outweighed my fear. "Then we should go find out what's happened."

He set a good pace and home drew near quickly. Walking down the middle of the street was an odd sensation, leaving me feeling exposed and grateful I could see anyone approaching at the same time. Jack and Gabe's job would be like this at times, as Henderson's was now. I respected all of them for being able to deal with the uncertainty and the danger day after day. This little taste was making me ill.

Tradesmen came out of the house across the street from ours and climbed into the back of the furniture van. They emerged with a chaise, covered in shocking blue damask and trimmed in white maple along the front edge. I watched them struggle up the front steps with the couch and wondered if thoughts of those they loved disappearing, or worse, ever interrupted their day. A normal life, free of worrying about ghosts and murderers, was still something I longed for with all my heart.

Henderson waved us through our front gate ahead of him. We hurried up the walk and the porch steps, pausing at the top so he could ring the bell. He kept the gun drawn, but held it half-hidden behind his leg.

A nervous glance behind showed the walkway clear of ghosts, somewhat of a surprise. The itch on the back of my neck told me Aileen was still with me, watching as always, but she'd chosen not to show herself. She often disappeared when Annie was near and I prayed that was the case now.

My knees sagged when Annie opened the door, whole and safe. Annie saw the gun in Marshall's hand and her eyes widened. She didn't waste a second shutting and locking the door once the three of us were inside.

Sadie hugged Annie tight, her hands visibly shaking. "Thank God you're all right. I was worried something terrible had happened to you and Mama."

"I'm fine and so is Miss Esther." Annie cradled Sadie's head on her shoulder, rocking her side to side as if she were a little girl again. She frowned and turned her sternest look on Henderson. "Explain what's going on, Marshall, and why that gun's in your hand. I need to know why both my girls come home scared near to death."

He stood his ground, not an easy thing to do against Annie. "I need you to answer some questions first. Is Aaron in the house with you? If not, do you know where he is?"

She patted Sadie on the back and let go. Annie took the roast from me, kissing me on the forehead before answering Marshall. Her frown grew deeper. "No, he left awhile back. Messenger came by and brought him a note saying he had to get back to the stationhouse. He came to the backdoor and told me he was leaving, but drove off right after. Is Aaron being gone what's got you all upset?"

"That's part of it." He looked past Annie and stepped closer to the sitting room until he could see inside. Marshall cast about, as if deciding whether to search the entire house. "Aaron shouldn't have left you alone, Annie. Is anyone else in the house with you other than Mrs. Larkin? Anyone knock on the door or ring the bell since Officer Casey left?"

Annie shook her head. "Not since he left, no. A man from the rail company delivered Delia's trunk earlier today, but Aaron wouldn't let him come inside. Made that man most unhappy. I guess he thought better of shouting at a police officer or got worried that his boss might hear about it. He calmed down after a minute, even said he was sorry. Aaron dragged the trunk in himself after the man drove away."

"I thought they'd lost my trunk forever." I set my handbag on the hall table. On the surface all was well, but a calm surface hid many things. I was too unsettled, too restless to relax. "I'm glad that's not the case."

"I'm going up to Mama." Sadie glanced at Henderson and touched my shoulder on her way to the stairs. "Call if you need me."

Henderson finally holstered his pistol and hung his hat on the hall tree. "I hate to impose, but I think it best if I stay in the house with all of you. The only officers with the authority to pull Aaron off this detail are Lieutenant Ryan or Sergeant Fitzgerald. I can't imagine either of them doing that, not without sending someone to replace him."

"No, neither can I. They'd send a patrol car, not a note." The sick feeling in my stomach returned. Gabe and Jack would stand watch themselves before leaving the house unguarded. Marshall's instincts ran true, something was wrong. "Annie, where did Officer Casey leave my trunk?"

"It's still on the utility porch. Aaron said that he and Marshall would bring it up to your room later." Annie shifted the roast to her other arm, eyeing me and Officer Henderson both, but didn't ask any more questions. At times I was sure Annie saw right through me and divined all the thoughts I tried to keep hidden. "I best get this meat in the oven if supper's going to be on time. Jack and Gabe are both coming to eat with us. Are you meeting your girl tonight, Marshall?"

He blushed, his neck and cheeks turning a deeper red than his hair. "No, not tonight. She's going to a family wedding. One of her cousins."

"Well you're more than welcome to stay for supper, too." She handed him the roast and smoothed down her apron. "I could use an extra hand with the potatoes. Come along now, both of you."

We followed her from the entry, across the formal dining room, and through the swinging door into her domain. That she ruled the kitchen was a fact none of us contested.

Annie was never shy about putting people to work. The young officers watching the house were no exception, but she fed them well and none of them ever complained. I suspected that secretly, most of them liked helping her.

Henderson set the roast on the oak worktable in the middle of the kitchen. He slipped off his uniform jacket, draping it over the back of a chair and began rolling up his sleeves. "Do you know what time Lieutenant Ryan is coming by this evening, Miss Martin?"

I grabbed an apron off the peg near the icebox and slipped it over my dress. "If Gabe and Jack are coming for supper, I imagine not later than seven."

"Right after shift change." He sat in front of the potatoes Annie had piled on the table and started peeling, tossing the ones he'd finished into a mixing bowl. "Edwards and Thompson are on tonight. Maybe I can call in a few favors and pull more men in for overnight. I don't think the lieutenant will mind."

Annie was in the pantry, gathering ingredients for biscuits and singing one of her favorite hymns. I moved closer and lowered my voice. "You think someone lured Officer Casey away for a reason. That's what really concerns you."

"I don't know that for sure." Marshall Henderson glanced up at me and for an instant, all the worry showed in his eyes. This case had aged him in just the few weeks we'd known each other. "But it is a possibility."

Annie took a tray up to Esther so Sadie could help her mother eat while our supper cooked. Esther ate less each day, all soft foods easily swallowed. I set to work cutting up turnips and resolved not to think of how near Esther's end drew, hour by swift hour.

With three of us in the kitchen, supper had come together quickly. Potatoes and turnips bubbled on the stove and the smell of roast beef filled the kitchen. Biscuits sat on the cutting board, covered with a flour-sack towel, ready to bake at the last minute.

I patted the last of the pie crust into a tin. Henderson was still peeling and cutting up apples, eating one wedge for each that he added to the mixing bowl. Until he finished I wouldn't be needed. I washed flour from my hands and opened the door to the utility porch.

My trunk sat on the chipped brown linoleum floor and filled most of the small porch. The last anemic rays of sunset found their way through the window, glinting off brass hinges, and the wide metal-bands that reinforced the rounded top. Given the time the rail company had the trunk in their keeping, I'd expected it to come back to me scratched and dirty from weeks spent in baggage cars. Instead, the wood and fittings looked cleaner than when loaded on the train in New York.

Officer Casey had shoved the trunk into the room and turned it sideways to let the outside door close again, and the latch faced the backdoor, out of reach. Squeezing between the trunk and the laundry sink was a tight fit, but I managed. Having my own things again would be a treat and I wanted to change before Gabe arrived.

The etched nameplate on the front was gone, something Aaron Casey wouldn't know to miss. A neat square of pale blue paper was wedged into the frame in its place, the words Miss Delia Martin written out in sharp, black ink.

I backed away until the wall behind stopped me, remembering at the last instant not to open the door and run. Clamping a hand over my mouth kept me from screaming, but only just.

"Oh, God . . . oh, God . . . oh, God." I sucked in air, fighting to stay calm and not retch. "Marshall . . . Marshall!"

He hit the door at a run, a hand on his gun. Relief flashed across his face as he saw me, but he leapt the trunk to reach me, his long legs clearing the rounded top with ease. Annie appeared in the doorway right behind him. Her eyes went wide as she saw me huddled against the far wall.

"Are you all right?" Marshall turned me to face him when I didn't answer. "Miss Martin— Delia, tell me what's wrong."

"He was here. He brought my trunk." Breath caught in my throat and I choked, trying not to sob. I pointed at the blue envelope bearing my name. "Marshall . . . he was here."

"Son of a—" He put an arm around my shoulders, holding me up as my knees gave out. "Annie, call the stationhouse and have them send two cars right now. If Lieutenant Ryan isn't there, tell the desk sergeant to find him. Give the sergeant my name and make sure he understands this is urgent."

Annie hesitated, twisting her hands in her apron and staring at me.

"I've got her, Annie." His voice was calm, reassuring, and reminded me of Gabe. "Call the lieutenant."

Henderson helped me around the trunk and sat me in a kitchen chair, leaving me only long enough to close the door into the porch and fetch a glass of water. I heard Annie's voice from the parlor. She was speaking to Gabe. He and Jack would be here soon.

Esther's ghosts, Teddy and the little girl, Beryl, shimmered into view, blocking the door onto the porch. Aileen and her sister ghosts appeared next to Teddy, and a new face, a young man I'd not seen before. Shutting my eyes didn't prevent me from knowing they were there or sensing their anger. More would come as well, all determined to stop this man.

An army of ghosts haunted me, haunted Sadie and Esther,

spectral guardian angels standing between us and the darkness a murderer cast over our lives. So many spirits, aware and purposeful, had gathered together for a reason. I couldn't look into Aileen's eyes and not believe that to be true.

The thought brought me comfort.

Gabe

Gabe swallowed his anger, struggling to remain detached and professional. Letting go of Delia to do his job was one of the hardest things he'd ever done.

Jack stood with him, taking notes as Marshall Henderson gave his report. Each angry scrawl of Jack's pencil on paper was a reminder that his partner fought the same battle between duty and the need to be with Sadie.

Neither of them wanted to stand in the cold on unmowed grass, dampness from last night's rain soaking into their trouser cuffs. Supervising the collection of evidence was the very last thing Gabe wanted to be doing. He knew Jack felt exactly the same. Neither of them had a choice.

Too close, too close. He couldn't get the words out of his mind. Gabe looked from the side yard to the utility porch and the door into the house; he turned away again to keep from punching a wall. He was angry with himself for being careless and taking half measures, no one else. Ignoring the killer's pattern put people he was supposed to protect in greater danger. People he cared for deeply.

Henderson wasn't to blame for leaving the house unguarded and Gabe was determined no one would hold his promising rookie responsible. The young officer had done everything right. Aaron Casey was the one who'd disobeyed orders, but even so, Casey hadn't let the stranger inside.

Gabe was extremely grateful for that second chance. He'd be willing to give Casey another chance and let him make up for his mistake—if they found him alive. That seemed less likely as more hours passed without word.

One man to watch the house and one to drive Sadie and Delia on wedding errands was at least one man short. He'd known that from the start, but Gabe had let the captain bully him out of having three to four men on each detail. That ended now, tonight. Extra men were already on the way to Isadora's house.

"Lieutenant?" Maxwell stood at the top of the back steps. "Baker's finished taking his photographs. We're ready to open the trunk when you're finished."

Gabe stuffed clenched fists deeper into his trouser pockets. "Did Turner find any fingerprints?"

Maxwell leaned back inside thc door to ask. "He says the prints he found won't do us any good. They were smeared one set on top of the other and spread all over the outside. Rail company baggage handlers or Casey's most likely. Nothing we can use to identify our man."

He'd known, but he had to ask "Thank you, Maxwell. Sergeant Fitzgerald and I will be right there."

Gabe glanced at the men working near him. His squad worked methodically and combed the ground in the side yard for clues, their kerosene lanterns casting flickering yellow islands of light around their feet. A depression in the soft ground near the porch showed where the stranger dropped the heavy trunk. Deep parallel gouges marked where Casey dragged it to the steps and mud left behind on weathered wood told how he'd walked the trunk up one step at a time, struggling with the weight.

No grooves marred the ground from the street to that telltale depression. The killer had carried the trunk, at least until Casey confronted him and refused to let him inside. A man that strong was more than capable of overpowering Terrance Owens or any of the other murder victims.

Annie had heard Aaron threaten to shoot if the angry stranger took another step. The shouting stopped then and when she'd peeked out the kitchen window, Aaron still had his gun drawn. Without Casey's pistol pointed at him, the killer might have tried to force his way into the house.

Too close, too close.

Gabe clapped Henderson on the shoulder, signaling an end to questions. Marshall was tired, the corners of his mouth drooping and bruised circles darkening under his eyes. "That's enough for tonight. We'll pick this up again in the morning. Use the front entrance and go back inside. Annie's keeping supper warm for you."

"Yes, sir." Henderson started to leave, but turned back. "I know Annie got a glimpse of him through the windows. But the deliverymen out front or the ice man might have gotten a better look at the man who brought the trunk."

Jack stuck the pencil stub behind his ear. He glanced at Gabe before speaking, taking the lead. "We took the name of the furniture company from the people across the street and Annie knows the ice man. If they saw anything, we'll know by morning. You did a good job today, Marshall. The lieutenant and I are both grateful to you for taking good care of Sadie and Delia. Let the rest of the squad take over now. Go eat your supper before you get me in trouble with Annie. She made me promise not to keep you long."

That made Henderson smile. "Yes, sir. I wouldn't want Annie mad at you."

Officer Henderson headed toward the street and the front of the house, feet dragging with fatigue. Gabe started up the back steps, muttering so only Jack could hear. "You're better at that than I am."

"What? Making the rookies feel less guilty about needing to

eat and sleep?" Jack clomped up the steps beside him and pushed the door open. "Set a better example if you want the squad to take you seriously, Lieutenant Ryan. Most of them feel they need to work double shifts just to keep up with you. They're all afraid of letting you down."

He stopped on the threshold and stared at Jack. "Jesus . . . I'm turning into my father. I swore to myself after Victoria died I wouldn't do that."

Jack put a hand on his shoulder and pushed him the rest of the way inside. "I won't let you. I'd be willing to wager that Delia won't, either."

One bare bulb dangled from a wire in the ceiling, harsh white light that made Gabe squint until his eyes adjusted. Fingerprint dust covered the outside of Delia's trunk, fine black grains clumping around the oily mass of prints near the latch and the handles on each end, fuzzy as mold on spoiled bread. He slipped out of his overcoat and hung it on a hook near the backdoor with his fedora. Jack did the same with his coat and hat.

"Turner, do you have a cloth I can use to wipe away the fingerprint powder?" The porch was warmer than outside, but still too cold to take off his suit jacket. Gabe compromised and pushed up his sleeves. "I'd hate to get it all over Miss Martin's clothes."

Turner dug in his case and came up with two pieces of soft flannel. Gabe wiped the trunk front clean and took the second cloth to do the same to the latch and the rounded top. Fingerprint powder stuck to his fingers, but a splash of water from the sink and a handkerchief solved that problem.

He went to his knees on the cold floor, a worshipper at the altar of the murderer's cleverness. This man had repeated his pattern exactly, proving to Gabe as he'd proven to Matt Ryan that he could take anyone he wanted. He counted his blessings again. *Too close . . .*

Sweat trickled into his collar, down the back of his neck and between his shoulder blades. Gabe traded looks with Jack. He silently counted to three, took a breath, and flipped open the lid. The top layer showed nothing but neatly folded stockings and petticoats, exactly what he'd expect to find in Delia's traveling trunk.

After the surprises the killer had left for them in the past, Gabe didn't trust that in the slightest. The only small bit of relief he allowed himself was that they hadn't found a body stuffed inside.

He began laying some of Delia's things inside the rounded top, but the bottom of the trunk was twice the size. Not everything would fit. "Jack, does Annie have a wicker basket, one she uses for laundry?"

"I'll ask. Be back in a tick." Jack slid between the trunk and the edge of the sink and disappeared into the kitchen.

Gabe removed pieces of clothing carefully, unfolding blouses and skirts to make sure nothing was hidden inside. He felt funny about handling her undergarments and nightdresses, but that was just the place the murderer would hide something terrible.

Jack returned with two deep baskets and raised an eyebrow at the cluster of young men crowding the utility porch. "Out, all of you. Talk to Officer Morris and find out what he needs done. The sooner you get through his list the sooner you get to go home. The lieutenant and I will take care of this."

His partner refolded everything Gabe handed him and Jack laid Delia's clothes in the deepest basket. Toward the bottom of the trunk, Gabe found a layer of shoes, books and jewelry boxes of different sizes. He handed the jewelry cases to Jack to search.

One by one, Gabe shook the shoes out and dropped them into a basket. He'd almost finished when something small and wrapped in brown paper fell out of the toe of a black shoe, clinking on the floor with a metallic sound. He set the shoe aside, heart thumping against his ribs. "What are the odds of Delia hiding trinkets in her shoe?"

"Not very good I'd say." Jack sorted through the largest of the jewelry cases. He frowned and lifted out a slim parcel, wrapped in a large man's handkerchief and tied with a ribbon. "Probably the same odds of her keeping books in a jewelry box."

"It might be a diary." Gabe couldn't have explained why, but he knew that was wrong as he said it. He poked at the paper around the trinket and began to work at untying the string holding it in place. "Open it. We can tell Delia we're sorry later if that is her journal."

He ended up tearing the paper off rather than fight the string. An old-style police sergeant's badge lay in his hand, the brass tarnished green and pitted. Gabe rubbed at the front with his damp handkerchief, trying to make out the number. "Badge seven forty-eight of the San Francisco Police Department. That's an early number, Dad was badge eight ninety-one. This one was issued before he joined the force."

Jack gave up trying to slip the ribbon off and dug a penknife out of his pocket. The ribbon cut easily. "The department lost a lot of records in the fire. Any chance that your father might know who that number belonged to?"

"He might remember. Dad knew almost everyone on the force back then." He turned the badge over in his hand, staring at it and trying to deny the icy knot forming in his middle. He needed the information in his father's files. Visiting his parents might draw the killer's attention toward them, but the risk was there even if he stayed away. Gabe couldn't bring himself to say aloud what both he and Jack knew. The killer had hidden the badge for them to find, taunting them again. "I'll take it to show Dad tomorrow. This means something, I just don't know what. About the only thing I'm certain of is that Delia didn't pack this in her shoe."

"This isn't Delia's journal, either. It's some sort of history book." Jack flipped through the book, glancing at a few pages before turning back to the flyleaf. "It's inscribed to Augustus Whitfield, from his loving sister and dated March, eighteen eighty-three."

Gabe tucked the badge in his inside jacket pocket and took the book from Jack. "The first series of murders started in June of eighteen eighty-three. That was only a month after my parents were married."

The book was a combination of memoir and a recounting of his service to the British Empire by a man named Brewster. Chief interpreter and secretary to the intelligence department in Egypt in the mid-eighteen hundreds, Brewster had recorded his travels and adventures. Faded lithographs and line drawings recorded images of pyramids, temples, and statues of Egyptian kings.

Gabe flipped through pages, stopping at a series of drawings near the end. Images of Anubis, Osiris, and a scale balancing a human heart against a feather stared back at him. A few pages further on, the Court of the Dead was explained in gruesome detail, much more horrific than Colin had outlined in front of Delia. He handed the book to Jack and waited silently while his partner read.

Jack snapped the book shut. "He wants us to know what he's doing. What I still don't understand is why."

"Why he wants us to know? Or why he treats the city as his own personal hunting ground?"

"Either." Jack let out a long, hissing breath. "I'd take anything you have to offer right now. He got too damned close today. I'm not ashamed to admit this guy scares me."

"He scares me, too. But this man thinks he's smarter than us and that's leading him to take chances." Gabe sifted through the few things left in the bottom of the trunk, but nothing was hidden there. They'd found the killer's message. He began repacking Delia's things. "He made a mistake today. Annie didn't get a good look at him, but enough that we can put out a flyer describing him.

I'm betting that either the iceman or the deliverymen saw him, too. They'd have gotten a better look."

Jack helped him pull the trunk lid closed. "And if they did, we can add a sketch to the flyer. Tacking flyers up on every lamppost and storefront in the city might slow this bastard down."

"Maybe." Or make the killer so angry he retaliated. That was a risk, but one they'd have to take. Gabe stood and brushed at the knees of his trousers. "It's a start anyway. Are you ready to help me carry Delia's trunk to her room?"

"I've got a better idea, let two of the squad take it upstairs. Annie saved supper for us, too." Jack handed Gabe his coat and hat. "Set a good example and eat, Gabe. I'm sure Delia will be happy to sit with you while you do."

"That is a better idea." Gabe snatched the book up off the floor and eased past the end of the trunk. All the carefully suppressed need to be with Delia, to see and talk with her hit him at once. "It's been a long day for all of us. Let's not keep the ladies waiting any longer."

CHAPTER 14

Delia

I laid awake a long time after Jack and Gabe left, unable to stop myself from dwelling on all that had happened. Imagining horrible things was all too easy.

Each time I shut my eyes, I saw Aaron Casey's face. Finding him alive and unharmed might take a miracle, and I prayed for one. Gabe made sure Sadie and I knew that the killer had found a method to lure an officer away from his post. Knowing would remind us to question everything that didn't come from him or Jack directly. Questioning kept us safer. He had the same talk with Annie before going home.

What worried Gabe and Jack most was that they'd no idea how this man managed to fool Casey. What worked once might work again.

The big clock in the parlor chimed two in the morning, a hollow, lonely sound. I turned onto my side, wide awake and mind racing. Aileen's ghost stood in front of my door. I'd spent months wishing her away, wanting to be free of the burden of knowing she was always there. Now the sight of Aileen standing watch at my door was more of a comfort than knowing half a dozen officers guarded the house. I didn't understand what changed or why, just that it had.

I fell asleep soon after, dreamless sleep that left me more rested than I'd a right to be. Annie let me sleep until seven. We'd talked it over the night before and decided the trip to see Gabe's parents, and giving Dora access to his father's files, was more vital than ever. I stumbled around my room and yawned until my jaw ached, but managed to dress and eat breakfast before Gabe arrived at nine.

Annie sent him to find me in the kitchen. I was still lingering over my coffee and trying to wake up, more than a little afraid I'd fall asleep on the drive to Santa Rosa. Gabe pushed through the swinging door and took the chair next to me. "Good morning. Did you sleep well?"

I traced the dark, bruised looking skin under his eye with a fingertip. His cheery smile didn't fool me. Gabe looked exhausted and I was certain he felt worse. "At a guess I slept better than you. So no, not well at all. Any word?"

He shook his head. "No sign of Casey or the car. We had men out searching all night."

"What now?" I took his hand. Gabe held on as tight as I did, both of us needing comfort. Aileen and the other ghosts were victims of this killer, but I'd not known them as living, breathing people. I knew Aaron Casey, remembered the sound of his voice saying hello and how he tipped his hat to Annie with a smile.

"Jack is pulling men from other stations to search the warehouses by the docks. Captain Parker is giving him trouble, but he'll handle it. Once Jack has extra men, he can widen the search area. If we don't find him today . . ." Helplessness and the knowledge he couldn't save Casey filled Gabe's eyes. He'd never lost a man under his command before. But he shut grief away, the professional mask that allowed him to do his job falling into place.

Gabe stood, pulling me up, too. "We should go. Dora is expecting us by ten."

I put my arms around him, determined we weren't going anywhere until I was sure he'd be all right. "Don't you dare pretend this is all part of the job, Gabriel Ryan, not with me. Losing one of your squad like this is horrible. You can't make me believe you don't care. I know you too well."

He held me awkwardly at first, silent, breathing hard and arms stiff. Then Gabe sighed and pulled me closer. "Thank you. I made some promises to myself after Victoria died. One was to never allow this job to shut me away from people I cared about, not the way my father did. Jack said you'd never let me. Don't tell him he was right."

"Not a word. Promise." Learning all there was to know about Gabe Ryan would take time. I grew more certain each day the time would be well spent.

We clung to each other for a moment before Gabe let go. He brushed a finger down my cheek. "I shouldn't let you walk into my parent's house completely unprepared. We can talk on the way to Dora's house. Is that all right with you?"

"Yes, of course." My nerves had increased tenfold, but I'd put on a brave front and hope he wouldn't notice. Distraction was always a good strategy. I put my coffee cup and saucer in the sink, and turned to face him with my most serious expression. "Keep in mind Dora will be with us all day. I imagine your parents will either be completely taken with her special charms or speechless with shock. They'll take no notice of me at all. That should work out well."

Gabe grinned and held the door into the dining room open. "That would work out well. But I know my mother and you shouldn't get your hopes up. Mom will notice you."

I took a breath and brushed by him into the dining room. "I'll try to find some charm of my own then. Be sure to let me know how I'm doing."

"Delia." The door closed behind him and he reached for my hand. "Stop worrying. I promise you, my parents will love you."

After all that had happened, hauntings and murders, and all the danger stalking us, losing my composure over whether his parents would like me or not was silly. I knew that, but I panicked anyway. Panic was the normal thing to do in this situation and I needed a moment of normality. "How can you know that for sure?"

"Because I—" He halted in mid-sentence. A bit of his own panic filled Gabe's eyes, but vanished again in an instant. "Because I know they won't feel any differently than I do. My parents will love you because I do."

"Oh . . ." I couldn't think of a single thing to say in the face of his declaration, not one. Quiet happiness stole over me and all I could do was smile, hoping I didn't look utterly witless.

Annie came into the dining room, her arms full of linens. She stopped and stared at the two of us, shook her head and continued on into the kitchen. I saw her smile and wink at Gabe before the door shut. Annie never missed a thing that went on in our house.

Gabe cleared his throat. A flush showed above his collar. "We should go. Dora's waiting and it's a long drive."

I held tight to his hand and led the way. My handbag was on the front table, my coat hanging on the hall tree. Gabe opened the door to speak to the officer on the porch as I gathered my things. The day outside was bright and sunny, the sky a perfect late-June blue.

A shimmer at the foot of the stairs caught my eye as I slipped on my coat. Aileen rippled into view as did a smaller ghost, faded to the point of being no more than a faint glimmer against the dark carpet on the staircase.

Victoria's ghost come to say good-bye, the tie holding her in this world frayed and unraveling. Gabe had let go.

Aileen met my eyes, sorrow and gladness both in that knowing gaze. She took Victoria's hand and led her up the staircase. One step from the top, the ghosts crumbled. A veil of glimmering dust lifted toward the ceiling, spreading thinner and thinner until I lost sight.

"Delia?" Gabe frowned and wiped a tear from my cheek. "Is something wrong?"

"Nothing new. All the things that were wrong five minutes ago are still wrong. I'm just tired." I found a smile for him and stepped out into the sunlight. "It's a marvelous day for a drive in the country. Let's pick up Dora and get started."

Gabe

Gabe shifted position, hoping to ease the cramp in his arm without waking Delia. She'd fought a valiant battle against sleep, but the drone of tires on pavement and the monotonous countryside conspired with exhaustion until her eyes closed. He'd wrapped an arm around her and pulled her head onto his shoulder.

The next two hours were spent ignoring Isadora's amused smirks each time he glanced her way. He supposed that was to be expected. She'd try to bait him until she grew tired of the game or realized she couldn't embarrass him. A game was all it was, born of the need to maintain the pretense of being a free spirit. He'd spent enough time with Dora by now not to take her teasing seriously.

He went back to staring out the window. Apple and plum orchards lined both sides of the two lane road, fully leafed out and only a straggling pink or white blossom in evidence. Tiny green apples and plums, no bigger than the end of his thumb, hid among the leaves. He'd bring Delia back in August to see the trees heavy with plums, their skins a deep, dull purple.

Apples would wait until the early fall harvest, filling farmer's roadside stands with reds and golden yellows. If they waited until October, they'd find pumpkins heaped in teetering, orange pyramids as well. He knew his landlady, Mrs. Allen, would appreciate him bringing back newly picked fruit for pies, jellies, and applesauce. Annie would, too.

Whether he'd have time or not to make another trip with Delia for pleasure, not work, hinged on solving this case. He glanced down at her sleeping face, imagining having breakfast with her each morning and coming home to her at night, raising children and becoming as comfortable in each other's company as his parents were after a lifetime together. Although he'd only known Delia for a short time, each day he became more certain that was what he wanted.

Too many things hinged on solving this case. Having a life with Delia, one without an undercurrent of fear, was at the top of Gabe's list.

"How much further?" Dora lounged against the seat, legs crossed and hands resting easily in her lap. The rapid bobbing of her foot spoiled the picture of ease. She didn't fool him. The relaxed pose was as much of an act as her teasing interest in him.

Moving the book and the badge into the front seat with Henderson didn't keep Dora from sensing them or grimacing in pain. The killer had touched them too recently. That he'd no choice but to bring the book and badge into the car didn't ease Gabe's guilt. Isadora's discomfort was obvious. "Another fifteen or twenty minutes. No more than that."

She nodded curtly. Not for the first time, Dora's gaze drifted to the picnic basket at her feet. The dangling foot bobbed faster.

"Dora, it's my fault you're uncomfortable. Open the brandy if you need a drink."

"And greet your father with liquor on my breath?" She arched an eyebrow. "It's only just past noon. I'll save my debauchery for the trip home. My task will be easier with your father's cooperation and that's unlikely if I begin drinking before we arrive."

Delia stirred in her sleep, but settled again right away. Gabe tightened his arm around her and lowered his voice. "I'm sorry, Dora. I need to show Dad what we found in Delia's trunk. I never thought . . . I should have warned you first."

She waved away his apology. "No lasting harm done. I've survived worse, Gabe. Your duty doesn't coincide with my comfort and catching this killer is more important. He's becoming bolder, taking more chances. That's not a good sign."

The quiet authority in her voice spoke of experience and knowing that what she'd said was true. He'd put a great deal of trust in Dora, he needed to stop worrying about giving offense and get some answers. How she'd gained that knowledge was important.

"I've wanted to ask this question for a long time. Forgive me if I say this badly, I don't mean to make you think I don't trust you." Gabe looked Isadora in the eye and plunged ahead. "How does a society medium know so much about murderers? You didn't learn that on Nob Hill."

"Very good, Gabe." Dora beamed as if he'd won a school prize for being the brightest pupil in class. "I wondered when you'd ask."

Cops honed their instincts over time and learned when a person wanted to evade a question. Dora was doing her charming best to evade his. "I'd appreciate an answer."

She smirked again, still playing it for a joke, but the telltale bob of her foot told a different story. "I may as well. You'll continue to be tiresome otherwise. Before coming to San Francisco I lived in Atlanta. Homicide Detective John Lawrence and I worked together on murder cases for nearly seven years. We trusted each other. A new chief of police took command and decided I was a fraud, or worse, covering up my involvement in the crimes. The chief threatened to fire John if he consulted me again."

"And you left town after that."

The bright, teasing edge left her smile. Dora plucked at the front of her jacket and avoided looking at him. "Not right away. Six months later three officers pulled me out of bed in the middle of the night. John was dead, killed by a murderer we'd been hunting for the past year. The chief tried to implicate me in John's death and planned to press charges. Luckily, I wasn't sleeping alone that night."

She looked him in the eye, daring him to comment. Gabe didn't flinch or turn away, and did his best to hide the horrified sympathy welling up inside. She wouldn't want that. "I can't begin to imagine how difficult that was for you. That never should have happened, not to you or anyone. I wish I could say that rank guarantees personal integrity in a senior officer, but I can't. There are examples I could point to in my own department."

"I've heard of the infamous Captain Parker from Jack." Dora's teasing half-smile returned. "You should wake Dee soon. Give her a chance to collect herself before we arrive and she meets your parents. She'll be mortified otherwise."

"I will. Let her have another minute." Gabe brushed an errant strand of hair off Delia's face. "Thank you for all you've done for her. This can't be easy for you."

"It's not. I swore I'd never get involved in a murder case again. But gossip to the contrary, I'm not selfish enough to leave Delia to cope with spirits on her own." Dora stared out the window. "Now that I'm in up to my ears, I'll do what I can to help end this. Just promise me you won't do anything rash like getting yourself killed. I don't think I could live with watching Delia grieve. Sadie, either, for that matter."

That was an easy promise to make. "You won't have to. I have no intention of dying. Neither does Jack."

Dora tipped her head to peer at him, the brim of her hat casting a shadow so that he couldn't see her eyes. He grew uncomfortable at the way she stared before she turned away again. "Belief is half the battle won and often makes things true. Hold tight to that conviction, Lieutenant Ryan, and this will end well."

Delia

My embarrassment over spending the entire trip asleep on Gabe's shoulder was minor compared to how much better I felt. I was calmer, more relaxed. The thought of yawning in his mother's face while saying hello was much worse.

We pulled off the narrow dirt road into his parent's front yard and Henderson parked the car. I was wide awake by that time. Despite Gabe's assurances, my welcome was not guaranteed and I worried they'd see me as an intruder. Victoria's ghost had moved on, but her memory would still loom large in his parent's minds.

Gabe was nervous, too, perched on the edge of the seat like a sprinter in the starting block. His father went strictly by the book in terms of police work. Dora's abilities were far outside the bounds of what Matt Ryan was used to and even further away from anything he'd consider believable. How his father would react to Gabe calling in a spiritualist to consult on the case was a real concern.

Dora would weather the former Captain Ryan's scorn if and when it arrived, and likely give as good as she received. She'd dealt with such things before. I worried how well Gabe would come through the same storm. He was his own man and good at his job, but his father's opinion and respect still mattered.

A large chicken coop stood near the house, one of four in a line leading to the barn. Tiny yellow balls of fluff followed the hens around the fenced-in chicken yard and scratched in the dirt. Roosters crowed from atop the chicken house nearest the barn. Others answered, the calls muffled and distant.

The farmhouse was two stories, painted white and with a wood-shake roof, weathered to a soft gray. Pink roses climbed a trellis on one end of the deep porch, their sweet, peppery scent competing with the smell of ham and candied yams coming from the house. A large calico cat lounged on the top porch step, flipping her tail and eyeing the visitors invading her yard.

Henderson helped Isadora from the car and handed her the canvas shopping bag of white candles and sage. She swept her gaze across the house and the yard, turning to stare at the old carriage house attached to the barn. Gabe's father had fixed the carriage house as an office and stored papers, case files, and boxes of evidence there, out of his mother's sight.

I'd learned that from Gabe on the drive to Dora's house. That she somehow knew without being told didn't strike me as overly strange, not in light of other things I'd seen her do. My world had changed.

Gabe buttoned the book and the old badge into his pocket and took my hand. "Ready?"

"No and neither are you." I gave him a sidelong look and smiled. "But we should get on with it. I'll be brave if you will."

The screen door slammed and the cat scrambled away, disappearing under the porch. Mrs. Ryan bounded down the steps, swiping her hands on her apron as she came. "Gabe!"

He released my hand and met his mother halfway. The top of Mrs. Ryan's head barely reached Gabe's shoulder. Doubtless used to farmwork and slim as a result, her flowered cotton dress looked overlarge. Locks of gray hair escaped hairpins, and curls as unruly as Gabe's coiled around her sun-browned face.

Gabe swept her up and swung her around, hugging her tight and both of them laughing. He set his mother down and kissed her cheek. "You get prettier every day, Mom."

Blue eyes peered up at him in mock sternness. "Nonsense. I get grayer and more wrinkled and both of us know it. Now introduce me to your friends."

Henderson, Dora, and I had remained clustered next to the car, out of the way while Gabe greeted his mother. Dora threaded her arm with mine and moved forward with a smile, leaving me no choice but to follow. Henderson trailed behind.

"Mom, this is Officer Marshall Henderson and Miss Isadora Bobet. Miss Bobet is helping me with my investigation."

Henderson doffed his hat and nodded. "Nice to meet you, Mrs. Ryan."

Dora smiled and extended her hand. That she didn't hesitate to touch Gabe's mother said much. "I'm very pleased to meet you, Mrs. Ryan. Gabe speaks very highly of you. Thank you for having us here on such short notice."

"Call me Moira." His mother shook Dora's hand and smiled. "Living this far out from the city I don't get to meet many of Gabe's friends or the people he works with. This is a pleasure."

Gabe stepped closer and took my hand, so that I stood with him, not apart. He looked into his mother's eyes and smiled. "And this is Delia Martin. I plan to bring Delia back, so be nice to her."

Mrs. Ryan's smile faltered and she looked from Gabe's face to mine, and back into his eyes. Wanting to be sure, as I'd wanted to be sure.

She must have found the reassurance she needed. Her smile brightened, became warm and welcoming, and she grasped my hand. "I'm very happy to meet you, Delia. Don't pay any attention to Gabriel, he's a terrible tease. I have every intention of being nice."

"It's a pleasure to meet you as well. Gabe's told me wonderful things about you." I couldn't resist some teasing of my own. "And never fear, Mrs. Ryan. I seldom pay attention to Gabe."

Gabe blushed, bright red blotches showing above his collar and burning his cheeks. Not laughing at him was difficult.

His mother did laugh. "Come inside now, all of you. Dinner's almost ready and Matt will be along any minute."

Gabe took the steps two at a time and held the door open. "Where is Dad?"

"Delivering eggs to some of his customers." Mrs. Ryan touched his arm in passing. "He left early so he could get back and have most of the day free for you."

The inside of the farmhouse was larger than I'd pictured, but still homey and comfortable. Chintz pillows in pale green and yellow graced a dark-green roll-backed sofa. A rag rug in the same colors sat just inside the door, and a large carpet woven in black and gold covered the center of the front-room floor.

Photographs sat in small, oval frames on the mantel over the fireplace. Some were pictures of Gabe as a boy and I longed to go closer and investigate. Manners kept me in the overstuffed chair Mrs. Ryan offered. She took coats and hats back to the bedroom, and insisted on treating Gabe like a guest despite his protests. "Sit with your friends and keep them company. Dinner will be on the table in a few minutes."

Gabe perched on the arm of my chair and leaned in to whisper. "I told you my mother would like you."

"So you did." I ignored Dora's imploring glance heavenward. If we were being adorable again she'd just have to endure. "With luck I won't run out of charm before your father arrives."

A dog began to bark, the sound faint at first, but growing

louder. The creak and squeak of springs bouncing over ruts in the dirt road drew closer as well, cumulating in the backfire of a motorcar engine. I leaned to look past Gabe and through the front screen. A mud-splattered, Model-T truck was parked next to the police car and a large, flop-eared dog stood in the back, barking loudly.

"Lucky! Be quiet." The driver's door slammed shut, rocking the truck. Matt Ryan leaned into the bed and worked at untying the rope holding the dog. The hound whimpered and licked Mr. Ryan's fingers, making it difficult to work the knots loose. "Hold still, Lucky. Hold still!"

I sat back and folded my hands in my lap. Meeting one parent I'd handled well, the prospect of conversation with two and finally meeting his father loosed a flock of hummingbirds in my stomach.

"I'm going to go help Dad. Sit tight, I'll be right back." Gabe started to get up, but he saw the alarm in my eyes and stopped. "Don't be nervous. He's gruff and makes a lot of noise, but he doesn't mean any harm. I promise he'll take to you right off."

Dora had claimed one end of the sofa and settled in to pose as if she sat on a throne of gold, not chintz cushions. She leaned forward to see Gabe's face, obviously amused. "Are you speaking about the dog or your father? You'd do a better job of putting Dee at ease if you made that clear."

It was absurd and irreverent, and exactly the right thing to say. The hummingbirds fled, letting me breathe. "Don't be silly. He's talking about the dog of course." I stood and waved Gabe to his feet, and out the door. "I'll go with you. I want to meet your father."

I stepped off the porch and shaded my eyes. Gabe's father was broader through the chest and a few inches shorter, but the two of them were cast from the same mold. If I could brush aside the years ahead and peer into the future, I was certain Gabe would look just the same: sun-browned, strong, and wearing his age lightly.

His father's eyes lit up at seeing Gabe and he rushed to greet him, leaving the dog to bark. "Gabe! You made it. I was afraid work might keep you away."

"We made it." Gabe grinned and held out his hand. "How are you, Dad?"

The last of my nervousness vanished watching Matt Ryan take the offered hand and pull Gabe into a bear hug. His eyes squeezed shut, the relief he felt at seeing his son hale and whole sitting raw on his face. More than anyone, he knew the dangers of Gabe's job. That his son was now the one facing those dangers changed things between them, but I suspected Matthew Ryan's need to protect Gabe hadn't changed.

Gabe and his father stepped apart, both still grinning. "Dad, there's someone I want you to meet. This is Delia Martin."

I took that as my cue, moving forward to offer my hand. "I've heard a great deal about you, Captain Ryan. It's a pleasure to finally meet you."

He wiped his hand on the front of his coveralls and glanced at Gabe before shaking mine. "Nice to meet you, Miss Martin. I'd like to return the compliment, but I'm afraid my son is rather tight-lipped when it comes to his friendships. Gabe hasn't spoken of you to me."

"Please, call me Delia." I wasn't at all sure how to approach Mr. Ryan, other than head-on. "I have high hopes that you and I can be friends as well. If there's anything you'd like to know about me, ask. I'm rather fond of your son and he claims to be fond of me as well, so I'm sure you'll be seeing me again. If we're to be stuck with each other, we might as well make the best of it."

His father grinned and clapped Gabe on the back. "Then it's

about time he brought you to meet us. Call me Matt, Delia. Let me finish up here and we can talk more. I don't want to make Moira hold dinner."

I put my hand out for the dog to sniff, the only member of the family whose friendship was still in question. Lucky licked my fingers and wagged his whole body, hoping to convince me to rescue him. His silky fur slid through my fingers. "Can I help with anything?"

"If you like." Matt held out a stack of empty wicker baskets, similar to what children carried for egg hunts at Easter. "If you thread the handles over your arm it's easier to carry the whole lot at once."

Gabe finished untying the dog. Lucky leapt to the ground, excited at finally being free and the chance to race in circles around all of us. Matt lifted out a nested stack of wooden trays, leaving the last of the baskets for Gabe. The dog knew the routine. Lucky led the way across the yard to the barn, stopping every few feet to make sure we were following and racing ahead again. He pranced in front of the door until we caught up.

"I dug out the files you asked about last night." Matt took the baskets off my arm, piling them in a large wooden bin just inside the barn door. "You and I have been over them a hundred times, son. Do you have a new angle to try?"

"I brought someone with me to look at them. A fresh perspective." Gabe caught my eye, nervous and unsure how his father would take things. "Miss Bobet worked with the police force in Atlanta and consulted on murder cases for seven years. Isadora lives in San Francisco now and she's volunteered to lend a hand. I have something new to show you, too, but that can wait until after dinner. I don't want to keep Mom waiting."

Matt nodded and made a noncommittal sound deep in his throat. It was too much to hope for that he'd let things pass that easily and I waited for him to question Gabe about Dora. He held off long enough to finish stacking the trays on a shelf. "What exactly did Miss Bobet do for the force in Atlanta? For that matter, what do you expect her to find in thirty-year-old files? Those cases are cold."

Gabe took a breath and braved the lion's den. "I'm not sure what she'll find. Maybe nothing, maybe something that will lead me to this man. Isadora's a spiritualist, Dad. She won't be looking for the same things as we did. I know you don't believe in those things, but give her a chance before you dismiss her. She's not a con artist or a fake. I give you my word."

"A spiritualist?" Matt yanked his hat off and ran fingers through his hair, the gesture a mirror of the one I'd seen Gabe make a hundred times. "God Almighty, Gabriel, have you lost your mind?"

"No. I haven't lost my mind." Gabe's voice was tight and controlled. I took his hand, letting him know I was there and presenting his father with a united front. "This is my case now and in my judgment, this is the right thing to do. At the very least, letting Dora look at the files can't do any harm."

Matt didn't attempt to keep the scorn off his face. "And just how much are you paying this miracle worker?"

I stepped forward, still clinging to Gabe's hand. Matt might stop and pay attention if I answered. "Nothing, not a dime. She's not doing this for money and I promise you, she's not a fraud. People Dora cares about are in danger from this killer." My voice cracked. "I'm in danger. And Dora refuses to stand idly by and do nothing. Hoping this man doesn't carry through on the threats he made won't stop him."

"He threatened you directly?" Matt's eyes widened and he raked fingers through his hair again, breathing faster. "When?"

"Yesterday, Dad." Gabe put an arm around my shoulders.

"He's following the same pattern he did when you were working the case. He left a letter addressed to Delia with the same kind of threats he made against Mom."

He outlined the story for his father: the false deliveryman, the confrontation with Officer Casey and Casey's subsequent disappearance, and the letter addressed to me, prominently displayed on my trunk. Matt looked up sharply when Gabe told of finding the book and badge hidden in my things. By the time Gabe finished, his mother could be heard calling, telling us that food was on the table.

"Your mother worked hard on this dinner. We shouldn't keep her waiting. After we eat you can show me the badge and book you brought. And I want to hear more about what Colin said about the hieroglyphics." Matt motioned us out the door and swung it closed behind us. "Your friend can look at the files, too. I don't have any faith that her hocus pocus will do any good. But you're right, letting her look can't do any harm. Just promise me that no one in the city will get word of this. I still have friends on the force and they'd never let me live it down."

"I promise, Dad." Gabe scuffed the dirt with the toe of his shoe and looked up to meet his father's eyes. "Jack knows why I'm here, but he won't say anything. Not a word to anyone else."

"All right, that's fair enough." We started toward the house and Matt shortened his stride to walk next to me. "I'm sorry you got tangled up in this mess, Delia. You can trust Gabe and his partner to do their best to get you clear again. Don't tell him I said this, but he's a good cop."

I glanced at Gabe and smiled. "I trust him. He is a good cop. And it's not Gabe's fault I'm involved. He's not to blame for any of what's happened to me."

Aileen's ghost appeared at Matt's side, pacing us. She was alone, dressed neatly as I'd first seen her and staring straight ahead.

I'd think her unaware of us, but that sense that let me experience her emotions told me that wasn't so.

She turned to me and her green eyes were anything but placid. I couldn't look away; Aileen's rage filled me to bursting. That her anger had something to do with Gabe's father was clear.

Matt hadn't saved her. She couldn't forgive him for that or for his failure to find the man who murdered her. But there was more to Aileen's anger, another layer beyond bitterness over being the killer's last victim.

The last until this man returned to San Francisco and began to kill again. Matt hadn't saved Aileen or any of the victims in the newest series of murders. He hadn't saved Aaron Casey.

Aileen's ghost blamed Matt Ryan for many things, that much was clear. What I still didn't understand was why.

CHAPTER 15

Delia

Dinner went well, a huge relief. I'd worried that Matt's doubts would make it difficult for him to speak with Isadora and put a strain on conversation, but I needn't have worried. He was pleasant if a trifle distant. I saw where Gabe learned his professional demeanor.

Dora was charming and restrained, but I'd worried less about her than Matt. She chatted about Sadie's wedding and minor society gossip, and helped me describe the fair to Gabe's mother. We both chimed in to help Moira convince Matt it was worth taking a trip to San Francisco for the exposition. Moira was obviously taken with Dora and I was glad. Friendship smoothed the way for many things.

Gabe hadn't been able to visit his parents for months. Neither he nor I wanted anything to spoil our visit for his mother, especially conflict over how to handle investigating a murder case. The hunt for this killer had shadowed most of Moira's life. One bright and happy meal with her son wasn't too much to give her.

Matt and Gabe talked baseball, pulling Henderson into the conversation without any trouble at all. Plans for expanding Matt's barns to raise ducks were also a topic of discussion. Mr. Ryan had conceived a clever scheme to supply young ducks to the markets and restaurants in Chinatown. Watching Gabe and his father trade ideas gave me a great deal of pleasure.

Henderson volunteered to help Moira clean up and do the dishes. I doubted that Marshall knew how much time he'd spend in kitchens when he joined Gabe's squad, but I didn't think he minded, either. He seemed right at home and I imagined him helping his mother the same way. We left him heaping scraps into a tin bowl for the dog, happily keeping Moira company.

The afternoon was warm, the sky clear and free of clouds. Bright sunlight washed out colors in the farmyard and on buildings, sharpened shadow-corners to a knife edge. Dust hung above the horizon in hazy brown clouds. Farmers plowed their fields out of sight, evidence of their labor painted on the sky for us to see.

Matt unlocked the door to the carriage house office, going ahead to turn on his desk lamp and the bigger lights hanging from the ceiling. We'd need all that light. He'd sectioned off the space, but the room was still large, with high shadowed ceilings. The double, swinging doors made to accommodate four horse carriages had been boarded over to become a windowless wall.

Shelves and deep cabinets filled the space on either side of the door and the entire back of the office. Matt's desk sat against the wall opposite the door. The only window, and the only source of natural light, was right above the desk.

A cage of iron bars was bolted to the frame and encased the window glass. Breaking the glass wouldn't give access to the office or the files stored inside. It gave me pause to realize that even this far out in the country, Matt felt the need to put up barricades to safeguard the evidence he'd collected. His decision not to store his records in the house took on new meaning.

In the center of the room a long, low pine table held a double line of pasteboard evidence boxes. Dates were marked on each one in thick, black grease pencil. The oldest boxes were scuffed and faded, and showed hard use. Gabe's stories of going over letters and reports with his father hundreds of times were illustrated by each bent corner and smeared grease pencil date.

Matt rummaged inside his desk. He took a folded sheet of clean butcher's paper out of a drawer and covered the desk blotter. "Let's see what you found, son. Put them here where the light's best."

"The book has an inscription in the front, but I'm not sure if that means anything or not. Maybe you'll recognize a name that I don't." Gabe unbuttoned his jacket pocket and glanced at Isadora. "Are you all right with this?"

"I'll be fine, Gabe." She gave him a fond smile and moved to stand near the table in the middle of the room. "Distance will help, but I don't want to go too far. I'm curious to hear what Captain Ryan thinks about what the killer left for you."

Gabe removed the book and the badge from a creased brown envelope. The badge was brighter than last I'd seen, much of the corrosion polished away. He laid them on the butcher paper and stood back, giving his father room. I stood with Gabe, hopeful that Matt could shed some light on this part of the puzzle.

"Son of a bitch." Matt grabbed the badge and held it under the desk lamp, turning it to catch the light and inspecting the back as well. He glanced at me and gave a shame-faced apology. "Beg your pardon, Delia, Miss Bobet. I forgot there were ladies present. This was my partner Thom's badge number."

"Thomas Brennan, your partner?" Gabe's expression changed, curiosity replaced by his cautious policeman's face. He reached for my hand and held tight. "I remember you telling me he quit the force during the investigation. I don't remember why."

"I never told you. I didn't think his reasons for leaving had anything to do with your case." Matt clamped his hand around the badge, squeezing until his knuckles turned white and bloodless. "Parker was a sergeant back then, same as Thom. The two of them were at odds from the day Parker transferred into our squad. Twice he tried to bring Thom up on charges for taking bribes. They didn't stick because they weren't true. Parker went after Thom's son Ethan next."

I'd heard of Parker from both Jack and Gabe. Captain Parker seemed to relish making life difficult for both of them, but Gabe was never able to explain why, other than Parker's hints of conflict with Matt in the past. I'd thought it especially petty to continue a feud with the father by visiting trouble on the son. Listening to Matt's story, Parker's sins multiplied.

"And that caused your partner to leave the force." Gabe's voice remained calm, nonchalant, but his arm was stiff with tension. "What reason did Parker give for going after Sergeant Brennan's son?"

Matt looked up sharply. "I taught you how to question a witness, Gabriel. Don't think for one minute I don't know when I'm being interrogated. Thom's wife died when the boy was five. His son was all he had left and Parker was trying to ruin the boy's life. I didn't blame Thom for packing up or moving out of state."

The two men stared at each other, expressions grim and bordering on angry. Gabe broke the silence first. "Dad, this is my case now. My responsibility. There's a connection between the killer and Thom Brennan's badge. I can't afford to brush it off as coincidence or not question why he left it in Delia's trunk. I wouldn't be doing my job otherwise. Did the killings stop before or after Thom Brennan left town?"

"He's not your killer, Gabe." Matt sighed and dropped the badge on the desktop. It spun in a circle, brass glinting in the lamplight. "Thom died more than five years ago. His sister wrote to me and sent a copy of the obituary from the paper in Glenrock. He bought a cattle ranch out in Wyoming after he left San Francisco. Thom was still living there when he died."

"I had to ask." Some of the stiffness bled out of Gabe's stance, but not all. He was still troubled by something. "Thom's son, Ethan, he couldn't have been that old. What made Parker go after a boy?"

"I never figured that out." Matt picked up the book and flipped through, glancing at a few pages before tossing it back on the desk. "Ethan was sixteen, maybe seventeen at the time. He worked on the docks and I guess he got in fights with the older men once in a while. You know how it works there, Gabe. Nothing I heard from Thom or anyone else made it sound serious enough for Parker to go to the chief the way he did. Thom resigned the next day."

Gabe let out a long, hissing breath. "We'll talk about this more after Dora's had a chance to look at the files. I'm missing a connection between Sergeant Brennan and the killer, other than Thom being your partner. I'd really like to know how this man got his hands on the badge to start with. This killer never does anything without a reason. Maybe between all of us we can figure out why he wants me to have it."

"Maybe. You have more faith in there being reasons for things than I do." Matt gestured toward Dora, mouth twisted as if he couldn't rid himself of a sour taste. "I think your friend started without you. You've got faith in her, too."

Dora circled the long pine table at a distance, wary as a cat with a snake in the garden. Her heels clicked on the flagstone floor, each steady and determined step echoing off the ceiling. Whiffs of her lilac perfume mixed with the dry scent of dust. The smell made my nose itch and I fought hard not to sneeze.

Matt perched on the front edge of his desk to observe, arms folded over his chest and frowning. Gabe and I kept well back and out of her way, too, but not for the same reasons. Ghosts tended to cluster near me and I feared having them too near might interfere with what Dora sensed. I didn't want to be the cause of this attempt failing.

She came to a halt on the farside of the table. Dora concentrated on the pasteboard boxes as if they could speak. Perhaps for her they did.

Her shoulders relaxed the smallest fraction. Dora glanced at Matt and smiled. "Try not to be quite so loud while thinking about me, Captain Ryan. The money-grubbing charlatan can hear you and it's very distracting."

I told myself sternly I wasn't allowed to laugh and bit my lip to keep from doing so. Matt Ryan's face turned the most spectacular shade of red. He stared, first at Dora and then at Gabe.

Gabe lounged against the wall, hands shoved deep in his pockets. He shrugged. "Don't look at me, Dad. I told you she wasn't a fraud. You should work at trying to believe that."

Dora winked at me and went back to circling the table, arm outstretched to hover over the boxes. She paused in front of different pasteboard cartons, but never touched them before moving on again. The third time around the table, her pauses were longer and the expression on her face strained. "Gabe, be a dear and help me for a moment. I'm going to show you which boxes are safest for me to work with. Stack the rest against that back wall, please."

Gabe moved all but four of the boxes to the far end of the room. He and Dora circled warily around each other, each careful not to accidentally brush against the other and send sparks shooting between them. I knew full well what they were doing and why, but Matt was clearly puzzled by the odd dance to keep out of each other's way. Unless he asked, I thought it best not to attempt an explanation. Disapproval radiated from Gabe's father as it was.

"Delia, I need you as well." Dora motioned me to the table.

She kept her back to Gabe's father and spoke quietly. "It seems I was too optimistic about how much the killer's presence and the victim's pain would fade. I did what I could to prepare, but I never expected this much anger. Not after thirty years. I'd planned to keep you out of this. Now I don't see another choice."

"Tell me what to do." I wasn't eager to touch the belongings of long-dead victims, the killer's letters, or riffle through reports detailing the conditions under which a body was found. Subjecting Isadora to the pain appealed to me even less.

"The less I handle some of the items in these boxes the better, otherwise fainting is a very real possibility. I doubt that would overly impress Captain Ryan." She shut her eyes and concentrated. "The box on the far right, open that one first. Her name isn't on them, but the files about Aileen Fitzgerald's murder are inside. Some of her belongings are inside as well, her ring and some buttons. You'll know when you find them. Lay everything out on the table. We'll go from there."

Jack's father had never reported Aileen missing for reasons of his own and the police had never found her body. There was nothing to connect Aileen Fitzgerald to the letters taunting Matt or the items sent as proof the killer held another victim. Of course her name wasn't on the file.

I scolded myself soundly for trembling. After all these months of wondering about Aileen, of having her ghost following me night and day, the thought of touching things that belonged to her in life shouldn't come near to undoing me. That was silly and I knew it. Isadora's wan face and the strain around her eyes gave stark testimony that this was much worse for her.

Lifting the lid sent the odor of musty old paper and smells I couldn't name into the air. Dora was right. I knew which envelopes and files contained Aileen's things as soon as I touched them: a small wooden box, a thick folder stuffed with papers, the now familiar pale blue stationery, and a small brown envelope, full of lumps I took to be a ring and buttons.

Three more times I did as Isadora instructed, lifting out files or envelopes, and spreading them out on the scratched and gouged pine table. Dora knew the name of a victim in each box and what scraps of their lives remained to tell their tale. My hand went to the right files each time. I didn't know whether I acted under silent guidance from my ghost or Isadora's influence. I wasn't certain I wanted to know.

Gabe cleared the boxes off the table once I'd finished. The four piles left behind struck me as very sad, a poor, cold memorial to symbolize a person's life. I desperately wanted justice for all of them, for Aaron Casey and all the other victims I didn't know. This man left too much grief and terror in his wake. That needed to end.

Dora threaded her arm through mine. "I'm going to ask one more enormous favor of you, but only if you're willing. I'd like you to act as a buffer between me and the victim's belongings. There's no danger, Dee, but I can't say for certain how uncomfortable this will make you. You're sensitive enough I can't predict that with any accuracy."

My first night back in San Francisco I'd walked through ghost after ghost in the train station, experienced the death of person after person. I could think of little worse than reliving someone burning alive. Bravery grew a bit easier in the face of that. "I've survived living with ghosts most of my life, I can survive this. How do we start?"

"Ghosts? Now you're dragging ghosts into this?" Matt scowled and moved away from his desk. He looked between me, Dora, and Gabe, all of us unsmiling and sober, and shook his head. "Never mind. You've all lost your minds if you believe that load of hogwash. Get this circus over with. I'd like to talk to Gabe in private."

Dora gave Matt her brightest, most guileless smile. "I understand your skepticism, Captain Ryan, but there's no need to insult Delia and your son. Perhaps I can convince you to apologize. Would you have more faith in my hocus pocus if I told you exactly how this murderer hurt each of these four women? How much pain they suffered at his hands, the bones he broke, or how long it took each of them to die? Or perhaps you'd like a description of what it was like for Sarah Miles as he cut her heart out. I can do that for you."

Matt's jaw tightened and his ruddy complexion turned ashen. "No one other than Thom and I knew about what happened to Sarah Miles. Her father was a fellow police officer. We kept the condition of the body out of the files so he wouldn't know. Finding her dead was hard enough on her parents." The conviction in his eyes that Dora was a fake began to crack. "I never told Gabe, either. Is this the kind of thing you did for the department in Atlanta?"

"This is exactly what I did for them and equally as painful." Dora's smile faded and she held my arm tighter. "I came here to help Gabe discover this man's identity. I'd appreciate you staying quiet so I can get on with it."

Dora turned her back on Matt and ignored the muttered conversation he had with Gabe. I had a harder time pretending not to hear. Matt's tone was distinctly sharp and unhappy, Gabe's expression tight and controlled. I felt partly responsible.

"Delia? Did you hear me?"

I blushed and shook my head. "Sorry. What should I do?"

"Open your hand and lay your palm flat on top of each item. I'll put my hand over yours." She wiped her palm on her skirt. "You're already attuned to Aileen. We'll start with the killer's letters from her file. Maybe we'll get lucky and not have to go any further."

She didn't believe that nor did I. I sucked in a deep breath and set my palm on the small stack of blue envelopes. Nothing happened. Not until Isadora laid her hand over mine.

Jumbled images filled my head, boats on the bay and a house near the water, and flashes of the face I'd seen in my dreams, a man with cold blue eyes, dark hair and a chipped front tooth. Each glimpse chilled my blood and brought a stab of pain behind my eyes. Uncomfortable, but bearable. I hoped it wasn't any worse for Dora.

We moved from small pile to small pile, each group of letters tied to a different victim. The angle I saw his face from was different, the light sometimes behind or to the side, but I'd no doubt I saw the same man each time. This was the face of Aileen Fitzgerald's murderer, the same man who'd killed all the people in Matt and Gabe's files.

The pale blue envelope on the stack marked with Sarah Miles's name was marred with rusty brown stains, larger streaks smeared and smudged on the corners. I laid my palm on top as I had with all the rest. All the agony of Sarah Miles's death was concentrated in that one small square of paper. I jerked my hand away immediately, cradling it to my chest and panting for breath. "Oh, God . . . oh, God."

Gabe frowned and started toward me, but Dora waved him back. She put an arm around my shoulders and whispered in my ear. "I can do this alone if need be, Dee. Just say if the pain is too much."

"No. I'm all right." I scrubbed my palm against my skirt, the gesture a twin of Isadora's. Breathing was easier with her arm on my shoulders. "I was surprised, that's all. I'll finish what I started."

"This one will be the hardest for both of us. More of Sarah Miles's presence remains and she didn't go easily." Dora smiled, but that did nothing to lessen the strain and fatigue in her face. "Together, then."

Our hands came to rest on the envelope simultaneously. Pain overwhelmed all else, at least at first. Images were sharper when they came and focused on the killer's face. Sarah Miles memorized everything about the man murdering her, every scar and imperfection in his features. She held tight to the anger of being helpless and not being able to fight free. She carried that rage into the grave.

Anger grew in me as well. I understood why Gabe and Jack spoke of this man as a butcher. He'd taken his time with Sarah Miles.

What the dreams and glimpses of Aileen's memories hadn't shown was how big he was, tall and broad-shouldered. Muscles in his arms told of days at hard labor. Her killer was very young, not much past boyhood. His pale blue eyes were even colder and spoke of nothing but death, his face unsmiling and marked by deep, fresh scratches. Sarah had hurt him. I took grim satisfaction in that.

And Sarah Miles's memories were strong even after thirty years, as if her blood splashed on cheap paper held the essence of all she'd struggled to remember, all the rage she'd nursed. I suddenly knew who the murderer was with a certainty that startled me. Ethan Brennan had killed all these women. Ethan Brennan was still murdering people.

Sarah's father was a policeman. She'd known him, too.

Isadora pulled my hand away with hers. The room spun in dizzying circles and I held the table edge to keep from falling. I couldn't rid myself of the pain, the feel of his knife cutting through Sarah's skin and her terror. Sucking in air as quickly as I could unsettled my stomach more. I stumbled along the length of the table, out the door, and behind the carriage house to be sick in the weeds.

Gabe followed. He wrapped an arm around my middle, holding me up until I'd stopped heaving. I was embarrassed, shaking and sicker than I could remember being since childhood. Spitting to clear the bitter taste from my mouth was even more humiliating, but it was that or vomit again.

He helped me into the patch of shade stretching out from the carriage house. With the wall at my back and his hand on my arm I could stand, but only barely. Sliding down rough clapboard siding to the ground was a real danger.

Gabe wiped my face and mouth with a handkerchief, his professional mask and any semblance of calm shattered. "Are you all right? Talk to me, Dee. You're scaring the hell out of me."

How naïve I'd been hit home. There were worse things in the world, much worse, than the brush with death contained in a ghost's touch. "No, I'm not all right. I may never be all right again. Sarah was in so much pain and . . . and he kept hurting her. But she fought him until she didn't have any strength." I burst into tears, drowning in Sarah Miles's memories. "Ethan Brennan killed her. He murdered all those people. That's why Thom Brennan left town. He knew, Gabe, and he lied to your father. He knew."

Gabe stared, reaction held in check, searching my face for the core of truth that would let him believe. I was a sniffling, tear-stained mess, but I didn't flinch or look away. I was asking for a great deal of trust.

"Are you certain?" Gabe didn't ask how I knew or for proof, but his job demanded he hear the answer. People's lives, including my own, hung on finding this man.

And both of us knew what this would do to his father. Neither of us relished hurting him, Gabe least of all.

"Yes. Sarah Miles knew him." I swiped the heel of my hand across my eyes. "Ethan is the man you're looking for. Dark hair, pale blue eyes, and a chipped front tooth. Ask your father."

Gabe pulled me into his arms. He petted my hair and let me cry on his shoulder, but didn't offer false assurances or try to pretend the revulsion crawling over my skin wasn't real. But he'd seen enough of the killer's handiwork to build nightmares of his own. He wouldn't dismiss mine.

Gabe

Gabe couldn't decide which scared him most, how shaken and ill Delia was, or the prospect of telling his father Thom Brennan had lied.

He couldn't have talked Delia out of helping Isadora and wouldn't have tried. She'd been determined not to let Dora tackle the files alone. But he'd never wanted this case, his job, to touch her this deeply. Holding her was the only way Gabe knew how to help, other than giving her time. Time might be the only cure, letting the impact of what she'd experienced soften. Living through the days after the quake had been like that for him. He never forgot, but remembering got easier.

His father came around the corner, Dora leaning hard on his arm. She was shaky and pale, but on her feet. Her full attention was on Matt Ryan, speaking to him in low, urgent tones that kept Gabe from hearing what she said.

He'd pushed thoughts of Dora into the background, too consumed with Delia's collapse to worry about both of them at once. Concern hit him full force now. If Delia was shaken this badly, by rights Isadora should be shattered. Likely she was, but she'd had a lifetime of practice hiding pain. What he saw on the surface wasn't the entire story. His respect for her resilience rose another notch.

Frazzled was the only word that fit his father's appearance and demeanor. The haunted, lost look filling Matt Ryan's eyes was one he'd seen each time they went through files or talked about old cases, but a hundred times worse. Gabe didn't need to be told that Dora had broken the news about who the killer was and that, somehow, she'd convinced his father to believe. The anguished expression on his father's face was enough.

That his father had stopped scoffing long enough to listen was nothing short of miraculous.

"I owe you and Delia both an apology, son." His father wouldn't meet his eyes, staring resolutely at some point near Gabe's shoes instead. "I've already told Isadora how sorry I am for what I said to her. Your mother's always said that I dig my feet in like a Missouri mule about all the wrong things. I should have pushed Thom harder for an explanation, but I trusted him. He was my partner."

Thom Brennan had been more than his father's partner. The two men had been best friends both on and off the job for fifteen years. He couldn't imagine how he'd feel if Jack betrayed him. "You did what you thought was right at the time, Dad. No one can blame you for that."

"I can blame myself." His father wiped a hand over his face and sighed. "I could have stopped Ethan all those years ago. People died because of me, Gabriel. Probably more than the ones we know about. I was so damn blind with hating Parker I shut out everything he said. If I'd been half the cop I thought I was, I'd have listened."

Dora patted his father's arm. "You can't change the past, Matthew. Gabe knows who to look for now and that makes all the difference. Let's get Delia back to the house so she can lie down."

Delia stepped away from him, shaky and sniffling, but able to stand. "No need to fuss, I just need a few minutes. I'll be fine."

"Nonsense. Never turn down a chance to be pampered." Isadora swayed and the small flush of color remaining in her face bleached away. Gabe's father caught her before she fell, wrapping an arm around Dora's waist and holding her up. She shut her eyes and licked her lips, swallowing hard. "If Dee is going to decline the offer, perhaps I should lie down instead. I'm sure Moira won't mind."

His father clucked over Dora, sounding like one of the brood hens in the yard. "No, Moira won't mind. Let's get you inside the house. Slow and careful now."

Gabe pulled Delia deeper into the shade and back into his arms. He held her quietly for a moment, cringing at the small catch in her breath and half-swallowed sobs. "I can't imagine what you and Dora go through, or what experiencing someone else's suffering is like. Seeing the aftermath is bad enough. Promise me something, Delia. Don't shut me out. Let me know when the pain is too much for you."

"I'd rather not make dealing with death and suffering a lifelong habit. Not that I've been given a choice so far." Her voice was hoarse and still thick with tears. "But I'm not a hothouse flower. I don't want to be treated as such."

"I don't intend to treat you like one." He brushed fine strands of hair off her face. "All I'm asking is that you don't hide how much it hurts. Let me help sometimes."

Delia stepped out of his arms. She dabbed at her eyes with his soggy handkerchief. "That works both ways, Lieutenant Ryan. I'll promise if you will."

"You have my word on it. We'll help each other." He wrapped an arm around her shoulders and smiled. "Mom will start to worry soon. We should go back to the house."

"That might be wise." She put a hand to her stomach and grimaced. "Perhaps I do need to lie down. I could rest up a bit before sleeping on you all the way home."

"Tell me if I go too fast." That she was making jokes was a relief. Gabe shortened his steps and let her set the pace. Delia didn't lean on him much, but she let him help when necessary.

It was a start. He wouldn't ask for more.

CHAPTER 16

Gabe

Gabe studied the street map on his office wall. Map pins, black for his father's cases and white for his, marked the locations where each of Ethan Brennan's victims had been found. The rounded tops reminded him of tombstones, worn down by wind, rain, and time. Appropriate given the circumstances. He kept hoping that if he stared long enough, the widely spaced pins would resolve into a pattern.

All he'd managed so far was to give himself a headache. Ethan had left victims in every part of the city, from the shipping docks and alleys near the bay, to Chinatown and every well-to-do neighborhood in San Francisco. There was no pattern Gabe could find, no cluster of victims left in one district or obvious hunting grounds. Ethan flitted around the city, a dragonfly that never settled among the cattails.

A cursory knock was all the warning Gabe had before his partner charged in and swung the door shut again. Jack brandished a sheaf of telegrams in his hand. "We finally heard back from the sheriff in Glenrock."

"Why do you bother to knock, Jack?" He counted black and

white pins again. Fifteen bodies for his father, eight for him, and twice that many letters claiming victims they hadn't found. "It only slows you down."

"Decorum, why else?" He dropped the stack of paper on Gabe's desk. "Come take a look at these."

One more quick survey convinced him the map wasn't going to yield its secrets easily. He sank into his creaky desk chair, feeling far older than thirty. "Did they find anything at the ranch?"

Jack dragged the visitor's chair over and made himself comfortable. He flipped through the telegrams, plucking some from the pile and handing them to Gabe. "Six graves so far, all within a mile or less of the house. No one from town's gone missing, so the sheriff is pretty convinced the bodies belong to drifters or people passing through no one would miss. Thom Brennan's ranch is over forty-five hundred acres. Leeds is afraid his men will find dozens of graves."

"They will. Ethan moved his hunting ground, but he never stopped killing." The Glenrock sheriff's description of the graves and the bodies was detailed and extremely thorough. All male from the clothing and effects found in the graves, and all older murders with bodies in advanced stages of decomposition. Likely they were men looking for work or travelers who met the wrong person on the road. The sheriff's theory seemed valid. "Have they started tearing up the floor of the house yet?"

Jack held out another telegram. "They didn't have to. Leeds ordered a search of all the buildings on the property first. One of his deputies fell through the floorboards of an old barn on the south end of the ranch. Sheriff Leeds says the barn was used to store winter feed for the cattle. They found a room dug out under the floor just like the one in Delia's dream."

Gabe slumped back in his chair and rubbed his throbbing temples. A room just like the one where he killed Jack's mother,

Sarah Miles, and who knew how many others. Neither of them wanted to say it, but they both knew. Hidden away somewhere in the city, Ethan had a new room. "I don't suppose his deputies found any photographs of Ethan. Knowing what he looks like now would make finding him a hell of a lot easier."

"All the photos from the house are on a train and on their way to San Francisco. The box should arrive in a couple of days." Jack neatened the stack of paper, fiddling to align the corners just right. "Sheriff Leeds can't tell us if any of the pictures are of Ethan or not. He never met either of the Brennans."

"Dad will know. I'll send a car to bring him into the city tomorrow. He can stay with me for a day or two. Helping might make him feel better." Gabe rummaged through the paper tray on the corner of his desk until he found the duty roster for the week. "Send Lawrence, Schaffner, and Polk. Tell them to draw straws for who stays with my mother. I don't want her on the farm alone. Dad refused protection, but he can't argue about officers looking after Mom."

"I'll tell them to help her with the chores, too. Feeding chickens and collecting eggs won't hurt them." Jack continued to arrange the telegrams, making minute adjustments. "If I thought Esther could survive the trip, I'd move her, Annie, and Sadie out to your parent's house until this is over. Delia and Isadora, too, for that matter. At least then he'd have a harder time getting to them."

He'd had the same idea and talked it over with Delia. Turning his father's isolated farm into a fortress was safer than his men having to treat every tradesman or stranger out for a stroll as a threat. Delia had agreed that they'd all be better off outside the city, but Esther's fragility was a stumbling block none of them could overcome. "Ethan won't get anywhere near Sadie or Delia, or Isadora for that matter. We'll make sure they stay safe."

"No, you're right. I'm worrying too much." Jack wandered over to stand in front of the map, staring the way Gabe had earlier. "Sadie's got her heart set on a church wedding and having her mother there. It's important to her, but I get a sick feeling in the pit of my stomach each time I think about all the people at the church. All the strangers. Any one of them could be Ethan Brennan and I'd never know."

A sharp knock rattled the frosted glass in the pine-framed door. "Lieutenant Ryan?"

Gabe recognized both the voice and the broad-shouldered silhouette. "Come in, Rockwell."

Jack turned away from the map, hands in his pockets and perfectly composed. His partner might let Gabe see how he felt, but never the men serving under them.

Lon Rockwell ushered a slight, dark-haired boy of about twelve or thirteen into the room ahead of him. The boy held a battered cap in one hand and the other clutched the strap of a newsboy's bag slung over his shoulder. His jacket and trousers were fairly clean, and the holes in his shoes patched. Gabe figured the boy had a home to go to at night and a mother to look after him.

"Lieutenant, Sergeant Fitzgerald, this is Jeff Murdock. I've known him going on a year now. His regular spot to sell papers is on my beat, right out in front of the Ferry Building." Rockwell patted the boy's shoulder. "Jeff's a good boy. Never causes trouble and takes his earnings home to his ma every night. It's just the two of them since his pa died last year. When he caught up to me this evening and asked if I knew you, I figured you should talk to him."

Gabe moved around to the front of his desk, sitting on the corner so he didn't loom over the boy. Rockwell wouldn't drag Jeff downtown and into the station without a damn good reason, especially now. He'd have wagered his far-distant pension that reason was Ethan Brennan. "It's a pleasure to meet you, Jeff. This is my partner, Sergeant Fitzgerald."

Jack flipped the visitor's chair around and scooted it closer to the newsboy. His partner straddled the seat, putting himself nearly at eye level with Jeff. Gabe sat back and let him take the lead. If anyone could put the boy at ease, Jack could.

"Good to see you, Jeff." Jack smiled and gestured toward the canvas newsboy bag. "What paper do you work for?"

"*The Examiner.* Lots of folk like to read on the ferry ride. A big paper lasts longer so I sell more." He pulled back against Rockwell, wary and scared. "Lon said I won't get in no trouble coming here. He promised."

"You're not in trouble." Jack grinned and raked fingers through his unruly hair, so that it stood up curly and wild. He looked younger that way, less like a cop and more like someone the boy would play stickball with. "If Lon vouches for you, that's good enough. We just want to get to know you."

Rockwell patted the boy's shoulder. "Go ahead and tell them the story you told me. Remember what I said, take your time and don't feel you need to rush."

Jeff stuffed his cap in a back pocket. "The noon ferry was gone, so there weren't many people around. I found a shady spot to sit and eat, hidden up next to the wall. I try to stay out of the way so I don't get bothered. My ma sends something with me near everyday. Says a boy my age needs to eat. That I work hard and shouldn't go the whole day on an empty belly."

Gabe smiled, matching Jack's friendly manner near as he could and burying impatience deep. Pushing the boy would frighten him and likely make Jeff forget important things. "Your mother's right. I ate all the time when I was your age and I didn't work half as hard. Did something happen while you were having dinner?"

He nodded, hazel eyes large and solemn in his grime-smudged face. "Yes, sir. A man came up and asked if he could hire me for an important job. I didn't want to talk to him. Some of the older boys told me to watch out for men who get too friendly and want me to go off with them. I thought he was that kind at first, or meant to rob me of the coin I'd earned. I told him to let me be or I'd be yelling for the police."

"That was smart, Jeff." Rockwell ruffled the boy's hair. "You did exactly right."

"What happened then?" Jack rested his arms across the back of the chair and leaned forward, his posture eager and attentive. "Did he leave?"

"No, he stepped closer and bent down so he could see me better. He promised he weren't asking anything to get me in Dutch with the cops. Said he just wanted me to deliver a message and that'd he'd pay me two dollars for the job." Jeff jiggled on his toes and clutched the canvas strap tighter. All his attention was on Jack, one boy telling another about his scary but exciting adventure. Gabe would never understand how Jack worked his magic with witnesses, but he was always grateful. "I still felt funny, but there's whole weeks I don't make two dollars. So I said if all he wanted was message carrying, I'd do it. That's when he gave me money and told me to ask any cop on the street for Gabe Ryan. He said they'd know where to send me."

"Jeff found me soon as I came on duty, Lieutenant. I brought him straight here." Lon Rockwell's hands rested easy on the boy's shoulders, but his expression was anything but relaxed. The boy had seen Ethan Brennan's face. He was marked now, they all knew that. The only one who didn't know was Jeff.

Gabe added the boy and his mother to the list of people he needed to protect. He crouched in front of Jeff, back against the desk and hands resting easy on his knees. "Lon's right. You did exactly the right thing. What message are you supposed to give me?"

"I made certain not to lose it." The boy dipped a hand into the canvas bag and came up with a pale blue envelope. He held it out to Gabe. "He said to give you this. He said you'd know what to do with it once I handed it over."

He forced a smile and took the envelope. "Thank you, Jeff. I do know what to do with this." Gabe stood and met Rockwell's gaze. "Take Jeff into the patrolman's lounge and see what you can find for him to eat. Better yet, send a rookie out for food and I'll pay for it. Then have the desk sergeant dispatch some men to bring his mother here. I don't want her to worry about him. Sergeant Fitzgerald and I will want to talk to him again before he goes home."

"Yes, sir." Rockwell ushered the boy out. Gabe counted to a hundred, giving them time to get out of earshot and battling for calm. He lost.

"That evil son of a bitch. Brennan thinks he's untouchable." Gabe flung the envelope onto the desk blotter. He paced the length of the office, shoving down the urge to rage and punch things. Hitting the wall might make him feel better, but he was just as likely to break his hand in the process. "Using that little boy is supposed to remind me he can take anyone he wants."

"He can. We know his name, but nothing else has changed." Jack cleared his throat and dragged the visitor's chair back to the side of Gabe's desk. "But he's getting cocky and that's his first real mistake. Open the letter, Gabe. Let's see how much he plans to up the ante."

Gabe yanked his chair out and sat, disgusted and disheartened at the same time. San Francisco was still a hunting ground for Ethan Brennan. The city was full of visitors come to see the Pan Pacific, with more pouring in each day as the warmer days of summer began. Ethan was just another anonymous face in the crowd, with little to fear in terms of being caught.

A sense of futility infused itself in every gesture, but Gabe went through the procedure they'd set, covering the desk in clean paper and wearing cotton gloves to open the envelope. Using Jeff to deliver the letter canceled any chance of fingerprints on the outside, but he couldn't dismiss the possibility of Ethan making a mistake and leaving a trace of himself behind. They knew who he was now. They still needed evidence to tie him to the crimes.

Evidence that would send Ethan Brennan to the gallows.

The crisp black ink was the same, the sketched figures of Anubis and Osiris in the customary place instead of a signature, but the message from Ethan had changed.

"He's offering us a challenge, Jack. A sporting chance as he calls it." He passed the sheets of cheap paper to his partner. "Ethan's warning us he plans to kill two people at the fairgrounds during the fireworks exhibition on Fourth of July. If we find him in time, they get to live."

Jack read aloud. "'Two will be chosen from the crowd and taken for judgment in my father's court. The beast waits to consume hearts heavy with sin.'" He thumbed through the rest of the letter and handed it back. "I don't know why I wager against Dora, I always lose. I bet her that Ethan was faking the obsession with the court of the dead, but he really is a madman. No wonder she laughed and told Daniel to take my money. What are the chances of getting the mayor to close the fair on the Fourth?"

"Probably about the same as you winning a bet with Dora." A sharp pain behind his eye joined the throbbing in his temples. Supper might help, sleep definitely would. "I'm hoping Jeff can remember the man he saw well enough to give us a description. Talking to him is your job, he'll be more comfortable with you and Rockwell. I'll talk to Jeff's mother. Once the box from Sheriff Leeds arrives and Dad takes a look at everything, maybe we'll have an idea of what Brennan looks like. We have five days to come up with a plan."

Jack tugged at his mustache and frowned. "I don't trust this. Why give us warning this time?"

"I don't trust this either, he still thinks he's smarter than us. Ethan has something planned." Something to make them look like fools. Gabe unlocked his bottom drawer and added the newest letter to the file. He prayed he wouldn't have to add more pins to the map. "Let's go talk to Jeff. Maybe he left us some food."

"Not much chance of that, Lieutenant. He's a growing boy and a skinny one at that." Jack pulled open the door and waved him out. "You'll have to wait and ask Annie to feed you."

"That would be a real hardship, Sergeant. But if there's apple pie involved, I think I could bear up." Gabe's mood lightened at the thought of seeing Delia and eating in the kitchen with her. Another habit he'd settled into with her, one he dearly loved and wanted to make a permanent part of his life.

After nine years of mourning and dwelling on the past, planning a future with Delia was exciting, if just a bit frightening. That was another hardship he'd bear gladly. The rewards would be more than worth any attack of nerves.

Now that he'd started living again, Gabe didn't plan to stop.

Delia

I carefully printed another name from Sadie's list onto a pink envelope, stuffed a wedding invitation inside, and added it to the stack. Sadie labored over addressing the outer envelopes in a neat, rounded hand. We'd nearly buried the oval table in piles of vellum inserts, creamy RSVP cards, and rose-tinted reply envelopes. Even a small wedding required more paper and writing than I'd ever thought possible. Ink-stained fingers and paper cuts had become the norm for both of us.

Mine was the easier task. Sadie had insisted on lettering all the addresses herself, refusing my repeated offers to help. The more wedding chores she took on, the less time she had to dwell on her mother's illness or what danger Jack might be in at any moment. I sympathized. We shared the same fears, the same worries.

Sadie was better at diversion and distraction. I tended to brood. And I'd other things to dwell upon aside from my worry for Gabe.

Since the trip to Matt and Moira's farm, more ghosts had come to occupy our house. They were quiet and didn't do anything beyond watching me, but the numbers grew daily. Aileen had brought them in over the last week, made sure I saw each new addition, and vanished again. Each phantom followed me as Aileen did. I couldn't escape them.

No one needed to tell me that each new ghost was another of Ethan Brennan's victims. The truth of that squirmed under my skin, grubs burrowing deep in a fallen log. They wanted me to find where he'd abandoned their bodies and see them placed in proper graves, bringing their loved ones a measure of peace. Knowing what the ghosts wanted didn't tell me how to find their earthly remains. Dora was my sole hope in this regard.

The doorbell chimed. Annie was forbidden to answer the door on Gabe's orders, another restriction on our lives. Noah Baxter set his book on the floor and moved to the dining room entrance, hand on his gun. One of the other officers opened the door, greeting Isadora and her cadre of guards. Noah relaxed and went back to his book.

Dora began flirting shamelessly with the man in the entryway almost immediately. Sadie rolled her eyes and kept at her lettering. Charming and enthralling each man in Gabe's squad, no matter how old or young, was a temptation Dora didn't attempt to resist. I suspected all of the single men had succumbed to one degree or another, while the older, settled men recognized she wasn't serious. They played along in any case, all of them flattered even if they didn't choose to admit to it.

It was a game to Dora, her own form of distraction, and she never carried any flirtation too far. The stress of aiding Gabe and Jack took its toll and she grew thinner, wan, and more fragile each time I saw her. I had enormous respect for her strength, but even the very strong break. This case needed to end soon for all of us.

Isadora swept into the room, dressed in scarlet and gold, the ostrich plumes on her hat bobbing in time with her steps. She winked at me and turned to Noah Baxter. "Noah, please be a dear and ask Annie to bring us some tea. Delia and I have private things to discuss and much as I adore you, I'm going to ask you to leave. I've complete faith you can keep us safe from the entryway. Why don't you see if you can win your money back from Corey? He brought his deck of cards."

"I won't play cards with any deck Polk's had to himself for longer than a minute or two. That's how I lost in the first place." Baxter marked his place in the book with a red ribbon and set it on a side table. He held a chair for Dora, getting her settled and comfortable. "I'll have Annie fetch your tea, Miss Bobet. Should I tell her to bring milk as well as sugar?"

"You remembered!" Dora positively beamed, turning all her considerable charm on Baxter. He stood straighter, preening under her praise and attention. "How thoughtful you are, Noah. Yes, please ask Annie to bring the milk if you would. Perhaps a little something to snack on as well. I'm absolutely famished."

Sadie rolled her eyes again and I bit my lip to keep from laughing. Before her engagement to Jack, she'd behaved just as outrageously. Not that she'd admit to such behavior now, but I remembered well.

Baxter bustled away, eager to do what ever Isadora asked. She slumped back in her chair, shut her eyes, and rubbed her temples. "I am starving. And this day has been positively draining. Touring murder sites with your charming beau gave me a raging headache, Dee. I may need a little time to recover before we tackle your problem. How many ghosts are there?"

Closing my eyes helped me concentrate and separate the essence of one restless soul from another. What I saw with my eyes wasn't always true when it came to ghosts. Dora had shown me the trick of seeing with that other sense inside, leaving anything within the house to me as a way to hone my skill. How quickly I'd learned was a frightening blessing. "As near as I can tell, at least twenty, but I feel sure there are more and I just can't see them well enough to count. A great many of the ghosts cluster together. That makes distinguishing between them harder."

Dora winced. "Ghosts that clump that tightly are often buried in a common grave and the bones jumbled together. Sorting that when the time comes will be difficult."

Light played across the wall behind Dora, reflections and shimmers rippling as if a ghostly river flowed through the house. The ghosts of Ethan's victims kept their distance from Isadora as they did Annie, reluctant to approach her too closely.

I understood why with Annie, she'd threatened to send Aileen away often enough that all the ghosts feared attracting her notice. That wasn't the case with Dora, but try as I might, the reason eluded me. Perhaps they knew she was stretched to the edge of endurance and didn't want to drain her further. That the dead might show her compassion was as logical and probable as anything else involving the spirits in my life.

Annie carried in an oval tea tray with deep, raised sides. The tea service and a plate of cookies were nestled into the center, slices of pale yellow cheese, pieces of bread, grapes, and a dish of strawberries wedged into the space around the silver teapot. She set the tray on the one end of the table we hadn't filled with wedding debris.

"Go ahead and start in. I'll be back in a tick with milk and sugar for the tea, and a jug of cream for the berries." Annie wiped her hands on her apron and hurried off. "Be thinking if there's anything else you might want. I need to get lunch up to Miss Esther soon."

I piled cheese, bread and grapes on a plate and set it in front of Dora.

"Bless you, Dee." The skin under Dora's eyes was the bruised purple of ripe plums. "I'd no idea our tour of the city would drag on so long. I'd have made provisions otherwise."

Sadie put down her pen and blotted dry the freshly inked envelope. "Did you make any progress?"

Feigning no more than mild curiosity didn't fool me. Sadie wanted this over as much as any of us. Ethan's shadow loomed over her wedding and her life with Jack. Progress in finding him was of more than passing interest to her.

"If you mean did we find Ethan's lair, sadly the answer is no. He's scattered bodies and left traces of himself all over the city." Dora broke off tiny pieces of cheese, nibbling each one slowly. As ill as I'd been after touching evidence from Sarah Miles's death, I could easily imagine how Isadora felt. "The only new thing we learned for certain is that he'd been to Elaine Meadows's cottage more than once. Ethan might have been seen, or so Gabe hopes. He and Jack have men talking to the neighbors again."

"They have a description from the newsboy now. That should help." I settled across from Dora with my own plate. The little boy had spoken of a tall man, dressed in calf-high black boots, gray trousers, a black bowler hat, and a matching black wool coat. Hack drivers and cabbies dressed thus, a uniform of sorts they wore winter or summer. Working as a cabbie explained much about how Ethan moved about the city, unnoticed and unseen.

The man who'd watched me the night I met Gabe was dressed just the same. That Ethan might have been that near was too horrible to think on and I didn't dwell on the possibility, dismissing it as too wild of a chance. He couldn't have known who I was then or picked me out of the crowd. The Pan Pacific grounds were filled with cabbies looking for a fare, taking advantage of increased custom. Ethan hadn't hunted me. He hadn't.

"Having a vague idea of who to ask about will help, yes." Dora shrugged and popped a grape into her mouth. "But people seldom remember tradesmen or cab drivers, not unless they deal with them repeatedly or they've cause to remember. Ethan is much the same as the killers I helped track in Atlanta. He'll go out of his way to avoid giving people a reason to remember him."

"That's why Aaron Casey disappeared. Ethan made a mistake." Sadie pushed her chair back and stood. "I'm going up to sit with Mama and feed her lunch. The two of you can talk ghosts to your hearts content while I'm gone."

Annie brought in the rest of the fixings for tea as Sadie hurried toward the stairs. Time not spent on wedding preparations or with Jack, she spent with her mother. Each hour and minute was precious to her. None of us knew how much time was left to Esther.

By the time Dora finished her second cup of tea, color was returning to her face and sparkle to her eyes. "Now that I'm not ready to expire, we can talk about your problem. The timing puzzles me a bit. My first thought is that the victims should have begun to gather around you as soon as you returned home. That they didn't is the most troubling part of this for me. It worries me that Aileen's ghost appears to be gathering the victims in one place. She might be stronger than I'd imagined." She frowned and made a dismissive gesture. "Or perhaps it's nothing more than all this poking into murder scenes and evidence has stirred up the spirits.

I shouldn't go hunting for trouble. The most important thing is preventing you from being swamped by their demands. We can determine why later."

"I'd like to help them, Dora. Banishing the ghosts seems cruel, considering." I toyed with the grape stems lying on my plate, plucked clean and bare as winter branches. The sweet scent lingered, mingled with the stronger odor of ripe strawberries. Both smelled of summer. "If there's a way to find the bodies and see them buried, I'm willing to try."

She folded her arms, leaned back in her chair, and smiled. Long, pale fingers drummed against the scarlet of her sleeve, rustling the stiff fabric. I'd amused her, but the deep-rooted cynicism that was so much a part of Dora never went away. "That's why these spirits haunt you and not me. I'm not willing to assign pure motives to any ghost, much less one that appears as focused and determined as Aileen Fitzgerald. We've had this talk before, Dee. You can't let your soft heart overtake good sense when dealing with ghosts. Protecting yourself comes first."

"I was hoping to find a middle ground. Somewhere short of self-sacrifice and not as extreme as leaving Ethan's victims unburied for eternity." I shoved my plate away and folded my hands on the tabletop. "I'm not naïve enough to think this an easy task. And I recognize the necessity of waiting to find their bodies until after Ethan is caught. All I'm asking for now is a way to keep my sanity."

She narrowed her eyes and her drumming fingers fell still. "All right. We'll see how long it takes for you to learn to build walls. Shutting Aileen and the others out is something you need to learn in any case. I've said as much before and I'm relieved I don't have to force the issue."

Aileen came into view behind Sadie's chair, standing alone for once. My ghost's normal serene expression had vanished, replaced by naked rage that truly frightened me. Her anger filled the room, rising waves that flipped envelopes, reply cards, and vellum inserts off the table and swirling to the floor. The spirit river flowing across the wall swirled, glints and glimmers brightening.

Anger was a pressure in my chest and behind my eyes, thudding with each beat of my heart. That Isadora was the target didn't spare me. I couldn't breathe.

"I warned you once, spirit. You'd do best to heed that warning." Dora stood and stalked closer to the ghost, all her weariness falling away. The angry wind scattering wedding invitations parted around Dora and left her untouched. "You have no place among the living, no place in this house. I won't let you force your will on Delia. Leave before I send you away."

The pressure pinning me to the chair vanished abruptly along with Aileen's ghost. I shook and gasped for air, immensely glad not to be the center of their battle of wills any longer. My tea was cold, but I drained all that was left in my cup.

Isadora began gathering the wedding stationery blown to the floor. I sorted what she laid on the table, determined to set everything to rights before Sadie could see the mess. This was my fault. I'd let the ghost have the advantage for too long.

The only permanent damage was the bent corner of a reply card. I straightened the last stack of envelopes and sat across from Dora. "Tell me how to start. I've been too stubborn to admit it before now, but I'm completely at the mercy of Aileen's ghost. Sending her and the others away still feels wrong. I'd like to avoid that if possible. Teach me how to keep the upper hand."

Dora dug a cigarette and matches out of her bag, and struck the match on the underside of the dining-room table. "I'll make a deal with you. Don't tell Annie I strike matches on her table and I won't go on about having told you this ghost posed a danger. We'll call it even and go from there." She sucked smoke deep into her lungs and blew thin, blue clouds toward the ceiling. "We'll start with something easy and refine the method if needed. Think of a room that is yours alone, one you don't allow anyone to enter without permission. Now think about shutting the door. Keep opening and shutting the door until I tell you to stop."

By the time Dora was satisfied, my hands shook and we'd drained the large, silver teapot, but I could shut the ghosts out with only a bit of effort. The peace of feeling alone in my own body was worth the strain of learning.

She snubbed another cigarette out in a saucer. "Very good, Dee. I'll worry less now. And I promise, this will grow easier with practice."

"I keep hoping that once Gabe catches Ethan Brennan I can forget about ghosts haunting me. Going back to brief glimpses of spirits or seeing the odd ghost on the street would be just fine." I rolled my shoulders, trying to loosen muscles knotted tight. "Or are you saying I should prepare for a career in séances and fortune-telling?"

"Don't give up hope, you might get lucky. But I'd be lying if I said that was a sure thing. Once the door opens wide to the spirit realm, it seldom closes again." Dora came around the table and tugged me to my feet. "Come on, Dee. Annie keeps a bottle of brandy in the kitchen for me. You can drink tea while I get a head start on being able to sleep tonight."

"Do I have that to look forward to as well?"

"God forbid. You can place the blame for my debauchery on my bohemian lifestyle." The bright, charming smile was a lie, I saw the pain in Dora's eyes. She stopped pretending when I continued to regard her solemnly, waiting for the truth. "If you must know, I didn't drink at all until after John was killed. Finding the courage to send his ghost away was difficult and I spent a lot of time looking for the strength in the bottom of whiskey bottles. I'm not as strong as I pretend, Dee. Not near as strong."

I wanted to cry for her, but Dora wouldn't want that kind of sympathy. We were much alike that way. "I'm sorry. He must have meant a great deal to you."

"For a time, he meant everything." She smiled again, eyes bright with tears. "Let's get that tea now. Gabe will never forgive me if learning to deal with ghosts leaves you too ill to enjoy his company."

CHAPTER 17

Gabe

The small box from the Glenrock sheriff arrived half empty. Gabe fought to quell his disappointment and unpacked what little it contained: a few framed pictures of an older man, a boy who looked six or seven, and a faded portrait of a solemn young woman in a wedding dress. Books, ledgers, and letters written to names he didn't recognize filled the bottom of the pasteboard container. The house had been emptied of the majority of its contents when Thom Brennan died, furniture sold and personal effects shipped to his sister in Missouri. What little in the way of personal effects the sheriff found was stuffed in a battered strongbox in one of the bunkhouses.

His father was on the way to the city from Santa Rosa. Gabe wouldn't know for certain that the pictures and papers had any connection to the case until his father arrived. The thought that the contents of the box might be worthless in terms of identifying Ethan Brennan tied his stomach in knots. He was almost out of time.

Tomorrow was the Fourth of July. Every patrolman in his squad and every officer he could pull from stations around the city would be on the Pan Pacific grounds. He'd planned on having at least a third of the men dressed as tourists to blend into the crowd and the rest visibly patrolling in their uniforms, a show of force even Ethan couldn't ignore.

But the fair would be teeming with people, both residents of San Francisco and tourists from all over the world, all of them focused on enjoying the holiday. Such large crowds would attract every cabbie and hack driver in the city, each eager for his share of the Pan Pacific windfall. Catching Ethan under those conditions, even with a detailed and accurate description, was long odds. Without one the chances of finding him in time fell to near zero.

Two more people would die tomorrow. Two more pins would sprout on Gabe's map, documenting his failure.

His office door stood open. Gabe heard his father's voice rumbling down the hallway, giving him time to pull himself together and stop brooding. He wasn't beaten yet.

The biggest surprise of Gabe's day was that his father and Sam Parker walked in together, deep in conversation and any lingering trace of rancor between them gone. Captain Parker and Matt Ryan had been rivals if not outright enemies all of Gabe's life. If he hadn't known better, he'd swear the two men were old friends now.

Jack trailed behind the two older men, toting an old evidence box and obviously amused. He caught Gabe's eye and shrugged, as if to say he was just as much in the dark about the change.

"Gabe, how are you?" His dad wrapped Gabe in an enthusiastic bear hug that was impossible to avoid and stopped just short of cracking a rib. His dad's grin was infectious. "And how's Delia, son? Still planning on staying around I hope."

That his father brought Delia up first thing lifted one nagging concern off Gabe's shoulders. Victoria's loss and the loss of their grandchild had hit both his parents hard, and they'd mourned deeply. Liking Delia was one thing, but he'd worried how well they'd accept someone taking Victoria's place. "I'm doing well, Dad, real well. Delia's fine, keeping busy helping Sadie with the wedding. I don't think she's tired of me yet, but you can ask her yourself. We're having supper at the Larkin house later."

"Don't think that I won't." His father walked the small office, touching file cabinets, folders stacked neatly on the corner of the desk and stopped in front of the pin-studded map. "I had a map just like this on my office wall. Remember, Sam? I must have stared at that thing for hours. The whole time, the answer I was looking for was at a desk in the next room."

Parker moved to stand next to Gabe's father and put a hand on Matt Ryan's shoulder. "Thom lied to all of us. No one can blame you for trusting your partner. The past is the past. The important thing now is catching Ethan."

Jack's incredulous expression was a perfect match for Gabe's own reaction, however swiftly hidden and buried deep. He'd give a month's pay to know how the two men had made peace, but unless his father volunteered the information, he'd let it lie. Having Parker on the same side, helping instead of hindering, could only be a positive thing.

He'd take all the help offered. Stopping Ethan from killing again was the most important thing.

"Jack tells me the box from Glenrock arrived this morning." The reluctant way Gabe's father forced his gaze away from the map was familiar. He slipped out of his coat and hung it next to Gabe's. "Anything I can help with, son?"

"I hope so." Gabe spread the merger pile of photographs along the edge of his desk, starting with the wedding portrait and ending with the photos of the little boy. "These are the only photos Sheriff Leeds found at the ranch. Do you know any of these people, Dad? He also sent a few books, ledgers, and a stack of letters. I don't recognize any of the names on the letters. I'm hoping you will."

"This is Abby, Thom's wife." His father brushed a finger over the fading image of her face. "Abby died in childbirth when Ethan was six. Their baby girl died with her and grief just about killed Thom, too. The little boy is Ethan. He might be five or six in that photograph. That picture used to hang in Thom's sitting room next to the picture of Abby. I haven't seen these in more than twenty-five years."

Jack held up the last photo, the older man. "Is this Thom Brennan, Captain Ryan?"

"No, that's not Thom. If I remember right, that was one of Abby's brothers." He gestured toward the photo of Ethan. "After Abby died, Thom agreed to let her brother take Ethan home with him for the summer. Thom was a mess, drinking more than he should and came close to losing his badge. Ethan ended up staying with his uncle more than two years. He was nine, nine and a half, when Thom brought him home again. The boy wasn't the same."

Gabe shoved his hands in his trouser pockets and leaned against the edge of his desk. The instincts his father scoffed about poked him. "What do you mean, Dad? How did Ethan change?"

His father hesitated, wiping a hand over his mouth. Guilt and regret settled on Matt Ryan's face, more than thirty years of hindsight coming to fruition with Gabe's questions.

"You don't have to say it, Matt." Parker cleared his throat. "I met him when I was still walking patrol and he was always in trouble. Real trouble, not the kind of pranks most little boys get into. One of the older ladies on the block complained he'd almost killed her cat, but Thom didn't take it seriously. The older Ethan got the more he liked bullying and hurting smaller children. I never knew the boy before he went to live with his uncle, but I'll take Matt's word that he wasn't always that way."

Jack hissed a breath out through his teeth and caught Gabe's eye. He knew his partner well enough to know that both of them were thinking the same thing. Ethan's time with his uncle did more than change him into a bully. Something that happened during those years turned him into a murdering butcher. "Captain Ryan, did the uncle live near San Francisco?"

"I know you're hoping Ethan might be holed up in his uncle's house, Jack. But you won't be that lucky." His father studied the uncle's picture, lip curled. "He lived outside of Portland when he took Ethan with him, but a year later he pulled up stakes and moved up into the mountains of Idaho. Took Thom months to find Abby's brother and another year to pry his son loose from the bastard."

"Dad . . . what about Thom's old house?" Gabe stood and began rooting through the papers in the bottom of the box from Sheriff Leeds, a memory and instinct both nagging him. He found the deed folded and stuck inside one of the ledgers. "There's a deed here in Thom Brennan's name for a house in San Francisco. Do you know if he sold the house, Dad? Or if it survived the fire?"

"Thom didn't sell out before he left, there wasn't enough time. I never heard much from him, so I don't know if he sold his property later." His father went back to the map, tapping an area near Lincoln Park and 30th Avenue. "He liked living close to the water. I don't think the fire got this far. That doesn't mean the quake didn't knock the building down. Thom had been in Wyoming for years and I never thought to see if his house was still standing."

The neighborhood was near Golden Gate Park, near the Presidio and the Pan Pacific. Every bit of experience gained during his ten years as a cop told Gabe that Ethan was hunting out of that house. He was certain of that.

Jack and Parker knew, too. He saw it on their faces.

"Round up a dozen of our men, Jack. Make sure all of them have sidearms." Gabe unlocked his desk and pulled his pistol out of the bottom drawer. "We leave in ten minutes."

"On my way." Jack paused in the doorway. He looked to Gabe and at a nod, finished mending fences. "Captain Parker? Should I sign out a pistol for you?"

"I'll come with you. The desk sergeant will move faster for me." He clapped Gabe's dad on the shoulder. "We'll catch him, Matt. He's not going to slip away this time."

Gabe locked file cabinets and drawers, securing the office and the evidence sent by Sheriff Leeds. He draped his coat over an arm and stuffed the old fedora on his head. "Grab your coat, Dad. You're coming, too."

His father licked his lips and eyed the pin-strewn map. "I'm a civilian, son. When I retired from the force I lost the right to go with you. You'd be breaking regulations taking me along."

"I have the authority to appoint deputies. Consider yourself deputized." Gabe tossed his father his coat. If anyone deserved to be there when they uncovered Ethan's lair, his father did. "I need someone to point me at Thom Brennan's house. I'm putting you in charge of making sure we don't break down the wrong door."

His father grinned. "I guess I can't turn down being deputized."

"Just promise me two things, Dad." Gabe waved his father out the door and into the hallway. "I can't issue you a weapon, so stay back until I tell you it's clear."

"I didn't lose my common sense when I retired, Gabriel. I remember how this is supposed to work, you won't need to assign me a nanny." His father frowned. "What was the second thing?"

Gabe locked the office door and dropped the key in his pocket. "Be careful. Mom will never forgive me if you get hurt."

"I can take care of myself, son." His father squeezed his shoulder. "But the same goes for you. Watch yourself."

The sun was low on the horizon by the time Gabe and his men arrived in Thom Brennan's old neighborhood. They parked the cars several blocks away and crept toward the house in small groups, using the cover of shrubs and plantings around the neighbor's yards to conceal their movements.

Two older women worked in a flower garden at the end of the block and Jack shooed them inside, issuing a warning to wait for an all clear before venturing out. All the other front yards on the dead-end street were empty. The evening was clear and warm, and the absence of children playing outside after supper struck Gabe as strange. That he didn't have to worry about keeping curious children out of harm's way was a blessing, but he still wondered what kept them indoors.

Proximity to Ethan Brennan could explain the quiet in the neighborhood. Ethan wouldn't hunt his neighbors, his every move was too calculated to draw that kind of attention to himself and where he lived, but Gabe doubted he could hide his nature completely.

Over time, the people on his block would recognize Ethan as a threat, even if they didn't know what kind of danger he represented. Parents would learn to keep their children inside and close after an encounter with the strange, menacing man down the block.

The house itself wasn't large, single-story with grayed cedar siding, a covered porch, and a long drive leading toward the back. One side of the yard butted up against open land, a part of Lincoln Park that ran clear to the ocean. The nearest neighbor on the other side was two lots away, with a tangle of windswept cypress and pivot hedge between the two properties.

More overgrown hedges stood between the house and the street, and a jungle of weeds and knee-high grass grew in place of a lawn. Night was coming on quickly and the dim, murky light worked to their advantage in the neglected front yard, helping to conceal Gabe's men from anyone inside the house. A break in the hedge offered him the perfect vantage point to observe the house.

What looked to be an old carriage house or a small stable sat at the end of the gravel drive, doors wide open and the empty interior still visible despite the gathering dusk. Ruts in the drive showed fresh mud, evidence of recent use. The house and building behind were perfect for a man working as a cabbie.

And perfectly isolated for a murderer. Gabe realized with a start that he'd never considered the possibility that Ethan didn't live in his father's old house. The certainty wiggled under his skin and burrowed to the bone.

A light came on inside the house and a woman's voice called out. "Andy! Time to wash up for supper. Hurry up now. You need to be sleeping before your papa gets home."

Gabe's pulse sped up, heart thudding against his ribs and a sour taste rising into his throat. Dora had warned that the killer might be married, a man with a family and the appearance of a normal life. Given what he knew of Ethan, just how "normal" the lives of his wife and child were was an open question.

But if his wife and the evidence of the empty carriage house were to be believed, Ethan wasn't home and likely out driving his cab. This was their chance. Gabe didn't plan to waste it.

"Dad, is there a backdoor?"

"There was. I can't imagine anyone would board it up. Three or four steps up to the back porch if I remember and the door off the porch opened into the kitchen."

His father's deep, gravelly voice was surprisingly soothing in the darkness. Gabe suddenly remembered his dad sitting on the edge of his bed when he was five or six, telling bedtime stories and how much he'd loved falling asleep listening to that voice. The memory was so strong Gabe shivered, but he didn't have time to wonder why he'd remembered such things here and now.

"Jack, take five men and work your way behind the house. Wait until you hear us at the front door before coming in the back." He chewed on his lip, weighing risks. "Weapons ready, but don't go in with pistols drawn. That little boy will be scared enough without us pointing guns at him."

"Count to one hundred and we'll be in place." Jack tapped five men on the shoulder and led them away.

He counted to one hundred and ten, just to be sure. Gabe waved half his men to either the left or right side of the yard, and went up the center walk with Captain Parker. His father kept his promise and stayed back, keeping low and following at a slower pace. He could only imagine what that cost his father's pride. He knew what it would cost him.

Gabe reached the porch and listened hard for a man's voice inside, holding his breath until Parker shook his head. The woman and the boy were the only ones inside. He beat his fist on the rough pine door, and yelled, "Mrs. Brennan! Police officers, open the door!"

He heard Jack go in the backdoor and the woman scream. The front door wasn't locked. Gabe shoved it open and led his men inside.

The little boy came streaking through the sitting room from the back of the house, crying and running as hard as he could for the front door. Matt Ryan caught the boy around the waist and scooped him off his feet before he made it outside. The boy fought to squirm loose, kicking his feet and yelling. "Let me go! Let go."

"All right now, calm down. No need to carry on like this. I

heard your mother call you Andy. That's your name isn't it? No one's going to hurt you or your mom, Andy. You've got my word on that." Gabe's dad wrapped Andy in his arms, holding him tight and patting his back until all the fight drained away. The little boy drooped, sobbing and limp. He carried Andy to an armchair out of sight of the window and settled in. "I'll take care of him, Gabe. Go."

Gabe's men filled the house and swarmed over the carriage house in the back, moving purposely and searching methodically for anything that might tie Ethan to the murders. Dressed in their dark blue uniforms, they reminded him of ants at a picnic, hunting for every last crumb dropped from the table. He edged past them and down the short hall to the kitchen. They knew their jobs.

The square table sat in the center of the kitchen, the remains of Andy's dinner cooling on a white glass plate. Dented tin pots and a cast-iron skillet were shoved to the back of the stove, presumably to keep the potatoes, spinach, and sliced pork inside from burning. The smell made Gabe's stomach growl. He'd be lucky to eat by breakfast.

Mrs. Brennan sat opposite her son's dinner plate, shaking hands folded on the tabletop, no doubt instructed by Jack to keep her hands in plain sight. She furtively watched the commotion of officers pulling open cupboards, drawers, and emptying the contents onto the counter and into the sink. Her lower lip trembled and she was obviously frightened, but she didn't cry. Small, fragile-looking, and much younger than he'd have guessed Ethan's wife to be, bruises—old and new—showed on both her arms.

A kitchen full of policemen was the least thing she had to fear or cry over.

Jack stood behind and slightly to one side, a buffer between Mrs. Brennan and the men gathering evidence to hang her husband for murder. His moleskine was in his hand, a chewed pencil stub tapping the edge. He caught Gabe's eye and nodded before he moved around to where Mrs. Brennan could see them both. "Lieutenant Ryan, this is Mrs. Maddy Brennan. She says her husband left for work a few hours ago and won't be back until after the fair closes at midnight. Mrs. Brennan says she has no knowledge of her husband committing any crimes."

"I'm sure she's telling the truth." Gabe pulled out a wobbly kitchen chair and sat next to Maddy Brennan. He'd be as gentle and compassionate as she allowed, but time was in short supply. "I doubt Ethan would confess multiple murders to his wife. But you still knew something was wrong, didn't you Maddy?"

She sucked in her lower lip, hands clutched together tight, and stared straight ahead. Gabe waited, hoping she'd say something and he wouldn't have to push her. His men continued to move around the kitchen, speaking in low tones. Maddy Brennan stayed silent and avoided looking at anyone.

Gabe gently took one of her hands and pushed up a sleeve, revealing more bruises. She cried then, tears rolling off her chin to spot the front of her dress, but still didn't make any noise or look at him. Maddy might have been one of the carved marble sculptures at the Pan Pacific. He sternly reminded himself that lives were at stake, that he had little choice.

He still felt like a bully. "Tell me if I'm right. Ethan hurts you. He gets mad if you ask questions about where he goes and when he's coming back. But you see things that scare you, blood on his clothes maybe, so you ask again. Does he hurt Andy, too?"

Maddy shook her head, sniffling and choking back sobs. Gabe released her hand and offered his handkerchief. She dried her face, teetering on the edge of sobbing hard, but managed to compose herself enough to speak. "No, Ethan would never hurt his son, that boy means the world to him. And I do my best to keep Andy clear. I take good care of my little boy. I'm a good mother."

Officer Polk hesitated in the doorway, shuffling his feet and clearing his throat. "Lieutenant? Could I have a word with you?"

His job pulled him in five directions at once. That was nothing new and he was used to delegating responsibility to Jack and others. Gabe didn't relish the feeling of cowardice as he left his partner to deal with Maddy Brennan. That was new and most unwelcome. "Stay with her, Jack."

He followed Polk to a small bedroom in the back of the house. Polished stones, seashells, and a robin's egg were displayed on the windowsill. A faded blue calico curtain had been pulled back on the closet, revealing a few neatly ironed shirts and a jacket hanging from a crooked rod. Small shirts. This was Andy's room, neater than the rooms of most small boys, but the trinkets and treasures testified to the fact that the room belonged to a child.

The bed was pulled away from the wall. A trapdoor gaped in the floor.

This was likely the room from Delia's dream, the last place Aileen Fitzgerald saw light before Ethan locked her in the dark and killed her. He didn't want Jack inside this room, to be this close to where the mother he never knew died, but Gabe knew what he wanted didn't matter. This was Jack's job as much as it was his.

Officer Dutton's head and shoulders poked up through the trapdoor. Under streaks and smudges of dirt, his normally ruddy face was chalky. "Lieutenant, we found two rooms under the house. He— the killer poured lime on the bodies in one room. We found two full sacks stacked against the outside wall. The other room—" Dutton wiped a hand over his face. "The other room is where he killed them."

Gabe jammed his hands deep into his trouser pockets, thinking of the job, planning what needed to be done to recover evidence and which men were best for each job. He concentrated on the necessary, the practical. If he let himself think of Maddy Brennan tucking her small son into bed each night, or of Andy playing with tin soldiers in this room, Gabe knew he'd put his fist through the window.

Captain Parker appeared in the doorway. His eyes swept the room, taking in all the details that marked this as Andy's room. He blanched and swallowed, but recovered quickly. "You're needed in the carriage house, Lieutenant Ryan. We found the remains of several victims."

Another room. Ethan couldn't bring prey into the house with his wife and child. "On my way, Captain. Give me one minute."

Gabe gave his orders. He trusted his squad to obtain the necessary photographs and he didn't need to stand over them. Tomorrow they'd begin sifting the ground for undissolved bone and belongings. Tonight his sole concern was making sure Ethan never killed again.

He checked his watch on the way down the hall. Less than three hours before Ethan was due home and they sprung the trap. Gabe didn't want anything out of the ordinary to tip him off. They needed to leave the carriage house undisturbed.

One patrolman stood guard by the backdoor and Jack was deep in conversation with Parker on the porch. His father sat at the kitchen table with Maddy and Andy Brennan.

Maddy's arms crisscrossed over Andy's chest and her chin rested on the top of his head. She rocked him side to side as they both listened to his father. Matt Ryan was telling Andy stories about his grandfather Thom, recounting adventures and mishaps from their days as rookies. The little boy listened with rapt attention, just as Gabe always had when he'd heard the same stories as a boy.

He wasn't sure if the stories were for Andy's benefit or if telling them made his father feel better. In the end, it probably didn't matter.

By sunup, Gabe was forced to admit that Ethan wasn't coming home. He went over every move they'd made since arriving at the house, every command decision on his part. The mistake that alerted Ethan to their presence, whatever it was, eluded him. He came to the reluctant conclusion he might never discover if he'd done something wrong or if Ethan planned to vanish all along.

As the night dragged on, the fear grew that Ethan's disappearance was tied to his threat to kill two people on the Fourth of July. Questioning Maddy Brennan revealed that there were occasions when he didn't come home for days at a time, reappearing again without explanation or any sign of remorse. Maddy had learned not to ask her husband questions about his time away.

Gabe spent hours pacing the darkened house. Time and again, he found himself compelled to make the trip down the short hallway to Andy Brennan's bedroom. The bed had been shoved to block the closet on the other side of the room, clearing the way for his men to work. Moonlight filtered through the curtains and the tin soldiers on Andy's dresser threw shadows on the wall behind.

He stood and stared at the gaping hole in the floor, imagining the suffering of each victim who'd died in the room below. Ethan allowed his little boy to sleep here, the child that meant the world to him, as if the bedroom were any other little boy's room. The thought made Gabe recoil in horror.

What Ethan might be doing in place of coming home to his family, the secrets yet to be uncovered, tied Gabe's shoulders in painful knots.

Two things he knew for certain. First, he needed at least a few hours sleep before going to the fairgrounds that evening. Tracking a killer when he couldn't keep his eyes open was courting disaster. Second, Ethan's threat still held and stopping him was all important, now more than ever.

The one advantage he and Jack had gained was that now they had pictures of Ethan Brennan: a grim and unsmiling wedding photo with Maddy, and a portrait with his wife and son Maddy said was only a year old. How much Ethan resembled the photograph of the uncle who took away a normal little boy and returned him changed was uncanny.

After all the time he'd spent working with Isadora and the talks they'd had, Gabe couldn't shake the thought of hauntings and spirits possessing another body. He wanted to talk to Dora, but there was no time.

And he wouldn't leave Andy and Maddy Brennan at Ethan's mercy nor let them stay in this house while his men recovered what was left of lime-eaten clothing and bone. That wasn't in question. Each time he looked at Andy curled up on the sofa with his mother, the need to protect the little boy hit him harder.

Finding a safe place to send them wasn't as easy. Captain Parker volunteered a solution, offering his cabin near Santa Cruz. Convincing Maddy she needed to go wasn't hard at all.

By the time all the arrangements were made and the Brennans were on their way with four armed officers, the majority of his squad had arrived and set to work. Gabe checked the time again. It was past noon.

All his plans called for being in place at the Pan Pacific before six that evening. If he were to get any sleep at all, he'd have to forgo seeing Delia before he left. He borrowed a page from Jack's notebook, scribbled a note, and dispatched one of his men to deliver it. Jack sent a note for Sadie as well. He'd promised that if work kept him away, he'd find a way to let Delia know he was all right. A note was the best he could do for now, but she'd understand. Catching Ethan and bringing him to justice was as important to her as it was to him.

Gabe and his father climbed into the back of a squad car for the drive to his rooming house. He pulled his battered fedora over his eyes and promptly fell asleep, and into dreams of a life with Delia, one without Ethan's shadow hanging over them.

A dream was all he had for now. He wouldn't allow it to stay that way.

Delia

I breathed easier once Officer Baker delivered notes from Gabe and Jack. That they hadn't caught Ethan was a disappointment, but knowing Gabe was all right let me unclench my teeth. Worrying took up large portions of my day and crept into my sleep at night, leaving me restless and unsettled when I woke. Putting on a cheerful face grew harder as the search for Ethan continued to cast a pall over my life.

The same was true of Sadie. She kept to herself when not tending to Mama Esther and the bright, chatty gossip so much a part of her had vanished. We rarely spoke of the strain and fear openly, but neither of us truly relaxed unless Gabe and Jack were with us. The day was something to be gotten through, endured, until time came for their evening visit.

This day was longest of all; the second in a row we wouldn't see Gabe and Jack. That this evening the two of them were hunting Ethan had us both on tenterhooks.

Dusk finally settled into the corners of the yard, the low angle of the sun lengthening shadows from the fence and shrubs. I drew the drapes over the parlor window and turned away, my fanciful imagination transforming tendrils of gloom into monsters that clawed their way toward the front steps.

Winds off the East Bay hills kept the fog confined outside the Golden Gate, leaving the darkening sky clear and sprinkled with stars. Firework displays all over the city would be visible from the upstairs windows, including the array planned for the Pan Pacific celebration. The newspaper proclaimed the program outlined by fair officials to be truly spectacular.

I wasn't sure I could watch. Ethan's threat to kill people during the display took the luster off the fireworks for me. I hurried back to the kitchen to help Annie with supper and making sure the men guarding the house were fed.

At first, I thought the sensation of ghosts leaving the house idle fancy as well. The constant itch on the back of my neck and the pressure in my chest eased, sliding away so gradually that their absence took me by surprise. I guessed what their leaving meant. Relief would come later, once I was sure. Keeping Sadie company while she fed Esther came first.

Supper with Esther hadn't been easy since my return home and grew more difficult daily. Her mind frequently wandered and she lost the thread of conversation, or she relived events from her past, speaking to Sadie and I as if we were people from that long ago time. Sadie's distress grew apace with each incident, harsh evidence of her mother's decline she couldn't deny.

Sadie needed me. Best friends didn't abandon each other in times of need or they were poor friends indeed. And even if none of that were true, I owed Esther Larkin for giving me a home and a good life. I struggled to hide my distraction with vanishing ghosts and steer around the shoals of Esther's fading mind. Each moment we had left was precious, no matter how difficult.

Esther spoke little, taking each bite Sadie offered without

comment or complaint. She rarely looked away from my face, her eyes bright. I couldn't interpret the expression on her face, but I knew Esther heard ghosts clearly and suspected that she saw more than I imagined.

Little surprised me anymore when it came to spirits and hauntings. That Esther would know when ghosts began to fill her house least of all.

"That's enough." Esther waved away the fork in Sadie's hand, suddenly grumpy and out of sorts. "They're making too much noise and I'm tired. How can I sleep when they all carry on so loudly?"

"Who's making noise, Mama Esther?" Fearing I already knew the answer didn't stop me from asking. I took her cold hand, holding it lightly. She bruised so easily. "I can't hear anyone."

She scowled and shook her head, becoming loud and agitated. "You're not trying, Delia Ann. That girl who follows you, she brought the strangers here. Tell her to make them stay quiet."

"Mama, don't shout at Dee." Sadie's voice was firm, but her eyes glistened with tears. More and more, she became the parent and Esther the child. "There's nothing she can do about the ghosts. Dora explained that to you."

Esther yanked her hand away. "Piffle. She can talk to that girl and make her take all these people away again. I shouldn't have to listen to them wailing over what to do."

The pulse inside that told me Aileen was near strengthened. My heart sped up to match, but the ghost hid from me and didn't appear. Aileen's ghost was afraid. Not the fear of being sent away by Annie or Isadora, that I knew and recognized. This was new, different. Aileen's terror churned inside my chest, scrabbled over my skin like a nest of spiders. I shut her out as best I could and fought not to drown.

"Esther, the girl who follows me isn't here. I can't ask her to help." I smoothed her hair back with a shaking hand. She glared at me, angry for reasons I couldn't understand. "And I can't hear the ghosts. I need you to tell me what they're saying."

She pressed her lips into a thin, tight line and peered over my shoulder for what seemed like an eternity. I thought she'd forgotten to answer. "Your girl's distracted, watching over her boy. She won't come out and talk to Teddy. He tried to ask the strangers to go, but all they can talk about is the jackal. He hid their bones."

The jackal; she meant Ethan. I understood now, Aileen's ghost was afraid for Jack. Sadie knew as well. She sucked in a sharp breath and turned her back, staying close but unable to watch.

Questioning Esther bothered me, but I'd no one else to ask. "And the strangers are lost and don't know where they are. Is that why they're upset, Mama Esther?"

"No, no, not because they're lost. They'd learned to rest until your girl stirred them up." She screwed her eyes tight shut and shook her head. "But the jackal came back. He's hunting tonight and now they don't know what to do."

Sadie knelt by the bed and took her mother's other hand. As hard as this was for me, listening to her mother convey messages from ghosts was infinitely worse for her. The rest of the world saw Sadie as a curly-haired gossip without an ounce of real character. They didn't know her or the courage lurking behind the flighty facade. "Mama, ask Teddy if he knows who the jackal is hunting."

Esther sighed and sank back on the pillows, limp and exhausted, all the fire she'd shown reduced to embers. "Teddy says the strangers fight and argue, but don't really say anything. I don't think they know."

I gathered the dirty dishes and cups, and carried the tray down to the kitchen. Sadie's voice followed me down the stairs, a child trying to soothe her mother to sleep and ease Esther's fear of the unknown.

Fear of what Esther didn't know grew as she lost more of who she was, who she'd been. She spent more and more time talking to Teddy's ghost, reliving a life with him I still wasn't certain was real. Forgetting everything would be kinder than this half existence, but there were certain kinds of mercy I couldn't bring myself to pray for. Not now, not yet.

The muffled snap and crackle of firecrackers came from the street, a first salvo from young boys in the neighborhood. Soon, too soon, the staged displays at the fairgrounds would start. Gabe would run out of time then.

Time enough to catch a killer; that I could pray for.

CHAPTER 18

Gabe

Strings of colored bulbs looped over teeming walkways, lighting up the faces of the crowd in blues, golds, and reds. Gabe studied the face of each man on his right, old and young, short and tall, confident that Jack did the same to his left. They'd both memorized the photographs of Ethan and the description given by his wife. Neither of them was willing to dismiss anyone they encountered out of hand based on either of those things.

Ethan was too smart, too confident in his ability to outsmart the police, for Gabe to take anything for granted. Assuming they knew what he looked like was a mistake.

Full darkness and the start of the fireworks display were only minutes away. Families, young couples, and lone men and women strolled the walkways, crowded the lawns and benches. Fourth of July was the highlight of the summer season and the sheer number of people in attendance at the Pan Pacific staggered Gabe.

He tried not to despair and hold on to faith in his men. Finding Ethan was difficult, he'd known that while making his plans, but Gabe refused to think of the task as impossible. He wasn't ready to admit defeat.

And he'd had misgivings and argued against the idea, but allowing his father to join the men patrolling the fairgrounds felt like the right decision. Partnered up with Captain Parker, the two older men stood the best chance of recognizing Ethan, even after thirty years. They'd known Ethan at seventeen and while age certainly altered faces, Gabe would take what advantages fate handed out.

Jack tugged off his cloth cap and raked fingers through his unruly mass of curls. He left the cap off, slapping the hat against his thigh with each step. "Ethan's laughing at us. I wouldn't be surprised if he was watching us right now."

"Let him laugh." Gabe angled his way through the crowd, sidestepping excited children and their slow-moving parents. The main promenade was well lit, but the more night and darkness settled in, the more difficult it became to search for Ethan and avoid stepping on a child. "I want him cocky and making mistakes."

"He hasn't made any yet." Jack's mouth twisted and he stuffed his cap into a coat pocket. "How much longer?"

The clock tower ahead was bathed in spotlights, a landmark for people trying to find their way around the grounds. He'd avoided watching the hands slide around, counting down the hours and minutes until the first skyrocket was launched. How little time they had left was a surprise. He smothered a flicker of panic. Ethan wouldn't win. "About fifteen minutes. Try and remember we're not the only ones looking. Dad and Parker, or one of the other patrols may have Ethan right now. We wouldn't hear immediately."

"Always the optimist, Lieutenant." Jack's shoulders were hunched, but he flashed a grin. "Do they issue that cheery outlook with the badge and promotion certificate?"

Gabe relaxed, the knot in his stomach untying a fraction. If Jack was joking life wasn't totally dire. "I'm not allowed to reveal that information to the lower ranks, Sergeant. Work hard and you'll find out for yourself."

They continued down the Avenue of the Nations toward the Marina and around to the livestock exhibits. Once the sun went down, crowds thinned and eventually vanished in this section of the grounds. Interest in farm animals waned as families with young children went home. Activities in the Fun Zone were a bigger draw most nights, but this wasn't most nights. People still milled about along the Marina, biding their time until the fireworks started. Not until they got to the farm exhibit buildings did Gabe and Jack find themselves almost alone.

That the area was isolated and not as well lit made this the perfect place for Ethan to make his play and carry out his threat. It was also the reason he and Jack had walked through the barns and down the pathways between livestock pens multiple times that day. He'd come through the area so often, Gabe was on speaking terms with the longhorn bull.

Twice he caught sight of his men, both uniformed and plainclothes officers patrolling in pairs as ordered. The same unrelenting tension that lodged between his shoulders, refusing to budge, showed on their faces. Holding to optimism grew more difficult. Time was running short.

With the first burst of fireworks, Gabe's spirits plummeted. He and Jack pushed on, both grimly determined not to give up until they knew they'd lost. His mind wouldn't accept that Ethan had slipped away again, but he winced with each awestruck noise from the crowd and explosion overhead. If they'd failed, he'd find out soon enough and be able to berate himself at leisure.

The fireworks were being detonated from an area inside the polo fields, cordoned off for the safety of tourists and San Franciscans attending the fair. Gabe's ears rang with the concussion of gunpowder explosions and the delighted squeals of the huge crowd.

They'd passed the pens of dairy cows, horses, and Texas longhorns. The blank fence of the polo field lay ahead and the path was empty of people. Gabe saw little sense in going farther than the padlocked gate.

He was about to say so when Jack grabbed his arm. "Did you hear that?"

Another rocket burst almost overhead. "My ears are ringing. What am I supposed to hear?"

"A scream." Jack pointed down a side path between the barns they'd passed. "I'd swear it came from that direction. Come on."

They moved back the way they'd come, listening hard and straining to hear anything out of place between the rolling boom of the fireworks. A few young couples, courting and craving privacy, stood in the darkness watching the overhead display. The couples paid no attention to the two detectives, absorbed in each other and the spectacle. Gabe was beginning to doubt Jack had really heard anything.

The sobbing woman tucked under the sheltering arm of her beau and rushing away from the hog barn convinced Gabe otherwise. He exchanged looks with Jack and broke into a run, muttering under his breath, *no, no, please, God, no.*

Blood smeared on rail fences, the bleachers around a tiny show ring, the back wall of the barn—that was all Gabe saw at first. The raw, meaty smell combined with the stench of pigs and manure gagged him. A pen of squealing hogs squabbled at the back of the open room, the din they made deafening.

On a platform behind and slightly to the left of the pen sat a stock scale. Captain Sam Parker's blood-streaked hand dangled over the side, fingers splayed and just out of reach of the milling hogs below. Matt Ryan sprawled facedown on the ramp used to herd animals onto the scale. His open eyes stared dull and lifeless.

Running the length of the barn happened to someone Gabe

didn't know; a grief-stricken and guilty man who forgot everything he knew about being a cop, everything his father ever taught him about evidence and investigations. He didn't know the person kneeling in blood, clutching a body already growing cool, rocking and sobbing, making desperate bargains with God.

No . . . no, please, God, no! Please . . . don't take him, too. The litany echoed in Gabe's head, drowning out bursting fireworks, the hogs fighting and the hammering of his heart. His fervent prayer became a small boy's sobbing plea for protection from monsters under the bed.

But these monsters were real and God wouldn't answer.

Delia

I came awake suddenly, heart pounding and not knowing why. Annie called out and rapped sharply on the door. "Delia! Wake up and unlock the door. Do you hear me? Unlock this door."

"Oh, God . . . Esther." I tossed off the blankets and bolted across the room. Fumbling at the lock with shaking, sleep-dulled hands took an eternity, but the latch finally clicked open. Annie didn't wait. She was inside before I stepped back.

"Get your dressing gown and house slippers on. Hurry up now." Annie switched on the lamp. I blinked away the dazzle and did as she asked, shivering with more than cold. She tore open the wardrobe, sifting through my things until she came up with one of my heavy shawls. "Wrap this around you, too. It's cold down in the kitchen. I lit the stove, but that takes awhile to heat."

"What's wrong?" She was crying, quietly and without calling attention to herself. I hugged the dressing gown over my chest, trembling harder. She wouldn't rush me to the kitchen if Esther had died. "Annie, please. Tell me what's wrong."

Annie bundled me in the big shawl, wrapping it around me twice and tucking the ends into the belt of my dressing gown. She sniffled and brushed the hair off my face. "Gabe's in the kitchen, sweetheart. He's not hurt, but you need to prepare yourself before you see him. He's got his daddy's blood all over him and his clothes are a frightful mess. Gabe needs you something fierce right now, Dee. He asked Jack special to bring him to be with you. Losing his daddy's got him all tore up inside."

"Matt's dead?" A witless thing to say, but all thought had deserted me. Numbness crept through me, the same feeling of watching someone from afar that I'd felt when my parent's died. "How?"

"Jack didn't say and Gabe—" She wiped her face on a sleeve. "You need to be strong for him, sweetheart. You need to be real strong. Can you do that for him?"

I nodded, unable to speak and barely able to breathe. Gabe had come to me, trusted me to help when the pain was too much to bear alone. I needed to live up to that trust.

Ghosts began to glimmer in the corners of my room, all the spirits still in the house crowding in to fill the space behind my chair and spilling over onto the fringed carpet next to my bed. Ethan's victims, the lost and the unburied, gathered to plead with me again to find them and lay them to rest. Aileen stood at the fore in the waiting stance I knew so well, hands folded at her waist and green eyes demanding my attention.

In all the long months of being haunted, I'd never been angry at my ghost. Frightened and confused, yes, but the rage welling up was new. Now was not the time to demand that I do impossible things, or accomplish tasks I didn't even have the first idea of how to start. Dora and I would find a way to lay the dead to rest, but not tonight.

Not now. All Isadora's warnings about the selfishness of ghosts came back. I shut awareness of Aileen out, using all the tricks Dora labored so hard to teach me.

My concern was for the living. I needed to go to Gabe.

I can't remember running down the staircase. Annie maintains that I dashed from the room, taking the steps two at a time and that only the grace of angels kept me from falling. I lost a slipper sprinting across the dining room and hit the swinging door without breaking stride.

Annie did well to warn me.

Gabe sat on a wooden kitchen chair, hands palm up in his lap and shoulders slumped. The chair was shoved back from the table, a lonely island in a sea of polished linoleum. His shirt and tie were blotched rusty brown, his trousers stiff with dried blood from the knees down. Splatters covered his face, plastered his hair flat and coated his fingers. He opened and closed his fists and stared at the blood caked in the creases of his palm, his expression one of confused horror. The blood flaked and cracked each time he flexed his fingers, fell into his lap, and floated to the floor.

Jack stood at the sink in his shirtsleeves, water running. He scrubbed at the rusty stains on the front of Gabe's overcoat with one of Annie's flour-sack towels, staining the fabric crimson and attempting to rinse it clean again under running water. His eyes were red and swollen, skin blotchy from crying. He saw me and relief drove a small portion of the grief from his face. "Thank God, Dee, thank God . . . I have to go back. He shouldn't be alone."

"I'll stay with him. He won't be alone." I took the towel and Gabe's coat, wanting to retch. The old penny smell turning my stomach was Matt's blood, the last, sad residue of a vital man's life. Putting the coat on the porch got it out of my hands, but didn't banish the scent; Gabe's clothes were drenched in the same blood. I couldn't think about that now. I couldn't cry yet. "Annie and I will take care of him. Don't worry."

"I sent Marshall and Noah Baxter to Gabe's boardinghouse for clean clothes. If— if he can't manage, Marshall will help him change." Jack caught sight of his hands, the pink stains soaking his cuffs and sleeves. He turned back to the sink and the bar of lye soap Annie kept in a cracked saucer. "He hasn't said a word since he asked for you. He just stares."

Annie pushed through the kitchen door, her arms full of blankets and my lost house slipper dangling from one hand. She dropped the slipper in front of me, taking charge and jolting me into action. "Put that back on and help me get some blankets around Gabriel. Best to keep him warm until we can get him into fresh clothes. I don't want either of you coming down sick." Annie brushed the hair off Gabe's face and attempted to smooth down his curls. She'd washed her face, but tears still glimmered in her eyes. "Sadie's waiting in the sitting room, Jack. She needs to see you before you go back out. Go on now and do what needs doing. We'll take good care of Gabe."

Jack hesitated, a desolate, lost look in his eyes. He retrieved his jacket from a hook hung with Annie's aprons and slipped it on, each move heavy with reluctance. "Make sure he understands. I have to go back. I don't have a choice."

"I know that. Gabe knows, too." She shook out one of the blankets and passed an end to me. We got the soft green wool around Gabe's shoulders and tucked behind his back. He only moved when we pushed or pulled, settled back once we let go. "You did your best by him, now let me and Dee take over. Gabe knows you've got a job to do. He'd be most disappointed if you leave it undone on account of him."

Jack lingered in the doorway another few seconds and left. Annie brushed away tears, shut her eyes, and muttered a prayer for his safety. She'd never let him see how much she worried. That wasn't her way.

I'd grown to admire the gift Annie had for knowing when the wounds were deep enough and she needed to mother Sadie or me, and when to make us stand on our own. At sixteen the insistence I handle problems on my own seemed unfair, the way all things adults insisted on was unfair. As I grew older, I saw the wisdom in forcing us not to depend on her or Esther to fix everything for us. She taught us to be strong and responsible, and how to cope with the harshness of life. For the first time, I saw what teaching those lessons cost her.

But caring for someone always came at a cost. If I'd any doubts about loving Gabe, the helpless panic that filled my chest swept them away. I didn't know what to do. Gabe continued to stare blankly at his hands and I wasn't sure he knew where he was. He was lost in a private horror I couldn't imagine. I was at a loss over how to help him find his way back.

Annie filled a basin from the tap and added hot water from the kettle on the stove. She set the basin and a clean cloth on the table, and dragged over another chair. "Sit with him, Delia. See what you can do about washing the blood off his face. He's bound to feel better."

"His hands first." I sat in front of him and wet the cloth, wringing it out over the basin. Taking his hand didn't garner a response beyond his eyes following the movement. I became sure I was right. "He needs the blood off his hands."

"You do what you feel is right, sweetheart." She made another attempt to neaten his gore-matted hair, a futile effort, and kissed Gabe on the forehead. "I'm going to see how Sadie's doing and check on Miss Esther. Maybe he'll talk if I leave you on your own."

I gently scrubbed his left hand, removing layers of blood and grime in the way I'd remove tarnish from silver. Talking was harder, but I needed to speak and make him hear. I feared Gabe sinking deeper and deeper away if not called back soon. Speaking grew easier the longer I forced words, retelling the story of the darkest days after I lost my parents, the sharpness of grief and how it dulled with time. His eyes closed, giving me hope he listened at least. "We made a promise to each other, Gabe Ryan. You made a good start on holding up your end by having Jack bring you here. But I need you to talk to me. Don't shut me out, Gabe. I'm here, please talk to me."

He didn't answer. I chattered away, outdoing Sadie at her best, turning the topic away from loss and sorrow, and told Gabe about my day. Keeping the bright, cheery note in my voice was difficult, but I did my best.

The water cooled before I finished washing both his hands. I stood, meaning to get clean, warm water. Gabe clutched my hand, hanging on tight and eyes wide with panic. Tears spilled over and slid down his face, cutting tracks in the mask of dried blood. "Don't go. Don't leave me alone."

"I won't, I promise." I pulled the chair around next to his and put my arms around him, ignoring blood and the stale stench of death that clung to his clothes. "You're not alone, Gabe. I'm not going anywhere."

He trembled, breath catching in his throat, and began to cry. Holding him seemed like such a small thing to do, but that small kindness wedged open the crack in the wall he'd built between himself and pain. He buried his face in my shoulder, each sob wrenched from deep inside. I held tight, crooning comforting nonsense in his ear as Annie always had for me, and let him cry out his grief.

Not all, not near all, but a start.

I lost track of time, but eventually his breath grew less ragged and the sobs quieted. Gabe sagged against me, limp and utterly exhausted. He'd reached the end of his strength. Even if he couldn't sleep, I hoped he could rest.

Annie opened the door quietly, but came inside nonetheless. She'd given us privacy and let me help Gabe as I saw fit. Now it was her turn. "Gabriel, we're going to get you upstairs to the washroom so you can clean up. Marshall and Noah brought fresh clothes, and they're going to help if you can't manage. The bed in the guestroom's all made up for when you're finished."

"I'm sorry, Annie, this . . . mess is all my fault. I made so much work for you." His voice rasped and cracked, but he'd heard and answered, a huge relief. He shuddered and clung to me, and I thought he'd cry again. "I should go home. Take care of things."

"Nonsense. You're not going anywhere, I won't let you." I pulled away and brushed the hair out of his eyes, smiling around the pain. "There's nothing you need to do that can't wait until morning. Get cleaned up and I'll come sit with you."

Annie put a hand under his arm and helped him stand. They shuffled toward the door, Gabe leaning on her arm and the blanket around his shoulders hanging to his knees. "You need to stop fussing and listen to Delia. Taking care of you isn't a scrap of trouble, Gabriel. You're part of this family far as I'm concerned. Leave these clothes on the bathroom floor and I'll see what I can do about making them presentable again."

"I don't want them back." New lines in Gabe's face aged him. "Burn them. Burn everything."

The door swung closed behind them, hinges squeaking softly. Water dripped from the tap and plinked into a dish, sound echoing hollowly in the iron and porcelain sink. Floorboards creaked upstairs, a trail of footsteps that told me others were awake and moving about, and the timbers of the porch roof groaned, releasing the heat of the day. The house shifted and settled, eager for sleep.

Someone set off a string of firecrackers, the sound of sharp pops, snaps, and sizzling crackles carrying from down the block. The scent of gunpowder and scorched paper drifted in the kitchen window. A skyrocket shrieked and raced heavenward, burst in a flash of dazzling white. Laughter, expressions of glee and appreciation followed, and excited voices called for more.

I slid off the chair to the floor and curled over my knees, rocking and breathing too fast, fighting the urge to throw open the backdoor and scream at the neighbors to stop celebrating, they should mourn the death of a good man instead. That was vastly unfair and unkind, but the desolation in Gabe's face haunted me. The careless joy of others was more than I could bear.

Sadie found me half under the table and huddled in on myself. She ignored that the floor was cold and damp, sat next to me and draped an arm over my shoulders. "Annie sent me to keep you company. She didn't think you should be alone. From the looks of things, she was right. Not that Annie is ever wrong, but I feel honor bound to check once in a while. Let's go to my room, Dee. You can wash your face and wait for Gabe in a nice warm chair."

A familiar pressure in my chest warned that Aileen and the remaining ghosts were near. I was never truly alone, no matter how I longed for solitude.

I leaned against Sadie, needing the warmth of the living and a reminder the dead weren't my only companions. "Did Jack say anything? Tell you what happened?"

"No, he couldn't talk about it." The cheerful, bright lilt to her voice, so much a part of Sadie, was muted and subdued. She hugged my shoulders and sighed, weary and sad. We'd all grown older tonight. "All Jack could do was hold me and shake. He's coming back once—once the coroner removes the bodies."

"Bodies." Ethan had carried out his threat, choosing and taking his victims right from under Gabe's nose. I brushed at my eyes. "Matt didn't die alone."

Sadie stood and helped me to my feet. "Marshall told me they found Captain Parker with Gabe's father. Parker was still alive and managed to talk, and gave a good description of Ethan. He's changed his appearance from the photograph they have. The captain died before they could summon an ambulance or get him to a hospital."

"May he rest in peace." Chance or bad luck had nothing to do with who Ethan had chosen as his victims. The letter to Gabe was a ploy—bait. He'd lured the only two people who'd known him at seventeen to the fairgrounds and hunted them at his leisure. Rage vied with grief for which would hold sway. "Maybe Gabe and Jack can catch that monster now."

Sadie held the door for me, her face grim and determined. "They will. Then that bastard can hang."

CHAPTER 19

Gabe

Gabe returned to work once he'd broken the news to his mother and the funeral arrangements were made. Jack tried to talk him out of going back to the case so soon, mustering all the right arguments, but accepted Gabe's decision gracefully.

Working gave him a chance to do something other than brooding or sitting alone in the guestroom in the Larkin house and breaking down. Neither Delia nor Annie wanted him to go back to his rooming house alone, and he didn't argue too hard. The truth was he couldn't stand the silence or that his father's suitcase still sat open on the chair near the chest of drawers, spare shirts and socks stacked neatly inside. He needed companionship and the noise of others moving inside the house.

Most of all, he needed Delia. He didn't have to pretend with her.

The quiet sympathy of his men was hard to take, at least at first. No one pushed, no one cornered Gabe to say how sorry they were or share memories of Matt Ryan with his son, but they arrived at his office door with coffee and grease-stained bakery bags, or takeaway food from the café down the street. He thought at first Jack put them up to playing nanny, but his partner denied any culpability. No one person was behind the conspiracy to keep him fed and functional, the whole squad was involved.

Boxes of his father's files, as well as old records retrieved from Sam Parker's house, filled Gabe's office. Most he'd read a hundred times or more, but he was determined to hunt through them all again. Now that they knew the killer's identity, details that once seemed unimportant might lead them straight to Ethan. He couldn't afford to miss anything.

He spent hours hunched over his desk studying piles of crime-scene photos, read all the reports and interviews gathered by his father's men years before, and nursed the rage simmering deep inside. Rage was new, unfamiliar, and Gabe couldn't find his way back to being detached and professional. Catching Ethan had always been imperative, but this case had become personal in a way he'd never imagined. The depth of his anger frightened him.

Good cops didn't dream of revenge or of making a suspect suffer the torments inflicted on victims. Gabe began to worry about how good of a cop he really was. He extracted a promise from Jack to make sure he was never given a chance to find out.

Five days passed in a blur. The morning of the funeral dawned clear and warm, a blessing. Saying good-bye in a damp, dreary fog would add more misery to a miserable day.

Matt Ryan's old friends in the department turned out in dress uniforms for the services and the department gave his father full honors. That his father was still so well liked and remembered after all these years made Gabe proud. He had a lot to live up to in order to come close to his father's reputation, but he'd always known that.

Staying strong through the eulogy had been difficult, holding his mother up at the graveside even more so. Dressed in widow's weeds, she looked smaller, frail, and old in a way he'd hoped never to see.

Gabe put his mother on a train the morning after the funeral, relieved his Aunt Bess waited in Boston to comfort and coddle her sister. Two officers from the department went along to act as bodyguards on the long, cross-country trip. Neighbors, all good friends of Matt Ryan, were tending the farm in her absence. He'd breathe a little easier with his mother on the other side of the country. Even Ethan couldn't reach her there.

His mother never looked at Gabe with anything but love in her eyes, but that didn't stanch his guilt or stop the churning in his gut. He couldn't escape the unalterable fact that he'd been in command and all the decisions—all the losses—were his responsibility. Realizations of how he and Jack had been played and how eagerly they'd walked into the trap came too late.

The letter warning of the Fourth of July killings was a ploy to lure the police, and Matt Ryan, to the fairgrounds. Ethan had hunted at his leisure, killing the only two people in the city of San Francisco who might know him on sight.

That wasn't by chance. Ethan would have found a way to kill Sam Parker and Matt Ryan whether they'd been at the fairgrounds or not. When he could think clearly, Gabe recognized the truth of that. He was damn lucky he hadn't lost his mother, too.

She was still in danger, as well as Isadora, Delia, and Sadie. The certainty that no one he cared about was safe fueled his anger. He'd search every boardinghouse and hotel in San Francisco to find Ethan, and if necessary, roust every cabbie and hack driver within the city limits.

And once he'd laid hands on Ethan, he'd do everything in his power to make sure the man who killed his father was convicted. Gabe dreamed of the day he'd watch Ethan Brennan hang, hate growing alongside rage and the need for revenge. He'd never hated anyone before or wished them dead. He didn't much like the feeling.

A sharp rap on the glass of his office door startled him. He opened the folder in front of him, sheepish at being caught woolgathering, and cleared his throat. "Come in."

Jack breezed through the door, whistling and holding another white bakery bag. "Henderson brought in scones and crullers. He was on his way to Sadie's for his shift, so he asked me to deliver them. Marshall didn't want to miss Annie's pancakes."

Gabe flipped the folder closed and cleared off the desktop. "The men get Annie's pancakes and we eat doughnuts in my office. That doesn't seem right. And when did you suddenly start knocking?"

"Just this morning, Lieutenant. In two days I'll be a married man. Time to stop acting like a carefree bachelor and get serious about promotion. Setting a good example for the men is important if I want to make detective grade."

Jack's good humor was infectious and Gabe's spirits rose in response. For one day he could put aside work and mourning, and forget everything but celebrating Sadie and Jack's happiness. He owed his best friend and partner that much and more.

"It's about time Sadie made an honest man out of you." The scone was full of chopped almonds that crunched as he chewed and overly sweet. His coffee was lukewarm, but Gabe drained the mug nonetheless. "Is there anything the best man needs to do on Saturday?"

"Your job is pretty simple. Make sure I get to the church early and keep me from panicking. Delia remains convinced I'll faint as soon as I see Sadie in her wedding gown. She could be right." Jack set his half-eaten doughnut aside. He flattened crumbs with a finger, methodically moving from one to another. "I booked a suite at an inn in Sausalito for the wedding night. I'm hoping the ferry ride will be romantic. Sadie deserves a bit of romance. The owner wasn't exactly overjoyed that a group of armed policemen would arrive with the bride and groom, but I finally won him over. The extra twenty dollars I gave him for the night probably helped."

The coffee soured in Gabe's stomach. He added another entry to his list of Ethan's sins. "The two of you deserve a honeymoon. I'm sorry you won't get one."

"I promised Sadie we'd have a honeymoon and we will. She understands why we have to delay the trip." Jack tossed what was left of his doughnut into the wastebasket. "Ethan Brennan and this case aside, going away later is probably for the best. Sadie would spend all her time worrying about Esther. I don't think we can have a real honeymoon until her mother passes on. If something happened while we were gone, Sadie would never forgive herself."

Gabe cleared away the remains of their makeshift breakfast, uncertain of what to say or if he should say anything at all. His life was as much in limbo as Jack's. He loved Delia and wanted to spend the rest of his life with her, but couldn't bring himself to take the next step. Not until Ethan was in custody.

"Don't look so glum, Gabe. He can't stay ahead of us forever." Jack stared at the pin-studded map on the office wall, his expression impossible to read. That he wasn't joking said much. "Sadie and I will be together, and that's what I care about most. She's the most important person in my life. I'd do almost anything to make her happy, but both of us want a future where Ethan Brennan is nothing more than a horrible memory. The honeymoon can wait."

He didn't know what to say to that, either. Discussions about the future left him shaky. Gabe recognized the fear and uncertainty for what it was, a reaction to his father's death and how easily Ethan could take Delia from him, too. Loving someone wasn't enough to keep that person safe. He turned the conversation to practical matters. "Do you need help getting your things out of Katherine's house?"

"Katherine had one of the servants move them a few days ago. I have a few clothes in her house and my wedding suit. Nothing else." Jack divided the pile of reports between them and flipped open a folder. "If I didn't know my dear stepmother so well, I'd swear she was eager to be rid of me."

Gabe sorted through his own stack of folders, choosing one of Captain Parker's files at random. He couldn't abandon the hope that some hidden nugget of information lurked in Parker's files. "Has Katherine decided if she's coming to the wedding?"

"No, she won't be there. We quarreled over my father lying to me. Katherine swears she didn't know, but I don't believe her. I learned to tell when my stepmother was lying by the time I was nine." Jack shrugged, pretending a nonchalance Gabe didn't believe. "Sadie told me last night that Katherine formally sent her apologies. A conflict with another engagement or some such rot. I'd warned Sadie she'd find an excuse not to come, but I think Katherine's refusal was still a shock. We have a bet going now about whether the gossip will be about her or us. My money's on us."

"I'm sorry, Jack."

"Don't be. I'm not." Anger and bitterness flared in Jack's eyes. "Ethan took my mother from me before I had a chance to know her. If I was going to be sorry about anything, I'd regret all the things my mother and I never got to say to each other. Katherine isn't my mother. I won't miss her at my wedding."

Gabe couldn't disagree. He went back to burying himself in thirty-year-old files, making notes of things he wanted to know more about or follow up. But as the morning wore on, he found himself thinking more and more of things unsaid, and regrets over never having said them.

He had things to say to Delia. Fear of the future was a poor excuse for silence.

Delia

I woke late on Friday morning. The night had been full of dreams, frantic and unsettling, and memories of what I'd dreamed vanished as soon as I opened my eyes. That added to my restlessness. I'd forgotten something important, I was sure of that.

Jumping at small sounds was unlike me: the creak of floorboards in another room, sun-heated roof timbers moaning, a tradesman slamming the rear gate of his wagon. None were out of the ordinary. Yet each noise from outside my room startled me. I couldn't decide if the nervous drumming of my heart was a gift from the ghosts still occupying the house, or if the pressure of completing wedding preparations on time was the culprit.

Placing the blame on the need to finish a thousand and one tasks before the ceremony was reasonable. I dressed, going over lists in my head, and tried not to acknowledge how wrong the simple, reasonable explanation felt.

My unease grew on the way down to breakfast. Ghosts lined the staircase and clustered on the landing. Most sunk back into the wall to avoid touching me, projecting fear that penetrated the edges of my defenses. The air chilled far beyond what was normal for July, becoming cold enough that I saw my breath.

My attempt to cling to reason shredded and vanished. Something was wrong. The number of spirits confronting me was far greater than I'd imagined left in the house. I'd though the majority of the ghosts had gone, banished and laid to rest with the discovery of their bones.

Aileen's ghost stood in the entryway, hands folded at her waist and her shawl draped neatly over her shoulders. She stared intently, asking for my attention. I'd shut her out the night Matt died and had no intention of opening the door for her. Before I braved letting Aileen inside again, I'd need Isadora near.

I swept past, ignoring the pleading in my ghost's eyes, and growing more anxious by the minute. That I was still angry and a bit frightened of her might speak ill of me, but Isadora taught me ways to protect myself for good reasons. Ghosts weren't to be trusted. I'd deal with Aileen Fitzgerald on my own terms, not hers.

The kitchen held more restless dead, strangers who'd died at Ethan's hand as well as the two haunts I thought of as Esther's ghosts, Teddy and Blythe. Teddy seldom allowed me to see him, Blythe almost never. They stood in the open with the other spirits, radiating the same fear and turmoil.

That everything appeared normal didn't ease my mind. Annie stood at the sink, washing dishes and singing one of her favorite hymns. The kitchen was empty but for her, a rare thing with all the men guarding the house and how much joy she took in feeding them. Rare, but not ominous.

"Annie . . . where is everyone?" Sadie wasn't upstairs; I'd expected to find her in the kitchen with Annie. I swallowed, trying to moisten a mouth suddenly gone dry. The ghost's fear took root and became mine.

She smiled over her shoulder, mischief twinkling in warm brown eyes. "Well, you certainly took your time coming down this morning. Gabe's been gone to work for hours. You missed having breakfast with him."

I'd grown used to having him in the house and she'd every right to tease me. Annie couldn't know how terror gnawed at my middle or how the ghosts' silent regard affected me. How much I needed Gabe here, right now, right this moment, startled me. I braced my hands against a kitchen chair and held tight. "I'll see Gabe at supper. Sadie wasn't with Mama Esther when I peeked in. Where is she?"

Annie grabbed an old towel and wiped her hands. "She went out nearly two hours ago. Marshall went along with her. That dressmaker's helper called first thing this morning and said there was a problem. Told Sadie to get right down there or she might not have a dress for tomorrow. She was upset and rightly so."

"Who else went with them? I've forgotten who's on duty today."

"No one. Two of the other boys came down sick last night and there's only three of them to keep watch this morning." Annie frowned. "Marshall argued with Sadie about waiting until he could get somebody else out here, but you know how she can get. Once she started crying, he ended up agreeing to take her to the dressmaker on his own."

Pressure built in my head and in my chest, making me dizzy. Aileen's ghost appeared and crowded me up against the table. She stared, angry and baleful one instant, and imploring me to do something the next. Her emotions battered me, real and impossible to shut out.

"They shouldn't have gone alone. Gabe needs to know." I couldn't deny that something was dreadfully wrong or that Marshall Henderson had disobeyed orders. Understanding why was more difficult. Aileen attempted to touch me, but I stumbled backward to stay out of reach. "And Dora . . . she'll help me. We have to call both of them right now."

The temperature in the kitchen plummeted. Frost formed on windowpanes, the rim of the sink, and ice crystals crazed the wet countertop. A frigid wind, sharp-edged and smelling of pine, slammed open the swinging door, and bounced it off the wall. Dishes rattled on the shelves and a glass tipped, rolled off, and fell, shattering on the linoleum.

Annie hugged herself against the chill, narrow-eyed with anger. "That ghost's acting up again. I knew right from the start letting her stay was a mistake. No good ever comes from letting a spirit linger."

Other ghosts appeared around Aileen, standing in a half-circle behind her. She drew power from the other spirits, but Aileen Fitzgerald was the center and the focus of the chaos whirling through the kitchen. Accusation burned in her eyes. I'd failed somehow and she held me responsible.

My fingers went numb, cold creeping up my arms to lodge over my heart, and I dropped to my knees, shivering. Darkness crept around the margins of my vision and my throat closed, leaving me unable to breathe. The ghost meant to kill me.

"Stop it. Stop!" Esther appeared in the doorway, a specter in her own right. Arms braced against the doorjambs, her white cotton nightgown flapped around her ankles in the phantom wind and milkweed-pale hair whipped around her face. "Teddy, make them stop. Force that girl to leave Delia alone or I'll never forgive you. Do it!"

The wind diminished to a whisper and died, taking the cold away as well. Annie helped me stand and brushed the hair off my face. "Speak to me, sweetheart. Tell me you're all right."

A strangled croak was all I managed the first try. I coughed and cleared my throat, but my voice was still rough and barely recognizable. "See to Esther. I just need a moment and I'll be fine."

Annie hesitated, but Esther's frailty decided her. She slipped an arm around the older woman's waist, preventing her from sliding to the floor, and ignored the way Esther continued to rail at people who weren't there. "Let's get you back to bed, Miss Esther. I think we've both had near enough excitement for one day."

"I want that girl out of my house." Esther strained against Annie's hold, reaching for Aileen's ghost. Her small, fragile hands appeared skeletal, fingers hooked into claws. She began to weep. "This is all her fault. Don't make excuses for her, Teddy! That barmaid led the jackal to my Sadie and Delia. If he hurts either one of them, I'll drop that girl's bones into the bay myself. Get out, the lot of you! Find my Sadie and bring her back."

"Take her upstairs, Annie." I held in panic, smothered grief newborn and refused to believe. Belief would make Esther's raving real. "I'll call Gabe."

The kitchen door swung closed behind them. One by one, the ghosts around Aileen came apart. Motes of dust sparkled in sunbeams and rose toward the ceiling, the last visible evidence of how many haunts had filled the kitchen. The last to go was Teddy, Esther's champion. He went reluctantly, sharp-eyed and aware of me in a way I'd not sensed before. I was left alone with Aileen's ghost, serene and mild without the others at her back.

Dora had been right from the first. I couldn't afford to trust the motives of a ghost or allow sympathy to creep into how I dealt with spirits, especially one as powerful and determined as Aileen.

She might have killed me, with no more thought or remorse than Ethan Brennan showed his victims. I hardened my heart, finally seeing the ghost for what she truly was and not some lost, maligned soul. Aileen Fitzgerald wanted revenge far more than justice or peace.

My defenses thickened as well. That internal awareness of Aileen, and the pulse echoing my heartbeat that I'd grown accustomed to, disappeared. Being alone in my own head after so many months was an odd sensation. I shoved through the kitchen door and ran to the parlor, praying that the desk sergeant would summon Gabe to the phone without questions or delay.

And once Isadora arrived, I could decide about banishing my troublesome ghost for good.

CHAPTER 20

Delia

Furniture in the parlor wasn't meant to be comfortable. The thinly padded, high-backed chair I sat in near the front window was no exception, but I'd chosen this seat for the view of the street and the front walk. Policemen milled about the front yard aimlessly or clustered in small groups to talk, the entire squad waiting for orders of where to go and where they might begin to search for Sadie. The cheerful, smiling young men I knew all wore angry scowls.

Jack stood alone off to one side of the front yard, faced closed off and fists clenched. The squad had stern orders not to allow him farther than the front gate. As long as he stayed put, not one of the men approached him. As tight as Jack was wound, I couldn't blame them.

I'd never waited well or gracefully. As time passed without word, my annoyance rose and my tolerance vanished. I needed to do something, to feel useful, but anything I might do required Dora's help. Waiting for her strained what little composure I'd maintained. My mood was a carefully balanced house of cards and the threat of collapsing into inconsolable weeping too real.

Gabe had given up all pretense of patience. He paced the

room from end to end, pausing at the window to brush aside lace curtains and peer out, repeating the circuit again almost immediately. Frustration at not knowing where to begin, and fear of what might happen if delayed too long, chased him around the room.

Annie had tried to explain and make excuses, but that only fueled Gabe's anger and fed his guilt. Marshall Henderson was a rookie, inexperienced. He'd put too much responsibility on Marshall's shoulders, too soon.

Esther's heartbroken crying echoed through the house. Her sobs were punctuated with angry shouts, commands to do something, and for someone to bring her daughter home. Annie's repeated attempts to soothe her came to nothing. Esther's distress tore at me, but in an odd way her pleading gave me hope. The ghosts spoke to her, conveyed information I wasn't privy to, and she'd understood what was happening long before I was sure. If she believed Sadie was alive to be rescued, so could I.

The phone jangled, sounding two long bells and one short, the ring for our line. Gabe spoke to the operator briefly and she connected him to the person calling. He ran fingers through his hair and said little, listening hard to catch each word over the static on the line and Esther's cries.

"Thank you, Polk. Canvas the street and see if anyone saw anything." The call was bad news. His pained and stricken expression said as much before he spoke. "Sadie and Marshall never arrived at the dressmaker's shop. A foot patrolman found the car abandoned on a side street a mile or so from the shop. The rear wheel had come off."

Ethan's handiwork. I laced my fingers together tight, hiding how my hands shook and pretending calm wouldn't slip away if I trapped serenity in the palm of my hand. "What now?"

"I have every available man in the department out on the streets. They have orders to keep an eye out for Ethan's cab. I have a dozen men checking every location mentioned in Sam Parker's files and another ten poking around the taverns Ethan's wife said he frequented. That's all I can do for now." Gabe pulled aside the curtain, watching Jack as I had. He was always in control around his men. Only with me did he let down his guard, letting his worry and sense of futility show. "It doesn't feel like enough, Dee. Not near enough. We've covered this same ground a dozen times or more, and I don't have much faith this time will be any different. Ethan has the knack of vanishing when he chooses. I'm starting to believe Isadora's theories of guiding spirits."

Another patrol car pulled up to the curb. Dora barely waited for the car to stop rolling before leaping out and striding toward the house. She stopped long enough to embrace Jack and exchange a few words before continuing up the front steps. Baxter trudged behind her, struggling with a large picnic hamper.

"Dee . . . Isadora's here."

"I asked her to come." I took a breath, my fingers clenching tighter before slowly relaxing. "Dora and I spoke on the phone after I called you. She suggested something and I agreed to try. There are . . . there are ways we might be able to find Sadie in time. I know you believe that the ghosts are real, but I need more from you than simple belief. I'm asking you to trust that everything I tell you is true. And I need a promise you won't interfere."

"I trust you." Gabe offered his hand and I took hold. "But I'd like to at least know what you have planned before I give my word. You wouldn't be asking for promises unless this was dangerous."

Dora strutted into the room, heels clicking on the wood floors and silk shantung summer coat swirling around her ankles. Even in a crisis, Isadora dressed to the nines. Baxter followed a few steps behind and she pointed him at the settee. "Put the basket there, Noah. Now be a dear and keep Sergeant Fitzgerald outside. I'll call if I need you."

She plopped down on the settee, as tired and worn as I'd seen. Dora crossed her legs, one foot jiggling at a furious pace as she peeled off her gloves and shrugged off her coat. "Life is dangerous, Gabe. Dee and I need to take a calculated risk in order to reach Sadie in time. The danger to either of us is miniscule compared to what Ethan will do. Once we know where he's taken her, you and Jack can do your job."

Isadora was right, but I saw Gabe struggle with accepting. We asked much from him in terms of faith and trust. That he gave it said a lot about Gabe's character. "I agree, we have to find Sadie quickly. But I still want to know what you're going to do and why it's dangerous."

"Nothing for you to fret about, Lieutenant. It's simply a matter of control." She smiled, bright and guileless. Gabe's expression made it obvious that he didn't believe for an instant. Neither did I. "We have an overabundance of powerful spirits connected to this house and the people who live here. Dee and I are going to send two of them out to seek Sadie. This only becomes dangerous if control slips away from either of us. You've my promise, I won't let that happen."

"I don't understand." Gabe frowned, more annoyed than bewildered. He knew Dora well enough to sense when she kept secrets. "How can you find Sadie, but not Ethan?"

"Sadie is anchored to this house. So is Delia for that matter. Ethan isn't. It's the unique combination of spirits and place that gives this a chance of working." Dora rummaged in the picnic hamper, coming up with white candles, a large square tablecloth, and bundles of dried herbs. "Be a pet and hold these for me, Dee. I'll take them back as soon as Gabe and I clear a space on the floor."

Gabe ended up moving all the furniture and rolling up the parlor carpet under Dora's direction. I'd no doubt that was her intention all along, to keep him too occupied to ask questions. Once the floor was clear, she and I spread the white tablecloth, set candles at each corner, and laid sprigs of herbs along all four sides. Dora lit the candles and stepped back.

"Stand here, Delia. This will work just as I explained on the phone." She positioned me outside the square of herb-ringed damask, my back to the window. Dora squeezed my hand and the smile I got was warm, encouraging. "Remember I'll be here with you. It's important that you don't move unless I say. You're an anchor point, a beacon for the ghosts to return to the house. The herbs act as a barrier to keep them inside the square until I send them out, so it's vital you don't cross that line. Are you ready?"

Fear threatened to turn my knees to water, but I remembered Sarah Miles's pain and knew my worries were nothing compared to what Sadie might face. "I'm ready."

Dora walked the edge of the cloth, concentrating on the margin of polished oak floor showing and muttering under her breath. I trembled, reminded once again of arcane rituals and witches of old, and astonished at being deeply involved. She ended the circuit and nodded, satisfied.

"Gabe, please shut the door and stand in front of it. This is a lot like the séance, but more . . . delicate." Dora frowned, subdued and completely serious. She took her place to my right and we joined hands. "An interruption at the wrong moment could be dangerous. I'm counting on you to stand guard."

I shoved aside trepidation and did my best to shut out the sounds of Esther's grief, and the deeper chatter of policemen just outside the window. Dropping my defenses as Dora had instructed earlier and opening myself to the ghosts was an act of faith. Doing so was also a measure of my desperation to find Sadie. I feared losing my best friend more than losing myself to a spirit's control.

Dora squeezed my fingers and began. "Two spirits I call who

dwell in these walls, two spirits only should answer. In life you were known as Aileen Fitzgerald and Edward Coleman. We seek aid for a child of this house. Your task is to help us find her."

Three times Isadora repeated the call, each louder than the last. After the third time, mist began to coalesce over the center of the damask square. Tendrils of foggy gray and cigarette-smoke blue swirled around a pivot point, intertwined and separated again, but the shapes I'd come to associate with the ghosts never formed.

Teddy's ghost tried to take shape. Aileen's ghost resisted, blocking him. His tie to the house and family was greater, but she was still the more powerful spirit.

"Come to my call, Aileen Fitzgerald." Dora's control tightened and her voice became iron-hard. "A child of this house needs to be found."

"Find Sadie for me." Isadora stiffened at the sound of my voice, but didn't tell me to hush. She hadn't told me not to speak, just not to move, and this felt right. "Sadie belongs here. She needs to come home, Aileen. Don't let Ethan take her from Jack the way he took you."

The wall of resistance crumbled and both ghosts took shape, nebulous and barely there. Aileen's ghost gazed into my eyes and I opened the way wider. The parlor, familiar and safe, vanished. I traveled with the two ghosts and saw the world as they did, but this wasn't a dream of the past.

We walked along the bayshore, pushing through reeds and splashing across marshy spots of wetlands, following a well-worn path. Gulls keened in a cloud-brushed blue sky, wheeling across the sun and diving toward the choppy surface of the bay. The air was full of the tang of salt and the reek of seaweed rotting in the sun.

The reeds ended on a spit of dry land. Beyond was open water. The pristine sails of pleasure craft and the dingy sails of crab boats billowed in the stiff breeze. A ramshackle pier extended a few yards from shore before ending in a wrack of broken, sharp-edged timbers and rotting pilings.

On the landward end sat a small boathouse. The roof had fallen in closest to the sea and the door hung by one hinge, swinging in the wind. A small cottage sat farther back, safe from the incoming tide and the surge of storm waves. Behind and stretching to either side, a tall, sea-grass topped dune hid the house from view. Traces of a dirt-topped road wound around the dune to the grass-tufted land in front.

A black, two-horse hack, anonymous and nondescript, was parked near the front door. Ethan's cab.

The two ghosts turned to me. Teddy's eyes filled with tears and he crumbled, dust scattered on the wind off the sea.

Aileen pointed toward the house and spoke in soft, lilting tones. "Tell Jackie to hurry if he'd save his bride. I'd not like that bastard to take us both from him."

I turned in a circle, trying to remember the landscape and unsure if this was a dream. "Where are we?"

"The fishing shack. Jackie and that man of yours will know where it is." Aileen reached out to brush my cheek. Her fingers were warm, an impossible thing. I was dreaming. "He kept me in that other place for days before bringing me here. This is where he cut my heart out and tossed it into the sea. I wanted to lead you here from the first, but I couldn't force you to come, you had to be willing. I'm just sorry we left it so late. Make sure Jackie knows his mother's real proud of the man he's become. Now back with you."

Aileen Fitzgerald's patient green eyes were the last I saw. The bright, sunny beach faded and dimmed to featureless gray. I fell and kept falling.

When I opened my eyes, I was stretched out on the floor of

the parlor. Dora knelt next to me and stroked my face, calling my name, again and again. She let out a huge sigh at seeing my eyes open. "Oh, thank God, Dee. Are you all right?"

I tried to sit up, a mistake. The world spun and only shutting my eyes again kept me from being sick. "Gabe . . . I need Gabe."

"I'm here." He took Dora's place, kissing me on the forehead before clutching my hand. "I'm right here."

"The fishing shack. Ethan is there and he has Sadie. I saw his cab." Confusion clouded Gabe's eyes and the sour taste of fear rose into my throat. She hadn't lied to me, she wouldn't lie about this. Not even ghosts were that cruel. "There's a house on the beach and a ruined pier . . . and I could see boats on the water. The ghost said you and Jack would know where to go."

I knew the instant he'd remembered. Surprise replaced the confusion in Gabe's eyes.

"Damnation, there was a boathouse in Parker's files. Take care of her, Dora." Gabe hugged me tight before he ran from the room. "Jack! Jack!"

Dora yanked one of Esther's needlepoint pillows off the settee and slipped it under my head. She took another one for herself, blew out the two candles still sputtering and flopped down on the floor next to me.

"We've done all we can do, Dee. The boys will get there in time." Tears rolled down her face, smudging her makeup. "They must. I promised Daniel I'd stop drinking myself into a stupor at night. He'll be extremely disappointed if I can't keep my word."

Teddy and Aileen shimmered into view by the windows, looking out toward the street and standing vigil. Madam Isadora Bobet shut her eyes and began to sob in earnest. I held her hand, listening to the sound of Annie singing spirituals to Esther, car engines in the street, shouted orders, and the silence that followed once Gabe and all but a few of his men left.

Silence pressed me into the floor and held me there. Each breath became a prayer, a plea.

Please . . . bring her home. Please, God . . . not Sadie, too.

Gabe

Gabe motioned half his men to the left of the beach house and led the rest around to the right. The mares harnessed to Ethan's cab danced in place and shook their heads, tack jingling, but settled once Baker got a hand on their noses.

He'd brought the squad up from the road behind the house, using the shelter of the dunes and long, blue shadows of late afternoon to conceal their movements. Ethan had finally made a mistake, trading isolation for a clear field of view. Only one small window showed in the back wall and that was boarded over. The house didn't have a backdoor. One way in and one way out meant their quarry had nowhere to run.

If all went well, they'd have Ethan before he realized they were there. But Gabe had learned not to count on anything when it came to this case. He wasn't going to take any unnecessary risks, not with Sadie and Marshall's lives at stake.

"What are we waiting for?" Jack crouched next to him, fingers flexing on the grip of his pistol and voice tight with strain. "We know he's in there."

"And we know he has Sadie and Marshall, too. Surprise is the only advantage we have and might make the difference." Gabe squeezed his partner's shoulder. "I'd like to take Ethan alive, but don't hesitate to shoot to kill if necessary. Sadie's safety comes first. We go in the front on three, slow and careful."

"Hey there! What are you doing around those horses?" The old man hurrying toward them down the beach had the sun at his back, rendering him difficult to see. He shouted again, waving the fishing pole in his hand at Baker. "Too damn many thieves running loose since the fair opened. Skedaddle before I get the police after you."

Rusty hinges on the front door gave a tortured squeak. The door slammed shut again almost immediately, rattling windows and vibrating through the walls. Gabe swore and sprinted toward the front of the house, Jack right with him. "Maxwell, Finlay, get him out of here!"

Two of the biggest men, Coen and Thomas, threw themselves against the weathered cedar panel door. It rattled in the frame, locked and likely bolted on the inside. They tried again, putting all their weight behind their assault, but the door didn't budge.

Low windows sat on either side of the door. Gabe smashed the butt of his pistol against the glass, shattering the pane. Jack wrapped a hand in his coat sleeve, knocking away shards of window glass that clung stubbornly to the frame. Once the space was clear, the two of them scrabbled through the opening, pistols drawn. Officer Polk followed.

Dust laid thick on the furniture in the front room. Sadie's handbag and hat were tossed into a chair, but that and the metal bar dropped over the front door were the only evidence anyone had been in the house for years.

Polk began to work at getting the door open. Gabe cautiously made his way toward the back of the small house. Only the very real threat of Ethan getting the drop on him and Jack kept him from running. The first bedroom was empty, as abandoned and neglected as the main room of the house.

In the very back of the house was a larger room. A trapdoor in the floor stood open, identical to the one they'd found in Thom Brennan's old house. Rusty-brown blood splattered the walls and soaked the torn mattress on the iron-framed bed.

Marshall Henderson was sprawled facedown in the far corner, hands bound behind his back. Gabe swallowed the bile rising in his throat and knelt to turn Henderson over and search for a pulse, never taking his eyes off the trapdoor or lowering his pistol.

The relief of Marshall groaning and his eyelids fluttering left Gabe's knees weak. His face was swollen and already purpling with fresh bruises, evidence of the beating he'd suffered. A gash over one eye bled freely, as did the split in his bottom lip, but his injuries would heal. Gabe's promising young rookie would live to regret disobeying orders.

Jack fidgeted, fingers flexing around the grip of his gun and weight shifting side to side, but he held his position until Gabe stood and waved him to one side of the trapdoor. His partner's restraint was more than admirable.

In many ways, Jack was a better cop. If Delia was down in that hole, Gabe didn't know if he'd have the strength.

He took the two steps down in a rush, trusting Jack to cover him. This room wasn't as long as the one discovered under Thom Brennan's house, but still deep enough they could stand upright. Lanterns hung from pegs mounted in the house foundations, casting a flickering, yellow light across the floor.

A jumble of bones, aged and yellowed, filled one corner. Eyeless skulls stared accusingly, remains of the ghosts begging Delia to be found and buried.

Ethan stood in shirtsleeves and butcher's apron less than ten feet away, knife in hand. He'd shaved the beard from his wedding photograph, revealing a broad scar that ran from the corner of his mouth down his chin. Gray speckled his hair. Other than being tall and heavily muscled, he looked nothing like the description given by his wife.

Sadie was injured, but alive. A gag had been stuffed in her mouth and the rope around her wrists looped through a metal ring, and tied to the post driven into the ground behind her head. Gabe shut out seeing the blood on her face, the crooked angle of fingers on one hand and the bruises on her face. He damped down rage and thanked God she was still breathing.

Most of all, he pretended not to see hope flare in Sadie's eyes or that she watched him. Gabe concentrated on keeping his gun pointed dead center at Ethan's chest. "Step away from her, Ethan. Put your face to the wall."

"My uncle entrusted me with a duty and taught me what it meant. I can't just turn away on your word, Lieutenant Ryan. I am Anubis." Ethan smiled. Light glistened off his chipped tooth and emotionless blue eyes. "Osiris will judge her, as he judged all the rest."

"Step away, Brennan!" Jack circled slightly to the right, drawing Ethan's attention, his pistol aimed rock steady. He pulled back the hammer. "Move now before I forget I'm a cop and not an executioner."

The change in Ethan's smile or the twitch of his fingers around the knife, or the movement of a hand toward his pocket, Gabe was never sure what prompted him to shoot. He pulled the trigger, cocked the gun, and pulled it again.

Again and again he put bullets into Ethan's chest until he'd emptied his gun, each shot striking with a dull, wet sound. Blood blossomed and bubbled with each impact, telling Gabe he'd found his target. Ethan staggered and swayed, but kept his feet.

Fear snaked its way up Gabe's spine, accompanied by the momentary doubt that Ethan was capable of dying.

The last shot belonged to Jack. Ethan touched a hand to his forehead in surprise, staring at the blood on his fingers. His eyes closed and he collapsed, limp and boneless as a puppet with severed strings.

Jack stared, breathing hard, and passed his gun to Gabe.

"Watch that son of a bitch and make sure he's dead. I'm getting Sadie out of here." He snatched the knife from Ethan's hand, cut the ropes and scooped Sadie into his arms. Tears rolled down Jack's face as he carried her up the steps, into the light.

Gabe stood over Ethan, watching. Dead men twitched, moved, a reaction of muscles not willing to admit they'd been claimed by death. All his years of experience told him Ethan Brennan was dead, that there was no doubt.

But he couldn't ignore the cold fingers brushing the back of his neck, the whisper in his ear not to turn his back and walk away. He'd learned too much of ghosts from Delia and Isadora not to heed the warning.

Gabe put the muzzle of Jack's pistol to Ethan's temple and fired. The twitching stopped, but he fired twice more.

Being allowed to leave Ethan's body to rot in the dark would be right and just, but officers in the SFPD were constrained by law and society's idea of justice. Despite everything, he still wanted to be a good cop and someone his father would have been proud of.

Gabe contented himself with walking away and taking the lanterns with him. Someone else could drag Ethan's body into the light.

CHAPTER 21

Delia

My tea was long cold. I'd lost track of time as I'd sat at the table, hands wrapped around a fragile porcelain cup, and pointedly ignoring the ghosts clustered near the backdoor. Dora did much the same in the chair next to me, her tea laced with whiskey and a pile of discarded, half-smoked cigarettes on the saucer in front of her. Light continued to fade outside the kitchen window, as did my hopes. Gabe hadn't returned nor sent word of Sadie.

Annie pushed through the swinging door, the tray of sandwiches she'd carried out to the officers in the yard empty of everything but crumb-strewn plates and dirty napkins. Feeding people was her way of handling uncertainty. "Boys always have an appetite no matter what's going on. Both of you should try to eat something. Sadie's going to need the two of you to lean on once Jack brings her home. You won't do her a lick of good if you come down sick."

Isadora and I traded looks. Annie's faith that Jack and Gabe would find Sadie in time was unshakeable and absolute. We wouldn't say so aloud, but neither of us were as certain. "I won't get sick, promise. How's Mama Esther?"

"She's stopped crying, praise the Lord. Miss Esther was sleeping last time I looked in." Annie stacked dirty plates on the drain board and wiped down the tray. "She kept on saying that Teddy told her not to cry no more, that things would work out fine. Whatever let her rest, I'm plenty grateful. But I'll be glad when all the old ghosts are gone from this house and life settles back the way it was."

"We all will." Dora lit a fresh cigarette. "I'll do my best to make that happen, Annie. That's a promise."

The front door banged open, bringing the sounds of cheering, feet stomping up the stairs, and Gabe shouting my name. "Delia! Annie! We found her!"

He rushed into the kitchen before I'd taken more than a step toward the door. Gabe gathered me into his arms, his voice thick and choked. "We got there in time. Sadie's hurt and needs a doctor, but we got there in time. She's safe. Jack took her upstairs."

"Well done, Lieutenant Ryan." Tears glimmered in Dora's eye. She put her cigarette aside and covered her face with a hand. "Well done."

I hugged Gabe fiercely. "And Marshall?"

He hesitated, just for an instant, and my heart sank. "Ethan hurt him pretty badly, but I think he'll make it. Maxwell and Finlay took him to the hospital in another car. Jack wanted Sadie to go, too, but she insisted on coming home. He decided not to fight with her."

"He'll make it." I wiped my eyes on a sleeve. "And Jack knows better than to fight with Sadie. He always loses."

"Dee . . . Ethan Brennan's dead. We don't have to worry about him ever again." He brushed stray wisps of hair off my face with shaking hands. "It's over."

"Over . . ." Even with the specter of Ethan Brennan looming over us, I'd have gladly spent my life with Gabe. A brighter future opened up before me now, one not marred by fear and always looking over my shoulder. Relief and gratitude swept over me as well. No one else would die at Ethan's hands.

Annie shut her eyes and breathed a quick prayer of thanks. Then she took charge. "You did the right thing bringing Sadie home, Gabriel. I can take better care of my girl than the nurses at any hospital." She began to bustle around the kitchen, collecting soap, towels, rolls of bandages, and a basin to hold hot water. Annie paused long enough to wave me toward the door before filling the kettle. "Dee, you go up and sit with her. I'll gather what I might need and send one of the boys to fetch Doctor Miller. I'll be up soon as I can. Go on now."

"Go be with Sadie." How tired Gabe was showed in the lines around his mouth and the way his shoulders drooped. "She needs you. We'll talk later."

"I'm coming with you, Dee." Dora stood and smoothed the front of her dress. She smiled brightly, but I saw the way she studied Gabe's face and searched the corners of the room. "Prying Jack away so the doctor can tend Sadie will require all of us. And I want to make a start on keeping my promise to Annie. Insuring no other ghosts creep in seems like a good way to begin."

She meant Ethan's ghost. The thought that Ethan Brennan might haunt Sadie or Gabe was horrifying. He'd hurt them enough already.

Dora led the way to the staircase. Ghosts filled the entryway as they had earlier, but the spirits I saw were changing, becoming translucent and fading as I watched. She paused at the foot of the stairs, surveying the diminishing contingent of ghosts. Isadora spoke quietly, but the command in her voice rippled over my skin, raising gooseflesh. "Hear me spirits. Nothing holds you here, no ties to kith and kin, nor debt to the living left unpaid. You are free to seek your rest. Leave this house and be at peace."

Some ghosts went quickly, here and gone in the space of a breath. Others thinned and trickled away slowly, holding on a little longer. Even now some of Ethan's victims were reluctant to quit the world of the living.

The last glimmering ghost vanished from the entryway. I closed my eyes and listened to the house, searching for traces of spirits and an itch along my skin. Searching for Aileen.

I couldn't find her. That didn't mean she was gone.

"Dora . . . if spirits are going to continue to seek me out, I need to know how to send them away. Teach me to do that." My hands were balled in my skirts, clinched tight enough my fingers ached. "I don't want Annie, or Sadie and Jack, or Gabe tormented, or in any danger because of me. Show me how to protect those I love."

She frowned, one long nail tapping on the banister. "I never said that ghosts would continue to seek you out, Delia, I can't say that with certainty. But I can't deny that you'd be safer with more knowledge. Are you sure this is what you want?"

How sure I was surprised me. "I'm certain. I hate feeling helpless."

"Very well then. Consider it settled. I'll teach you anything I can." Dora threaded her arm through mine. She trembled slightly and tight lines appeared around her eyes. "Let's get upstairs to Sadie. Dramatic as it sounds, I need to reassure myself that the house is free of evil spirits and haunts. I won't feel easy about going home until I do."

Strong emotions sought Isadora out, wormed their way past her defenses and under her skin. I'd no doubt that the freshness of Sadie's memories and lingering terror came near to drowning her. "Is there another way to check for spirits, aside from going to Sadie's room? You're already in pain, Dora. I can see it in your face."

"Not near the agony I'd feel if we'd lost her, or Jack and Gabe.

Don't fuss, I've weathered far worse." Dora patted my arm and we began to climb the stairs. "I've few enough true friends in this world. I can endure a bit of pain for one of them."

I heard Esther singing before we reached Sadie's room at the far end of the hall, her thin, reedy voice breaking on the notes of an old lullaby. She sat in a chair next to the bed, tiny and frail, wrapped in a heavy shawl to ward off the chill. Esther held Sadie's uninjured hand and sang her child to sleep, chasing away fear of the dark and the monsters who lived there.

Teddy's ghost stood behind Esther's chair, a hand resting on her shoulder. The ghost didn't fade away when he saw me but stood firm, looking me in the eye before turning back to Sadie and Esther. I hadn't felt him leave, but he wasn't a stranger. He belonged in this house.

And he waited for Esther, that was clear to me now, patient in the way only ghosts can manage. Who he'd been in life and what they'd meant to each other was still a mystery, but in the end that didn't matter. She wouldn't be alone.

Jack had climbed up on the bed with Sadie, heedless of muddy boots on the counterpane nor anything but the need to be close to her. That Sadie had fallen asleep after all she'd endured was miraculous. She slept propped up on his shoulder, her broken hand cradled on a pillow in her lap. He stroked her hair and fussed with the blanket wrapped around her shoulders, as if tender gestures might make the bruises on her face vanish or knit broken bones.

Dora blew Jack a kiss and shut her eyes. Her forehead crinkled in concentration and she muttered under her breath, the words rushed and indistinct. She sighed and sagged against the doorframe. "Nothing rode home on Jack's coattails. Nor Gabe's for that matter. We can rest easy."

I watched Sadie sleep, trying to banish an image of Ethan's

other victims and the punishment inflicted on Aileen Fitzgerald, struggling to see my friend instead, that she'd survived and would heal. Dora put an arm around my waist and laid her head on my shoulder. "Don't let the past and old ghosts hide what's in front of you, Delia. We got our happy outcome."

Two weeks after her ordeal, Sadie and Jack were married in the front parlor. Annie, Esther, Dora and Daniel, Marshall, Gabe, and I were the only guests in attendance, but that was just fine with Sadie and Jack.

Gabe arrived early to help me clear away furniture and decorate. Sadie had ordered enough flowers to fill the church and a reception hall, and bouquets for several bridesmaids. She couldn't bring herself to cancel the entire order, so we filled the house with yellow and pink roses, lilies and carnations, sprigs of baby's breath and maidenhair fern. Vases and urns sat on every table, lined the oak mantel, and a garland of yellow roses draped an arched trellis we'd set in front of the parlor windows.

We moved the last overstuffed chair into a corner. Gabe wiped his face with a handkerchief. "Holding the wedding at the church would have been less work, but I think they made the right decision. Is Sadie still worried about the gossip?"

"No, I don't think so. Jack managed to convince her that worrying about what others said was foolish. If I recall, his exact words were to 'hell with all of them.'" I smiled and moved a vase of lilies so that it was framed by the roses draping the arch. "He was rather loud, too, so his statement was quite memorable. The two of them agreed that getting married was the important thing, not putting on a show for San Francisco society."

"He's right." Gabe's face flushed and he grabbed his jacket off the back of the settee. "I should get cleaned up before Dora and Daniel arrive. Unless you need me for something?"

I took one last look around. "No, I think everything is ready. Just make sure to have Jack here in less than an hour."

"I promise not to misplace the groom. Sadie would never forgive me." He kissed me on the cheek and left.

An hour later we were all in our places, dressed in our wedding finery and waiting on Sadie's entrance. Reverend Heisten stood in front of the rose-covered arch, ready to sanctify the marriage. At a nod from him, Annie began to play a hymn on the parlor piano.

Sadie came in on Daniel's arm. She wore her beautiful dress and didn't worry overmuch about hiding fading bruises or that one arm was in a sling. Jack didn't faint when he saw her, but it was a near thing. The stunned expression on his face gave me a great deal of satisfaction.

Reverend Heisten pronounced them husband and wife and we all applauded as Jack kissed his bride. I couldn't help sniffling and dabbing at my eyes with a hankie. Sadie had never looked so happy.

The pearly glimmer of a ghost, pale and barely still in this world, appeared behind Jack and Sadie. Aileen Fitzgerald reached for Jack, longing for all she'd lost stark and raw on her face. She'd not had the chance to know him or see him grow, to say good-bye or make peace with leaving him behind. He didn't know she was there, but he'd never known his mother watched over him.

Jack embraced Sadie, the two of them laughing and brimming over with joy. Aileen smiled, than she was gone.

"All right, folks, everybody find your place at the table. Dee, you and Gabe help Miss Esther to her chair if you would." Annie tucked her handkerchief up her sleeve. "Marshall, you come help me get this food out so we can eat. Sadie and Jack have a ferry to catch."

Annie outdid herself with a huge dinner and a magnificent wedding cake. The afternoon was filled with food, happy talk, and laughter, fueled by the relief that Ethan Brennan no longer cast a shadow over all our lives.

I stood on the front porch, hand in hand with Gabe, and waved good-bye as Jack and Sadie drove away. Their honeymoon trip was still in the future, but they'd have three days alone now to start their lives together. As frail as Esther had grown, that was all the time they were willing to risk being away. Sadie said they'd their entire lives to travel. Jack was just as content to wait.

Gabe lingered long after everyone else went home, helping Annie and I clean up and put the house to rights. The last bit of work for the evening was in the kitchen. Annie hummed under her breath while wrapping leftover food and stacking plates in the icebox. Gabe and I washed and dried the last of the dishes. He was quiet and often lost in thought, but I made little of that. A lot had happened.

We finished and I reached for the towel in Gabe's hand, meaning to hang it to dry. He took both my hands in his. "Dee . . . I've rehearsed what I want to say a thousand times, but now I can't remember any of it. Not a word. After losing Victoria I thought I'd always be alone. You changed that." He got down on one knee and cleared his throat. "I love you, Delia Ann Martin. I want to spend my life with you. Will you marry me?"

I stared, unable to answer. Annie clucked her tongue and shook her head, a sure sign that I looked utterly witless. I shouldn't have been surprised, but I was. "Marry you . . . Are you sure?"

He grinned. "I'm sure. Say yes. Marry me."

Tears filled my eyes, but I grinned right back. "Yes, Gabe, yes. I can't think of anything I'd like more."

Gabe stood and slipped the ring from his pocket onto my finger.

I stared at the pearl and emerald ring, unable to speak. Annie left us alone when he kissed me.

I didn't notice that she'd gone.

Esther died quietly in her sleep a week after Sadie's wedding, surrounded by family and without pain. I'd thought I was ready, but the loss of someone you love is never easy, no matter how long you have to prepare. She'd come back to herself, just a little, in those last few days, and we'd been able to say good-bye. I was grateful for that.

The day of the funeral was bright and sunny, cheerful in a way that made loss sharper. Wind brushed through the trees shading the hillside cemetery, leaves whispering softly in the voices of ghosts long laid to rest. The family stood at the graveside, Isadora and Daniel, Esther's friends, and neighbors ranged behind us. Gabe held my hand as Reverend Heisten intoned the words of the service, words meant to comfort the living and soothe grief. His words meant nothing to the dead, wouldn't bring peace to lost and wandering souls. I knew that better than most.

I couldn't help but think of Aileen Fitzgerald and Matt Ryan, my parents and Victoria. Life had been ripped away from them without warning or a chance to reconcile themselves with leaving loved ones behind. They'd never gotten to say farewells. I prayed that they'd found peace nonetheless.

The service ended and friends and neighbors drifted away. Men in coveralls arrived, leaning on their shovels and waiting to fill the grave. Marshall helped Annie down the slight slope, letting her lean on him for the walk back to the car. Jack and Sadie laid the lilies they carried onto the casket and followed. Gabe did the same, but stopped a few yards off to wait for me.

"Good-bye, Mama Esther." I laid a yellow rose amongst the white lilies. "You needn't worry. Sadie and I will be fine. Rest and be at peace."

I hurried to join Gabe. He kissed my cheek and frowned. "Are you all right? You took so long I was starting to worry."

"I'm fine. Just saying good-bye." All my ghosts were laid to rest. I took his hand, fully in the world of the living. "Let's go home. We have lots to talk about. And a future to plan."

TELL THE WORLD THIS BOOK WAS

GOOD	BAD	SO-SO
great!		Stupid ending